MW00626474

The wall of fire *was very close now upon her left. She could smell the smoke and feel the heat. The Carratril was only a score of strides away, but the fire was almost as close. She put her whole being into the desperate race. Her hair whipped wildly in the wind, and her lungs cried out for air.* **Then the fire caught her.**

Her hair took furious flame immediately, and all the rest of her felt scorched. Her worst fears about the pain were short of the reality. She felt she had run into Hell. She screamed out her breath, and then sucked scorching air into her straining lungs. She was still running, but she knew that in an instant she would collapse into even greater agony, until death relieved her.

But suddenly there was nothing beneath her feet, and she was falling through blessedly cool air. With a fearful crash, she plunged into icy water.

Blackness closed over her head, and a swift current swept her away.

About the Author:

Homeschooled from first through twelfth grade, Ari Heinze holds astronomy degrees from Caltech (B.S. 2001) and the University of Arizona (Ph.D. 2007). He's passionately interested in astronomy, but equally so in storytelling. Even in early childhood he entertained his two younger brothers with stories, and now, besides writing with obsessive delight, he invents stories for his own children: Petra, Eleazar, and baby Brogal, born in January 2010. He and his beloved wife Jane live in Houston at present, but plan to move to a more starry and adventurous locale when they have opportunity.

The Author's Favorite Books:

Fiction: *Cry, the Beloved Country,* by Alan Paton
Green Dolphin Street, by Elizabeth Goudge
The Jacobite Trilogy, by Dorothy K. Broster
Jane Eyre, by Charlotte Bronte
The Lord of the Rings, by J. R. R. Tolkien
The Napoleon of Notting Hill, by G. K. Chesterton
Northanger Abbey, by Jane Austen
The Space Trilogy, by C. S. Lewis
Till We Have Faces, by C. S. Lewis

Nonfiction: *Confessions,* by St. Augustine
Desiring God, by John Piper
The Reason for God, by Tim Keller
Jeremiah, by the Prophet Jeremiah
Galatians, Ephesians, Philippians, and *Colossians,* by St. Paul

Rain, Wind, and Fire

THE EPIC OF KAROLAN

THE THIRD BOOK AMONG FOUR

Ari Heinze

SOLI DEO GLORIA

Copyright © 2008, 2009(completed draft)
and 2011 (edited text) by Ari Heinze
Cover art by Ari Heinze
Published by Hopewriter Publishing
ISBN: 978-0-9825543-3-3

All rights reserved. Neither this book in its entirety, nor any portions thereof may be copied, reproduced, or transmitted in any form whatsoever without prior written permission from the author, except as provided by U.S. copyright law. Brief quotations included in a well-reasoned review, whether favorable or unfavorable, are expressly permitted by the author – but this express permission does not apply to reviews whose primary aim is to mock or denigrate the book or its themes.

The Scripture quotation used in the dedication is from THE HOLY BIBLE, NEW INTERNATIONAL VERSION®, NIV® Copyright © 1973, 1978, 1984, 2010 by Biblica, Inc.™ Used by permission. All rights reserved worldwide.

CONTEXT WITHIN THE EPIC OF KAROLAN

This is the third book in ***The Epic of Karolan***. While Book Two followed only Jonathan for some months after the end of the Norkath War, this book returns to follow the other characters, until Jonathan re-enters the story at the appropriate time.

The first book, **Bright Against the Storm**, told of the adventures of Jonathan the blacksmith and Sir Ilohan during the time preceding the great war between Karolan and Norkath, and of the love that was between Jonathan and Naomi the shepherdess, whom he left behind in Glen Carrah.

The second book, **Ashes of Our Joy**, told how Ilohan and Jonathan acquitted themselves in the Norkath War and its aftermath.

The fourth and final book, **Darkness Gathers Round**, describes how a new threat, first revealed in Book Three, came upon Karolan and was resisted with great heroism. It concludes the story of Ilohan and Jonathan, and of others, no less significant, who were caught up in their adventures. For at the last, though darkness gathered round, their stories did not end in darkness.

To explore Karolan further, visit http://www.hopewriter.com.

Acknowledgements

Thanks to my dear wife, Jane, for supporting me in writing and publishing this work, for believing it was possible even if I didn't, and for invaluable suggestions and insights at every step of the process. Thanks for reading it aloud to help with editing – until 2 AM the day before it went to the printers.

Thanks to my parents, Dan and Judith, and my brothers, Ky and Dar, for being my first readers, and for making me believe I could write something publishable.

Thanks to Daniel Song for detailed editing suggestions for the whole series.

Thanks to four-year-old Eleazar, who gave up three Tuesday afternoons' worth of fishing for this book. Apologies to the real Brogal (age ten months) whom I have sometimes sadly neglected to attend to the fictional one.

If I start naming those who shared with me the adventures I have drawn on to write my epic, this page will never be enough – but thanks to those who stood with me on icy mountains, hiked to hidden valleys, ventured into baked but splendid deserts, and dared enough heat and cold, hunger, thirst, and danger that my portrayals of these things have some taste of the reality.

Thanks to those whose love helped me dream of Ceramir, and whose courage and faithfulness helped me dream of heroes.

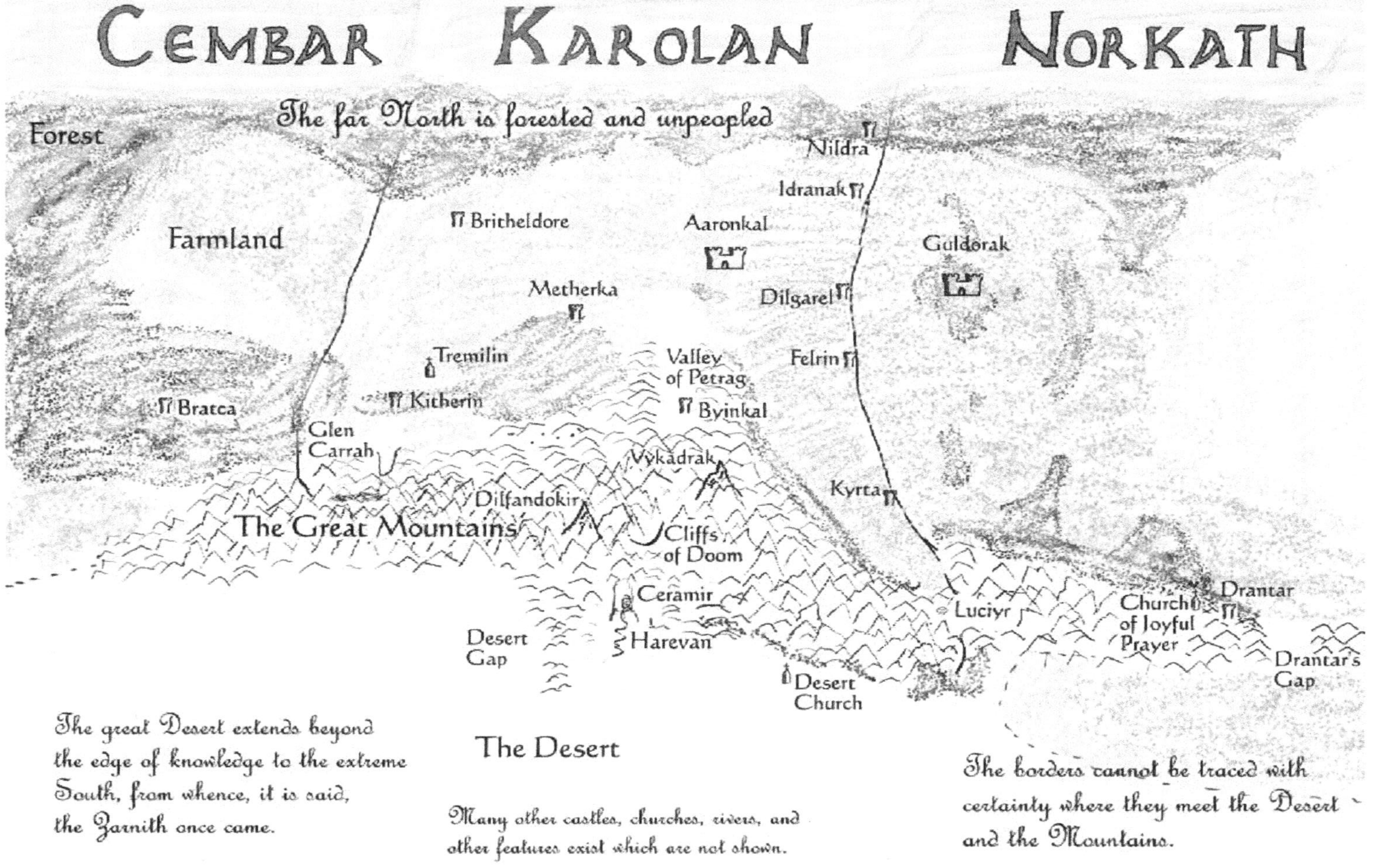

Cembar Karolan Norkath

The far North is forested and unpeopled

Forest

Farmland

Britheldore

Aaronkal

Nildra

Idranak

Guldorak

Metherka

Dilgarel

Tremilin

Valley of Petrag

Felrin

Kitherin

Bratca

Byinkal

Glen Carrah

Vykadrak

Kyrta

Dilfandokir

The Great Mountains

Cliffs of Doom

Ceramir

Luciyr

Church of Joyful Prayer

Drantar

Desert Gap

Harevan

Drantar's Gap

Desert Church

The Desert

The great Desert extends beyond the edge of knowledge to the extreme South, from whence, it is said, the Zarnith once came.

Many other castles, churches, rivers, and other features exist which are not shown.

The borders cannot be traced with certainty where they meet the Desert and the Mountains.

To my beloved wife, Jane:
No words I could write would truly express
how great a blessing you are to me.
I thank God for you with all my heart.

"Many waters cannot quench love;
rivers cannot sweep it away.
If one were to give
all the wealth of one's house for love,
it would be utterly scorned."

Song of Solomon 8:7, NIV

Chapter 1

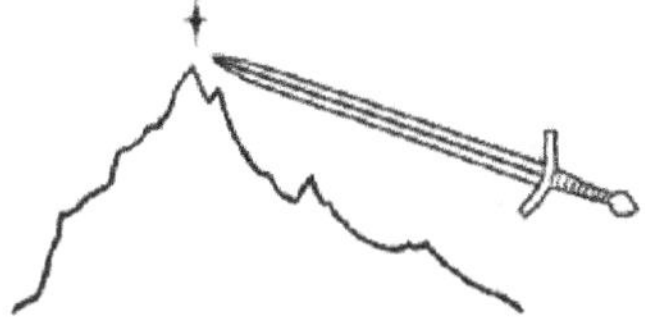

The Shepherdess's Life

WARM NOW FROM RUNNING TO AND FRO, NAOMI OF Glen Carrah flung herself down on the grass in the midst of her flock. It was the day after Karolan's heroic victory at the Battle of Petrag, but few who had not been there had heard the news. Naomi knew nothing more of it than of her own future – and yet there was peace in her heart, as she lay in the golden grass. The sun was warm despite the strong, steady wind from the north. She watched the heads of grass toss wildly in the wind above her, with the immeasurable blue sky beyond them. The calm footsteps of her sheep told her they were grazing contentedly around her.

She was thinking of Jonathan, her beloved. She had heard that his journey with Prince Ilohan had taken him far away, beyond the ravages of war. Yet she did not believe he was safe. Jonathan had wanted passionately to fight for Karolan, and for her. A weary journey over wild lands would not have stopped him. He had returned, she believed: he had returned somehow to fight in the war. He was in great peril, not only his mortal life but also his soul, for he had not given himself to God as she had.

"Father," she prayed, "You have heard my prayers for Jonathan, over and over, scores of times in the days he has been gone. I know you love me. I love you, and I pray that one day he will love you as well. Today I give him to you, and commit him wholly to your care, for I know that you have heard me and have done what was best."

She lay still among the grass stems, her peace deeper than before. She did not need to pray for Jonathan any more, she felt: that task was done. God had heard and acted. He had done the very best, by his own, ultimate, definition, and she trusted him. She was held in peace as in a loving embrace, and she knew it came from beyond the world, not from her own heart or mind. She wondered why it had come to her now, and what its purpose was. Then she noticed that the sheep had stopped eating, and were hurrying about uneasily. She rose swiftly to her feet to see what troubled them. Below her, spanning the full width of the glen, was a wall of fire.

It rushed up toward her, blown by the swift north wind, with a speed she could never hope to outrun. Already the crackling roar of it was loud in her ears. She stood still, her hair blowing in the wind, and looked at it. So the war was lost, and the land conquered. Her village was sacked and burnt. Jonathan was dead. Her father was dead. Barnabas was dead. Even Hannah was almost certainly dead. The children whose blankets she had folded that morning were dead, or captives. Her own death rushed on with the speed of the galloping fire.

She knew now the reason for the peace that she had felt. God had heard all her prayers. She was sure, beyond doubt, that Jonathan on his travels had come to love him, and that when in a moment the flames took her life, she would find him waiting to welcome her at the gates of Heaven. The flames roared closer, devouring the glen at a fearful speed. She smiled at them, and knelt down on the grass. They had no power over her. They would take her at the height of her beauty, with no shadow of fear in her eyes. The glen, too, on this bright day of autumn at the edge of winter, seemed to face its destruction undismayed, at the peak of its loveliness.

"Your life is not your own to set aside."

She did not know from whence the thought came, and it was not welcome. At the same time it came to her, she begin to feel afraid of burning. The fear was unconnected with the thought, but both pushed her in the same direction. She resisted it.

"There is no escape," she said.

"You must try something." Again, the answering thought did not seem to come from her own mind.

"I would rather be with you," she said, for she believed that God himself was speaking to her.

"Set aside what you desire, and follow me."

"Lord, I will," she said, and it seemed to her that she had never said a harder thing. Yet as soon as she had spoken, she saw that she had a chance: the Carratril, the cold, swift stream that watered the glen. A prayer passed through her mind like lightning: "I am yours, Lord; take care of me." Then she was running as she had never run before, flying over the golden grass toward the river.

The fear of burning was hot and terrible within her now, and the surrender to death that she had felt only a moment before seemed inconceivable. Yet through the midst of her fear there ran the awesome confidence that she had spoken with God, and was obeying him. It was his business, and his alone, to deal with all that happened to her.

The wall of fire was very close now upon her left. She could smell the smoke and feel the heat. The Carratril was only a score of strides away, but the fire was almost as close. She put her whole being into the desperate race. Her hair whipped wildly in the wind, and her lungs cried out for air. Then the fire caught her.

Her hair took furious flame immediately, and all the rest of her felt scorched. Her worst fears about the pain were short of the reality. She felt she had run into Hell. She screamed out her breath, and then sucked scorching air into her straining lungs. She was still running, but she knew that in an instant she would collapse into even greater agony, until death relieved her.

But suddenly there was nothing beneath her feet, and she was falling through blessedly cool air. With a fearful crash, she plunged into icy water. Blackness closed over her head, and a swift current swept her away. A prayer that never found words was the last of her fleeting thoughts.

*　　　*　　　*

Sir Drantar's face was grim and cold as he surveyed the burning village and the trembling captives. At any other time he would have been happy to hear that Sir Cygnak was dead, but now it left him in command of a mission he despised.

He looked at the cold, swift river, and thought with a sick heart of Cygnak's last deed. He had raped and murdered one of the most beautiful of the captured women, and flung her body into the icy stream. He had considered this his due, as the leader of the mission. Soon afterward there had been no sign of him but a bloody patch of ground beside a covered well. Drantar did not know who had murdered him, and did not care. Cygnak had deserved such a fate for long years, and it had come to him at a very fitting moment – if only he, Drantar, had not had the misfortune of being second in command.

A dark object came floating down the stream as Drantar watched. He was soon fairly sure that it was a dead body, but he himself would not have attempted to recover it. One of his knights pushed it to shore with a long spear, and lifted it out all wet and dripping. It was a dead woman. The knight laid her on the bank, and Drantar approached to examine her. Her hair, hands, and feet were badly burned, but her face was almost unscathed. It was clear that she had been very beautiful.

The knight turned to Drantar, and asked, "What shall I do with her?"

Drantar cared little. He hated slaughter and debauchery, but the Karolans were enemies: he did not have to respect their slain. He disliked the sight of this woman lying dead on the charred stream bank. She was like a trampled lily – a silent and damning witness against Norkath and all its servants. He would have her removed and thrown somewhere else where no one would see her. "Tie her over your horse," he commanded the knight sternly. "We will not leave them even the consolation of burying their dead."

Drantar scanned the wider scene. The destruction Fingar had ordered was complete, but the knights he must now command looked a disordered rabble. Some of the captured women and children were not even properly bound yet. He mounted and rode through the smoldering village, barking out imperious orders.

At last he had his troop organized. The captives were blindfolded, their hands were bound securely behind their backs, and each one was tied on a knight's horse ahead of him in the saddle. The knight who had recovered the dead woman had draped her behind his saddle like a sack of flour, with ropes clumsily tied around her waist to hold her on. It was a sloppy, undisciplined job, but Drantar let it pass: he was in haste to leave the scene of devastation, sell the captives in Cembar, and rejoin the main Norkath army. He shouted a command, and the whole cavalcade moved off at a brisk trot. The only sound besides the horses' hoof-beats was the suppressed weeping of the captives.

*　　　　*　　　　*

As consciousness slowly returned to Naomi, her first awareness of herself was as someone badly hurt in several different ways. She was not dead, as the Norkaths had thought her, but for a long time she felt that she was very near it. Her hands, especially her left hand, ached and burned almost as though they were still in the fire. Convulsive coughing racked her: her lungs had filled with water, and not all of it had drained out immediately when she was tied head downward on the horse. The jolting trot, the knotted ropes pressing into her stomach, and her awkward position draped over the horse all increased her misery as she became aware of them.

She remembered that she had fled from the fire and been washed away in the Carratril. It was strange that the strong current had not dashed her to death against the rocks. But it had dashed her against them, for she knew she was injured by more than simply fire and near-drowning. Her head ached badly. Her arms and shoulders seemed to be full of bruises, and without knowing exactly why, she had the impression that she had been struck much harder far down on her back. In sharp contrast, her legs did not seem injured. They did not hurt, at least. In fact, she could not feel them at all, or move them.

It took her a moment to realize how strange this was. She could not feel or move her legs. She tried her hands, and found that she could wriggle them, though they were stuck firmly under the ropes that bound her to the horse. She was never allowed the slightest doubt as to whether she could feel them. But her legs were different. They were numb as she had not known any part of her body could ever be. It was as though they were not there at all, but she knew they were. Looking under the horse's belly, she could easily see her feet hanging limply down, badly burned, on the other side.

She groaned, and coughed again. For a moment her vision went black, but then she recovered and could think again. She had been horribly injured and half-drowned in the Carratril. Now she was tied to a horse. Whose horse? Some Norkath knight's, she guessed – one of the victorious Norkaths who had burned Glen Carrah. From the sounds, she knew that there were other horses near her. She raised her head and tried to see them, but immediately pain stabbed through her and she grew dizzy, so she dropped her head and tried no more. She wondered what the Norkaths would do to her. She wondered what had happened to Hannah and the children. Perhaps they were dead, and therefore safe from further harm – as she herself was not.

Suddenly she remembered why she was still alive; why she had not been burned to ashes with the beauty of Glen Carrah. She remembered the voice that had called her to run, the voice she believed had been God's.

"Father," she groaned, "what have you done to me?"

She was silent for a while, in her misery, not trying to think or understand anything. The horse jostled her continually. She felt more helpless and hopeless than she had ever imagined possible. Presently, a memory came unbidden into her mind, prodding her dulled consciousness. It was not a vivid memory of time and place, color and motion, but only bare words and the voices that had spoken them, long ago: "...what if God places in your hand an adventure whether you want it or not? Could you accept it with trust?" Her father had spoken those words, in his kind, deep voice that she longed to hear again with all her heart.

And she, Naomi of Carrah, had answered, "Knowing that my life is God's, I can trust him for all that comes into it." She had said that in a voice of absolute confidence and courage, as if she were a martyr. She had not known what she was speaking of. Now she knew. Now she knew what an incredible thing she had said she could do.

She considered that for a long moment, as best she could. Every jolt of the horse sent a fresh pang through her aching head. Her thoughts themselves were painful also. She had been proved a fraud. She was not what she had thought herself.

Yet the merest hint of another train of thought flitted through her mind, and she caught at it. She had not intended to boast when she had made that reply to her father. Perhaps she had been boasting, without being aware of it – in her present weariness and agony she could not judge. But she knew there had been another reason for her words, and she clutched at that reason with all the strength she had left, determined to understand it.

She had said she could trust God, because she had believed that he would help her trust. Why had she believed that? It was hard for her to think through her headache and her pain, but at last the answer came. She had believed that God would help her trust him, because it was right to trust him, and he would always help her do what was right and avoid evil. When her own strength failed, God's strength would be there to sustain her. She had believed that. It had not been in her own strength that she was boasting, but in God's.

Then she came to the great question. It burned in her mind as hot and painful as the fires of Glen Carrah. Was it true? Would God really help her? Could she trust him even now? It did not seem very likely. He had hurt her so much. She had wanted to die. He had called her to live, and her life had become full of agony.

But the whole question turned on who he was. If he was all that she had always believed him to be, he had indeed the right to do this to her, and the power and wisdom to turn all her pain to blessing in the end. From childhood she had known God's promises from the Books of the Travelers, and as one of his people she had applied them to herself. God had never promised her a life without pain. He had promised that he would work everything that happened to her together for her good. Nothing that she was experiencing now proved him a liar.

Back in Glen Carrah she had believed that whenever anything God did or allowed seemed strange to her, it was only because she did not have his wisdom or understand his plan. It was much harder to believe that now. It was much harder to believe that he was truly good, when with every step of the horse she wished for death, yet feared its approach, and when she drew every breath with teeth clenched against her pain. Was God what she had always thought him? Was he loving and good, wise and powerful and faithful?

A sudden realization changed Naomi's thoughts completely. She need not try to determine whether God was good. She need only wait and see, for the moment of crisis had come. Here, now, God would prove himself or fail to do so. If he was with her now, if he was helping her trust and hope in him now, he was proven faithful. If he had forsaken her, he had broken his word and was proved a liar.

And then for a second time Naomi's world changed in a moment. The change was a return to her spirit's habitual attitude. She had been thinking about God, as if God were in her mind, awaiting her judgment. But the habit of her life was to turn outward to him, in love and supplication, not inward to her own thoughts and judgments. He was wholly beyond her. Her whole being waited on his will and choice, but he did not wait on hers. She felt that all her painful speculation was simply irrelevant, swept away by the reality that descended upon her.

"I am yours, Lord," she had said when he had called her to run. All her thoughts and questions were shallow nothings compared to those four words. She belonged to him, and he was her Lord and God.

"Father," she prayed, "come to me and help me trust you. Be with me and comfort me, and do with me as you will." Though it seemed right to her to speak the words, she felt she was asking for something that had already been granted. Through all her wondering and questioning she had still been trusting, though she had not known it. She had still been his. He had not left her.

Naomi remained miserable, fading in and out of full awareness of her surroundings, but there was a core of peace in her because of her restored trust in God. As time went by, her coughing subsided, but she grew colder and the aches in her back and shoulders grew worse. At last twilight began to fall. There came a shouted order from the captain of the Norkaths, and the cavalcade bunched up and came to a halt. At last, looking beneath the belly of her horse, Naomi could see some of the others in the company. She could hear bustling and the unloading of horses, and also the soft weeping of women and children.

She felt the knots around her loosened, and she was carried ungently to a forest clearing just off the road. The Norkath who carried her dumped her down carelessly near the edge of the clearing. "I would have sworn she was dead, but she isn't," she heard him remark to a comrade. "I heard her cough and groan behind me as we came along. She still breathes even now, but I doubt she'll last much longer."

Naomi felt that he was probably right. She lay awkwardly huddled and unable to adjust her position, shivering in her damp clothes. Her head was against the leaf-covered ground, and she did not even try to raise it. She could see the Norkath knights taking their blindfolded captives off the horses, binding their feet, and laying them in ordered rows on the ground. She recognized many of the captives, but she did not see Hannah or any of the children she had been caring for. She supposed that they were dead. The Norkaths built a large fire in the center of the clearing. Naomi felt only the feeblest touch of its heat where she lay. She longed to be closer, and to feel warm again.

She heard the leader of the Norkaths speaking imperiously to his troops. "I and five others will go off in search of a house where we may ask our way to Bratca. All the rest of you must stay here. Set a strong guard armed with crossbows, and keep a sharp watch. Conduct yourselves like knights at war. I will return soon. Farewell." He and the knights he had chosen rode away into the falling twilight. Ten other knights took up crossbows and posted themselves as guards all around the clearing.

The rest of the party sat around the fire eating and drinking. They drank a good deal, and their talk grew louder. The watchmen were annoyed at being kept away from the merry meal, and the one nearest Naomi actually set down his bow and joined his comrades at the fire. Some of the men there began dancing about, while others boasted loudly about impossible feats of arms.

Naomi saw all this, fully aware of what was passing, but feeling that it meant nothing to her. She was not thinking now, only watching and feeling. She was going to die and leave this world, and nothing in it mattered anymore. She watched it dully, cold and hurting and helpless at the edge of the light.

A loud and confident knight stood up, boasting that he would prove himself a stronger man than any other there. He was drunk, no doubt. Yet the wine did not make the evil in him – it only released it. With raucous laughter he strode to the row of captives, and chose one for himself. He heaved her up by her bound arms, and carried her roughly into the circle by the fire. There he stripped her quickly, ripping her clothes away with strong and ruthless hands. She screamed for help, and prayed and struggled frantically, but he only laughed at her. The other men sat around, unmoving, each watching with his own mixture of admiration, envy, and horror. None moved to help the woman.

Beyond the circle of the firelight, Naomi also watched – and could not watch unmoved. What was happening by the fire mattered now, whether she felt it or not. If there were something she could do to stop it, she must do it. But there was nothing. She was helpless and mortally hurt. Yet no – the guard's abandoned crossbow lay beside her on the ground, loaded, only a step away. Reaching it seemed impossible, but she could see no escape from her duty to attempt it. She might be dying, but she could still act – and she must. "Lord, I am yours," she said. "In your strength let me save her."

Naomi stretched herself out across the fallen leaves, trembling with pain and effort. As she had expected, her hands did not reach the crossbow. She tried to push herself toward it, but her legs would not move. She felt anchored to the ground. Furious anger at her helplessness rose in her heart.

She dug frantically through the leaves with her hands, trying to find some purchase. Her scorched fingers met a root, and she grasped it in both hands. She gave an involuntary gasp of pain as she began to pull, and blood seeped out through newly-opened cracks in her burned hands. She strained with all her strength while waves of feverish weakness broke over her. Yet she felt herself sliding across the dry leaves. A moment later her hands closed around the loaded crossbow.

She could not lift it, so she aimed from the ground. She sighted along the straight, smooth arrow, aiming for the center of the Norkath's body as he struggled with his captive and pranced around her in drunken lust. Naomi wondered if she had the strength or courage to force down the hard iron trigger in cold blood with her scorched fingers. She wondered if the bow would shift with the effort and kill the woman she had hoped to save. She aimed as best she could, gritted her teeth, and pulled the trigger with a whispered prayer.

She heard a horrible scream of pain and rage, and found she had unconsciously closed her eyes at the moment of shooting. She opened them again and saw what she had done. The arrow had struck the Norkath in his stomach and pierced him through. The woman was unhurt. The man staggered a few steps, groaning and gripping the arrow, and then fell on the ground and lay there writhing. The woman crouched down and tried to cover herself with the ripped pieces of her clothing, ineffectually with her bound hands. None of the other

Norkaths moved for a long moment. The watchmen looked fearfully into the woods, their crossbows ready.

No one noticed Naomi, lying like a dead thing on the ground, her bleeding hands still clasped around the crossbow. It seemed to her that a long time passed, and still nothing happened. A few men moved by the fire, and a few drank stoically from the wineskins, but none spoke or laughed. The half-naked woman shivered on the ground, despite the nearness of the fire. Naomi thought vaguely that she should let go of the crossbow and push it away from her, but she did not. She felt she had spent the last of her strength.

She heard the sound of footsteps on the leaves, both of men and of horses. Several Norkaths leading their horses passed by her, just between her and the fire, almost near enough to trample her. In fact, the first man to pass her stumbled over the crossbow and kicked it cleanly out of her bleeding hands.

Sir Drantar and his five scouts had returned. He left his horse at the edge of the clearing, walked up to the fire, and stopped. The wounded man, who had already begun to unclothe himself before he was shot, lay at Drantar's feet. Drantar looked around the camp with a cold gaze. He pointed to the man and woman on the ground before him.

"This man intended to rape her?" he demanded of one of the soberest of his knights.

"Yes, Sir, he intended to," said the knight.

"Did he do it?" asked Drantar shortly.

"Sir, he did not," said the knight. "He was shot, Sir."

"Who shot him?" asked Drantar sharply.

"I do not know, Sir,"

"None of my watchmen shot him?" asked Drantar.

"They did not, Sir."

Drantar reached down and lifted the wounded would-be rapist from the ground. He had bled a good deal, but was still conscious. Drantar slapped him in the face. "Stand up like the man you are not," he shouted. The knight stood, on unsteady legs. Drantar stepped back.

"Look!" he cried in a commanding voice. "Here is a knight of the great land of Norkath, exhibited before you. He is drunk, and has exposed himself. He is bleeding from a bolt that has gone through his guts. He intended to rape a bound captive whom he had been ordered to sell as a slave in Bratca." Drantar raised his voice in thundering denunciation. "This is not a man!" he cried. "This is not a knight, or a soldier. This is a craven, a fool, a weakling who cannot control his lust. Could he not have found harlots enough to content him at a time when we are not at war? Could he not conduct his own raids of rape and murder when they would not hamper the wars of Norkath? Could he not have the honesty to be an outlaw and a bandit, since he has one's heart? But I intend to lead men and knights, and I will."

His sword leaped from its sheath and in a single motion he beheaded the man standing before him. The body and head fell together on the ground. Drantar's blade ran with blood in the light of the fire. His voice was strong and cold. "Take warning!" he said. "You are no longer under Cygnak's command. Thus shall all be served who cannot conduct themselves as knights of Norkath, and as men."

Drantar roused several of the most drunken of the knights around the fire. He slapped them with the flat of his sword, cursed them coldly and got them on their feet. "Go find an inn, and buy clothes for this woman," he said to them. "And if you are mistaken for Karolans and taken as slaves, it is a small loss! I give you no gold; the price of the clothes you must take from your pay. Now go! Or I will have more heads yet this night!" He turned to survey the rest of his men. "Bring all that remains of the wine, and pour it in the fire," he said. "Cygnak thought a cohort of knights should be supplied like a wine-merchant's caravan, but I do not. It was my folly that I did not pour it in the stream at Glen Carrah."

Some time after this Naomi felt herself lifted, almost gently, and carried to the fire, where she was laid down again on the dry, warm ground. She was sure she would have died of cold if this had not been done. As it was she slowly sank into an unconsciousness that was not much like the sleep she had known when her body was whole, but was much, much better than waking.

* * *

The first thing that Naomi was aware of when she woke up in the morning was that she was still very badly hurt. The second thing was that she had just been lifted in someone's arms. A hood was over her head, and she could see nothing.

"She it was who shot the craven last night," said the man who carried her, whose voice she recognized as the Norkath leader's. "She – a crippled woman – proved herself better than any of you, for she stopped an evil thing that you watched with leering grins! But she must die, for we cannot sell her as a slave, and she is guilty of shooting a Norkath knight, however deserving he was. I will take her into the woods and kill her, and hide her body so it will bring no trouble on us. I return soon! Conduct yourselves like men in my absence!"

Naomi felt herself being carried a substantial distance at a fast walk. Now and then tree branches whipped against her, so she knew they were going through the forest. Finally the

Norkath cursed, set her down, and took off her hood. The moment of her death had come, she supposed. Her heart was beating fast, but she felt little fear. Yesterday she had wished for death, and if God willed that it should come to her today, that did not seem to her an evil. Still, she did not wish to meet death completely helpless. With a painful effort, she freed her arms from the new cloak that had been wrapped around her, and then looked up at the Norkath. She was surprised to see that he had not drawn his sword.

Naomi looked straight into his eyes. "Are you not going to kill me?" she asked.

Drantar pulled her to a tree and sat her up against it. He sat against another nearby. "I have not before seen courage like yours," he said. "I chose, last night, to save you, though it is against the orders of my king. There was supposed to be a pony here, tied to this oak. The Cembaran innkeeper from whom I ordered it has played me false. I would have tied you on it, and sent you back to Karolan with a veil to hide your face. But now it cannot be, and I have no more time."

"What will you do with me then?" asked Naomi.

"That must be your choice," said Drantar in a voice that had become cold again. "There are no houses or inns to which I could bring you in the little time I have. If you will, I will lay you on some woodland path, and wrap you in the cloak again. If you are found before the night you may be taken to a warm place. Then your life will be saved. But I warn you that you are not likely to be either free or happy with those who find you. The other choice is death. I will kill you now if you wish, to spare you further suffering. A death stroke carries no pain, and much is in store for you if you make any other choice."

"The life of those who belong to God is not their own to lay aside," said Naomi. "Take me to a forest path, and go back to lead your men. I thank you."

Drantar lifted her again and strode swiftly off through the forest. He soon found a little footpath that ran beside a frozen stream. He set her down on it, and put a skin of water and some food beside her. Then he turned away and left without a word.

Naomi lay still and silent where he had left her. She thought only a little of his strange, callous mercy. The strength she had mustered to face his sword-stroke, and sustained to make the choice he gave her, faded quickly. The day was cold, and her body deeply hurt. Her pain did not cease or ease. She prayed that she would be found and cared for. Than she prayed that she would not be found; that she would die quickly and gently of cold as the night fell. She prayed that Jonathan was alive, and looking for her. Then she prayed that he was dead, but had loved God before his death and was now safe in Heaven. She did not know what to ask for, so in the end she said, "Father, do with me and those I have loved as you will. I trust you." She drank from the cold, clean water Drantar had given her, pulled the hood of the cloak over her head, and lost awareness of herself.

She did not exactly fall asleep, but she rested, and her thoughts wandered dreamlike around a hundred irrelevant, nonsensical paths. She became aware of her surroundings again a little after sunset. She was deeply chilled. She realized that the day had passed and she had not been found, and so she guessed her death was imminent. She was very hungry, but her hands were too numb with cold to open the bag of food that Drantar had left her. She gave it up and tucked them as best she could back into her cloak. Her consciousness slipped away, and she gave herself up for dead.

* * *

In the chill dawn, two women came along a forest path in Cembar to draw water from a stream. One of them was old, hunched over and darkly hooded, while the other was very young, dressed lightly for the weather, and shivering with cold. The sight of a dark bundle lying on the path brought them to a sudden halt. The young woman quickly bent over it and carelessly drew aside the hood. "Here's a strange thing, Varga," she exclaimed in the Cembaran language. "A pretty woman, mayhap just your sort, alone sleeping in the woods. But she's dead of cold, or looks it."

"And not much use to me then, Brint, would she be?" asked Varga gruffly. Nevertheless she knelt beside the body and put her hand gently across the mouth. The next moment she had wrapped the cloak tightly around the motionless figure, and yelled to Brint, "Go and fetch the horse! She is still alive! Hurry, or I'll make you as cold as she is."

Brint ran as fast as she could back to the narrow wooden house where she and Varga lived, for there was nothing she feared more than being shut out in the cold. She came back panting hard and leading a lame pony. She and Varga together heaved the woman's inert form onto the animal's back.

They laid her in an upper room of their tall, narrow house. They made up the fire, and gave her a hot, strong drink when she was conscious enough to swallow it. They removed her clothes, which were burned and dirty, and tended the scorched skin they found beneath them before dressing her in new, clean clothes that fit her well. They cut her hair, removing all that was burnt and frazzled. Then they left her alone, in the bed beneath a heavy blanket, and went back to other business.

Naomi had submitted to all of it, semi-conscious and vaguely surprised to be alive, but very thankful for the kind actions and the warmth that gradually crept into her body from the roaring fire and the drink. When her rescuers were gone she slipped from partial consciousness into deep sleep, or the nearest approach to it she had had in some time. Her dreams were uneasy and shot through with lingering pain, but she slept a long time.

Chapter 2

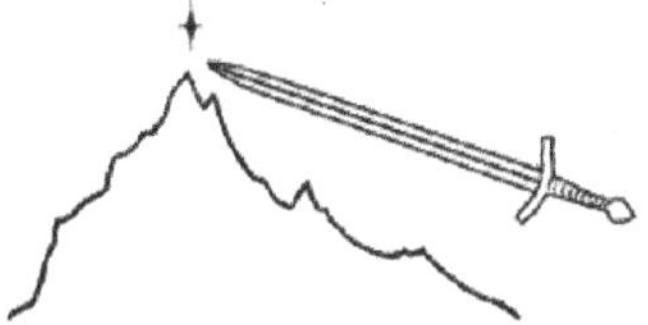

The King's Coronation

LEAVES THAT HAD GLOWED RED AND GOLD TO GREET Jonathan and Ilohan in Ceramir now lay brown upon the ground, and the branches above them were gray and bare. The wind down from the mountains could be cruel. But the plague was beaten, and the blue caps were gone, together with the restraints that went with them. Roaring, welcoming fires always burned on the wide hearths of the stone house. The children were rosy-cheeked with the cold, but never chilled or sickened in it. On clear days their laughter rang out brightly through the crisp, cold air. Clouds and towers of billowing white mist wafted off the warm lake, and the boldest of the sons of Ceramir still swam in its nearly undiminished warmth. When they reemerged into the freezing air they ran dripping and shivering into the house to dry before the glorious fires. Food was plentiful and good, and with harvest over there was less work and more time for merriment.

Yet there was one figure the laughter never touched. It was seventeen days since Ilohan had left the Valley of the Undismayed. On the tenth day, Princess Eleanor had sent Skykag, but he had returned hungry and messageless: clearly, he had found the tower room at Aaronkal empty. On the fifteenth day Eleanor had sent him again, and today she expected him back.

Eleanor was gentle and loving still to all who came to her for comfort or conversation. But her thoughts strayed far away, beyond the awesome rampart of the mountains – sometimes even beyond the grave. She seldom smiled or laughed, and was often found in some secluded place where she had been praying for a long time.

Today, as the short afternoon drew to a close, she was kneeling on the roof of the stone house, draped in a warm shawl with her crutches lying beside her. She was praying for many people, in many ways, for though her heart was consumed with hopes and fears for Ilohan, she could not pray for him alone – not when the fury of war was being unleashed on so many others also. The afternoon darkened to evening around her, and she, lost in her prayer, did not notice it.

A piercing scream slashed down from the clear, cold air above the valley. Eleanor started up and struggled to her feet, her prayer forgotten. She was hurrying to leave the roof when the scream was repeated.

Brogal caught her on the stairs. He had saved her from a bad fall. "You must be careful, my Lady," he said. "Your bones were broken enough times already, long ago in Karolan. The eagle will wait. But ah! Let me lift you up, and I will carry you."

Eleanor smiled at him as well as she could. "I thank you," she said. "I know that anyone may trust you fully."

"You, at least, may always do so, Lady Eleanor," he said, and with that he reached the foot of the stairs and began to run, still carrying her. He was surefooted and strong, and he knew every tree and bush in the woods of Ceramir. At last they came out into the open fields, and he set her down beside a small bush in which perched Skykag, the golden eagle who could soar to unguessed heights of bitter cold, and bear a message from Ceramir across the great mountains in a single day. His talons were clean: he had not killed on the way, and therefore must have been fed at Aaronkal. The scrap of parchment wrapped around his leg now was larger than the one Eleanor had sent.

Eleanor untied the string with trembling fingers, and spread the parchment out in the failing light. "I and Jonathan are alive," she read, and her heart seemed to burst with joy. She staggered to her feet to raise her hands in worship, fell down to be caught by Brogal again, and then lay back on the dry stubble laughing and crying all at once.

She bowed her head to read the parchment more carefully. A firm, clear hand that reminded her of her dead husband's had written:

I and Jonathan are alive.
We braved the mountains and came safe to Karolan.
Beyond hope Karolan triumphed over Norkath.
Wonderful things have befallen me, which I cannot write here.
Fingar is dead, and Andokar his heir is a good man.
I rule as best I can, with trust in God who helps me.
Pray for our people.
Our dead are many, though fewer than we dared to hope.
May God bring you joy, my mother.
Ilohan of Karolan

Eleanor raised her eyes up to the heavens. "Father," she said, "it is so much more, so much more than I have ever deserved. I had even given up asking for so much. Father, I thank you – oh Lord, help me thank you forever!"

She knelt, and raised her hands again, and gazed up into a twilight sky now pricked with stars. Her whole spirit sang for joy. Dimly she heard Brogal blessing her in heartfelt tones, and saying he would go back and bring her crutches. She remained lost in worship, swept by wave after wave of thanksgiving and wonder. Ilohan was his father's son, a hero of the realm – yet living! As Thomas and Sarah and she herself had hoped through long, hard years, he was reigning at Aaronkal at last. "The Lord has done great things for us," she whispered, "and we will rejoice in him forever."

After a long time Brogal returned with her crutches, and she followed him back through the woods. Though she might have expected it, she was astonished to see a banquet of celebration prepared beside the lake, and she laughed aloud. "Welcome, dear Princess," said Imranie, coming forward. "It is good to hear your laugh again, that has been silent through the days of waiting. Tonight the whole valley shares your joy."

* * *

Naomi lay sick and helpless for many days, only vaguely aware of her surroundings. At last there came a time when she felt stronger, and her mind was more clear than it had been. Still it was not easy to sort dream from reality. She knew, or thought she knew, many things about her surroundings without knowing how she had learnt them. She believed that two women had tended her, and that their names were Varga and Brint. Varga was stooped and wrinkled, but still seemed strong. Brint was no older than Naomi herself – perhaps a good deal younger. Since they spoke only the language of Cembar, of which Naomi knew nothing, she could not converse with them. She believed they had taken good care of her.

When Naomi came to consider the events that had brought her there, her memories were blurred and mixed with dreams. She remembered a great fire that had burned her, and then there had been misery and cold. Something terrible had gone wrong with her body, but she could not remember what it was. She supposed it was now healed. There had been another fire, she thought, with evil visions around it. It was not the fire in this room, which merely kept her warm. Someone had carried her, but not Jonathan. Jonathan was dead, and Karolan had fallen. But did she know that, or was it only a dream? She thought she knew that her father was dead also, along with Barnabas and Hannah. Everyone she loved was dead, and Karolan had fallen, and Glen Carrah was burned to ash – or were some of these things only dreams? She did not know.

When she turned her mind farther back, she could remember everything perfectly. She remembered days with Jonathan before there was any shadow of separation or of war. She remembered running through the golden grass so vividly that the scent of it seemed still in her nostrils and the feel of it across her hands. She remembered her father's bountiful love for her. She remembered the night he rode away to war. Even if some of her later memories were only evil dreams – even if her loved ones were not all dead and her home were not all destroyed, yet surely they had been in great danger and her home had taken great harm. And she might never return there. The pain of loss seemed to stab her until she had no more breath.

Something relieved her, some other memory, still lost in confusion and dreams. Something else had happened, that meant she need not despair, that meant there was something good left for her in the world, even if all her fears were true. She could not remember, but she was comforted, and she slept.

She awoke in early morning. Her mind was clearer and her body more at ease than they had been for many days. Her fever was gone. She lifted one of her hands and looked at it in the combined light of the fire on the hearth and the dawn filtering through a shuttered window. Her arm was smooth and strong, and her hand, though scarred by fire, was healing well. Already she could move it freely.

She drew her blankets aside and lifted her head to look down at herself. She had known she was not in a nightgown, and had been prepared to find herself naked. She was surprised to see that instead she was dressed in odd, very short garments that she supposed must be what all Cembaran women wore to sleep. Her legs had been burnt badly, especially her feet, but from what she could see in the dim light, they were healing well. She guessed that she would soon be whole. Already she felt very little pain. Her hands ached a little; her feet not at all. Even though she was not really decently dressed, she thought she would get up and sit by the fire. There could be no harm in that, since only Varga or Brint would enter to see her.

A wave of fear went through her. She was looking at her legs and trying to swing them out of bed, but she could not move them. Not even a little. She reached out a hand to touch her bare right knee. She pinched until the blood came. She could feel nothing. Naomi lay back in bed, and pulled the blankets over her. So that was the terrible injury, dimly remembered. She was paralyzed. Since she had remained so for many days with no hint of recovery, she supposed she would be a paralytic for life. And this had come upon her, along with the fall of Karolan, the burning of Glen Carrah, and the death of everyone she loved. It was all clear in her memory now, and the grief and loss overwhelmed her. For a long time she felt that sorrow would kill her. She was frail and injured already, and now she would simply die.

But her memory was fully clear now – even the moments before she had raced to the Carratril, even her miserable journey slung over a Norkath horse. And so she could not die of grief. She remembered that she belonged to God, and that it was only because of him that she had run, and lived. So she might rail at God, but she could not simply fall beneath her losses and die. God still had some business with her mortal life.

"This life is yours, Father," she whispered through her pain. "I wanted to die, but you made me live. So you must be with me. Even though I cannot see it, you must have some purpose in my life, though I have lost my people, my home, and even my legs. I cry out to you – you must be with me. It is only because of you that I live, and you must make something good out of this my life."

Her thoughts turned away from her terrible losses, almost without her will – as though her mind simply shied from the agony to consider other things. She remembered the Norkath camp, the pain of the cold crossbow trigger across her scorched hand, and the rape she had prevented. That was some good that God had brought out of her survival.

She remembered the leader of the Norkaths, whose name she thought was Drantar. He had despised and killed the would-be rapist, who had been a slave to lust – and yet he himself had obeyed the cruel commands of Fingar. It was very strange to her. She remembered the kindness of his arms when he had carried her to the fire and saved her from dying of cold. Yet the next morning he had been unwilling to sacrifice more than a very little to save her life. His voice then had been cold.

She thought of Jonathan in any similar position. The agony of his loss threatened to overwhelm her again, but again she turned from it. She would think about who he had been, not about the fact that he was dead. If Jonathan had decided to save someone's life, he would have saved it or died in the attempt. No single mishap could have discouraged him. His manhood was deeper and better than what the Norkath captain had preached to his underlings.

And yet Jonathan did not love God – or had not. That had been her greatest sorrow before her life was shattered. No one could attain the fullness of what he was meant to be without God. She thought of Joseph, her father. He had been a man. He had been a hero. Here again grief swept over her: she felt the awful emptiness of her life now that he was dead. But she turned to consider his joy rather than her sorrow. All was well with him. He had faced his greatest challenge, and been proven faithful by his God. Her heart rejoiced as she thought of his welcome into Heaven. Her mother and father were together now, before the throne of God.

There, and there alone, men and women at last were made truly themselves, as they were meant to be. There, said the Books of the Travelers, there was joy, there was an eternal weight of glory, compared to which all the worst sufferings of earthly life were not even worth considering. That was her own destiny, despite the depth of her present loss. Only a little while ago, this very morning, she had cried out to God, "You must be with me," as though she could demand it of him. Now it came to her that indeed, he was with her – that his call to life rather than death in Glen Carrah had carried an implicit promise. In obedience to him she had remained on earth to suffer pain and loss, but that very act had bound her to him in a new way, with new awareness of his immanent presence and care. She had demanded of him only what he had already steadfastly intended to give. He was with her, every moment, comforting her, guiding her, and using everything that touched her, both pain and joy, to make her the creature he intended her to be; the Naomi who at last would be with him forever. She lay in the shuttered room for a long time, her soul seized alternately with the pain of her staggering loss, and with the awesome certainty of God's presence and power in her life.

The sound of footsteps on the stairs leading to her door pulled her back to consider her immediate situation. Brint and Varga came in, and soon recognized her new alertness. Naomi, in turn, was shocked to realize that Brint was dressed in the same scanty clothing as she was herself, though the young woman certainly seemed to have been up and at work in the house for several hours. Brint and Varga made it clear that they expected Naomi to get up, and she undertook the unpleasant task of trying to communicate to them that she was paralyzed. Varga was the first to understand what she was trying to say. The old woman took a glowing coal from the fire with a pair of tongs, and moved it toward Naomi's thigh to burn her and test if she was truly numb. Naomi was shocked and scared, but could not move to escape. She reached out her hand to stop the tongs, and Varga said something that sounded like a curse. Brint began to speak very fast in the language of Cembar, and her words seemed to convince the older woman to relent. Varga's angry look faded, and she smiled and laughed. The two Cembarans left the room.

Naomi was slow to recover from her fright. She thought Varga could easily have overpowered her if Brint had not spoken up in her defense, and it occurred to her for the first time to wonder what Varga's motives were in caring for her. She did not like the look of the old woman's smile, nor the sound of her laughter. Neither did she like the impression she had that Brint obeyed Varga through fear.

Varga and Brint soon returned, and at Varga's word, Brint lifted Naomi from the bed and set her down in a chair near the fire. The Cembaran girl crumpled to the floor, panting, after this effort, for Naomi, slender and wasted from illness though she was, had been a heavy weight for Brint's small frame to bear. Varga handed Naomi knitting needles and a skein of yarn, and smiled at her. Some of Naomi's distrust faded. Perhaps Varga was only thoughtless, not cruel. Yet there was still something wrong with her smile.

Naomi took up the needles and yarn in skilled hands. She had knitted even in early childhood, and the money her shawls and blankets earned had often been a blessing to her and her father, before... but she would not think of that. She began to work, and found to her delight that the flames of Glen Carrah had not taken away her skill or her speed. Brint and Varga marveled together at her flying needles. They left her a shawl to copy, and passed out of the room together.

The swift motion of Naomi's hands seemed to bring peace to her heart. She had lost almost everything, she thought, yet God was still with her. Life was hers to use as well as she could, and lose when she could no longer keep it. It seemed foolish to fear either death or further harm, when she had already borne so much.

A gust of wind blew wide the east facing window above Naomi's bed. The morning sun streamed through it and fell full upon her face. If Jonathan had seen her then, though her lovely hair was cut short and the scars of burns could still be seen on her face, he would have loved her more than he ever had before. He would have dared all to find her, and forgiven all when he had found her. But he wandered despairing in the winter woods of Karolan, hidden from help and hope, and knew nothing of her.

*　　　　*　　　　*

Late at night in an inner room of Aaronkal, Prince Ilohan hunched forward over a table, in earnest conversation with Sir Benther. "You know that you must be crowned king by the Servant of God from Tremilin, as is written in the ancient law," said Benther. "To delay any longer speaks of weakness and indecision, doubt of your own right and power."

"I wanted it to be a great celebration, with thousands filling the field of Aaronkal with joy," said Ilohan. "I wanted to take my title when I felt I had more right to it, when Karolan was nearer to full healing."

"You will never feel ready, Your Majesty," said Benther. "And we have already chosen not to gather the people at Aaronkal, lest the winter journey add to their hardships. The time has come – indeed, it has long been come, and now is very late – to take the crown that Thomas left you."

"You have said that I doubt my right and power, dear counselor," said Ilohan. "I do not, for I know both. I know the right is mine by birth. I know I do not have the power or wisdom to be king. And it seems wrong to claim the crown, when many of my people cannot claim a roof above their heads."

"Your Majesty," said Benther, "you yourself say that all good power comes from God, and that he has blessed you with strength equal to your days. If that is true, do not say you lack power or wisdom for the throne that is yours by right. And as for your people, how does being kingless help their plight?"

"You are a wise counselor, Benther," said Ilohan, "and I do ill, to keep the man of God from Tremilin waiting, when he has come a swift journey through the snow at my request. Call him in."

To Ilohan's surprise, a spasm of pain passed across Benther's features. "Again I must say that I believe Your Majesty acts unwisely in keeping me as counselor," he said. "Was that not my father's role, which he most vilely disgraced? And is it not folly for you to harbor the son of such a viper near you?"

"Behold, who delays and doubts now?" said Ilohan. "And have I not declared you fatherless? Before the throne of Karolan, Tulbur the Unknighted is not your father, nor are you his son. Now bring in the man from Tremilin as I have commanded."

Benther rose and admitted a man, white haired but beardless, and bent with age. He was dressed in a white robe, but it was made of coarse, rough cloth, and secured around the waist with a rope. Ilohan stood as he entered. The man did not bow, but only stepped forward to stand still a few paces in front of the prince.

Ilohan had never tried to cow anyone with majesty or coldness, yet now he stood straight, with his crowned head high, his red royal robe around him, and the sword of Kindrach at his side. He felt that several others – Eleanor, Mudien, Imranie – each had far more right to crown him with God-given authority than this man, appointed by the ancient law though he might be.

"You are the Servant of God from the Church of Tremilin?" asked Prince Ilohan.

"I am an old man who has not prayed as he was meant to pray," came the reply.

"How were you meant to pray?" asked Prince Ilohan, startled by the strange humility of the answer.

"With faith and diligence, and hope. With certainty that no time spent in prayer rather than an easier task is wasted. I have wasted much time in silence and in foolish words. I have been unfaithful to my calling."

"Are you worthy, then, of your honored place?" asked Ilohan.

"I am worthy in myself only of Hell," said the old man.

"All men deserve Hell," said Ilohan. It was a catechism answer, but also one he fervently believed – not because he had deep vision of pervasive evil in the hearts of men, but because he stood in awe of the purity and holiness of God compared to his own, representative heart.

"So it is written," said the old man, "but I have the right to speak only of myself, for I know myself."

"Have you even that right?" asked Ilohan. "Must you not reserve even your own judgment to a higher Judge than your own heart?" The old man's answers were astonishing him, and the conversation reminded him oddly of speaking with Veril in Ceramir: there was the same raw honesty, the same swift delving into profound truth.

"I must indeed relinquish even the judgment of myself to God, and praise the mercy that finds a different verdict than my own," said the old man. "The years are long, but I am slow to learn – and this, perhaps, is the last of many lessons."

"For what have you prayed? I wish that God had spared the farms of my people that lie burnt, and the thousands who fell at Petrag." Even as he spoke it, Ilohan was ashamed of the complaint, for he felt that God had indeed granted miraculous rescue to Karolan, and the cost, though heavy, was far less even than had been hoped before the war.

"It is not ours to know," said the old man, "but perhaps if it had been as you wish, some who died free and strong would have fallen into evil or suffered greater pain with the passing years, and some who were rude iron would never have been tempered. But I have prayed for many things, the goodness and power of your throne, and the peace and blessing of your realm neither least nor greatest among them. Even for a swift and easy victory I prayed, but not with hope."

"What are the greatest things you pray for?" asked Ilohan.

"What is the greatest matter with which I could be concerned? The rescue of a single soul whose troubled, foolish path has touched my own. I spent the day of Karolan's rescue chiefly in prayer for a miller's son, too young to fight, who was afraid of Satan. In some, such fear might be irrelevant, or even a cause of prudence. To him it was deep darkness, the greatest challenge of his soul in the years that change him from a child into a man. His fear is passing, and Karolan is saved. Who can say which victory was the more difficult? Or if that can be said, who can say in which battle an old man in a drafty churchtower should ask God's help? I matter little. And you, Prince of Karolan though you are, may matter less than you fear."

"Or more than in my deepest nightmares," said Ilohan. "God needs none of those he has created, but he uses them for greater things than they know, and when they fail him who can tell how much is lost?"

"No one can tell that," said the old man, "nor can any say how much may be redeemed. We only know at every moment that we must follow him."

"I am not at peace with all that you have said," said Ilohan.

"That is good. I am not free from fault. But are you now at peace with my station in the ancient law?"

"I am," said Ilohan, "and I am glad to know that such a one as you lives, to pray for millers' sons in the most beautiful churchtower in the world." Ilohan turned to Benther, who stood straight and grim beside the door. "Sir Benther," he said, "bring us the crown."

Prince Ilohan knelt before the old man, and felt the crown of Thomas descend gently on his bowed head. Then the man's voice filled the room, stronger than seemed possible from one so old. "God, be with this man, and never leave him. Be at his side his hope and strength, his conscience and his guide, his justice and mercy, his glory and his joy. Hear my blessing, Savior of my soul, merciful Listener to feeble prayers." He paused, and then said, still louder and in a different tone, a tone of command. "Ilohan, son of Kindrach, son of Thomas, rise King of Karolan. Bright in sun, rich in grain, sweet with peace, sharp with joy, and long be the years of your reign. Turn not away from God, nor cry against him if the path is dark. As your days, so shall your strength be. Dawn comes to end all darkness, and winter falls before the grace of spring."

King Ilohan rose slowly, then looked up to thank the Servant of God from Tremilin. It was too late – already he had gone out, and the door was closing behind him.

There was a long silence. Neither the new-crowned king nor Benther seemed able to put into words any comment on the coronation or the man who had performed it. At last Benther said, "Does Your Majesty still intend to ride for Petrag at dawn, despite the heavy snow?"

"Yes," said King Ilohan, "but before we set out, send swift messengers to all parts of the kingdom proclaiming that I have taken the crown at last. Proclaim that I pledge before God to rule them well, by his help, and to do them good all the days of my life, at any price that I can rightly pay. Proclaim that I will never betray them, and that I expect their loyalty and honor in return."

"It shall be done," said Benther.

A caravan departed for Petrag at dawn, as the king had ordered. He and Benther rode with it, heavily cloaked and hooded, after only a small modicum of sleep. Before them and behind them went wagons full of food, wood, and iron mining tools. Now and then as he passed to and fro among the wagons Ilohan heard men who did not know he was near complain that he was a hard master, ordering them out to make grueling journeys in any weather. It was true, he knew: he drove himself and others hard, and he and they were weary.

Yet he would not rest more than he must, while so many hurts remained unhealed in the land. The miners' halls at Petrag were full of widows and orphans, and not full of either food or winter fuel. Their horses and even their mining implements were sadly depleted, thanks to their heroism in the war. Every time Ilohan went to Petrag he felt the terrible price of victory. So many lives were broken, and the healing was so long... For now, they had hard work simply keeping the miners' valley supplied with basic necessities.

There were many other needs. Fingar had burned thousands of farms and homes in a wide swath leading from Aaronkal to Petrag, through some of the most fertile land in Karolan. And Glen Carrah, far from Norkath and the battle, had been utterly destroyed in an act of pure malice against Jonathan – who had now disappeared. Ilohan was weary. There was so much beyond his power to heal; so much brokenness and evil. He seldom considered his own loss or hardship, as he labored to lessen that of others, but sometimes his thought strayed to Thomas, and he marveled not that the old king had perished of weariness at last, but that he had lived so long.

Chapter 3

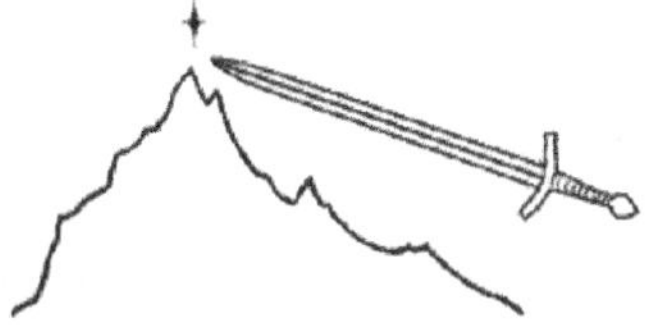

The Kindness of Cembar

EVERY DAY NAOMI GREW STRONGER, AND HER BURNS healed. She ate hungrily of the food Brint brought to her. She begged for the window to be kept open all day long. The changing beauty of the sky, seen through a tracery of bare tree branches, was like new life to Naomi, wounded child of Glen Carrah. She did not know of the new danger to which her growing health exposed her.

Brint knew, however. A night came when she rose from her bed, tormented by her knowledge, and crept stealthily into Naomi's room. She went with noiseless steps to her bedside, and stood looking down at her sleeping form. Brint trembled with fear, and also with a fever that was coming on her.

The Cembaran girl was young, but she was already deeply broken. She was a prostitute, a slave of Varga. The knowledge that something was wrong in her life seldom surfaced to her conscious thought, but it was always there, deeply buried in her mind. Every time she surrendered her body to the lust of a man who had bought her for the night, she laughed and teased him, and glossed over the gnawing wrongness that she felt. The men considered her a good whore, and paid Varga well.

She was young and healthy, and her body gave much pleasure. She was always full of laughter, as if she did not care. Even Brint herself hardly knew that she cared: she only felt a deep ache above which all her laughter was a farce.

But Brint cared about Naomi. She wanted Naomi as a friend and sister, but not as a fellow whore. She knew somehow that Naomi would care far more than she did. She knew Naomi must escape, or share her defilement. Her aching, untrained mind did not suggest any plans for escape. The thought of Naomi's leaving saddened her. She had decided at last that she would simply warn her. It was the bravest thing that Brint had ever done. She was defying the wishes of Varga, who could throw her out in the cold to die. So it was that she stood trembling at Naomi's bedside. She knew that Varga spoke no idle threats.

Brint shook Naomi gently awake. Each had learned a few words of the other's language in the preceding days, but nowhere near enough for this night's purpose. Brint had to resort to signs and gestures, many of which shocked Naomi. At last she was shocked into understanding the truth.

Naomi shuddered and closed her eyes, swaying a little as she sat in bed. So that was the explanation of the scanty clothes, the fear, the wrongness of Varga's smile. She might really have guessed it, but in her innocence she had not. It was one more crisis, one more horror. But God was with her, and thanks to this brave girl – brave almost, Naomi thought, as her father had been – she had warning. She reached up her arms, drew Brint down against her, and kissed her. The poor prostitute girl left the room with tears streaming down her face, almost forgetting to be afraid. Varga did not wake up.

Naomi lay in bed thinking about what Brint had told her. Brint was a prostitute, Varga her slave-mistress and the collector of her fees. Varga had rescued Naomi herself to share Brint's work. Until now she had been too sick, or too scarred, to be desirable. Yet now she was mostly healed, and Brint herself was falling sick. Varga intended to use her as a prostitute, for the first time, tomorrow. She would send up a man, and...

Naomi had to fight with fear. She did not believe that it was better to die than suffer rape, but she felt she might prefer death. Suicide passed fleetingly through her thought, but then was gone. Her life was not her own to lay aside now, any more than it had been in Glen Carrah.

Yet she was Jonathan's beloved, though he was dead. She thought of his iron determination, and she knew that she would not give up her body without a fight, hopeless though such a fight might seem. It seemed almost absurd; a paralyzed woman could not hold off a strong man full of lust. She could not even get out of bed without help. Yet she would try something. She would fight. She would do her best. And now was the time to plan, while Varga slept.

* * *

The next evening the window was shut at the usual time. Brint was in a pitiable state with the fever, but still she somehow managed to lift Naomi into bed before staggering back to her own room.

Meanwhile, Varga was explaining to a customer that the new whore was ready. "She is a virgin," Varga said, "and she does not yet even know why she is here. I will let you explain that."

The man turned suddenly on the stairs. "What if she does not like it?" he asked. "I can overpower her, of course, but that is not the kind of pleasure I desire tonight. You must give me back half my gold."

"Oh, no, Sir," said Varga, "she is well worth the whole. She will not fight you, for she cannot move her legs. You will move them for her, and she will be helpless against you. There is no disorder in the parts that most concern you. She will give you all the pleasure you desire."

"Nevertheless, I must consider her paralysis a defect," said the man. "We will say her virginity compensates for it, and you may keep my gold, for the present. Yet you had best hope that I find her beautiful, and that she does indeed give me pleasure!"

The man halted before the door to Naomi's room, out of sight of Varga who had remained below. His hand went to a hidden knife. "Long ago my father taught me not to kill, save only at the direst need," he whispered. "Though the evil here is horrible, it has yet to press me with such need. Otherwise, Varga, you would not see tomorrow's dawn."

Then he opened the door to Naomi's room.

She was not in bed. Instead, she was kneeling unsteadily beside the hearth, looking up to see the intruder as he came through the door. They stared a moment into each other's eyes. He saw the firelight flickering over her beautiful face and form. She saw calm eyes empty of the lustful hunger she had expected, but still she tensed her grip on the heavy tongs she held – tongs that gripped an oak log flaming in the hottest part of the fire. She was trembling, but not with fear only. She was like a captured warrior, condemned to die, preparing to seize his last chance of escape.

"In the name of God, I command you to leave me," said Naomi of Glen Carrah. Her voice did not waver. It was clear and strong, and seemed to the man to carry an edge like a polished sword. The words came with the absolute resolve of her soul, from a hidden courage he would underestimate at his peril. "I will not give you my body," she said. "I will not surrender to you my purity. Depart from here, before you find to your grief how God defends the weak. Take another step, and none of your days from now until you lie in your grave will be free of pain."

The man swayed at the door, amazed. She was weak and crippled, he thought, not sure of her balance even on her knees. She was like a crumpled flower there beside the fire. Yet her words were as brave as swords flashing in the sun. Her voice rang clear, unwavering, womanly and yet hard with authority and command.

The man closed the door behind him, but did not move forward. His heart exulted, for before him was a game he could play for a mighty stake, with good hope of winning.

"I know your speech," he said in perfect Karolan, as gently as he could. "I understand you. You are not what you seem to be; not a broken whore like too many whom I have met. But I also am not what I seem. You need not fear me. I would not take your maidenhood from you, even if you offered it."

"Do not move, except to leave!" said Naomi, as he moved to approach her. "I am afraid; afraid that you will make me trust you. But surely I cannot. Shall I believe, on your word, that you hire whores and do not use them?" Her voice was dangerous now. She was very near the desperate act she had planned.

"I am a wanderer in the desert, and a lover of the God and Father of Jesus Christ, who redeems my soul," said the man. "I obey the Father's law, and I will lie with no woman until the day comes, if it ever shall, when I bring my bride to a home filled with joy. I have not come to use you, but to free you, if you will accept freedom. I am devious; a spy; a thief, but my heart is full of laughter, and in all things, hidden and revealed, it is my desire to serve my God. This promise I offer you: I will do nothing to you that you do not permit. I will swear this by any oath that you think more binding than my word. But I do not break my word."

"Any man could say what you have said, and might, guessing from my words the best way to deceive me," said Naomi, her voice now trembling indeed. "My heart would believe you, but I know that none who come where you have come and pay what you have paid are innocent. What you have said is so strange that it would be folly for me to believe it. I would that I could trust you, but I cannot. I beg you, go away and do not return."

"Do you know my name?"

"You say that as though it were the name of an angel," said Naomi wonderingly. "Who are you, that I should know your name? I am a shepherd girl of Karolan, and know little of what names may be praised in the taverns or widely known among the great."

"I am Brogal, son of Mudien, a child of Ceramir. I would take you there – to the Cloth of Joy, the Valley of the Undismayed. There you may find healing from all that you have suffered. I would bring you to a new life, to freedom. You would use them well. Do not throw them away now. I swear to you that I am trustworthy."

Naomi wept. Her tears shone in the firelight as they fell hot and fast down on the wooden floor. "I do not know which to choose!" she sobbed. "I am afraid; I do not know." Then she raised her head again; her tears had stopped and her eyes were clear. "I cannot trust you," she said. "You have offered me too much, and I do not believe it is real. Go away from me, or come near at your peril."

"Lady of high courage," said Brogal, for it was he indeed, "is there no way I can persuade you? Is there no way I can prove the truth of what I have said? If I go now, tomorrow another man will come to you. If I wanted your body, I could buy you from Varga and keep you as my slave for life, raping you, despite your courage, whenever I chose. I ask for your trust, the only thing I cannot take, because I do not wish to take the rest. Will you not trust me, and let me bring you to freedom and healing?"

"God may provide me with escape from all that you foretell, Brogal," she said. "And if he does not, the one who takes my maidenhood will do it by force, against the utmost striving of my will, and I will be innocent. I will not surrender myself to your power. I will not trust you."

Brogal stood still beside the door for a long moment. At last he said, "Perhaps I am false," and Naomi's face filled with horror at the change in his voice. "Perhaps all I have told you was lies," he went on. "You are beautiful, and your clothing is short. I am a man, not a eunuch. Perhaps indeed lust consumes me. Perhaps I will take you now, by force, since I could not do it by deception."

He sprang toward her across the room. She cried out, and with all her strength she flung the log of blazing coals from the fire straight at him. Sudden flame leaped from it as it flew, and sparks scattered like red stars in the dimness of the room. Brogal raised his cloak to shield himself, and the log, which had broken in several pieces as it came free of Naomi's tongs, struck full against it. The pieces fell back on the floor and shattered again into a myriad of small, hot coals. Brogal was unscathed, but the cloak he had used as a shield burst into flames. He threw it off him and into the fire. He seized the glowing tongs from Naomi's hands even as she tried to strike him with them, and he used them to put the largest pieces of the log back into the fire. The others he stamped on with his boots until they were dead and the fires that some of them had started in the wooden floor were extinguished.

He stood in the center of the room, catching his breath. It had been a near thing. Had he not guessed where Naomi would throw the log; had he scattered any of the coals onto the straw mattress of her bed, the outcome might have been far different. He did not care. When he failed, then he cared; near misses had no power over him. But his game was far from over.

He stared down at Naomi, who had fallen over with the effort of her throw and was now trying to pull herself up again by grasping her bed. She was trembling, but there was no surrender in her face. "Now," he said, "the conqueror may turn to his prey. You see your defense was not all you hoped, my whore!"

Naomi was wholly unprepared for this. She had been sure that God would save her, and he had not. Her defense had failed. And this terrible stranger, this Brogal, who had almost made her hope that he was telling the truth, had proven false. But she did not give up. She cried out, as loud as she could, "Father, will you not save me? Is no one near to help?"

Brogal gathered her in his arms and lifted her, holding her tightly when she struggled. He was very strong. She noticed that he did not hurt her, but she found no hope in that. She loathed the feel of his arms against her bare skin, where her scanty clothes did not cover her. "Anyone!" she screamed, loud enough to make the house ring; to wake Brint to miserable terror; and to make Varga sit up in bed and cackle softly to herself before lying back again. "Help me, anyone who hears!"

Brogal threw her down upon the bed. She clawed at the mattress to roll herself onto her front, then buried her face in the pillow. She felt the blanket gently pulled across her – and then, nothing. She lay beneath the blanket, breathing hard, wondering dully why a rapist would cover his victim. The silence in the room grew deep. Naomi realized that nothing was happening to her. Gradually she became aware that Brogal was kneeling beside her bed, with his head bowed on his folded hands. She began to wonder what he was doing, and then at last to hope. Finally she spoke.

"If that was all to prove to me..." she said, and then stopped as he raised clear, pained brown eyes to meet her gaze. There was sorrow in those eyes, but not a shade of lust.

"It was, my Lady," he said. "I am sorry."

She did not know whether to laugh or cry, to thank him from the depths of her heart or to scream at him for what he had let himself appear. Her mind and heart reeled. She wondered if he was mad, or if she herself was; she wondered if even now she should trust him. "Why did you call me your prey, and your whore?" she asked. "Why did you prolong my agony? Why did you not stop with blocking my attack and taking my tongs?"

"I thought I might win your trust best by showing you most clearly what a liar would have done, and then not doing it. I feared you would not trust me if I stopped with merely foiling your defense. I thought I had best carry on the charade a little longer, and then break it and wait for you to see that it was broken. Now you have seen. I am not false. You are within my power, but I will do nothing to you that you do not permit. Will you permit me to take you to Ceramir, to healing and to freedom?"

Naomi was silent for a long time. All that had happened and all that she had done came over her, and she was deeply weary – too weary, she felt, to speak or think. Brogal still knelt beside her bed, waiting with worry in his face. At last she spoke, slowly and in a low voice. "That was bad," she said. "That was one of the worst things I have ever known. It is hard to leave it behind, to feel that all is well."

"I am sorry," said Brogal. "I ask your forgiveness. Yet I did not come to bring you pain. I came to bring you freedom, if I could, whatever the cost. If there was a way that would have caused you less pain, which I was too foolish or too proud to see, I ask your forgiveness."

"Tell me that all is well," she said, slowly.

"All is well," he said. "If evil has been done it is I who have done it. You are brave and faithful. You made the best choice that you could, and fought with all your strength. It is as you said before: even if I had taken your maidenhood, you would be innocent and undefiled. Yet I have done nothing to you. You are innocent, and you retain your maidenhood. You are not defiled, my Lady, and you are safe. All is well. Please believe me when I say that all is well."

"Let me rest a little," she said, and she lay back on the bed and closed her eyes. She lay still and silent for a while, and then great sobs began to shake her body, though she made no sound and no tears came to her eyes. Finally the sobs subsided, and she was at peace, though weak; as if she had swum with all her strength against a mighty river, and had come safe to shore, barely. She opened her eyes. Brogal still knelt beside her.

"I thank you," she said. "I am not sure you have wronged me, but if you have I forgive you. I will come with you, to seek healing in Ceramir. Can you bring me a drink of water?"

Brogal left the room and went down to his horse, his heart singing. His hand was shaking as he untied a waterskin from his saddle, and he realized how desperately he had wanted to save this maiden from Karolan. He always wanted to save them, of course, and though he called these endeavors a mighty game, he never forgot that the stakes were lives and souls. Yet this woman was special. Had he failed with her it would have been the most grievous failure he had ever known.

Naomi drank deeply of the water. She tried to sit up in bed, and Brogal helped her slide backward and lean against the headboard. There was more light and life in her eyes now, and Brogal knew all would be well with her. "This rescue is beyond my hope," she said, still in a low voice. "Almost, to my shame, beyond my prayer: I scarcely ever dared ask something so wonderful. Can you truly take me from here, and bring me to a place of healing and freedom, a place where I even… a place where I may be able to walk again?"

"I can," he said. "I can buy you from Varga, and take you to Ceramir. I do not know if we can heal your legs, but we may be able to. Such things have happened among us before, to the glory of God."

"What of Brint, Varga's other slave?" asked Naomi. "She is deeply hurt, and needs healing even more than I. She has been very kind to me. Can you not take her as well?"

Naomi saw a shadow pass across Brogal's face. "I tried once," he said. "I could not find her." The pain in his face deepened with the words, and Naomi thought he was not saddened only, but also afraid. She guessed already that few things could frighten him, and that what he was speaking of had touched him deeply. His voice was low and grim as he went on. "I could not find her. I know that in her captive body there is a captive soul, but I could not reach her. She would not understand me. I learned more of the power of evil than I ever wished to. It can break those it claims deeply, so deeply... She is beyond the power God has given me to awaken and to rescue. My call did not reach her. I could not make her see what I was offering her. She only laughed, and beckoned me to her bed, and was hurt when I would not come. I have never met a greater tragedy."

Naomi had listened to Brogal's words, but now her eyes blurred with weariness, and she felt too exhausted to reply. The firelight in the room was fading as the last flames sank into coals. What had happened to her was beyond her comprehension. She grasped only that she was rescued, and that Brint could not be. Yet she believed that God could rescue anyone; forgive anyone; heal anyone.

"There may be a time for her," she whispered.

"Yes there may, Lady," said Brogal. "But now is the time for you, and you are saved. Now you must sleep, for we have a long ride tomorrow."

He helped her lie back in bed, and smoothed the blanket over her. His last words echoed in her thoughts as she fell asleep. "... a long ride, a long ride tomorrow..." For fifteen days she had not been able to move from her room. Tomorrow she was going on a long ride. The very word meant freedom; freedom to go where she wanted to be... Ceramir, the Cloth of Joy...

* * *

In the windy gray dawn, Naomi sat on Brogal's large brown horse in front of Varga's house. She wore a long, warm dress that Brogal had brought for her, and over that a thick cloak. The voices of Brogal and Varga arguing came to her from the house. She knew they were bargaining over her, though she did not understand the words. She did not worry, for she was sure Brogal would buy her freedom.

With that miraculous word, her thoughts took a wider range than she had allowed them in many days. She thought of Karolan, firmly subjugated by now, she guessed, under the iron fist of Fingar. And yet it no longer seemed certain to her that those she loved were dead. She wondered if Jonathan might perhaps have survived – if he might be searching for her – if he might someday find her in Ceramir.

Brogal came out of the house. He was not smiling. "Varga bargains hard," he said. "She barely let you go at the price of all my gold. I hold your freedom worth all that and more, yet the coins I sought to spare might have aided us in crossing Cembar. Still," and he smiled again, "we shall ride like the wind, to hope and freedom."

He looked through his saddlebags and brought out a rope. A look of concern crossed his face. "I would like to tie you on my horse, my Lady," he said, "for you cannot hold on with your legs, and I fear you may fall if I do not. Yet if ropes remind you of capture and slavery, I will dispense with them and ride with care, more slowly."

Naomi smiled at him in the growing light. "I am not afraid," she said. "I know the difference between ropes that bind and ropes that protect."

Despite her words a momentary chill passed through her as he bound her, gently but securely, to his horse. But her hands were free, and the free wind blew in her face and raised her hair, and she knew that all was well.

A hoarse scream from the house shattered the windswept peace of the gray morning. Naomi heard only, "Ya cieloradca varka Brint! Varkaradra! Ya varkaradra bonbar, zash yon needeem breen!" Yet she knew from the tone that the speaker was full of hatred and fear. She guessed that it was Varga, but what had angered her she could not imagine.

Brogal, flawlessly fluent in the Cembaran language, heard, "Brint is dead! Murderer! You are a murderer, and I will get justice!"

Thankful with all his heart that Naomi had agreed to be tied on the horse, Brogal leaped into the saddle himself and spurred the horse forward with a great cry. They flew down the narrow forest path, with bare tree branches whipping them as they passed. "What did she say?" Naomi cried back against the wind of their going.

"She said I have murdered Brint, and she will get justice," said Brogal loudly into the wind. "She is insane. Last night she told me Brint had fever, and I did not go near her. But Brint is popular with the men of the neighboring villages, and they will hear Varga's cries and come after us for vengeance. Perhaps she thinks to keep my gold and retake you – but we will thwart her."

"Is Brint dead, then?" asked Naomi.

"I think Varga must have looked in on her and thought so," said Brogal against the wind. "I do not know. Perhaps she was only unconscious. Even that would mean her illness was worse than I gathered from Varga last night. I hope you have not been near her."

"She lifted me into bed the day you came," said Naomi. "She was feverish, but I certainly did not think she was dying."

"You have been near her, then," said Brogal, "but sickness is but of one of many perils that may or may not come upon us. In the blessing of our Lord, we need fear neither death nor life."

Naomi was silent for a long time, and then she only said, "Poor Brint..." in a low voice below the wind of their riding.

The winter woods flashed by them as they passed onto larger and larger trails, tending east and south. Bitter cold reigned, and no birds or animals could be seen. A cold, dry snow lay thinly on the ground, swirling up now and then in eddies of the wind. Naomi drew her hooded cloak close about her to shut out some of the bitingly cold air that struck her face. So far there was no sound of pursuit.

They struck a major road, and Brogal turned onto it. It led them south-southwest in a nearly straight line. The road was narrow, paved with hard stone, and fenced on either side with thick, tangled forest. Naomi could feel Brogal looking back often now; scanning the path behind them for pursuers. The clatter of the horse's hooves seemed to violate the winter calmness of the world, the silence broken otherwise only by wind sighing in bare branches, and the soft hiss of eddying snow.

"Are we in much danger?" asked Naomi calmly after a while.

"If we are caught here on the open road, yes," said Brogal. "Horses cannot go through the forest here, and side paths are few. But if we make it through this stretch," he laughed aloud in the cold air, "we reach the open mountain woods, and I could escape a thousand expert hunters there, though all were sworn to kill me. If I can get you there, you are as good as in the Cloth of Joy, though it will be ten more days of riding before we reach it."

Naomi's heart sank at the thought of the weary road that would separate her from Jonathan, if, perchance, he was still alive. She was about to ask Brogal for news from Karolan, when suddenly he gave a loud cry, spurred his horse to greater speed, and bent over her as the wind of their going roared past. "Lay your head against Merya's neck," he said to her, "she must fly as she has never flown before."

Realizing after an instant's confusion that Merya must be the horse, and that Brogal had sighted pursuers behind them at last, Naomi obeyed. Brogal bent down over her. He spoke calm words to the horse in a language Naomi did not know, and the animal seemed to go even faster. The breathless moments passed very slowly. Naomi dared not move, lest she slow Merya or get in Brogal's way as he urged her to her utmost speed. She listened intently for noises behind them, but she could hear nothing above the roaring wind in her ears.

After a long time, Naomi felt Merya falter. The powerful horse seemed to have reached the limit of her strength, and she could not bear them much farther. Brogal spoke calming words to Merya again, and Naomi felt her steady and push forward, but it did not last. Brogal reined her in to a slow trot.

"We cannot get away," he said. "That pace will kill Merya, and if she dies we are lost. Yet I will not break faith with you. I will hide you and let them take me. No rope or prison has ever held me yet. Ah, here is the place I sought!"

Brogal guided the horse off the road and onto a side path that led to a small, frozen stream. He stopped the horse and jumped down from the saddle. Swiftly he cut the ropes that held Naomi to Merya's back. He yanked a blanket from his saddlebag, wrapped it around Naomi, lifted her down, and laid her on the frozen ground beside the stream.

"I will return when I have escaped and thrown off the pursuit," said Brogal. "If I do not come by sunset, this creek leads to a mill, which is not far away. It is not a brothel, and you may find more honest shelter there than Varga gave you, though in any case you will be taken for a slave. I think you can reach it by pulling yourself along the ice. But I will come. Do you trust me?"

"I do," said Naomi. "God go with you!"

"Farewell," said Brogal, and he leaped back into the saddle and returned to the road. Naomi lay still and silent beside the ice, her heart aching with her suddenly clouded hope. After a few moments she heard the sound of many hooves back on the road, and then a babble of foreign voices, and then nothing more. She covered her head with the blanket to hold her warmth, and prayed, and waited.

* * *

Brogal had ridden into the center of the road and stayed there until the pursuers were very near. Then he spoke a sharp word of command to Merya, and she reared up on her hind legs and threw him down upon the stone. He lay motionless, even as the riders drew up and surrounded him.

"Well, we've caught him at last," said one in Cembaran.

"He's dead, though, Wyknas," said another. "He's got his due for poisoning poor little Brint."

The man called Wyknas knelt beside Brogal. "No, Purnaf, he isn't dead," he said. "He's only stunned. The punishment for murder is mine-slavery for life. I suppose we should take him back to Varga so she can have the price of him."

"Varga's an old witch," said a third man. "I say we get the price of him ourselves."

"You're forgetting Varga's the only one who can prove the murder, Skegit," said Wyknas. "We need her to get anything at all."

"We need her to get anything from a legal mine-slaver, you mean," said Skegit. "Why not sell him for something else?"

"And have a murderer who might get free or murder again any time?" asked Wyknas. "What do you suppose mine-slavery is for? It keeps 'em safe forever."

Purnaf dismounted and stood beside Wyknas. "Varga's crazed," he said. "Like as not Brint only died from cold or ill-care while she was sick. I'll take him for my own, and run the chance of being murdered, and I'll pay all of you your proper share of the price for a field-slave."

"I call that handsome," said a fourth man. "But what about the horse?"

"I'll take that too, for thirty gold bits," said Purnaf.

"Purnaf always was an honest dealer," said Wyknas, standing up. "I say accept payment all around and let's go home where it's warm!"

This proposal was unanimously accepted. Some of the men grumbled a little about revenge and justice, for they would have liked to have the blood of the man who had deprived them of their laughing little prostitute. But Cembar's murder laws were strict, and no one liked to suggest killing when it did not look like winning general approval. Also no one trusted Varga, and Purnaf's implication that Brint's death might well be her fault seemed plausible. The little group soon dispersed, most of its members jingling a little extra gold in their pockets, and one of them leading the weary Merya, with Brogal's inert form draped across her back.

*　　　　*　　　　*

Purnaf had gambled, taking trouble and risk on himself to win what might turn out to be a very useful slave, as well as a powerful, well-bred mare. He was quite aware of the possibility of loss: the strange man accused of murdering Brint might be permanently injured, or untamable and vicious. The discounted price he had paid his companions represented his judgment of the relative likelihoods.

The outcome of his gamble turned out even less profitable than his most pessimistic estimation. The first loss happened as he approached his home. After lying senseless across the mare for weary hours of slow riding, the new slave suddenly came to life, leaped from the horse, and began running wildly across a field – only to fall headlong into a deep well. Purnaf called several of his slaves to bring rope and a grappling hook, but two hours of diligent effort did not suffice either to rescue the new slave or to recover his dead body. Purnaf gave him up for lost – and reflected bitterly that the well, too, must be regarded as poisoned for a full year, according to the established principles.

Disgusted with the slave's senseless death, but thankful that it was not his only well, Purnaf consoled himself with the thought that at least the horse had been a bargain. The mare was indeed a fine animal: strong, but gentle and intelligent, with rich, glossy hair. He gave her a place of honor in his stables.

Purnaf's stables were well-watched during the day and locked at night, with a stable-boy sleeping inside the door to give the alarm on any would-be horsethief. The thief that came that night did not use the door, however. Somehow, he removed four planks of wood from the rear of the stable without waking the boy, and stole three horses. Two of them wandered back in the morning – but the fine brown mare never returned.

Purnaf was left with a dead loss. But Brogal, though he had escaped his captors as always, knew that he could not reach the place where Naomi waited until nearly dawn.

*   *   *

Naomi waited past sunset and long into the bitter night, straining her ears for the sound of distant hooves. It did not come. Finally she stirred herself wearily, and rolled down the low bank onto the ice.

The movement partly opened her blanket, and the freezing air stabbed her wide awake. The sky above was starless. She could barely distinguish between the white ice of the creek and the darker bank. She felt clumsily along the bank with numb hands, gripped a root, and pulled herself forward. She slid across the ice, as she had expected, but the force she had to use surprised her. She had imagined that the ice would be smooth, polished, and slippery. Instead it was covered in a thin blanket of gritty snow, through which frozen-in twigs and other debris poked upward, making the sliding still more difficult. She tucked her freezing hands back into the blanket and nursed them awhile before continuing to drag herself along. It was grueling work, and she had to pause time after time to warm her hands and catch her breath.

At times Naomi felt the nightmare quality of the journey: her friendlessness and peril, the starless darkness, and the weird experience of sliding along half-seen ice in an unfamiliar land. Yet she was wide awake, and homely smells of forest leaves and wood smoke came to her despite the cold. Above and beyond all, she remained aware of the love of God.

There came a moment when the sliding was easier, and then suddenly she found herself slipping forward uncontrollably down a steep rapid of the stream. She skidded to a stop in the middle of a smoothly frozen pool. At first she felt relief that the invisible rapid had not been the start of a frozen waterfall, but then she realized it had left her in real difficulty. She could not reach the bank in any direction: there was nothing she could grab to pull herself along. For several moments she thought she would not be able to move at all. Finally she found that her fingernails could find just enough purchase on the hard ice to move her. The ice of the pond was blessedly smooth compared to that of the creek above the rapids, and at last she reached the shore.

But the creek narrowed again below the pond, and the ice again became rough. To move the distance a whole person would cover in a single step, she had to pull herself forward two or three times – and each time her hands had painfully to seek new purchase on the frozen bank. The strange journey began to seem endless, but she could think of nothing to do but go on. Dark as it was, she could not possibly miss the mill and waterwheel Brogal had spoken of.

At length it occurred to her to doubt that she was going the right way on the creek. Going downstream had simply seemed the obvious thing to do. Now she wondered if, in the anxiety and haste of Brogal's departure, he had pointed the other way and she had forgotten or had not been watching.

Many times she thought she saw the sky lightening toward dawn, but each time she had at last to acknowledge herself mistaken: the night was passing far more slowly than she thought. She was deeply weary, and chilled despite her exertion, when she saw the dark shape of a building looming ahead and to her right, vaguely seen against the scarcely less deep blackness of the sky. It was tall, almost like a low tower. She pushed herself up to the bank beside it.

The tower was only a few steps back from the shore, but the bank here rose half a man's height from the surface of the creek. She wondered if she could ever make it up, but, desperate to find a place of shelter, she determined to try.

Her groping hands found a large tree root protruding from the bank, and she used it to lift herself part way off the ice. With a trembling effort, she reached higher and caught at another root – only to find the blanket slipping off from around her shoulders. If she lost that, she would die. She sank back upon the frozen creek, and knotted the blanket tightly around her. She breathed deeply, gathering herself for an effort, and then reached up again to grasp the large root. She pulled herself upward using a sequence of several roots, and even a low branch of a sapling, until at last she was sitting triumphantly upon the creek-bank, panting hard in the icy air.

Regaining her breath, she dragged herself painfully toward the building. Her probing hands met walls of frost-covered wood. It seemed to be a round tower about three paces across, and at least two stories high. There was no sign of life within. Naomi called out, loudly, several times, but her voice only echoed futilely in the frozen forest. She pulled herself around the base of the tower, feeling for a door or window. She found a wide, heavy door, but it was fastened with an iron lock. A few steps further, her hands came upon something she had not expected: a sturdy ladder of round wooden rungs, built into the wall. She looked up, and it seemed to her that the ladder led up to a dark opening high in the side of the tower.

Naomi thought for a moment in the bitter cold and darkness. Then, without coming to any conclusion, she put her hands on the highest rung she could reach, and began to climb.

The rungs were close together, and in the blessed, vanished days in Glen Carrah her arms had been strong. She thought she had a chance. But since those days she had been weakened by injury and illness, and now she was tired and cold. Her arms shook and her breath came fast and short before she was a dozen rungs up. The building towered over her like a mountain. Each rung cost her a trembling effort, and with each rung gained she wondered if she had the strength for the next. She wondered to what she was climbing.

Then she caught a glimpse of the square of deeper darkness above her, and she struggled upward with new strength. Her left hand came up over an edge of wood: the square was indeed an opening, and the sweet, healthy smell of dry hay came from within. Groping with her right hand for chinks between planks in the wooden floor, she found purchase at last and pulled herself in with a final effort, her legs sliding uselessly behind her.

She lay still, breathing hard, for a long time. The loft smelled clean, and she heard no sound of movement in it. She slid herself forward, and immediately her hands struck dry straw, piled knee deep upon the floor. Wishing for nothing more than sleep, she piled straw against the opening to keep the cold wind out, wrapped her blanket close around her, and fell asleep dreaming of the home that she had lost forever. Outside, long-threatened snow began to fall, obscuring the marks of her laborious journey.

Chapter 4

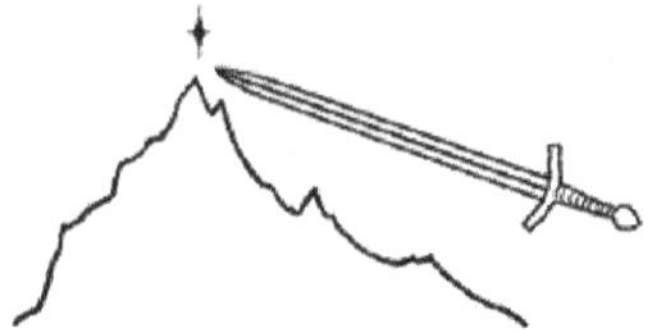

Her Time May Come

THE BLACK SKY CHANGED TO A COLD BLUE-GRAY, AND A brisk south wind welcomed the icy dawn. Despite the early hour, a man was seen trudging from house to house in the vicinity of the mill, hooded and muffled against the cold. He walked a little wearily, and some thought he was old, but his gruff voice when he spoke was strong and clear. At every door he asked the same question, "Have you seen my crippled daughter? She was riding near here yesterday, and her horse returned without her. I am afraid she will be mistaken for a slave, for since her injury she speaks only Karolan. But besides this her mind is clear. She is kind and good, and I love her." Then he would lean against the doorway, as if overcome with sorrow, and say, "I beg you, tell me you have seen her. Please... I must find her."

But she whom he sought had completely disappeared. He searched the woods and the stream where he had left her, but the snow had hidden all trace of her. There was no blanket or piece of clothing to suggest her movements, no corpse to tell of her death. He looked for her all that day, and continued the search on the morrow. Some of the local gossips wondered where he had slept, for none could trace him to an inn or house.

The second day closed equally fruitless. He began to look in the face the idea that he, Brogal of Ceramir, had failed to keep his word, and had lost one whom he had pledged to save. He wept that night in his secluded camp, in a forest glade where he had found some dry grass for Merya. He had failed before, many times, but never after having given his word; never after having come so close. He had not before been so confused. It was as if an evil miracle had taken her from the face of the earth at the very moment when she was about to be saved. He prayed a long time beside his fire, then slept at last and dreamed of Auria, his sister, long ago when they had been children together in the Cloth of Joy. He dreamed that she was teasing him, as she had often done, about some foolish action or idea of his. She had always had good sense, and he thought it possible that much of his healthy laughter had come from her, in the days when they had frolicked together in the flower-bright forests of the Cloth of Joy.

When he awoke, he knew what he would do. He prayed once more by the ashes of his fire. He asked God for forgiveness for his failure, and for peace and strength. He asked him to protect the woman he had failed to save, and bring her healing and rescue, wherever she was. Then Brogal of Ceramir mounted Merya in a bound, and rode north and east at a gallop, laughing in the wind. His errand was no jest, but he laughed for joy and hope, and for the preposterous things that he attempted. He would strip off his disguise before Varga, and for once stand forth as who he truly was. And he would take Brint, if she lived. Auria would have urged it, had she been there.

* * *

He came upon Varga on a forest path even before he was in sight of her house. He dismounted and faced her. The very fact of his return was sufficient to frighten her, but besides that he had drawn his hidden, razor-sharp knife. She fell at his feet, trembling and begging for mercy. He caught the front of her cloak in one hand and raised her up against a tree. "What do you know of mercy?" he asked. "I know of mercy. Varga, do you know who I am?"

He threw his outer garments back on the snow. The full, even light of the cloudy sky lit his whole form. His face was resolute, and his clothes were vibrant green and gleaming white, cut handsomely in a form unknown in Cembar, Karolan, or Norkath. To Varga he was like an image of uncorrupted manhood, bursting on her long experience of evil as something forgotten yet instantly recognizable when seen. He was brimming with life and laughter, strong in his youth, mirthful and wild, yet trustworthy and wise. She knew suddenly that she was powerless: she could compass neither his seduction nor his death. She shook her head, trembling. "I do not know," she whispered. "You are... you are strange to me."

"I am Brogal, son of Mudien and Imranie, a Son of Ceramir," he said. "I have deserved Hell and been forgiven. The Master of the world has loved me and healed me, and chosen me as his forever. His Spirit, the Spirit of God Almighty, is in me. I have been in a dozen prisons, and none has ever held me. Twice I have been condemned to die, and twice I have run free as the wind. I have set free the innocent from darkness and spoken words of forgiveness and hope to the guilty. I have knelt beside beds of plague and fever, and the sickness has not touched me. I have stood faithful and pure beside the beds of whores, and offered them freedom. I have laughed at those who would destroy me, and ever I have escaped. Varga, do you understand me?"

She only stood and trembled.

"I now do something which comes from God, for my own wish is to slay you without mercy. Varga, leave the life you have known. Even for you there is forgiveness and healing. In Ceramir you will find life that is truly living, such as in all your long years you have never known. Varga, come with me, and I will take you to freedom. For you are a slave, Varga, as much a slave as your whores have ever been. Do I not guess rightly that you were once a whore yourself?"

Varga trembled, shook her head, and then spat in his face. "I will not come," she said. "I have the power here."

He did not move in response to her action, but only stood looking into her eyes. "Varga, I will not come again. Will you go with me now?"

She only spat again.

Brogal's knife flashed coldly in the air, but struck only the tree above Varga's head. "I offered life," he said, his voice loud with authority such as she had never heard, though in the words of evil men she had heard its distortion. "I do not offer death. But Varga, you will give me Brint, even if I have only come in time to bury her. Varga, tell me where she is. I am taking her."

Brogal knew that Varga had rejected his appeal on her own behalf – though he did not know how powerful the appeal had been, nor how significant was her rejection. Now he watched carefully, seeking clues to Brint's fate in her face as she hesitated. "She has lain senseless and dead these three days," said Varga at last. "Now…" Varga paused, and Brogal saw a smile that seemed both dreamy and evil come into her face.

"She always feared coldness... she will not be cold now..." Brogal followed Varga's gaze in the direction of the house. A thick column of smoke could be seen climbing above the trees. Brogal released Varga, snatched his knife from the tree, hastily gathered his cloak from the ground, and leaped on Merya's back. He spurred her to a gallop as he did so, and a moment later he stood before Varga's burning house. In places, tall flames already flickered above the roof and licked at the branches of overhanging trees.

He stood still an instant before the house, thinking about Brint. "She is broken," he said aloud. "She is scarcely even human now. Her ruin haunts and frightens me; I hate to know that God's creatures can be shattered thus by evil. I would not like to have her near me all the long journey back to Ceramir. And surely by now she is dead." He wavered only the time of a single breath, and his thoughts changed.

"Yes, that is what Brogal is, a coward. I am jester, and a fool. But I am a fool in the hand of God." And he ran into the burning house.

The bottom of the stairway was in flames, and the first step broke beneath his weight. He raced out of the house and saw a tree near Brint's window. He climbed it with speed and grace, and leaped like a giant squirrel to catch the windowsill. He pulled open the shutters and clambered through. The room was very hot, and the wall opposite the window was all in flames, but the floor was still sound. The smoke was thick but not blinding. Brint's bed was on his left, and she lay there pale and unmoving. One end of the mattress was just taking fire, but she had not yet been burned.

He lifted her up. She was not stiff in his arms, so he knew that if she were dead, she had not been so long. He looked at the window. It was too high; he could not leap down carrying her and walk away – they would both be seriously hurt. He kicked at the burning door, and it burst open. The floor of the short hallway beyond was not yet on fire, but both walls were burning. Brogal ran down the hallway and came to the top of the stairs. The whole stairway was on fire, but fire was catching the floor behind him and he took his only chance. He was halfway down the stairway when it collapsed beneath him. He landed on his feet amid the burning wreckage, and ran forward into what seemed a wall of flame.

An instant later he was rolling over and over in the snow outside the house, coughing hard, with Brint still held close against him. He was free. He came to a stop. His clothes and Brint's had been burning, he knew, but now they were extinguished. He lay still in the snow for a moment. A massive beam of the house collapsed with a roar and a shower of sparks. Smoldering fragments rained down around him and Brint. He stood up and took her in his arms again. He walked to where Merya stood patiently, not far away. It took him a few moments to realize fully that he had escaped without harm and that the rescue, so far, had succeeded. He looked down into Brint's pale face, wondering if she were dead or alive. Her eyes opened at that very moment. "I am cold," she said.

Brogal laughed aloud beneath the winter sky. "Mother, and Lady Eleanor," he called, "what a charge I am bringing you! Yes, it will be a long road. But at last she is started on it!" He wrapped Brint in a thick cloak, lifted her to Merya's back, and mounted behind her. Together they rode away from madness, fear, and evil – toward life, sanity, and home.

*　　　　　*　　　　　*

Naomi lay in the dark hayloft. It was her third day there, but she was not troubled by hunger or thirst. Against all expectation, when Brogal had not returned, another friend had come to her. He had come in late morning on the first day: a young boy called Brekon, perhaps ten years old, with a quiet light in his eyes that spoke of peace and understanding beyond his years. Yet in other ways he was very much a child, and Naomi was not sure how he thought of her.

He had crawled up into the hayloft – to cry, she suspected – and had been shocked to find her there. Yet rather than being frightened or curious, he simply asked her to tell him a story. He had spoken the language of Karolan clearly, though as an untaught child. She had replied to his request, truly enough, by saying she could not tell a story without eating and drinking first. He had gone out, and returned in minutes with a fine meal of bread, porridge, and cheese, along with clean water. She had eaten and drunk gratefully, and then tried to remember the stories she had used to tell, now and then, to children back in Glen Carrah. At last she had begun, and her tale had delighted him. On the next day he had brought her more food, and she had told another story.

Brekon was very thoughtful, glad to provide her with all she needed, but she wondered whether he considered her a real person, or only a source of stories. She wondered if it occurred to him that if he were to betray or abandon her, she would die or be enslaved. And yet she did not want such heavy thoughts to quench his boyish laughter. She could be to him simply a storyteller. She could thank God for the food Brekon brought her, and wait on God for further rescue, if that was his intent for her.

She was grateful to hear his light footsteps on the ladder now, heralding this morning's visit. He pushed aside the hay and crawled in, bringing a gust of clean, icy wind and a burst of white light from the snowy world outside. "I have brought you a good breakfast, Naomi," he said, his eyes sparkling and his cheeks rosy. "Now, can you tell me –" he broke off as she gazed at him reproachfully.

"That is right," said Naomi. "First I eat, and then you have your story."

She ate gratefully, looking over at him now and then and smiling. She had no idea how he got the food. Wild thoughts sometimes passed through her mind of asking him to help her escape to Karolan, but she put them from her. It was folly: she would bring trouble on the child – and anyway she would be enslaved, or worse, long before she reached the border.

She finished her meal, and Brekon sat silent for a long moment, eagerness struggling with patience in his face. Finally he could bear it no longer, and spoke in a low yet pleading voice, "Naomi, have you a story for me today?"

She began to speak, and in the dark, narrow hayloft her story seemed to gain life and depth beyond any of the tales she had used to tell in Glen Carrah. Her words carried her and Brekon together into a brighter, more laughing world, far from the grim winter, and slavery, and fear. In this unfamiliar power as a storyteller she saw the blessing of God, to provide for her and lighten her gloom – to let her, crippled, exiled, and imperiled though she was, still bless another human soul.

When her story was over, the boy picked up the chamber pot that he had given her two days before, and carried it carefully down the ladder to empty it in the woods. Naomi wondered again who he was and what his future held. He carried the stinking pot without a hint of revulsion. "He does not know disgust," she thought, "and he has the heart of a willing servant." He brought the pot back not only empty but clean, rinsed with snow.

"I thank you," she said. "Did you like the story?"

His eyes shone. "Yes," he said. "It was the best I ever heard. Can you tell me another one tomorrow?"

"I will try," she said, "if you bring me more food and water."

"I will!" he said. "I thank you."

He turned to go, but before he began descending the ladder, Naomi asked, "Brekon, do you know God?"

Brekon turned back and looked at her. The bright square of winter world seen through the door silhouetted his head. "Of course," he said. He sat down with his back against the wall beside the door, as if to explain things to her in more detail. "My big sister taught me," he said. "When she was dying, I asked her if I could give her anything before she left. She said, 'tell me if you think you will see me again.'

"I said, 'Of course I will, when Jesus takes me away as he is taking you now. I will see you above the stars.'

"She said, 'But why should he want me, who have been such a wicked girl?'

"I said, 'I don't know, but he was tortured to death to have you, so he must want you very much. I mean, he went to die of torture for his people, and you and me must be some of them, since we love him. And you have not been a wicked girl, truly."

"She said, 'I have been a wicked girl, Brek, but you are right. He will take me. Brek, you have given me what I wanted most. Now I know that you know God, and I will see you again.'

"Then I had to leave her, and I did not see her again, but I know God.

Naomi was silent for a moment, and Brekon got up to leave as if nothing important had happened. She halted him once more with a question, "Brekon, are you an orphan?"

He smiled at her. "All slaves are orphans," he said, and was gone.

* * *

The wind from the desert blew strong in Brogal's face, and in spite of the winter it carried a ghost of warmth from the sun-baked sands across which it had blown. High above him the first stars shone, though the bright sunset still glowed on his right. Brint, riding before him in the saddle, did not seem to notice. Brogal knew that her mind was clear enough: she was no longer feverish, and when he gave her instructions she obeyed them. But she seemed blind to the beauty through which they rode, and every night when they camped she would beckon him to use her as a whore. She always looked confused and hurt by his refusal, no matter how he explained it. On some of these occasions he had heard her murmuring hopefully to herself afterwards, but at other times she wept, as though she feared she must have lost her beauty.

When he stopped to camp, he stood still for a moment beside the horse, breathing the desert air. This vast, barren wilderness was his, and he loved it. He knew it could kill him. He could die in its pathless, waterless dunes, or its sudden canyons of jagged stone. It held snakes with deadly venom, and briers with thorns as hard as nails. But it was fair, wild, clean, and beautiful. Nothing in it sickened his heart or stifled his laughter. He loved it, and the home it guarded. He breathed its clean, dry, air and laughed aloud beneath the brightening stars.

He had chosen to camp near one of the scarce watering places that he had found long before: a little stream that rose from a spring and chattered merrily down a short channel to lose itself in desert sand. The water was chilly, but much warmer than snowmelt even in winter. After lighting a campfire, he led Brint over to the stream. "Please to wash yourself," he said.

She dipped a hand, then huddled in her cloak. "It is cold," she said. "I will not go."

"Brint," said Brogal gently, "you are dirty, and must wash."

"I am dirty, but I am warm," said Brint. "That water is cold… as cold as death."

"Do you know that I am not your master?" asked Brogal. "That if you wished, I would take you anywhere you chose – even back to Cembar, and slavery?"

She shuddered and crouched on the ground, as if in fear of the stroke of a whip. "No… no! I do not wish that!"

Brogal smiled and knelt before her to meet her eyes. "I rejoice that you do not wish it," he said, "and you will never have cause to regret your choice. Yet will you not do as I ask, since you ride with me willingly?"

She crouched even lower. "To wash… in cold, cold water? No, please you… No, I will not."

Brogal said no more to her, but piled dry wood on the fire until it was a glorious blaze, illuminating the darkening land with a ruddy, warm and welcome light. He lifted Brint gently in his arms, and carried her away from the fire to the stream. He took off her clothes, and put her into the cold water. She resisted a little, but he easily and gently overpowered her.

She was still afraid of the cold, but she had been sorry to resist his will, and was almost glad to find her obedience forced. The water was piercingly, numbingly cold, but looking up from it, she saw that the sky was full of brilliant stars. She knew she was dirty, and that Brogal was making her clean. She liked the feel of his hands in her hair, combing out the tangles and washing the dirt away in the swift water. He washed every part of her, but his hands were not as other men's hands. At last he raised her up, and she stood beside the creek. She was deeply chilled, and she shivered, but not cringingly as she had before. "Walk back to the fire and stand near it," he told her. "I will stay here and wash your clothes."

She obeyed him, and stood naked before the glorious fire. The heat danced and shone and beat against her skin, and she reveled in the feel of it. She had always loved warmth, but she felt now that all the warmth she had known before had been dead, inert and dry like withered leaves. This heat was alive: it laughed and leaped and danced. She stood still and soaked it into her chilled body and heart. In her mind new thoughts and dreams awoke. They were things she had never known before, or had long ago forgotten, touching her now like strains of music from another world. She felt hope for which she knew no name.

Brogal returned with her clothes, and spread them out to dry before the fire. She met his gaze across the fire, and though his eyes were warm and full of life, they lacked something she had thought was universal in the eyes of men. She knew for the first time what it was. He did not lust for her; he only cared for her. And yet she stood naked, with only flames between them. And yet she was beautiful, and he was a man, not a eunuch. She still did not understand it, but now, for the first time, she believed it. Later that night, when she lay beside the coals of the fire clothed in fresh, warm garments, she did not beckon to him as she had before. Instead she looked up at the stars, and wondered if they had shone on Varga's house all the years she had been there, and she had never known it.

*   *   *

In a small stone room hewn out of the living rock in Petrag, King Ilohan was speaking with Therinil, the widow of Yalron. "You cannot give us back our dead," Therinil was saying, "and we do not expect it. Do not reproach yourself with our misery." For a long time, Ilohan sat silent. The torchlight that illuminated the room cast flickering shadows over the white shawl that covered Therinil's head, and shone reflected in the diamonds of the king's crown. Not far away was the room in which the miners of Petrag had loyally hoarded the vast wealth of their accumulated tribute through ten scores of years, until at last Ilohan, seventh from Corzogad, came over the mountains to lead them.

The gold was now in the treasury of Aaronkal, but Ilohan never forgot from whence it had come. "You have given me everything," he said at last. "You gave me your loyalty, your gold, your lives. And what have I done in return? What could I do in return? Nothing."

"The choice of a hero is his own, Your Majesty," said Therinil. "You did not choose to let them die for you. My husband and all the others stood up to defend the people and the land they loved, at any cost to themselves. You did not take their lives; it was not even chiefly for you that they gave them. They gave them for us, for those they loved, for those they left behind in a land kept free by their courage and their blood. It is not your task to undo the past or fill the gap they left. It is your task to rule the land they saved. They did not save it so that one good man named Ilohan could have the honor of the throne. They saved it so that those they loved could live free. You brought us hope, but you were not our reason for fighting. You brought us hope because it is only during the reign of a good king that the people are truly free. You can do nothing more than not disappoint that hope, and that is enough for any king."

"But my Lady, you are starving here," said Ilohan. "And down along the Petrag road, on burned farms half-rebuilt they are starving. And the winter is so hard… so hard… I have seen people burn the wood with which they should have built their homes, in order to keep warm. All that I can do is not enough. Will you only stand so patient, so brave and still, and never reproach me?"

"How could I or anyone reproach you, Your Majesty, when you are doing all you can?" asked Therinil. "But look at me, King of Karolan." She knelt down on the stone before him and spread her arms out so that her fingers touched both walls of the narrow room. Her arms were thin and her fingers white with cold, but she was not weak or gaunt. There was light in her eyes, strength in her voice, and she was upright and undismayed.

"I am hungry," she said, "and we are all hungry, but we are not starving. I am bereaved, as many others are, but God has not left me without comfort." She bowed her head a moment as if ashamed, and then raised it with joy shining in her eyes. "I did not believe it, but at last I can no longer deny it," she said. "I am with child."

Ilohan heard the depth of joy in her voice. He did not fully understand why the coming of a child into this bitter world should bring such happiness, but he felt an irresistible echo of it in his own heart. There seemed no more to say – but he had one more duty to her. He put in her hand a tiny thing, one of hundreds he had had made by a fine goldsmith at Aaronkal.

She unfolded it carefully and lifted up a slender golden chain, from which hung a many-pointed star fashioned of gold and diamonds. "I have never seen anything so beautiful," she said. "Why does Your Majesty give it to me?"

"I give it in honor of the hero whose child you bear, whose wife you were for so desperately short a time. May the child be blessed from the moment of its birth with strength and hope, courage and faithfulness, love and laughter and joy. May it bring you joy all the days of your life, and may you together be loved and upheld by God your Father, Christ your Savior, and the Spirit who seals our hope."

He departed swiftly, leaving her with that blessing but giving her no time for thanks. He joined Benther, who had been waiting for him, and together they passed through the labyrinth of tunnels that comprised the miners' great home and fortress. Benther looked at his friend and king as they walked. "There is a light in your eyes that I have not often seen of late, Your Majesty," he said. "It more often happens that you come away from your private interviews grim-faced, with the ghosts of tears in your eyes."

"You are very shrewd and keen eyed, Sir Benther," said King Ilohan. "I did not know you stared so hard at me."

"Hard enough to catch many things you would rather hide, perhaps," said Benther. "You would be wise to send me away from your service, or banish me from your kingdom. I have my father's shrewdness; I inherit his shame. I am a dangerous counselor, Your Majesty."

"Are you contemplating treachery, then?" asked King Ilohan, as he had a dozen times before.

"I swear on my life," said Benther, "that I will never betray you, and I would die or be banished for you without thought or hesitation."

"Then I do not see my danger," said the king. "Sir Benther, friend of my childhood, forget your father – I mean, forget the Unknighted – and forget your crime! Live true. Live free. Forgiveness is real, and if it were not who could stand?"

They emerged from underground into the frosty night, and mounted their horses to ride for Aaronkal. Benther noticed that though the king held himself regal and upright in the saddle for the most part, now and then his head nodded. He would shake himself fiercely each time, and sit up even straighter than before.

"You are weary, Your Majesty," said Benther.

"It is not important," said King Ilohan. "I will not fall."

"May I commit an impertinence, Your Majesty?" asked Benther.

"You may, Sir Benther; I trust it will be an impertinence which may become a knight."

"Then, Your Majesty, I would ask you if you know the reason King Thomas reigned longer than any other king among the last ten."

"I know it well," the king said reverently after a moment's silence. "Sarah."

"Yes," said Benther. "And now comes the impertinence. You spent a long time tonight speaking with a beautiful and faithful young woman who is a widow. When you had finished, there was hope and peace in your face such as I have not seen in many days. Am I to draw no conclusion from these facts?"

"None," said Ilohan. After a long silence, he continued. "Therinil of Petrag will never be my queen, though she would greatly honor the throne of Karolan. I do not think she will marry again."

"And you yourself will die without an heir?" asked Benther

"Perhaps," said the king. "But not without having loved."

"Your Majesty, tell me as a friend who you love. If she can marry you with honor you must not give up hope of her."

"She is free and pure," said Ilohan, "but she is far away… I cannot go to her, and if I did, I could not ask her to share the throne. That weight I will not lay upon another's shoulders."

"Glen Carrah, Luciyr, Ceramir," said Benther. "In which of these places does she live?"

"It does not matter," said King Ilohan. "In this you cannot persuade me. Let us ride faster."

They pushed on through the cold, barren night, and when they reached Aaronkal midnight had passed and dawn was not far away. The king climbed quickly to his tower room, and entered to find Skykag perched upon his chair. He wearily called a servant to bring food for the great eagle, and unwrapped the note that was upon its talon.

All is well with us.
I long for more news of you,
but your first duty is to your people.
Remember Veril.
A mother's prayers go with you always.
Eleanor

King Ilohan wrote,

I am weary.
The healing of the land is hard,
and the winter has no mercy.

My trust is in God.
Your blessing holds true.
A rider shall bring you the story
of wonder that was Karolan's rescue, and mine.
I cannot forget her.
Be assured of my great love for you.
Ilohan

Well fed, Skykag winged his way up into the frozen sky with the new message, and the weary young King of Karolan slept without a dream.

*　　　　*　　　　*

It was not long after dawn when the king and Sir Benther met in a council chamber before a good fire. Neither had slept enough. They ate breakfast hurriedly, discussing the troubles of the kingdom.

"All the slain of the battle of Petrag have been honorably buried, except the Norkaths who were crushed beneath the slab," said Benther. "Your Majesty's plans to rebuild the knighthood of Karolan are prospering. We have nearly fifteen score young men training to be knights, and even though most of these were peasants, they are swiftly progressing not only in the skills of war but also in those branches of scholarly learning that are required for knighthood. I must acknowledge myself astonished at the peasants' wisdom and the swiftness of their understanding.

"Moving on to matters of supply, Petrag and the burned farms have two weeks' worth of food on their current rations. A cargo of wood planks is ready to send to Glen Carrah at the request of some who wish to rebuild there. Thus far all is well – but no farther.

"Meaning that after two weeks, we will have no more grain to send?" asked Ilohan.

"Yes," said Benther. "Not only that, but even here in Aaronkal we may soon be hungry. In the villages that were not burned there is grain enough, mostly, but little to spare when the seed-grain of the new spring is set aside."

"There are rich farms to the west and north that saw nothing of the war," said Ilohan, "yet they have responded to our requests saying they have no grain to spare. Their sons died in the war, they say, and their grain is their own to withhold."

"Four thousand men of Karolan died in the war, mostly from the south or east," said Sir Benther. "There must be five thousand farms in northwest Karolan alone. They cannot all have lost a son. And I know that they reaped a good harvest."

"Must we levy a grain tax against them, then?" asked Ilohan. "That has never been done in the history of Karolan."

"No!" cried Sir Benther, banging his fist on the sturdy table. "That is what my father would have told you. What do I advise? I do not know. What would Kindrach have done? Would he have gathered the farmers of the north together and given them a mighty exhortation to charity, so that they went away weeping in repentance and gave half their grain to Petrag and Carrah?"

The king smiled. "Perhaps he would have," he said, "but I cannot do that. Here is another thought: I could write to King Andokar to propose buying grain from Norkath."

"The Norkaths lost a score and seven thousands at Petrag," said Benther. "Will they give us anything but curses?"

"That is a score and seven thousand fewer mouths they have to feed," said the king. "And their farms were not burned. When did a Norkath ever refuse gold?"

"Your Majesty, it should indeed be tried," said Benther. "Neither Thomas nor any of his advisers would have considered buying grain from the enemy, I think, but why not? It is strange, perhaps, but neither foolish nor unjust."

"Norkath is not our enemy, not now that Andokar rules her," said King Ilohan.

They talked a little longer, and then Benther went out to dispatch the load of timber for Glen Carrah. Ilohan was left alone to write his message to Andokar of Norkath. For a long time he did not take up his pen. He bowed his head on his hands on the council table, and wished with all his heart that he had more counselors, and that there were not so much to do alone.

The choices he had to make every day wielded immense influence over the lives of others, and because of his love for his people he felt this a heavy burden. Through speaking individually with some of them, as with Therinil the night before, he was growing to know them as well as love them. To him they were not just so many peasants, merchants, and nobles in each part of the land – they were people, each with a heart, with fears and longings, dreams and nightmares, loves and hatreds. Each had a face and an immortal soul; each had a measureless value. A few he had seen and spoken with, trying to learn how to serve them. Thousands more he could only imagine, but he did imagine them. He could see them in his mind, not as a faceless multitude, but as scores of thousands of people whom he would never know, each one a creation of God too complex to understand even with the study of a lifetime.

He remembered well his thoughts when he had stood upon the ridge before the ascent to Luciyr, and saw the vast expanse of Karolan spread out below him. He had thought then that the king's power was very great because of the staggering breadth of his realm, but then again very little because he could never have the strength to fulfill the entirety of his task. "I was right," he said now aloud. "In all that I thought I was right."

And yet he had wanted that power. He had wanted the authority and the responsibility of the king. He had wanted the chance to bless thousands of hurting souls, to rule them well and guard them, to lead a free people into strength and joy. He had wanted that which he now had, beyond his wildest dreams. "Thank you, Father," he said, against his ungrateful thoughts, against his wishes that any one but him might have the throne.

He longed for Thomas, for Britheldore, for the loyal Knights of Karolan who had advised the old king, and had perished to a man in Metherka's heroic, hopeless charge. He longed for Eleanor, for Mudien and Imranie, with their wisdom and their faith, but they were far away. He longed for Jonathan, with his love and faithfulness, his courage and confidence – and for the deep, calm insight of Barnabas. But Jonathan had disappeared, and Barnabas had chosen to be only a blacksmith of Carrah. He could not find them, could not ask them, could not raise them from the dead. He was alone, and Benther was his only counselor. Sometimes he felt he was a child trying to rule in the throne of ancient heroes, with another child as his advisor: two boys whose dreams were made terribly real before they themselves had grown to match them. And he was weary, with much to be done.

"Savior," he said, "you carried me through the darkness of the forget-me-not. When all was lost you were with me, and with my people. What right have I to be afraid now? Father, with you, a child can rule a land, and one hand can overthrow a thousand men. Keep us through this winter of our pain, into a spring of hope. Lift for us the flower of a new Knighthood, and in honor, strength, and glory let them surpass even the heroes we have lost. Sustain me in my weariness, and help me bless my people and never cause them harm."

He raised his head, pulled the parchment toward him, dipped his pen in ink, and began, "His Royal Majesty Ilohan King of Karolan, to His Glorious Majesty Andokar of Norkath: You must understand that the farms and barns burned in our sovereign realm of Karolan by the soldiers of Your Glorious Majesty's craven predecessor contained the grain and food required by large numbers of our people to survive the winter. Understanding that the grievous and deplored war so happily concluded in your current amity with us has left your people with a surplus of grain, I beseech your aid..."

The sun of a new day rose high above the battlements of Karolan's great fortress Aaronkal, and its rays seemed to tell the frozen land of the spring that would come at last. The blue and silver banners shone against the gray towers and the pale blue sky, and men looked up to the castle of the young king with hope. The long darkness of grief, cold, and hunger was not yet ended, but it was as though the morning star had risen to bring the hope of dawn.

Chapter 5

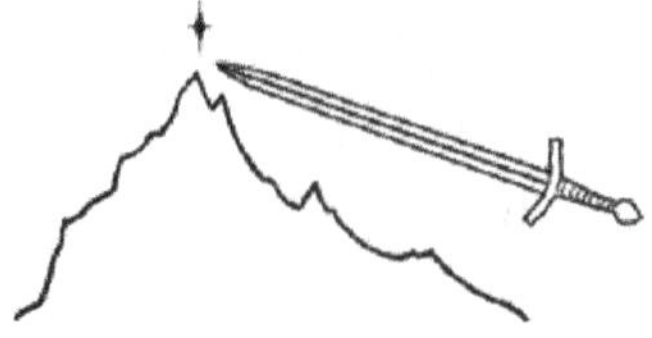

Veril's Choice

IN THE CLOTH OF JOY ANOTHER BANQUET WAS DRAWING to a close. The big waxing moon shone cold and bright in the high east, making a silver wonder of the thick mist swirling off the warm lake. The lamps of Ceramir burned bright and warm beneath the trees; their welcoming gold an earthly counterpoint to the cold splendor of the moon and stars. Warmly dressed, yet still crowded near one of the warm lamps, Veril, Eleanor, and Brogal sat talking at one of the tables.

"Lady Eleanor, put your arms around me," said Veril, "I have something to say, but I am afraid to say it."

Eleanor hugged Veril close, and Veril lay back against her like a child. "Lady Eleanor, if I went to Karolan to visit… the king, do you think I could bring him any blessing?" She shuddered with the relief of having finally said it.

Eleanor looked down at her. Her lovely red hair shone in the golden lamplight. In her fear and longing for comfort she was like a child, but her thought was a woman's. Her question was easy to answer, yet also hard – hard to know all that should or should not now be spoken. "Yes, child," said Eleanor. "Yes, you could bless him, more than you know. But if you go, there will, I think, be no returning. Are you ready to leave this place forever, and be the wife of a weary man who rules a land you have never seen? It will be harder than you know."

"I did not think of that, Lady Eleanor," said Veril, tears appearing instantly in her uplifted eyes. "I only feared I would be useless to him… I forgot that if it were otherwise, I would be his forever…I suppose I imagined I might sometimes come back. I thought Ceramir would somehow still be mine. I thank you, Lady Eleanor. Please to let me get up now."

Eleanor released her, and Veril moved her chair back and got slowly to her feet. She stood very straight, holding her head high, her tears shining in the lamplight as they fell.

"Yes," she said. "Yes. I love him, and I am ready. I will leave Ceramir. I will stand beside him all the days of his life, and bless him with all the strength that God will give me. I will go."

Brogal spoke now for the first time, his voice calm and almost trivial after Veril's words that had been spoken like a solemn vow. But he was not mocking her. "Are you sure of what will happen, Sister?" he asked.

She turned to him as if it were too much to bear, and stood absolutely still for a moment. Then she collapsed into a chair, crying and laughing together. "No, I am not sure," she said. "I know so little, and have dared to say so much. Maybe to him I am only a pretty girl, who dared a foolish thing on his account, whom he will always pity. Maybe he will be shocked and send me back home."

Mist swirled slowly off the lake in the following silence, while the lamp burned low and the silver light pressed in upon the gold. "He will not do that," said Eleanor at last, quietly. "But not the wisest of us knows the future. We can only love and hope, make our choices and keep our vows. No one can make this choice for you, Veril, nor can anyone foretell its outcome. I can say that you are worthy to be Karolan's queen, worthy as Sarah was, and more praise I do not have. I cannot say whether you will wear her crown indeed. I have already warned you of its cost."

"I like what you say, Lady Eleanor," said Brogal. "We can only love and hope, make our choices and be faithful. I call that Living, though it is a strange fact that some I have met on my travels do not do it, and still think themselves alive. Perhaps it is best to call it Adventure."

Eleanor smiled, and dreams and memories were in her eyes. "Perhaps," she said. "He who knows once said, 'I have come that they may have life, and have it to the full.' And that is how it is. We have life to the full, because Christ came. In my deep darkness still it was life, a thing worth living, because he came."

* * *

Veril set out two days later, and Brogal went with her. Imranie, Mudien, Eleanor, and Auria came down to Harevan to see them off on the desert road. It was a painful farewell. All knew that Veril might be leaving forever – or might soon return. Either way, she would know the grief of loss.

Yet hope shone in her face on that bright morning. Brogal, too, was in high spirits, ready to set out on a new adventure even though he had rested only four days in the Cloth of Joy since riding home with Brint. The morning sun made the snow-clad mountains seem an awesome rampart of dazzling purity, beneath which no harm or evil could possibly befall travelers on the desert road.

Brogal and Veril rode forth free and unafraid, he on his trusty Merya, and she on a beautiful black stallion called

Narlas. Far in the distance they turned together one last time and raised their hands and voices in a final clear farewell. They continued on their way, and those who watched saw them dwindle into mere dark specks upon the pale thread of the road, and vanish at last into the vastness of the desert.

The four watchers returned to the Cloth of Joy. If Veril could have hovered that day as in invisible spirit over her home, even she might at last have been persuaded of her worth. The gap she left was evident. Children she had cared for cried and quarreled, and her friends all thought in vain of a thousand things they would have liked her gentle council on before she left. Eleanor, Imranie, and Auria tried to fill her place as best they could, but it was a difficult business.

But not the most difficult. When Mudien and Imranie lay wakeful in bed that night, it was not chiefly of Veril that they spoke, but of Brint.

"People like her do not come here," said Mudien.

"Not unless they are brought," said Imranie.

"And then only when they are brought by force," said Mudien. "She did not choose to come. She only chose not to resist."

"Brogal has never taken anyone against her own choice before," said Imranie. "Yet one might say this was the choice of the fire. He could not let her die."

"It is written that we should, 'Snatch some from the fire and save them,'" said Mudien. "Seldom has the command been so literally applied."

"He has no caution," said Imranie.

"He has no fear," said Mudien. "It is all lost in his love and laughter. He has seen great darkness, but the darkness does not seem to touch him." He held his wife's hand more tightly. "Would that it touched us as little. Our task – or yours – is harder in this case than his. I am sorry. No one can ever guess what Brogal will do."

"Yet God's Spirit is in him with power, and little that he does goes amiss," said Imranie. "What you say of Brogal is also true of God: no one can guess what he will do."

"You are right, Imranie. Maybe Brogal is more important to the Cloth of Joy than we are."

"And maybe if all did not do their part, it would not be the Cloth of Joy. If we ever know whose task was most important, it will be after we have learned that it does not matter."

"Only God's approval matters, Beloved."

"And in his grace we have it."

They slept.

They were awakened in the dark center of the night by an unrestrained scream, full of fear and shatteringly loud. They rose and ran to the room from which it had come. Brint lay there, still in her bed, but she was rigid with terror. Her eyes were screwed shut as if to ward off some unbearable vision. Imranie thought with horror that her whole body could have been lifted from her ankles and held straight out, like a poker. The girl's lips moved swiftly as she spoke in a soft, desperate tone like a whispered scream.

"No, no, you don't understand," Brint was saying in Cembaran. "I've seen freedom now, and I know this is slavery. I won't be yours anymore. I won't, I won't! This isn't my life anymore. I'm not content, not happy – not anymore. This is horrible, you are horrible! You are evil! I've found you out: you are evil!"

She screamed again, then froze, rigid and silent with her screwed-up eyes. Imranie bent over her. Mudien lit a candle from coals on the hearth, and held it up to give them light. Imranie smoothed back Brint's hair, and gently tried to move her stiffly held arms. "That is all over, child," she said fluently in Cembaran. "You are not there anymore; you are in a good place now, the first good place you have ever known. You will not be cold here, and men will no longer come to you as they used to come. You have a new life, child. Awake and know it."

Imranie knelt and tried to raise Brint's head in her arms, but the girl would not relax. Then suddenly Brint's eyes snapped open and glanced for an instant at Imranie's face. "Leave me die!" she screamed, and in that instant she bit Imranie's right hand viciously and held it in her teeth.

Imranie cried out involuntarily, and her blood showed dark upon Brint's pale lips. Mudien threw the candle on the stone floor and reached down swiftly to pry Brint's jaws apart with both hands. Imranie pulled free her hand and stepped back.

Brint found herself suddenly gathered up in Mudien's arms, and held tightly. She struggled a little, but he was startlingly strong despite his age. His grip was like iron around her legs and shoulders, and she soon gave up all thought of escape. He carried her to the fire, and sat down upon the hearth. The light of coals shone on his face, and she relaxed in his arms. His grip did not relax.

"Brint," he said, "do you know who I am?" His voice, strong and clear and deep, echoed in the stone room.

She squinted at him in perplexity, slowly realizing that she had gone from a strange and horrible dream to a waking that might be merely strange. "Who are you?" she asked plaintively.

"Do you not know me?" he asked her again. "Look at me."

She stared long and hard into his face, but she had not been near him before, and could not recognize him. She remembered Brogal, and the absence of lust in his eyes, and felt safer. But she saw something more in Mudien's face, something her soul, not her mind, could recognize. "Father?" she said in a tiny, frightened whisper.

"Yes, my daughter," he said. "I am your father, and I love you."

"Father, why have I not known you before? For I think I have lived many years."

"You have been lost many years, Daughter, and it is only now that I have found you."

"Father, who am I?"

Imranie sat down beside them on the hearth, near Brint's head. She had wrapped her hand in a torn strip of white sheet. While Mudien sat silent, unsure how to reply, Imranie looked into Brint's eyes. She saw a momentary deep and desperate fear fly through the girl's face, and then yield to incredulous hope. "You ask who you are, my child?" said the mother of Ceramir. "You are one worth saving."

Brint's mouth moved slowly, but no words came. Then at last she spoke in a squeaking whisper, "You... You are not... Give me pardon, I hurt your hand, I thought... Alas, I hurt you, and you are not... you are not Varga!"

"No," said Imranie. "Varga is far away, and cannot come here. I am your mother. And you are forgiven."

* * *

Naomi always had a new story for Brekon, and he never tired of hearing them. Every day, in any weather, he appeared at the straw-stuffed entrance to the hayloft, bringing food and drink, and good cheer and laughter. As the days went by, they learned to trust each other, and Naomi gradually learned more about him.

He was a slave – the son, she guessed, of a slave-woman of Karolan descent whom he had never known. His master now was a prosperous Cembaran miller, who had bought him a month before Naomi first saw him, and for all practical purposes had adopted him as a son. In law only he was still a slave, since legally slaves could not be freed before their fifteenth year of life. His adoptive father was, as far as Naomi could gather, an eccentric old man who had liked him for the look of his face and now almost neglected him, giving him freedom to roam wherever he would in the frozen woods surrounding the mill. The only restraint upon him was that he had to study hard with a tutor every morning, to master the Cembaran language and learn his father's business. After this each morning, he would go straight to the little hayloft. Naomi suspected that she was the only person he knew with whom he could truly talk.

The greatest grief in Brekon's life was the loss of his older sister. Based on all that he had said, Naomi could picture her: brave, ignorant, tender, passionately protective, and physically fragile. At night when they had lain side by side in crowded slave quarters, Brekon's sister had used to tell him stories that enthralled him. He had been pining for one of these on the morning when he first stumbled on Naomi. He had asked everyone in the mill to tell him a story that morning, and all had rebuffed him with harsh words, especially his adoptive father's wife. And so he had come up to the hayloft to cry, and had at last met someone who would give him a story.

Naomi's situation sometimes seemed to her absurd and impossible. Sometimes she felt angry at Brekon for not seeing that her life was shattered. Yet she did not want him to see. Often she would lie awake in the night and pray for him, wondering what the end of their strange friendship could be.

She could not live like this forever. She thought of asking Brekon to tell his stepfather about her, but she feared what might follow. She could form no accurate idea of the miller from what Brekon told her. He might take her as his adopted daughter, and give her the best of care. On the other hand he might despise her and sell her to a brothel. Each time she considered it, she chose to wait, and pray, and not take the risk. Not yet.

Her promise to Jonathan was often in her mind. Her one-time certainty that he was dead had long deserted her, and she longed more than anything else to be back in Karolan. There might still be some there who would take pity on her and aid her in searching for him. Even if not, even if the people of Karolan were all slaves and the farms and villages all ashes, she would rather die there in the ruins of her home than here as a slave in a strange land. She would like to die in a search for Jonathan her beloved, even if that search never had a shred of hope.

At other times, when her fervent prayers melted into dreams, she imagined his firm and heavy steps pounding up the ladder, and his strong brown hands thrusting away the straw. She imagined him shouting her name, having found her at last after months of searching. "Naomi!" he would cry, and his voice would carry the joy of mountains in the sun, of water roaring over mighty falls. He would still love her, she knew. He would always love her.

Naomi could not know the vast distance of wintry wilderness that separated her from Jonathan. She could not know that at that moment he was leaving Jenn in a lonely cottage in southeastern Karolan – leaving her heartbroken, because he did indeed still love Naomi. But even in his dreams he did not imagine that she lived. He would never search the slave-land of Cembar for her. Instead he would go eastward, yet farther from her, driven by anger, seeking for revenge.

* * *

"Lance in rest! Take your place! Ride!" The horses' hooves kicked sprays of fine ice from the frozen ground as they rushed together across the field before Aaronkal. King Ilohan's lance met his opponent's shield square in its center, and threw him forcefully from the saddle. The king quickly dismounted and strode across the field to his side. The other young man had already risen a little shakily to his feet and taken off his helmet.

"Only a few more bruises to go with those I already have, Your Majesty," he said. "I cannot imagine how anyone could beat you – or Sir Benther either."

King Ilohan sighed. Benther had told him the peasants were learning quickly, but that did not alter the fact that they were trying to compress years' worth of training into months. "I remember when I was the least of the Knights of Karolan," he said. "And now none can surpass me. How the mighty have fallen! Thank God, at least, that there is no imminent threat of war."

The sun rose to the highest it would reach that day: bright and clear, but not warm. The frozen ground remained iron-hard, merciless to those who fell. Ilohan worked patiently among the young men he had chosen to train as knights, teaching them how to gird on their armor, how to sit in the saddle, and how to hold the lance – and then yelling out advice to them as they jousted with one another. Often he grieved for the heroes who had fallen in Metherka's charge, who could not now teach the young their skill. Far better knights than he or

Benther had died that day, he knew. He did not know how their prowess could be restored to the Knights of Karolan.

In the late afternoon King Ilohan left the field to Sir Benther, who would continue the training until the evening. Yet Ilohan stood at the gate of Aaronkal watching for a little longer. He remembered how Jonathan, with neither lance nor armor but only a sword, had defeated a Norkath knight. When he thought of his disappearance and of Naomi's death, it seemed to him a mockery to say that the war was won. It was lost. It was miserably lost. He would never again find a friend like Jonathan. Together they had done the impossible. Together they had fought hopeless odds and triumphed. Jonathan had broken the forget-me-not and saved his life. He loved him as a dear brother. And Jonathan would have been a knight like few who ever lived in all the world.

King Ilohan went inside to his other duties. Andokar had agreed to let him buy grain from Norkath, and he must write a letter of thanks. Then he must determine how much grain was needed in different parts of Karolan, and plan how he would bargain for it, how he would gather and transport it. Yet when he reached his room, he sat and stared out the window over the frozen land, while the parchments lay untouched on the table before him. He wanted someone to help him. He wanted some assurance that there was hope. He wanted to feel that the war was over, and that the war was won.

There was a knock at the door. "Enter," he said, and stood. A page briskly opened the door and stood aside to admit a dusty, weary messenger. The man knelt before his king, and without a word he presented a scroll of parchment tied with a cord.

"Accept my thanks. Who sent you?" asked King Ilohan.

"I come from a meeting of five score and six of the richest farmers of northwestern Karolan, Your Majesty. The message is from them."

The king untied the cord, and read:

We humbly request Your Majesty's pardon
for the lateness of our action.
We acknowledge the justice and wisdom
of Your Majesty's request for grain.
We assent to the request, asking pardon
again for our past refusal.
We have sent grain to Aaronkal.
Two score and eight large wagons
completely full should arrive before
the moon has reached its last quarter.
We hope to send another ten before the moon wanes out.
We await your orders. We will send more if it is required.
May Your Majesty's reign be blessed.

The remainder of the parchment was covered with the seals and symbols of the farmers from whom it came. King Ilohan turned to the page. "See to it that this man has bread and good ale," he said. "I will dispatch him with my reply before the day is spent."

The messenger stood, bowed, and followed the page from the room. King Ilohan took a parchment, dipped his pen, and began to write. The formal phrases of thanks and acceptance came easily to his mind, and he could say other words aloud even while writing them. "Thank you, Father, that there is always hope," he said. "Forgive my despondency, and may this new sign of your care help me to trust you more. Yet still I ask… I ask that Jonathan will be found, and that you will give him joy. I do not ask to have him in my service. It would be enough for me to know that he was well and safe. Father, please let it be so... Oh Lord my God, let it be so."

* * *

Nails glowed red on Barnabas' anvil in the falling dusk at Glen Carrah. The blacksmith returned them to the furnace, and pumped the bellows until they glowed a dazzling yellow. He poured them like a fiery avalanche into the tempering water, which quenched them with a furious hiss and many bubbles. Leaving the finished nails in the water for the present, he turned to make more of them. He heated a long wire that he had already made, and cut it into nail-length pieces using a sharp chisel. He gripped one of the pieces with special, heavy-jawed pliers, and held it at the edge of the anvil such that only a very short piece of glowing wire stuck vertically out of the pliers' jaws. With a single hammer-stroke, he crushed the protruding wire back against the pliers, creating the broad, flattened head of a nail. The other end was already pointed, thanks to the angled cutting edge of his chisel.

Nail-making was repetitive work, with less skill and interest than the forging of a sword. Barnabas did it gladly nonetheless: he had made swords to defend Karolan, and now he was making nails to rebuild her. He took a dazzling bright bar of metal from the forge and began to make a new length of wire: the most interesting part of forging nails. He pounded the broad iron with his heaviest hammer, and its end grew thinner and longer until the slender nail-wire looked like some fiery worm called out from the glowing metal by the magic of his blows.

At last the new wire was all cut and made into nails: the last set of the day. Barnabas re-heated them, tipped them glowing into the cold water, and went into to the cottage to Hannah. They sat together near the fire to eat their supper. "I am sorry we have so little bread, dear Barnabas," said Hannah. "Grain is in short supply everywhere, or so I hear. Yet the venison is very good: thanks to your skill as a hunter, we need fear no hunger."

Barnabas smiled at her. "Thanks also to your arrows, which always fly straight," he said. "And the cottage is warm and snug, and even after buying our neighbors' freedom in Cembar, we still have more gold than before the war."

"Yes," said Hannah, glancing at the third, empty chair at the table. "We have everything we could want, except..."

A long silence settled heavily on the little room. They had everything they wanted except Jonathan... and Naomi. "Perhaps I should have sought for him," said Barnabas at last.

"It was I who dissuaded you," said Hannah. "I was sure he had gone away to hide his grief, and still I think so. Even if you had found him, he would not willingly have returned, and you could not have forced him." She paused. "I was sure he would return at last of his own choice. Yet now the weeks are lengthening to months, the winter is bitter cold, and I do not know... I do not know where my child is."

Their meal was finished, and they sat side by side before the fading fire. Outside the wind was rushing cold and strong from off the mountains, and Barnabas knew that ice on his tempering water was already thick, freezing clear and hard over the new-made nails. He put his arms around Hannah and held her close to him. He had nothing to say in comfort, so he held her and was silent.

At last she spoke. "I visited Jemra today to see how their cottage was building. She told me something very strange."

Something in her tone made Barnabas think it was something wholly unexpected, and not good. "What was it, Beloved?" he asked.

"Jemra says that one of the captives was nearly raped by one of the Norkath soldiers at their first camp in Cembar. Jemra would not say who, for the woman herself did not want it known. Of course Jemra and all the others were blindfolded, so they could not see what happened. But as far as she could tell, the Norkath was shot with a bolt, and no one could tell who shot it. The next morning Jemra overheard the Norkath leader talk about a crippled woman among the captives who had stopped the rape while the other soldiers only gawked at it. But no one among those we rescued is crippled, and only two of the women of Carrah are missing."

"Hrelia, and Naomi," said Barnabas.

"Yes," said Hannah.

"Does Jemra know what happened to the cripple?" asked Barnabas.

"According to Jemra, the Norkath leader killed her as punishment for shooting a soldier of Norkath."

"Were none of the other women raped?" asked Barnabas.

"Jemra swears they were not," said Hannah.

"Then the commander must have forbidden it," said Barnabas.

"Yes! Jemra says he did; he forbade it on pain of death, and commended the cripple for her action."

"And did he kill her, after commending her?" asked Barnabas. "Does Jemra not see this as evidence that she does not know what really happened?"

"She says she has spoken only what she knows," said Hannah, "and that if it does not make sense that is not her fault. But I wonder... Oh, Barnabas, can it be that he did not kill her, and that she was... And that she was..."

Barnabas stared into the fire for a long moment. "I do not know," he said at last, slowly. "I can imagine a man who would commend her and yet consider it his duty to execute her. Such a man might think the rapist worthy of death, and yet still kill the one who shot him, by some merciless law of Fingar's fear-forged army. And even if he did not kill her... Even if he did not kill her, still two things oppose our hopes. The first is a wall of fire, from which no one could escape. The second is a bitter winter – bitter even for those with whole bodies, in a friendly land."

Hannah was silent then, staring into the glowing, ever changing coals. At last she spoke, and her voice was clear and sweet, as though years of darkness had been rolled away from her. "Do you know what I think, Beloved?"

"I do not, dear Hannah,"

"My heart soars against all reasons. I think Naomi lives."

"Shall I look for her in Cembar, Beloved?"

Hannah was silent for a long time. When she spoke her voice was low again, and fear was in it. "You would be captured," she said. "And you must not go without me, and I must stay here for Jonathan's return. No, please do not go."

"I will not, now," said Barnabas. "Nor ever, perhaps. But let us keep listening to any tales our neighbors have to tell, and praying, and thinking. For if indeed she is alive but crippled in Cembar, I must search for her – and with a good plan, the search would not be hopeless."

* * *

Every day the mountains showed a different aspect, as Veril and Brogal traveled east on the desert road. Even between morning and evening the view would change in ways that Veril could never predict. Though she had lived within sight of the great mountains all her life, she felt that she was seeing them for the first time. They had been a lovely image in the sky of her home, a backdrop for the Cloth of Joy. Now every passing hour brought into view new peaks and crags, new juxtapositions of gleaming pinnacles, dizzying cliffs, and steep valleys – and Veril knew that the mountains were no mere backdrop, but an awesome reality. They were high and wide beyond her comprehension, a glorious masterpiece of creation in hard rock and endlessly frozen ice. The beauty and awe of them seemed to fill the very air she breathed, and to rest like light on every moment of her journey.

Veril noticed that Brogal did not often look at the mountains. Instead he looked ahead with a keen and thoughtful glance, picking out the tenuous desert track they were following, and sometimes temporarily leaving it. Veril marveled at the way he found some shelter for her every night in the apparently empty desert, and how they seldom went more than a day without coming to some unlikely-looking place where digging up a few handfuls of sand brought them to water, clean and fresh.

On the fourth morning of their journey, Veril suddenly said, "Brogal, you have not laughed or spoken much on this our journey. Does something grieve you?"

"Certainly nothing you have done, dear sister," said Brogal. "I have been thinking of Mother and Eleanor, and the burden I have left them in poor Brint. My last adventure in Cembar lies heavily in my memory. But you, Sister, have laughed and smiled upon this journey far more than I remember in recent years, and to see this brings me joy."

"What will you do next, when you have left me with King Ilohan?" asked Veril.

"I want to do something I have never done before," he said. "I want to rest and run free before I go laughing again into darkness." He turned his face to the south. "I want to go there," he said, pointing, "far out into the unknown, wild and clean."

"But there is nothing there but desert," said Veril.

"I love the desert," said Brogal, "and no part of it is the same as another."

Veril gazed off into the desert, trying to see it as Brogal did: a place whose very emptiness and wildness were beautiful and healing. His voice broke in upon her thoughts.

"Veril, I ask you this in earnest. Do you think I should not go?"

She turned to him in surprise. "Why would I think that?"

"It is selfish," he said. "I want to go to please myself. It will help no one."

"It will help you, Brogal," said Veril. "You are not no one."

It was Brogal's turn to be surprised. He considered her words for a while in silence, until he was interrupted suddenly by her laugh, which made him think of clear water rippling down a fall. "Take your adventure, Brogal," she said. "Love God, and make your life a song and a jest before him as you always have. Not even the wisest of men know the future, as Eleanor said. Who can tell in what way you can do the deepest good?"

Brogal laughed with her. "Thank you, Sister," he said. "You always were wiser than I."

She looked at him calmly. "In that you are very wrong, Brogal. I have never known what to do in my life, but you have never doubted."

"That is because I have done what I liked," said Brogal. "You have tried to do what was best whether you liked it or not. Even when we were children together, Auria and I used to talk about how you were too good for us without knowing it. We said you would someday be like Mother, whereas," and he laughed aloud in his turn, "Auria would never be like Mother, nor I like Father. Our childish words have been proven right by the years, though God has led each of us to follow him in the way he gave us."

"You should not flatter me so," said Veril. "You do not know me as clearly as you think, if you think I have become like Mother. I will never be Imranie."

Brogal looked at her seriously. "I know you better than you know yourself, Veril," he said. "Or at least I see your quality more clearly than you ever will. Remember my words if ever you have need of them."

Veril looked at him and shook her head, smiling but not believing. Brogal turned back to the path and said no more, but silently he thought, "As you have said, Sister, you will never be Imranie. You will only be Queen of Karolan."

* * *

The king walked in the field of Aaronkal late at night. The frozen ground felt hard as stone beneath his feet. The waning moon was rising brightly, only a few days past its full, but the sky was still full of sharp, cold stars. Ilohan knelt in the center of the field and remained there silently for a long time.

At last he said, "My Lord, I remember the forget-me-not. I remember the greatness of your love and power. You carried me safe through the darkness, and beyond my hope you have set me on the throne. And yet I could wish to be back there, because you were so near me in the darkness, and because of the depth of my prayer in that place. I have not been able since to pray as I prayed then."

Ilohan sighed. "Lord God, this broken world is strange and terrible. I am not equal to it. Do not leave me. I know you will not abandon me, but I feel that I am drifting away from you. Hold me near you; hold me up. Let it be a hopeful spring."

He stood. In the bright moonlight the flags flying on the battlements of Aaronkal showed clearly. A strong wind from the mountains rushed and sighed through the sturdy oaks surrounding the field. "This is my place, and it is beautiful," breathed Ilohan. "This is my land, and the people of this place are my people. Lord, I offer myself to you for the service of this people and this land. I have called them mine, but they are yours. It is all yours: the moon, the earth, the stars. I thank you that you care for us still."

Frost crunched beneath his feet as he walked to the great gate of Aaronkal. The guards saluted him, and he felt that they were truly loyal. The halls and passages were dark and silent, but not stale or dank: Aaronkal was alive. All day long it was full of the bustle of servants, advisors, warriors, armorers, messengers, petitioners, and visitors of many kinds. Banquets filled its great hall in the evening, and young men destined for knighthood slept in its many chambers at night. Ilohan felt that he was fulfilling his duties as Lord of Aaronkal, and King of Karolan. He was winning the people's love. He was weary, but hope was in the air.

As he climbed the stone stairways, in his weary mind the rhythm of his footfalls seemed to chant back to him the hopeful news of recent days. The promised wagons of grain from the farmers of the northwest had arrived to feed the starving east, and Petrag, and Carrah. King Andokar had responded very graciously first to Ilohan's request for grain, and then to his report that it was no longer needed. There had been no misunderstanding; no hostility. There was good reason to hope for a spring of peace. And the young knights-to-be were progressing... Today, for the first time, one of them had unhorsed Sir Benther.

Ilohan reached his room, laid aside his robe and crown, and slipped between the finely woven blankets of his bed. The fire burned low as he drifted toward sleep, and images of the past day flitted vividly through his mind. He saw the candidates for knighthood, charging together across the field of Aaronkal, their armor shining in the sun, and their banners bright in the wind. And they rode not to glorious death, but to hope and freedom, to a spring of promise. The dead had not perished in vain, and Karolan would not be long without her knights.

Yet when Ilohan dreamed it was not of these pleasant things. He seemed to walk in his dreams in all the castles of his land: Metherka, Dilgarel, Kitherin, Nildra, Byinkal, and so many others. They were ruled now by widows or servants, and he did not know what to do with them. He was training new knights to replace those who had fallen – to replace them as defenders of Karolan. But he could not train the young men to take the places of the dead as husbands and fathers: he could not replace the lords of those desolate castles. In his dreams Ilohan seemed to see each of the widows meet him in her castle and say the same words to him: "How could you be worth the cost... How can you redeem the loss?"

Metherka had led the Knights of Karolan in their last great charge, into the wind, into the arrows, into the spears. Their courage had shone like the Morning Star, in the hopeless darkness when it was most desperately needed. The glory of that charge would be remembered forever. So would its cost.

Chapter 6

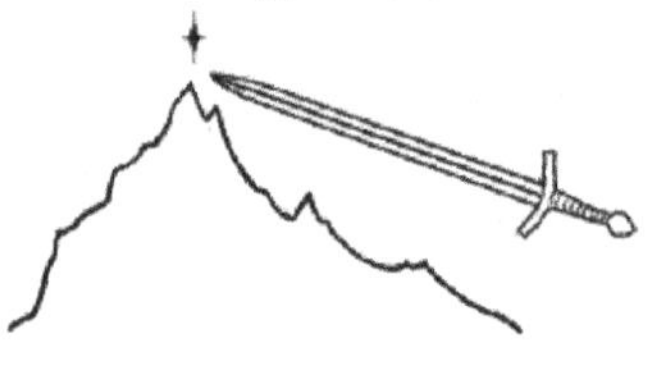

The Song of Winter's End

EARLY IN THE MORNING SOME DAYS LATER, ELEANOR ROSE and leaned out a window of her cottage into the cold dawn. King Ilohan's messenger had found her in Harevan the day before. She had stayed awake long into the night, reading and rereading the account her son had sent her. She held the manuscript out the window now, to reread its final words in the growing light.

"It has been so much more than I ever expected or deserved. In the Darkness I felt the love of God and the strength of prayer... I cannot express how much greater they were than I had ever known before. It is as though a man who had known water previously only through a dripping spring were suddenly plunged into a waterfall – or as if a man who knew no more of fire than a candle were struck by lightning... And I know you have been praying for me... I know it as surely as I know the sun shines, and I feel it as surely as I feel the heat of my warm fire. I love you, Mother. The night is cold.

"It is a hard winter, and there are many widows... The price of my crown was paid by too many, and it was too much, yet I can help no one by throwing it away. It cannot be sold to regain the lives of those who died to win it. All I can do is wear it as faithfully as I can, before God, and live to bless my people. It is hard, but I have put my trust in God. May this letter, though it holds tidings of mingled grief and wonder, bring you joy. I know no one more faithful. I seem to see your face in the darkness even as I write. You are beautiful and strong in love and prayer. It may be that you do not know the measure of the strength God has given you. Remember that I will love and honor you forever.

"Your son, in darkness and dawn, winter and spring, agony and hope, through earth into eternity,

"Ilohan, King of Karolan.

The dawn wind ruffled the pages in Eleanor's hand. Soft mist, still gray before the sunrise, lay across her barren garden. The morning star looked ethereal and immeasurably high as it faded in the dawn. She felt as though a great wave had swept over her, of mingled joy and sorrow, as Ilohan had said – but the greater part was joy.

She felt warmth and motion behind her, and a hand upon her shoulder. Turning, she saw Auria standing there, her eyes sparkling in her youthful face, and her hair disordered but still lovely. Eleanor felt suddenly that life was short. "You are spring and I am autumn," she said.

Distress flitted across Auria's face, but then she laughed, and her laugh was indeed like the laugh of springtime. "No, my Lady; we are both spring, and it is dawn, and hurts will be healed, and seeds will flower. Rangol has sent us bacon. Shall I cook it?"

Eleanor sat down and laughed, sounding just as young as Auria, though she did not know it. Auria got the bacon sizzling over the fire, and then rushed back to her room to comb her hair. Presently they sat down to breakfast together, while the sun turned the mist to gold.

* * *

Naomi shivered in the hayloft as she stared into a large bucket of water. The day before, she had decided that she absolutely must wash herself, despite the coldness of the winter. She had mentioned it to Brekon very hesitantly, thinking she was asking too much of him – but he had only smiled at her, and today he had brought the water. The bucket was so large that they had worked together to haul it into the loft using a rope. Now she gingerly took off her clothes, thinking how bitterly cold she would soon be. She took a deep breath, and plunged her head into the water.

It was warm. She was amazed and thankful. She washed her hair and face, and then the rest of her body, using a sponge Brekon had put in the bucket. Despite the weeks that had passed since her injury, it still shocked her when she wiped her legs with the sponge and felt nothing. The strangeness of her condition still frightened her. She could not run. She could not walk. She could not even crawl.

At the end of the bath she was intensely chilled, shivering hard despite the warmth of the water. Her hands shook as she reached out for her clothes.

Her clothes were filthy – she must wash them, and her blanket too. But they would not dry quickly, and she could not live long without their warmth. She hated the thought of putting them on again, unwashed. She paused a moment, shivering.

"Naomi, Naomi!" Brekon's cheerful call came to her from below.

"What is it?" she asked, staying out of sight.

"Do you need anything more?"

"I... I suppose you could not get me a clean blanket, to wear while I wait for my clothes to dry?"

Only moments later a heavy bundle of cloth flew through the hayloft entrance and lodged itself in the straw. Brekon's cheerful laughter came up from below.

Naomi draped the blanket across her shoulders. Working frantically, half naked in the bitter cold, she scrubbed her clothes in the bucket, wrung them out tightly, and spread them to dry on the hay. Finally she managed to get herself curled up, nestled in hay, with the blanket tightly wrapped all around her. As her violent shivering slowly subsided, she marveled at Brekon. He brought her everything she needed, and kept her presence secret, yet he did it only as another boy might conceal some romp or game his elders did not approve. She wondered again if he understood what would happen if she were discovered; if it ever occurred to him that without him she would probably die. Presently she remembered to call out that he could come and take away the sponge and bucket.

"I thank you with all my heart, Brekon," she said when he appeared. "I do not know how you do all that you do for me."

"I wish I could make you walk, Naomi," he said. "Someday you must tell me the story of what happened to you before this."

"It is not a story of the kind you love," she said. "In the real world, stories do not always have good endings. Where did you get this blanket, and what will you do if it is missed?"

Brekon looked at her questioningly. "I asked for it and Zerkela gave it to me," he said. "Why are you afraid?"

"I am afraid of what may happen to you, and to me, if someone discovers that you have been coming to me. Who is Zerkela?"

"She is my father's servant. I think he has told her to give me what I ask of her, even if she does not like to. My father loves me, and also he trusts me. Yesterday," his eyes sparkled, "he gave me a pony, to be mine alone. I would not have asked for such a great thing as that, never! I used him to carry your washing water, which Zerkela warmed for me. She does not ask why I do things, and no one watches where I go."

"It is a strange life for a boy as young as you are."

"Is it?" asked Brekon. "My father says I am a strange child, and his eyes smile when he says it. I wish I saw him every day."

"You do not, then?"

"No – sometimes not even once in a week. But today I will see him! I must go. Farewell, dear Naomi!"

"Farewell, dear Brekon. Tomorrow you will have a story." As his footsteps died away on the ladder, she thought his adoptive father was right about him: he was a strange child, but his strangeness was pure gold.

Nestled in the thick blanket, Naomi felt almost warm. She was glad in the knowledge that she was clean, and would presently be able to dress in clean clothes. Yet she was sick – sick with long inaction, with cold nights and sunless days – sick at heart. She was terribly vulnerable and weak. She felt half-dead, as her body was half paralyzed. Brekon was her only link with the land of the living – a tenuous link that might be exposed and broken any day. Though she had been almost happy when she bade Brekon farewell, now tears of desolation fell on the thick folds of the new blanket.

"Father, I am lost and lonely," she said. "I feel that my days on earth are drawing to a close in darkness, like this day. Brekon does not understand, and I do not know what to do. I do not know how to face death here." For a long time she lay still, spent and surrendered while the twilight faded, waiting for she knew not what.

"Jesus," she whispered at last. It was a name that seldom passed her lips. Of all her Lord's many names, it was, to her, the most laden with sacred mercy. It was the name of the holy Hero of all ages, of God incarnate come to earth to rescue doomed humanity at the cost of his own death. "Jesus," she whispered, "you promised never to forsake me. Be with me now. I think I shall soon leave this life, leaving undone all that I most hoped to do. Bless Brekon and comfort him. Help me to do whatever is best for him in whatever time is left. I am so weak. I have no strength to leave this place, I think, but I do not want to die here. Your will be done."

* * *

Near midnight that same night, Ilohan sat awake in a cold room in Aaronkal. No urgent duties kept him from sleep, only a deep agony of spirit. He bowed his weary head on his hands, and watched the events of a few hours before mercilessly replay themselves in his memory.

He saw again the final jousting match of the day's training. With light already fading from the west, two young men, fully armored, galloped across the field toward each other. Their speed was good, and their lances nearly level. But the moment of impact never came. One horse stumbled and crashed in ruin, throwing his rider head foremost on the frozen ground.

King Ilohan ran to the young man's side before any other could reach him, but he knew already what he would find. The man was dead. King Ilohan lifted the broken body in his arms. The cold twilight seemed to him an emblem of the event: no shining armor, no strong sun, only dull, cold death. One more tragedy of war and winter. One more bereaved mother, one more casualty of the cursed and broken world.

Yet he could not blame the world, or the dead man, or the horse. He had chosen the men to train as knights. He had ordered this final joust, when the men were tired and the light poor. His hands were sticky with the young man's blood; the corpse was in his arms.

There were things to do, and Ilohan did them. He ordered a stretcher and bearers for the dead man, and cleansed his hands and changed his robe. He consulted the records, and found that the bereaved mother was a widow who lived quite close to Aaronkal. Benther agreed that she should be informed at once, but to Ilohan's surprise he also said, "Do not go yourself, I beg you, Your Majesty."

"But to hang back seems cowardice," said Ilohan. "Shall I refuse to face this woman and acknowledge her grievance against me?"

"Your Majesty, it is that very thought of yours that makes me think you should not go," said Benther. "You did not kill this man, but you feel responsible. Do not, with these thoughts in your heart, go to face his mother. You will wound yourself without cause. Write that you share her grief, assure her that you will support her and her family, but do not go and say that her son's blood is on your hands."

"I will not say that, but I must face her myself," said Ilohan. "However, you may come with me if you will – indeed, I ask it."

When they reached the cottage, a gray-haired woman opened the door. She knelt in awe at the sight of the king and his torch-bearing entourage. He raised her up with a gentle hand. "Has Your Majesty come to bring news of my son?" she asked. "Is he to be knighted soon?"

Ilohan himself knelt before her and took both her hands in his. He met her eyes. "Your son is brave and strong, and I have found no fault with him," he said. "But, alas, he cannot be knighted. Today he was thrown from his horse to the frozen ground. He is dead."

She tore her hands away from him and screamed. The change in her was terrible to see. "Is the war not over?" she cried, tearing at her clothes distractedly. "For what did my child die? To defend Karolan; to defend his home and land from fire and conquest? No! He died for a dream, for a fool's dream that peasants can become knights. He died on a quiet day in winter, and all joy is gone from my life because of you... Your... Your Majesty!"

She pushed past him and ran out to the horsemen. The men who carried her son's body surrendered it to her frantic pulling, and she, by an effort beyond her strength, carried it into her cottage and knelt on the floor beside the hearth, staring down at it and sobbing wildly. She kissed the bloodless forehead, and then rushed out. Ilohan stood aside to let her pass, but Benther shouted, "Stop her!" in an imperious voice.

It was too late. She rushed over a low parapet and vanished with a final scream. When the king and Sir Benther reached the place, they found a deep, dry well.

Guilt and misery weighed so heavily on Ilohan that he almost wished he could have thrown himself down to share her death, but he thrust the evil thought far from him. He sent back to Aaronkal for ropes to retrieve her corpse from the bottom of the well. While waiting for them, he conferred with Benther over a new problem: should they find the dead woman's next of kin that very night, or wait till morning? Morning seemed the obvious choice, except that waiting inevitably meant a public funeral. The family might wish to avoid that, since she was a suicide.

"There will be no hiding it, with the guards and bearers as witnesses," said Benther. "This whole village will know how she died within the week. However, Your Majesty might spare the family some intensity of shame by offering a quiet burial tonight."

Ilohan chose to attempt this. The written roll of the village showed the woman had no living parents or siblings, save one married sister. They found her in a cottage nearby, and woke her and her family. Ilohan told her what had happened, and then she, her husband, and her children came with him, late though it was, to the graveyard attached to the little chapel where Ilohan had prayed so long before. They buried mother and son together, by torchlight.

All this Ilohan saw again, hours later, as he sat alone and cheerless in Aaronkal, still unable to sleep from the turmoil of his mind. Only two had died this afternoon, compared to thousands in the war, but for the first time he had seen someone die as a direct result of his orders – orders that now seemed pointless and insignificant compared to their horrible results. Benther had said he was not to blame. In part he believed it, but he could not make his heart accept it. He had spoken, his commands had been obeyed – and a young man, full of health and hope, had lain dead on the frozen ground. He had forced himself to do the hardest part of everything, but it was not enough. No penalty that he might pay would bring the dead new life.

He tried to remember the brief, torchlit funeral, which seemed blurred by guilt and sorrow in his mind. The dead woman's sister had had a calm strength, he remembered, and had spoken no word of blame. What had she said to him?

"Rhoda was never strong, and she let young Matthew be her all. I beg you, Your Majesty, to forget the bitter words she must have screamed at you before her death. It is not by such words that we would have Your Majesty remember us and our kin."

Yet her very patience increased his grief. Why could she not rail at him, as her dead sister had done? Ilohan knew vaguely that in his weariness his thoughts were straying toward destructive folly. He had indeed a duty to restore the Knights of Karolan as swiftly as could be. It was with prudence and diligence, not cruelty or folly, that he had pushed the training so hard. Yet such thoughts of sanity and hope seemed very frail against the restless sorrow that filled him.

One by one the low-burnt candles sputtered and went out, leaving him in darkness. He was weary. He knew the world was broken; broken and marred ever since the ancient tragedy of Eden, of which the Books of the Travelers told. He now held a position of great responsibility in this ruinous world. Full victory could never be won here. Joy was always threatened with grief, life with death, hope with despair, and beauty with destruction. His life stretched out before him, a long strife in which he would see much that was beautiful perish, and much that was good fail to reach its potential. And he must face this prospect alone. He could not confide his sorrow to Benther, or even to Jonathan if he (thought of fresh sorrow!) could be found. They would not understand; nor would it change anything if they did. A great weight of sorrow and weariness burdened his heart and dulled his mind. He did not even think of praying, and he was utterly alone.

The sound of hesitant footsteps intruded on his despondent thoughts. They paused a moment just beyond the door and then retreated; Ilohan guessed the servant had not dared to interrupt his royal solitude. Somehow the trifling event roused him a little. He lifted his head, and got wearily to his feet. Whatever new crisis those footsteps might portend, he must face it: he could not use an oak door and his servants' diffidence to hide from his duty.

He went swiftly to the door, confident even in total darkness in this familiar room. He stepped out into the passage and stood there a moment, blinking his dark-accustomed eyes in the torchlight. A strange voice was speaking in a room below. One of his guards replied, but he could not make out the words in either speech. There was silence for a moment, but from the tones of the voices he did not think the issue they had been discussing was settled.

In the silence a single voice began to sing. It seemed somehow more wonderful for being wholly unexpected. It made him think of sunlight on white flowers and green grass, of bright leaves fluttering in the wind, and of mist rising off the lake of Ceramir in the morning. Though he had not been able to understand the words of his guard, the verses of the song came to him clear and free through the echoing hallways of the ancient castle:

Brutal is barren ice and frozen ground,
Laughing streams beneath stone-hard prisons bound.
Keen wind reaches through cloak the heart to chill,
And moans in barren branches haunting still
The one who hears, though sheltered he may be.
Men and beasts shiver, pining to be free,
But Winter rules, in heartless tyranny,

Till hope itself she freezes icily.

The piercing wind and gnawing cold decry
The dream that spring shall bring a kinder sky.
And who can say if spring shall come again
Ere hand falls limp, and heart is still within?
The mournful wind's lament may triumph still:
No man – Alas! – so strong, but death may kill,
Or winter on the soul may fall as deep
As that which binds the earth in death-cold sleep.

Winter lies not, when speaking of her power,
Or of the step of death in his cold hour.
But death rules not, even in Earth the Broken,
And long ago his own sure doom was spoken.
The sentence stands: winter shall end in spring.
Lovers of light shall freed from darkness sing.
All Winters end: soul's shadows, or world's blight,
And spring shall come, as dawn shall end the night!

Ilohan knew the voice, and yet could not believe his ears. He saw a guard hurrying along a lower passage, and rushed down a stairway himself to accost him. "Your Majesty," the guard explained breathlessly, "a man and woman, newly arrived from a far country, asked for an audience with Your Majesty – at this hour! I told them it was impossible, of course, but I... I fear I let it slip that Your Majesty had not yet retired to your bedchamber. They insisted that if Your Majesty were not asleep they must see you. They have been very courteous, but very persistent. I in my turn have persisted in saying they must wait for morning. At last, rather than agreeing or pressing me further, the woman simply stood and began to sing. I do not understand them at all."

"You have done well," said King Ilohan. "I know them, however, and there is nothing to fear. Go and order our finest guest rooms made ready. I shall go and welcome them myself."

When Ilohan first saw her down the length of a hallway, Veril was still standing as she had stood to sing. She had a calm gravity about her that was only just beginning to fade into her underlying weariness. Yet there was peace in her face: the peace of one who has done what she must, and leaves the outcome to God. In a flash it came upon Ilohan that she was absolutely honest, that nothing about her was ever acted or faked. Nothing could have been more contrary to her nature than the part she had played in the Joseph Test.

He stepped into the room. She and Brogal started up and then knelt swiftly at his feet. Though he had known she was come from the first words of her song, still he found himself unprepared to meet her. He had not known how much he longed for her. Though she remained kneeling, she was too anxious and alive to be still, and the soft gleams of torchlight in her hair shimmered when she moved her head. It seemed to Ilohan that she brought with her all the love, laughter, and unassailable innocence of the Cloth of Joy. Yet she was far from home, and knew nothing of the darkness into which she had come. Suddenly, though with all his heart he wanted her beside him, he wished for her sake that she had not left Ceramir with all its peace and safety.

"Rise, Veril," he said, "and rise, Brogal. Welcome, dear friends. Is all well in the Cloth of Joy?"

"Yes, all is well there," said Brogal. "It was not for any trouble in Ceramir that we came this long journey."

"Your coming fills me with joy," said Ilohan, "but I must tell you that you have come to a place beset with many griefs."

"May our coming lessen them, Your Majesty," said Brogal, his eyes sparkling with their usual hint of mischief. "The war with evil does not end when kings make peace, but the very fact that it is still fought means, at least, that there are those still to be found on earth who stand on the side of ultimate victory."

"And what if one day they shall be found no more, Brogal?" asked Ilohan. The question seemed to come irresistibly from the remnants of the despondency that Veril's song had lifted – though he was sorry to make her stand waiting even for a moment while he spoke with Brogal.

"If there were none to fight against it on Earth, still the cause of evil would fail utterly in the end," said Brogal. "Our Captain needs no soldiers."

In the sudden silence Ilohan remembered a familiar carving on a chapel altar: Christ the Lord coming on the clouds, with a victorious host of angels in his train. Though scholars debated the prophecies' exact meaning, there was no doubt that the Books of the Travelers foretold the utter defeat of evil at the end of the world.

"But there will always be those who love our Lord Jesus, even to the end," said Veril softly. "He is the Light of the World, the Prince of Peace. How could it not be so?"

"You honor him well, dear Veril, daughter of the Undismayed," said Ilohan. "He is the Light of the World, and your song brought light into my darkness. Seeing you now brings healing to my heart."

She bowed her head, and did not seem to know how to reply. Seeing her confusion, Ilohan spoke again. "If you will forgive the poor hospitality of Aaronkal thus far, I will try to mend it."

He led Veril and Brogal up to a small dining room. He called his servants imperiously to stoke the fire, bring good food and drink, and prepare comfortable rooms for his guests. It was only as he sat with them at this midnight meal that he realized their true weariness, especially Veril's. She was too tired to eat much, and when he called a servant to show her to her room, she stumbled like one asleep upon her feet. Reminded that he, too, was weary, Ilohan went to his own bedchamber and found that he could sleep at last.

*   *   *

Veril came to vague awareness in the morning, but did not open her eyes. Warmth and softness surrounded her – wonderful, but inexplicable at first. Gradually she remembered where she was and how she had come there. She sat up and slid the blanket off her, exulting in the fact of the heated room. For many days before, pulling open her blankets in the morning had been the beginning of a cruel ordeal: icy air had flooded round her; she had leaped up shivering to pull on frost-stiffened over-clothes; and she and Brogal had eaten hastily with numb lips and ridden onward through the cold. Now the air of the room was deliciously warm, and her bare feet touched a soft carpet as she stood. She walked to the window and threw wide the heavy wooden shutters. Icy air did make her shiver then, but she stood and looked in the delightful consciousness that warmth was now at her command.

Her room was high in the castle wall. Below her, snow-clad trees sparkled in the light of the sunrise, while farther away the forest gave way to snowy fields and farmhouses with comfortable wisps of smoke blowing from their chimneys. Far beyond those, like a dream at the edge of the world, rose the majestic mountains of Karolan, a faint but impressive outline against the clear dawn sky. They were her mountains, the mountains of the Cloth of Joy – seen from the other side. Her heart leaped in wonder.

The chill reached deeply through her clothes, and she shuttered the window again and went to stand by the fire. A basin of warm water was on the hearth, together with a towel and a set of fine, clean clothes. Ilohan had thought of everything, it seemed. She washed, dressed herself in the warm clothes provided for her, and left the room.

Veril passed alone through chilly hallways and down one stairway. An early morning stillness seemed to fill the castle. Occasionally she encountered guards who nodded curtly to her and let her pass. Finally her attention was caught by an open door leading into a large room full of fresh morning light. She went in and stood awhile gazing out through one of the big, iron-grilled windows. There was no view of the mountains here, for the windows faced due west and the room was lower. She loved the sight of the frosty tree branches, however, blowing to and fro almost within her reach. It was the view a bird would have, she thought, skimming through the wintry dawn above the forest.

"My Lady," Veril heard a voice behind her speak the words. She turned. The king was standing there, with the cool, fresh light of morning all around him.

"Your Majesty," she said, and curtsied to him.

"Why did you come here?" he asked her.

"Do you not know?" she asked sadly.

"I do not know," he said. "I only hope – and fear."

"What do you hope, Your Majesty?"

"I hope an impossible thing. I cannot say what I hope."

"And what do you fear?" she asked.

"That which will destroy my hope. The darkness of the world, the weight of the crown, the pain of the throne."

"Shall I now tell you why I have come, Your Majesty?" she asked.

"I ask it, my Lady," he said. She noticed that his voice was not perfectly steady, but found, to her distress, that her own wavered much more as she answered.

"It... it seems horribly presumptuous, now that I stand before you, Your Majesty. Forgive me, I beg you. I came in the hope that I..." she knelt on the stone and continued, her voice now broken by tears. "I came in the hope that I might help you bear the weight of the crown, and the pain of the throne. I do not lust for power, I only want to love you. Forgive me for my folly. I am sorry."

He raised her up and embraced her, and held her close. "I love you, Veril," he said. "I love you with my whole heart, and it will be a great sorrow for me to send you away. Do not reproach yourself with folly or presumption, for I will always remember your coming as a great good. You understand why you must not stay?"

"No," said Veril through her tears, "no, I do not understand why I must go. If you truly love me... If you love me why may I not stay with you? Is it written in the law of Karolan that your bride must be a princess?"

"No!" said Ilohan loudly. "Were there such a law, I would defy it! But there is a far different reason. Do you truly not know it?"

"Your Majesty, I truly do not," she sobbed.

Ilohan's arms tightened around her. "Maybe, then, it does not exist," he whispered. At the barely-heard words, and still more at the glorious strength of his arms, Veril's heart sang – yet she did not forget his unspoken reservation, which might exist after all. He released her and led her to a bench beside a wide hearth, gratefully warm after the icy breeze before the windows.

King Ilohan sat down beside her. "You came so far because you loved me, Veril?" he asked.

She sat there calmly, her tears ended. "Yes, Your Majesty," she said softly. "Yes. I came because I love you. I love you with my whole heart. I thought I could bless you."

"You must go back, dear Veril, because I love you," he said. "I love you too much to wish upon you the crown of Karolan's queen."

She remained perfectly still, looking at the floor in front of her, but hope was like the sunrise in her heart. "Is that the only reason you want me to leave you?" she asked. "Because you think the life your queen will have to lead would destroy me?"

"I know at least that it would bring you great pain," said King Ilohan. "It has killed others. Queen Sarah died, I think, chiefly of weariness."

"I do not think myself unworthy to share Queen Sarah's fate," she said, raising her head and looking him in the eyes. "Of what did King Thomas die?"

Ilohan bowed his head and turned away from her. "Also of weariness," he said.

"And which of them had the easier fate?" asked Veril.

King Ilohan was silent.

"Of what will you die, Your Majesty, if you try to carry on alone, refusing the aid of one who would give her life to help you?" asked Veril, her voice trembling again.

At last Ilohan spoke, slowly, as if it were hard for him to get out the words. "You are a child of Ceramir, dear Veril. The Cloth of Joy is your birthright. You were born to a life of joy, hope, beauty, and true service. I was born a prince, out in the broken world."

"We were both born in the broken world," said Veril. "Ceramir is not beyond its confines. Do you truly love me? Would you marry me if you were not the king?"

He wrapped his arms around her and held her close. "I do. I would. You must believe me, for I speak the truth with all my heart."

"I trust you," said Veril. "Your Majesty, hear my words. I have never felt more right or safe than now when I am in your arms. Even the Cloth of Joy is not my home as this is, and will be, even if you banish me forever. You must give me a chance to prove my love and courage."

"It is not them I doubt, dear Veril."

"My strength, then."

"Alas, Beloved!" said Ilohan. "If I only doubted, my doubt could be proven groundless. But I know of what I speak. I know the weight of a crown. I know that in making you my queen I would take you from the most wonderful place in all the world, and bring you into the center of a hopeless fight. None pass through that fight unwounded. It is the war against the evil and the pain of a whole land, and it cannot be won. I will not bring you into it. Though I long to have you at my side, I would not have you go with me where I must go."

"I knew Your Majesty before you knew your title," said Veril. "May I address you by the name you were called then?"

"You may call me what you will, Beloved."

"Ilohan. You believe God has called you to your throne, do you not?"

"I do."

"And it is a hard and bitter calling, which will kill you before your time?"

"I believe so."

"Ilohan, do you know beyond the faintest shadow of doubt that God cannot have called me to be your wife?"

For Ilohan those words changed everything. They shattered at one blow his certainty that he must not let Veril persuade him to take her as his wife. If he had been called, so might she be. He felt joy like the triumphant blast of many trumpets – but his caution and his fear for her were not wholly dispelled.

"Veril, do you know beyond the faintest shadow of a doubt that God has called you to be my wife?" he asked.

"No," said Veril. "But I also am not sure that if I put my hand in the fire it would burn."

"You doubt both propositions equally little?" asked Ilohan.

"I am less certain about the fire," said Veril.

He released her, and stood. She stood beside him, and for a while there was perfect silence in the room. Then Veril turned, walked to a window, and stayed there with one hand upon the iron grating. She seemed still and patient as she gazed out into the bright winter day, but looking closely Ilohan saw that she was trembling. She turned toward him with a swift motion, but did not raise her eyes to meet his.

The clear morning light filled the room and washed over her face and form. The dress he had given her was long and white, with gold thread worked into the cloth in subtle patterns. The rich color of her hair glowed in contrast to the pure white dress. Unaffected grace was in all her movements. She was beautiful, more beautiful in Ilohan's eyes at that moment than any woman he had ever seen, even Naomi of Glen Carrah. He longed to bind her to himself forever – but at the same time her lovely innocence made him fear to see her burdened and broken even more than before. She suddenly knelt and looked up to meet his gaze. "Make your decision!" she cried. "I cannot bear it!"

He went to her and raised her up, and held her close while she wept against his shoulder. "I have made my decision, dear Veril," he said. "For a score of days you may remain with me, and I will show you the pain and bitter weariness of the crown. At the end of that time you must leave me, and return to the Cloth of Joy. The moon will be waning when you leave me; it will wane out and begin to wax again before you reach your home. You must stay in Ceramir and rejoice in all its goodness until the moon wanes out once more. In your heart you must compare the bitterness of Aaronkal with the joy of Ceramir. But if, having done this, you still choose to be my wife, and believe before God that you choose rightly, at the new moon you may set out to come to me again. Then I will marry you, and I will trust you, and my joy will be like the joy of Earth in spring: the joy of life and hope renewed."

Veril stepped back from him and met his gaze. Her face was very pale, and her voice calm and quiet when she spoke. "It is a hard doom," she said. "Yet for the hope that comes at last, I accept it. With Your Majesty's leave I will go to my chamber now."

Veril knew she had spoken with self-control, but also that she must fly swiftly before it broke. Ilohan made some reply, but she was too distraught to understand the words. She raced back up the stairs and passages to her room, where at last she could throw herself down on the floor. She lay there unmoving for a long time. "I accept it as I might accept a dagger-stroke that I could not escape," she whispered at last. "Ilohan, dear

Ilohan, why must you be at once so good and so foolish? Lord Christ, bring peace to us, and help us both."

Chapter 7

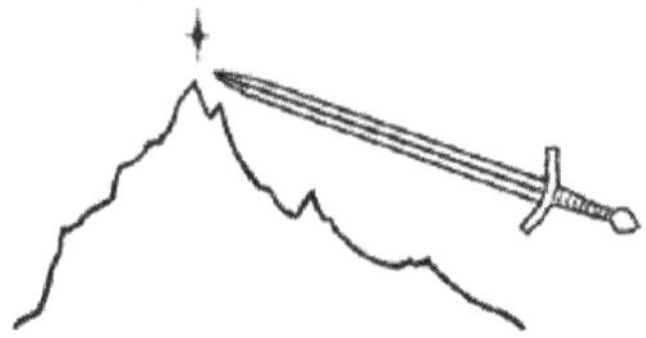

The Bird and the Storm

VERIL BREAKFASTED WITH ILOHAN, BENTHER, AND BROGAL later that morning. She saw that Brogal ate heartily: he was ravenously hungry after their long journey. She was hungry too, but she did not seem able to eat much, and she seldom raised her eyes from her plate. She stopped eating when the others had finished, although she had not had a full meal.

Veril remembered the things that she had said to the king earlier that morning, but she could not understand how she had found the courage or the folly to say them. She did not know which it had been: courage, or folly. She was sure that he truly loved her. But if she would be a burden to him, he had no right to marry her. She had assumed she would not be, and with strong and bold words she had declared her confidence that she was meant to be his wife. But that confidence was based on the belief that she could truly bless him, which now she doubted. She wondered if he doubted it too, and if his doubt was the real cause of his reservations.

She pushed this thought away behind her faith in his full honesty, but it would not stay down. It would not be the only cause. He might believe her likely to be a burden to him, and yet speak to her only of his fears for her wellbeing. That would not be dishonest, for she was sure he did sincerely fear harm for her if she married him. He had not lied to her; he had only refrained from speaking truth that would hurt her. Doubtless she was useless here, as everywhere.

Suddenly she realized that the three men had stood up, and were putting on warm hooded cloaks. A servant held a similar cloak out for her, and she put it on, not knowing what else to do. She had a vague idea that the day's plans had been discussed over the meal, and even that she had put an assenting word in here and there, but she realized with shame that she had no idea to what she had assented.

She followed the king, Sir Benther, and Brogal through a series of passages, arriving at length in the chill vastness of the throne room. Ilohan took his place on the throne, with Sir Benther on a lower seat beside him. Veril did not know where she was intended to go. She wanted to stand with Brogal, in a corner of the room near the door, but Ilohan motioned her to a seat just behind his throne. She was distressed to realize that she would be higher than all save the king himself; higher even than Sir Benther, the royal advisor. At least her chair was undecorated, and partly obscured by the throne itself.

Ilohan's knights-in-training filed briskly into the throne room and arranged themselves in a regular phalanx on the stone floor. As one man, they knelt, saluted, and then stood again. One place was vacant, and with a grim face the king stood to speak of the man who was lost.

He told what had happened, simply and directly, for those who had not been present at the accident. He told of the mother's suicide, and the midnight double burial. For the honor of the dead, he bound his hearers to secrecy concerning the suicide, but told them that he had believed they deserved to know the fullness of the truth.

He explained that he would require all the horses to be more closely examined before jousting in the future, and that he would have the field of Aaronkal carefully searched for anything that could trip or injure them. But he went on to say that he doubted these measures would have stopped the accident of yesterday, and that no precautions could protect them from all peril. Jousting was dangerous, but absolutely necessary for a knight's training, and he would confer knighthood on no one who had not mastered it.

Veril listened to the story with horror. She could not hear such a thing without feeling an echo of the pain of which she heard. Ilohan's description had been cold and factual. Yet Veril could feel the king's agony, when he bent to pick up the broken body of the young man killed in his service. She could feel the mother's unmanageable terror and frantic grief, rising like a dark wave to sweep her into the yawning well that seemed to offer sweet escape. She could feel the sister's quiet sorrow, understanding but forgiving the faults of the dead. Veril imagined even the children's awe and dismay at being roused from sleep to watch the burial of their aunt and older cousin.

But as she thought of these things, the king was finishing his speech. "All of you who yet dare to seek knighthood, I thank you and commend your courage," he said. "Sir Benther will lead you out for the day's practice. May your strength bring you joy. You who wish to return to your homes and seek a life of less danger, I do not reproach you. Go in peace, and in peace may God bless you, and grant that you never need bear sword again."

Most of the men turned and followed Benther from the room. Some hesitated, and as the dwindling crowd around them made them conspicuous, either turned at last, or stood still with their eyes on the floor. The king went down among these who still remained, and Veril followed him.

One man strode up to King Ilohan and bowed hastily, doing honor to convention rather than to the king. "Your Majesty warned us we might die in battle, not in peace," he said angrily. "Every day I have said to myself that your training was too hard, but I have silenced my own heart with the soothing message that all this was not too high a price to pay for knighthood. Now I see that the reward may be not knighthood but a useless death. You will not find me behind your banner again, in any rank!"

The king said nothing, but as the man turned and strode angrily toward the door, Veril cried, "Sir, do only what you never will regret!"

The man stopped dead. While he stood still, the others gathered around Ilohan, and thanked him for his kind words of blessing and release. Yet the choice they had to make distressed them, and they could not tell if cowardice or prudence made them wish to leave. "There are good reasons men could have to leave this training," said King Ilohan. "There are reasons that make departure the right and noble course. Consider well, but above all let no man be reproached for his departure!"

The man who had stopped dead at Veril's words turned at last, and walked into the midst of the little group surrounding Ilohan. "My brothers, and Your Majesty, hear my confession," he said. "I almost threw away a chance beyond my dreams: a chance to be numbered among the Knights of Karolan. In cowardice and bitterness I would have done it, and but for this great Lady," he gestured at Veril, "I would not have come to my senses until it was too late." He saluted and strode from the room. The others followed him without exception. Veril,

Brogal, and the king went out into the cold and sunshine to watch the knights-to-be at their training.

For Veril, weary from a long journey and a short night, the day passed into a blur of many sights: impressive, moving, sorrowful, and strange in their turn, all new to her but scarcely comprehended. Behind them all, draining her strength, pulling at her attention, there was her heartache. She was useless, useless to help a king. All that she saw of his great works and challenges and sorrows proved it again and again. And that, she was sure, was the real reason he was sending her away. In all her lofty arguments to him there had been nothing genuine but the fervency of her own love, and that was no sufficient reason for him to take her as his wife.

Late in the evening Ilohan came from his last council with Benther to dine with her and Brogal alone. As they ate, vivid memories of the day passed through her mind in a disconnected sequence: swords flashing in the sun; earnest instruction about armor, sword-fighting, jousting, strategy; a long, fast ride in the cold; a village of half-made houses built on burned ruins; shivering, hungry children; a sick old man who would die before the spring; a mother of small children (the old man's daughter, Veril thought) passionately crying for help; deep sorrow and grim determination in Ilohan's face; a long, fast ride back; more words, more councils. Now she sat near a warm fire, and all was peaceful except her anxious heart. She fought to keep her weariness at bay, to keep her head upright and her eyes open, to eat, and to speak when spoken to.

The meal was over before she understood it, and for some reason Brogal left the room. The fact that she was alone with Ilohan came upon her with force, but she could not say to him what was in her heart. The words simply would not come to her. Ilohan came around the table, took her hand and kissed it, and raised her up. She swayed on her feet.

"You are weary, dear Veril," he said kindly. "I have led you a hard road today, to show you clearly what my queen would have to face. I am sorry for the pain I see in your eyes. You see already why I must not marry you, though I desire it with all my heart?"

Her eyes filled with tears. Her hand trembled in his. "Yes, Your Majesty," she whispered, "because I love you!" She slipped her hand swiftly from his gentle grasp, and was gone.

Ilohan sat down upon the hearth. He also was very tired, and Veril had seemed distant from him and uncertain of her place ever since she came down to breakfast. The dawn meeting before that, when she had spoken of her love with bright courage, and nearly convinced him that he could marry her, was buried now in his mind beneath the later events. He did not understand her, and yet even aloof as she had been today she had lightened his burden and brought hope to his heart. He wanted her intensely – and loved her too much to take her. Think as he might, he could find no escape from it: he must send her back to Ceramir, and she should not return.

"Because I love you... Because I love you..." The words repeated themselves in his weary mind. Those had been his words to Veril in the dawn, his reason for not marrying her. And now she had said the same to him. From her, it did not make sense. What could she mean? He was too tired to solve the mystery, yet it struck him vaguely that it was very important.

"Father," he said. "She is beautiful, in heart more even than in body. If she were my wife, I could be many times as good a king as I must be else. Yet I know that she feels deeply, and this single day has struck her to her faithful heart. I cannot marry her. Yet I want to bless her, and I want to understand why she spoke as she did tonight, and then left me so quickly. It seemed as if she thought to marry me was not to bless me; as if she feared to bring me harm rather than good. Help her know the truth, my Lord. Bless her deeply, and help her to find joy in another life than the one she seeks for now. I cannot marry her, and I wish her joy of another husband, or a life unmarried in the Cloth of Joy. And yet... And yet... Oh Lord my God, if ever words kindled in my heart a passionate hope, her words this morning did, when she said that you had called her to be my wife. I cannot pray that it might be so, though I do greatly wish it. I say instead what your children may always rightly say: Father, your will be done."

He trudged up the long stairs to his tower room alone. Before he snuffed the one candle that stood beside his bed, he looked long by its clear dim light at Sarah's picture. The thoughts and feelings that the picture brought to him were varied and strong, and regarding Veril they tugged his heart both ways. He pulled up his blankets, and his thoughts of good Queen Sarah drifted into dreams: vivid, sometimes sad, but blessed.

* * *

On a wild night, when the wind howled around the hayloft and made the whole structure shake with its power, and when the hiss of drifting snow sounded high and cold in Naomi's ears, Brekon came to her. He came without a light of any kind. She knew his footsteps on the ladder and his faint silhouette as he entered. He piled up the straw behind him and moved hesitantly forward, seeking her in the pitch darkness. She reached out her hand and touched his. He sat down in her lap without a word, and she spread her blanket over him. He was trembling in her arms.

"What is it, Brekon?" she asked him.

"My father," he said. "He is very sick, and they say that he may die. He lies in an upper room of the house, and his breath comes hard, and he speaks fast in a whisper between breaths. All the people in the house gather round him, but I love him best, and they sent me out of his room. I could not go to anyone but you."

"It is so cold, Brekon," said Naomi. "You came out alone in the darkness and the storm to find me?"

Brekon was silent for a long time. He could feel Naomi's heart beating steadily behind him, and her arms around him were warm and safe. The loft was chilly, but Naomi's two blankets were thick and warm. Outside the wind still wailed – he could feel it shake the walls with its power – but the structure was sturdy and the wind could not come in. "I like being here with you," he said. "I hope I will always be able to come to you."

Naomi thought of his dead sister: the only person, she guessed, who had ever loved him before he was found by his adoptive father, who was now dying. And she herself would die, before the spring. Every day she was more certain of it. She bowed her head over his and hugged him tighter, grieving for him. He would be the last person she knew on earth; his the last soul she could love and bless before she left her crippled body and her broken world. She prayed faithfully every day that she would truly bless him; that her passing would not leave him heartache only.

"I know things won't be how I want," said Brekon suddenly out of a long silence. "You won't be here forever. But how long do you think you can be here?"

"I do not know, dear Brekon," she said. "As you said, not forever. Someday you will have to bid me farewell."

Brekon was silent again for a while, and then asked, "Where do you wish you could go?"

Naomi sighed, and once again she hugged him tighter. Even with that motion she felt her weakness. "I cannot leave this place in any way save one, dear Brekon," she said. "I have no strength to go where I wish to be."

"But if you could, Naomi, where is it?"

"It was called Glen Carrah," she said. "It is no more."

"What happened to it?" asked Brekon.

Naomi rocked him gently to and fro in her arms. "That story would bring you no joy, dear Brekon."

"You don't want to tell me?"

"No, dear Brekon," she said. "I will gladly tell you a different story."

Brekon was quiet awhile. Naomi still rocked him. "Just keep holding me," he said at last. "I love you. Tonight I do not want a story, I only want you close to me."

* * *

Two nights later, when Veril had retired to her bedchamber, Sir Benther asked his king for a private conference. As soon as the door of the council chamber was closed, he turned to Ilohan and said, "Your Majesty, you must find out what is wrong with her. She has hardly spoken to you these three days, and each day I read a deeper love for you in her face. She would die for you, Ilohan – forgive me, Your Majesty. She would die for you. And yet a deep shadow is on her; she will not show her love, and she will not trust her voice."

The room seemed very still after the passionate words. The candle flames burned straight without wavering. "You tell me to find out what is wrong with her," said Ilohan slowly. "It is not as though I have not tried. She will not speak to me. She only smiles, through tears, and says nothing. You are not the only one who has seen great love in her eyes. Yet I cannot marry her."

"Can you not?" asked Benther.

"Sir Benther, you know what this life is. Would you, by your own act, bring one you loved into it?"

"Suppose, Your Majesty, that it is best for a bird to roost in a tree during a storm, so as not to be exhausted and dismayed by the power of the wind. But if the tree is set on fire, what must the bird do?"

"You choose a strange moment for a parable, Sir Benther. I see that the storm is my life and Veril is the bird, but what do you mean by the fire?"

"Only her love for you, Your Majesty. It may be that any hardship she suffers at your side will be less hurt to her than living apart from you, even in peace and comfort."

"If that is true, Sir Benther – and I long to believe it – she will come back to me, even from Ceramir. But I must be sure. I love her too much to put the crown of Sarah on her before I am sure she is called as Sarah was."

"But that is in the future, Your Majesty. You must try to lift the shadow that is on her now, when her love should bring her joy."

The king stood suddenly, so fast that his heavy oak chair fell over behind him. He set it upright. He knelt beside the table. "Lord Christ," he said, "You carried me through the forget-me-not. You rescued Karolan when there was no hope. Be with me now, and bless Veril. Refine my love for her; gently weaken her love for me. I long with all my heart to bless her, and it seems I can only cause her hurt. Help me now, I pray."

He left the room without another word to Benther, and went swiftly through the halls and stairways to the door of Veril's room. Candlelight shone under it. He stood there a moment, then knocked. She did not open to him, and for a long time he heard nothing from within. At last he tried the door, and found to his surprise that it was unlocked. He opened it hesitantly. Veril stood in the middle of the room. Her face was pale and full of grief, and though a clean, modest nightgown had been laid out for her, she still wore the rumpled clothes of the day. She looked up, but made no motion to forbid him. Ilohan stepped in and shut the door behind him.

She curtsied to him. "Forgive my discourtesy in not opening to you, Your Majesty," she said. "I was confused what I should do."

"I ask your pardon for my discourtesy, coming in unbidden, my Lady."

In the silence that followed she did not stir, and Ilohan was forced to speak again. "Dear Veril," he said, "tell me from whence your sorrow comes."

She turned away. "I cannot," she said. "Leave me, I beg you, Your Majesty."

"Veril, I love you, and in love for you I have chosen as I have. If you return to me from Ceramir, I will marry you. I give you this promise with all my heart. Please do not be so sorrowful. If I alone can bring you joy, I will, when you return to me."

"I love you with all of my heart," said Veril. "If one thing were other than it is, I would have no greater joy on earth than to be your wife and helper. But…" she fell to her knees and looked up at him with anguish in her face. "But one thing prevents me. I will go to Ceramir, and I will not return…" she was perfectly still, and neither wept nor spoke for a long moment, "…and it breaks my heart!" She crumpled to the floor, and passionate sobbing shook her whole frame.

Ilohan lifted her gently in his arms. She shuddered violently when he first touched her, but then wept a little more calmly as he carried her. He laid her in the bed and drew a blanket over her, and knelt beside her. "Dear Veril," he said gently, "tell me what one thing it is that breaks your joy."

*   *   *

"Spring will come," said Hannah. She and Barnabas lay in their bed together, beneath their warm blanket, and talked while they watched the coals fade on the hearth and listened to the cold wind sighing round the house. The night was late, and they felt weary and at peace, but still they talked rather than sleeping.

"It is strange," said Barnabas, "but since we are bereft of Jonathan and Naomi, and even of Jenn, the barren winter seems to me a more congenial season than the spring. I am ungrateful. I am sorry."

"Do not accuse yourself, Beloved," said Hannah. "Springtime birdsong might fall strange on my ears too, and I feel no wrong in that. Yet I do not think that spring will come before God sends a lifting of our sorrow."

Barnabas took her in his arms. "What do you imagine that will be, Beloved?" he asked.

"I am certain that Jonathan will return at last," said Hannah, "and yet I have been thinking mainly of Naomi. I can see her…" Barnabas could hear tears in her voice as she continued, "I can see her standing among her frantic sheep, when the wall of fire rushed toward her. Sometimes I think I can almost feel her heartbeat, and hear her thoughts. What do you think she would have done?"

"I see two faithful courses," said Barnabas. "The first is to pray while death comes on – to pray in trust and hope, for courage and for mercy. The second is to turn and fly, to try to preserve the life God gave. I think I myself would have chosen the second, as I did when I was struck down at Petrag, before Jonathan rescued me. As for Naomi… I do not know. She loved life, but she had faith enough to see the joy of Heaven clearly. She might have tried to live, for Jonathan's sake."

"I think so too," said Hannah. "How do you think she would have tried to escape? Had she any real chance?"

"You saw the fire, Beloved, not I," said Barnabas. "But if she truly could not outrun it, her only chance was to run out of its way. To the west there is no hope: the Glen ends in a steep, wooded hillside. To the east there is the Carratril. There is only the Carratril."

Hannah shuddered. "That was my thought also," she said. "But she was not above the rapids, and in the rapids…"

"She could drown rather than burn," said Barnabas. "But there is barely a hope that she could live."

Hannah snuggled closer to him. "Barely a hope…" she whispered. "Barely a hope. That is not the same as no hope, Beloved."

"No, Hannah," he said, holding her close. "No, it is not the same. She could not come through uninjured, but she might come through alive. There is a tiny hope."

"Barnabas," whispered Hannah, "we have heard of a cripple."

"We know nothing, dear Hannah."

"Nothing," she said, with sleep in her voice at last. "No, we know nothing. But we hope."

She slept in his arms, but he remained awake, holding her, for a long time. It was so nearly certain that Naomi was dead. He could search for her in Cembar only at great risk of slavery or death for himself. Still, if he and Hannah came at last to believe that there was real hope in a search for her, he would go. Naomi was his daughter.

Barnabas looked down at his wife as she slept. If he went into Cembar again he would leave her. He might never return. "Ah, Hannah," he whispered, knowing she would not wake. "How long will we pass from shadow to shadow, you and I, and at what price will come the new hope of the spring?"

* * *

Veril and the king rode through the dusk, side by side, and stopped by the warmly lit stables of Aaronkal. Servants took their horses, and they dismounted and walked together through the great gate. The guards on either side saluted them. The hall had changed little in the two weeks since Veril came, but it seemed vastly different to Ilohan as he entered it that night. This great castle was no longer merely a burden to him, and a stronghold for his people. It was his home, because Veril was there. The crown was an opportunity to bless, because she saw it so; it was no longer only an impossible duty. Every day, in a thousand ways, she reminded him of what he had forgotten. She reminded him that hope is real and good and honest. She reminded him that every good act is a stroke against evil and a thing of lasting value. She made him remember not only the good he could not do, but also the good he had done.

She loved him, and he her, and all the darkness in the world could not dismay them. They found in their hearts the certainty that victory does not go to evil ultimately, not even in the broken world, not even before the final battle is won.

Veril and Ilohan went through the halls and stairways of Aaronkal together, until they came to a small chamber with a good fire, and three soft chairs arranged around a richly set table. They stood face to face before the fire, and Veril asked the question she had asked every night for thirteen nights before. "Was I a burden to you today, Your Majesty, or was I of some use to you?"

Ilohan embraced her and held her tight. "Dear Veril," he said, "that you can ever doubt it is beyond my understanding. You bring me hope. When you labor with me, I find that good things are done that I did not imagine. I can see your love for the people of Karolan. The young widow at Wrellin Farm today: have you no idea how you blessed her? At Castle Dilgarel, you helped old Lady Anlia hope for the future – you helped her think of young Jacob as one who may become her foster son, not as one who displaces her own dear child, Sir Dilgarel, fallen hero of Metherka's charge... There are many others, Veril, Beloved. Everywhere you go the people love you. You could be a queen such as Sarah was; even more beloved than Sarah. You never touch people's lives without blessing them, except when weariness keeps you back, and even then who can know what blessings your prayers – yes, I know you pray then! – leave behind you?"

He let her go; she stood near him, both her hands in his. He met her eyes: they were brimming with tears of joy. "Veril," he said gently, "dear Veril, you bless me more than you will ever know. I delight in your love, and I long for you. You are no burden to me; instead, you do at my side things I wish to do but never could. I love you with all of my heart."

The joy in her face told more than many words she had no voice to say. He released her hands; she turned away and went to her room to brush her windblown hair and change her riding dress for another. He lingered below, pondering. The days wearied her cruelly. The pain of every man, woman, or child they met had its echo in her heart. Mudien had banned her from the healing-work of Ceramir for good reason: she felt too deeply the sufferings of others, and the toll on her was too high. Ilohan loved her more than he had known he could love anyone, and his heart ached to its core at the thought of sending her away. Yet he would not turn back from the decision he had made. In six days Brogal would return to Aaronkal, and Veril would go back with him to the Cloth of Joy. Perhaps she would return at the new moon. Perhaps...

* * *

While talking with Ilohan, Veril had felt a joy so great it seemed it might burst her heart. Once she had left him and come to her own room, fatigue touched her. She lay down and did not move for a long time. She must get up and dress, she knew, but she would rest a little first.

She lay perfectly still, enjoying the softness of the bed that cradled her exhausted body, and the peace of being alone, with no one nearby whom she could try to bless. As she considered the events of the day, many thoughts and feelings assailed her – but behind their turmoil, her knowledge of Ilohan's love formed a background of peace and joy, a memory of goodness that would not be quenched or defeated.

She remembered the hurting people she had seen. She remembered the young, childless widow standing in the half-built frame of her new house, with the snow blowing around her feet. What she had done to help her she did not know. She remembered Lady Anlia and the other widows of the castle-knights, grieving in their cold, barren fortresses, uncertain of their future and their place. She remembered the beggar children they had met on the road, not war-orphans, but children who had never known anything but beggary even in peacetime – probably children of outlaws.

None of their suffering had failed to touch her, yet she no longer felt helpless and trapped in her experience of vicarious pain. All the force of her sympathy remained, but the bitter hopelessness of it was gone. She was exhausted, but not wounded. With Ilohan beside her, with his unbelievable words ringing in her ears day after day, she no longer felt helpless, but only humble, and the world seemed not evil, but only broken and twisted – someday to be remade as it was meant to be.

She rose. She was at peace, and her weariness was no hardship. She brushed and ordered her windblown hair, and exchanged her riding clothes for the beautiful dress Ilohan had provided for her. Every time she put on that dress, she felt it strange and almost wrong that she, a humble daughter of Ceramir, should wear it. Yet it suited her. It was not splendid or magnificent, but simple and lovely. Ilohan's choice had been wise. It was the dress of a humble, gracious princess, who would accept her station but never lord it over those beneath her. It was her dress. She opened the door of her room and went down to dinner.

Sir Benther and King Ilohan were already at the table. As soon as she was seated, the king called for the food, and servants carried it in in steaming dishes. She found herself eating hungrily, while Benther and the king did the same, and there was little conversation for a while. Finally they began to talk, but not of anxious or weighty things. They talked of the beauty of the mountains, of hidden places of loveliness nestled among them. They talked of how the stars of each season have their own especial glory. Then their talk turned to the heroes of the past, who had stood against evil, endured hardship, and shown unbreakable love – heroes who would be remembered forever. The stories delighted Veril. Through the years they had lost the edge of human pain and weakness, until one forgot that the heroes might have failed – that they had not known, when they were living, what would be the end of their own story. She could hold back her weary thoughts from imagining their ancient pain and fear, and remember only the triumphs they had proved could be won through love and faithfulness.

Presently the conversation became more serious. Ilohan was speaking of the people of Karolan again, the thousands throughout his vast realm, most of whom he would never meet face to face. Benther had pushed back his chair and seemed to withdraw, while the king leaned forward to speak to Veril alone. Her weariness forgotten, she listened intently. "They are scores of thousands," said Ilohan. "I do not even know their number. Of such a great multitude, on any day I am sure some hundreds are in grave distress, which I can not alleviate and will never even hear of."

"It is true," Veril said. "Most of your people will never speak with you face to face. You will still bless them by your wise governing, but bad things will happen to some among them that you have no chance to heal or to repair. But you were never made to heal everyone. Do not reproach yourself for not doing that which cannot be your duty."

"Perhaps I did reproach myself that way, dear Veril, before you came, but not now. Still, I am always wondering what ways there may be for me to heal more of the hurts of my people. I remember, before I was ever king, when I was going to Luciyr with Jonathan, I stood on a high mountain ridge and looked back over Karolan. I thought of all the suffering people there who could be healed if there were only someone to do it. I longed, then, for the power to heal them all: the power to match my desire. When I learned that I was the prince, I thought the crown might give me such power. You yourself have now seen, dear Veril, what the power of a crown is in truth: it is real, but very limited, and costly to those who wield it."

"I have seen your burdens, dear King Ilohan," said Veril, "and my only desire is to share them."

"I do not think you will ever understand how greatly your presence blesses me, Beloved," said Ilohan.

They were silent a long time, and then Veril said, "Regarding your people, I think you are doing nearly all one man can do. If you would bless them more, you must inspire others to follow your example."

"Yet the Karolans are not uncharitable even now," said Ilohan. "Few perish for want of neighbors willing to help them. It is only the isolated or hidden who suffer – except in times of war or famine."

"I see," said Veril. "There is the plague-stricken hamlet where none dares to bring help. There is the daughter whose mother's cruelty makes of her a silent slave." She shuddered. "I see those who are hidden from help. But Your Majesty, beloved Ilohan, is there not a charity that will seek them out, that will break their isolation? Is not this the character of your own love for them, and is it not this that must be inspired in others?"

They sat together in silence for a long moment. Then Benther broke in, speaking slowly, almost reluctantly. "You will indeed heal and rescue many who would otherwise perish alone, if your words tonight bear fruit in plans and deeds. Together you can do more, probably, than even in your dreams you imagine. Yet I give you this caution: remember that the free cannot always be rescued. You cannot save those who choose not to be saved, unless you would make them slaves without a choice."

Ilohan started at a sudden memory. Long ago, when he had just crossed the mountains with Jonathan, Master Joseph of Petrag had showed him the vast hoard of gold that would be his if he took the throne. He had thought it would give him great power to bless everyone in Karolan, but then he had remembered those he could not protect or rescue because of their own noble choices. The words that had run through his mind that night, over and over again, were the very same that Benther had just used: the free cannot always be rescued. Benther was warning him and Veril that they must not take away the people's freedom in the name of keeping them safe – that they must accept the fact that some would always be beyond their aid. It was hard to hear, but he trusted Benther's wisdom.

Just then he saw Veril's head nod: he had forgotten that she was exhausted. With a few words of love he gave her leave to retire. He dismissed Benther with thanks, and made his way to his own bedchamber. As he lay in sheltered darkness, the mournful refrain still seemed to be sounding in his mind: the free cannot always be rescued. Yet Veril loved him, and Benther had said they might accomplish more together than they dreamed. He cheered himself with these thoughts, and presently he slept.

*　　　　*　　　　*

Under the shadow of her coming departure, the last six days of Veril's stay went by. Ilohan sometimes wavered in his resolution to send her away, but he never spoke these thoughts aloud. There was no doubt that the days spent at his side exhausted her. If there was also no doubt that for both of them, the idea of their marriage seemed absolutely, incontestably right, that was no excuse for him to take her now, giving her no time to reconsider. She must see Ceramir again, and know that it could still be hers if she chose it. If, after that, her mind remained unchanged, he would take her with great joy.

Veril longed to ask him not send her away, but she never did. She was sure he would not change his decision, and she believed her part was to accept the wrong she could not reverse, and forgive him freely. She would go back to Ceramir in sorrow. When the moon waned out, she would set forth from there again, and nothing but death would keep her from his side.

Veril wandered far and wide with Ilohan on his journeys to oversee the works of rebuilding and to understand the desires and prospects of his people. The hardest day came when they went to a village, burned by Fingar and but half-rebuilt, where bandits had taken advantage of the disorder to conduct a brutal raid only the day before. The sight of the children whose parents had been murdered broke Veril's heart. Yet the grief she felt was not hopeless. There was real good to be done. She might feel worthless in the day, but with every evening came Ilohan's incredible words assuring her it was not so.

The twentieth day came, and Brogal rode into Aaronkal as he had promised. Veril could not sleep that night, and in the morning she was up before dawn drowned the stars.

She dressed herself for travel and went quietly down to the room where she and Ilohan had talked on her first morning in Aaronkal. It was a quiet early dawn, and there was no fire in the room. Ilohan stood by a window.

Though her footsteps on the floor made scarcely a sound, he turned toward her while more than half the width of the room still lay between them. For a moment neither moved nor spoke. They only stood facing one another across the room, while the faint but lovely light surrounded them. The still air was fresh but icy.

Then Veril came to Ilohan, walking slowly, half afraid to break the dawn stillness. Without speaking he led her down halls and stairways she had not seen before, and out a little postern gate that opened to the northeast. The guard was sleeping. Benther or the king would punish him later, Veril knew, but for now she and Ilohan let him sleep. They passed together into the icy freshness of the morning. The frosty grass was high about the little-used gate, and it crushed and rustled icily as they walked through it. They came into the open field in front of Aaronkal. The morning star was bright in the blue heavens, and beneath it a band of pale golden light shone pure and lovely along the horizon.

"Those children..." said Veril softly, "the orphans we saw... Their parents did not choose to die."

"No," said Ilohan. "Benther is right that the free cannot always be rescued, but often they can be. Many die or suffer greatly who could have been saved – who would have welcomed rescue had it come."

"So Sir Benther's warning does not destroy your dream, but only alters it."

"That is true."

Veril looked up. The morning star was like a tiny, hard diamond shrinking into the brightening blue, growing ever purer and more lovely as it faded. "How much do you know of my brother, Brogal?" she asked quietly.

"I hold him in honor and gratitude," said Ilohan. "There is real power and love beneath his laughter and seeming carelessness, I think. Yet I know little of what he does."

"There is much that I do not know myself," said Veril, "though I think that, except for my father and mother, and perhaps Auria my sister, I know more than anyone else. He has no dreams of helping a whole land, as you have, and he does not think of the pain of thousands he will never see. But he looks for those in need of aid, and renders it with laughter and cunning and great skill. He trusts in God and mocks all dangers, and always he has returned unharmed. Neither peril nor the sight of evil and unnatural deeds has dismayed him or dimmed his laughter. He does not count his triumphs, or his failures. I have never seen him either boastful or ashamed. I think even he does not know how many people he has helped since the first of his strange journeys four years ago. If he heard me speaking like this, he would laugh at me kindly, but he would not be pleased. Yet all that I have said is true."

They had been walking hand in hand through the freshness of the cold morning, but now Ilohan turned to face her and took her other hand, and they stood thus while the lovely morning brightened above them. "There is wonder in your face, Beloved," said Ilohan. "What is it?"

"Dear Ilohan," she said, her voice sunk to a whisper, "last night I felt I knew the answer to your dream. Now I want to say it, but I hardly dare, lest it be wrong."

"What is it, Beloved?" asked Ilohan. "Do not fear, but tell me."

"It is this," she said. "You could found a new order of knights... if knights they should be called, who would go forth, as Brogal does, to find and heal the hurts of the world."

Veril saw wonder touch his face in turn, along with the gathering light of morning. "With five-score men like Brogal, we might make all Karolan a Cloth of Joy," he said, "but I doubt one man in a thousand has such power."

"That is true," said Veril softly, "but I knew that, last night, when I was thinking of these things. It seemed that I brought all that might hinder your dream before God – almost as Sir Benther might in council speak of the flaws of a plan – and God showed me an answer to every concern. These men would not need all Brogal's skill to do great good. They must simply have humility, courage, and love. Set free by these, each one would be himself, as Brogal is. Each one would be himself, with the gifts God had given him. They could not heal all hurts: for that we must await the return of Christ our Lord. But they would do good in the land – good that apart from them would go undone. They would seek out those who are hidden: those stricken with disease, the weak, the starving, and all who live enslaved to fear of others' making. They would labor with all their strength, in humility and prayer and wisdom, to save them all. They would have little praise, but great power to bless, and their victories would bring them joy."

"There would be danger, even as Benther warned, of their becoming busybodies who seek to control and only imagine that they seek to bless," mused Ilohan. "And yet, dear Veril, as you have said, already God has given you an answer to this concern: They must, above all, have humility and love. The humble are not busybodies. But I fear I have no wisdom to choose such a band of men."

"That fear is yours to conquer, Beloved," said Veril. "I know that God will give you the wisdom to find them, if only you seek him with all your heart in prayer. He will show you how it is to be done, and he will fulfill your dream." The boldness of her own words shocked her, spoken thus to King Ilohan in his strength and royal authority. Yet the words seemed given her, and her voice was low and calm in the quiet that surrounded her.

Suddenly they were in each other's arms, and he hugged her tightly. It was so perfectly right that she cried tears of joy, but did not make a sound. "Dear Veril," he said, "you are right! I am sorry for my doubt, Beloved. You are right. It is what I have longed for. Do not forget that you have given it to me."

"God has given it to you, dear Ilohan," she whispered.

"Dear Veril, if you do choose to leave the Cloth of Joy again, and return to me, then together we will pray for wisdom. Together we will write the Code of this new order, and together we will choose its name. Maybe it will be a long blessing to Karolan, and far outlast us, even as King Nirolad founded the order of the Knights of Karolan and it exists to this day." He paused. "Yet perhaps instead it should end with our lives, lest kings arise who will not choose with prayer and wisdom."

Ilohan looked up, and the dazzling sunrise met his eyes over the eastward trees. The time was fast approaching for Veril to begin her journey, and he began to lead her back toward the castle. Veril looked up at him as they walked, her face and hair glowing in the sunrise-light. "I will return to be your wife," she said, her voice no longer soft but clear and loud in the new day. "I pray that I shall not prove barren, and in the grace of God I will give you a son as wise and good as the son of Kindrach." Ilohan felt her joy, and knew she would come back to him.

With startling vision, with joy like a great waterfall shining in the sun, he saw himself and Veril as king and queen of Karolan, humble lord and lady of a golden age, raising faithful children to take their places and carry on. It seemed to him for one instant that the darkness and brokenness of the world were nothing before the blazing power of pure and faithful love, striking down like lightning, and driving all the darkness back dismayed. Then the moment passed and he saw only the beauty of the earthly morning, and of the woman at his side, and the joy of both was shadowed by the ache of parting in his heart.

They went in to a hasty breakfast, and came out again into the still-early morning. Brogal already sat astride his well-laden horse before the great gate, with Veril's horse beside him. Ilohan helped Veril to mount, and then hesitated a moment, retaining her right hand in his. "I love you with all my heart, dear Veril," he said. "Do not forget your worth."

"I will return," she said. "Ceramir is not my home. God be with you!"

"And with you!"

He let go her hand, and she rode away into the icy morning, with the frosty grass sparkling beneath her horse's hooves.

Chapter 8

Of Brekon and Grigsy

BREKON'S ADOPTIVE FATHER HAD RECOVERED, AND Brekon's joy had been so great that Naomi had not been able to bear telling him what she knew: that she herself was falling sick. For four days she had continued to hide it, and had told stories he seemed to find as beautiful and enthralling as ever. But now the dreaded day had come. She could not eat, and her voice was hoarse and low: she could hide her illness no longer.

When Brekon came, she smiled and said, "I cannot tell you a story today, dear Brekon. You must bid me farewell, and not return to me, for a fever is on me, and it may come upon you if you stay near me. I told you I could not stay here forever. I did not want to leave you so soon, but it was not mine to choose." Against her will, tears blurred her vision as she finished.

Brekon came to her, pushed back her hair with his small, slender hands, and looked intently into her face. "You are going to die?" he asked her.

"I think so, dear Brekon," she said. "I think so, very soon."

"What do you want most in all the world, Naomi?"

Naomi answered him directly, strange child that he was, though she knew he would not understand her answer. "I want to see Jonathan again," she said, and her voice trembled with the depth of her longing.

"Who's he?" asked Brekon.

"If you want to know I will try to tell you his story," said Naomi. "But forgive me if I have no strength to finish, and do not stay too near me while I speak."

"Don't make yourself tired, Naomi. But do tell it short if you can. I want to know the story of Jonathan, and Glen Carrah."

"How did you know they were in the same story?"

"You love them both. It will be your story too, because Glen Carrah was your home. But please tell it, if you can. I can't leave you before I hear it."

"I lived in Glen Carrah, in Karolan, with my father, who loved me," said Naomi. She spoke slowly, in her hoarse whisper, thinking a little before each sentence. She curled up on the floor, resting her head on one hand. "The glen was very beautiful, and I was happy. I loved Jonathan, a blacksmith, one year older than I. My mother was dead. Both Jonathan's parents lived, and were very good to me. King Fingar of Norkath, which is a realm on the other side of Karolan, raised a great army to attack Karolan. My father and Jonathan and his father went to the mustering of the Army of All Karolan, to fight Fingar when he attacked. I never saw them again. Ten days later, while I was tending my father's sheep in Glen Carrah, Norkath soldiers came and set fire to the glen. I jumped into a river to escape the fire, and I do not know what happened to me in the river. I think I fell down a waterfall and something in my back was broken. After that I could not walk, or even move my legs. The soldiers captured me and took me into Cembar. Many strange things happened to me, and I was left alone on the ice of the creek the night before you found me.

I climbed here to escape the cold, and in the morning you came here and found me."

She took her hand away and let her head thud down upon the wooden floor. Tears rolled down her face and wet the dusty boards. "I am sorry, Brekon," she whispered. "I am so tired. I did want to marry Jonathan. I did at least want to die looking for him, in Karolan, and not so far from my home. But I should not be sad. I am going to be with Jesus, where your sister is, and that is good. I would not cry except that I am so weak."

Brekon knelt beside her and pushed back her hair again and raised her head in his small hands. He kissed her forehead, and held a cup of cool water up to her lips. She nodded slightly to him and drank as best she could, grateful for his kindness, despite her fear that he might share her illness. He smoothed the blanket over her, and bunched part of it beneath her head to cushion her from the hard floor. "Farewell, Naomi," he whispered. He walked with his usual boyish grace to the ladder, and descended out of view. For a moment she could still see his hands arranging the straw behind him to keep the cold air away from her, but then he finished, the patter of his feet died away, and darkness and silence were all that was left.

* * *

A cloudy dusk fell as Barnabas walked the last leg of a long afternoon's journey, and came to the door of his own cottage. He paused there an instant, and then he opened it as usual and went in. Hannah was carving by the fire as he entered. She was safe and well, and she put aside her work and stood to welcome him with quiet joy in her face. She came forward into his arms, and he hugged her longer and more tightly than usual. "I thank God that you are safe," he said fervently. "I thank God for your love."

When he released her, she stirred the stew that was simmering over the fire and then sat down beside him. She took one of his large, calloused hands in hers, and said, "Tell me what has troubled you, Beloved. Did anything threaten me today of which we did not know?"

He looked at her lovingly. "How clearly you see, Hannah, and how well you know me!" he said. "No, no new threat has arisen. It is only that I have seen things today that reminded me of the frailty of our lives, and in thinking of that I realized anew how precious your life and love are to me. I must speak of dark things now. Will you hear me, dear Hannah?"

She squeezed his hand. "I have always been willing to stand beside you, Beloved," she said, "in darkness as well as in light. Say what must be said."

Barnabas spoke gently. "You knew Hrelia well, did you not?" he asked.

"I used to speak to her often. Have you had news of her?" She spoke anxiously, for she knew that of all the women of Carrah only Hrelia and Naomi were lost, and she was now afraid of what Barnabas might have seen.

Barnabas took a slender gold ring of curious shape out of a pouch in his cloak, and laid it on the table. "Do you recognize that, Hannah?" he asked.

Hannah picked it up and turned it over and over in her hand. "It is Hrelia's marriage ring," she said. "I am sure of it. She is dead?"

"When I delivered the nails, they spoke of a body trapped below the ice above the beaver dam. They were all for breaking through to get it, and I helped them. It was a hard task: the ice was as thick as the length of my arm. We did it at last, and pulled the body out. The face looked like Hrelia, but it was somewhat mutilated. That ring was on the finger."

Hannah met his eyes, and she saw far more than he had said. "She was not only killed, dear Barnabas," she whispered. "I understand why you held me. Yet violation cannot harm the soul."

"You are right, Hannah," he said in a calm, low voice without expression. "She was not killed swiftly: it was done with a dagger, and we can be sure that she was raped first." He bowed his head. "It is so inexcusable," he said. "It is such a violation of beauty and love and the Law of God. The man who did this, doubtless now safe in Norkath… I could kill him a thousand times – I, who cautioned Jonathan against private revenge! But I submit to God, and leave to him the vengeance.

Hannah shuddered. "Perhaps he is already dead," she said. "Justice comes at last to all who reject mercy. But let us not speak of this more. The world is broken, but God loves us. The Norkaths and all their death and torture are gone, and will not come again while we live. It is merciful that poor Jongern was killed in Petrag, and never came back to miss his wife."

There was a silence. Hannah kissed the ring, in memory of her friend, and handed it back to Barnabas. "I am sure she never disgraced that ring, nor cast away the right to wear it," she said. "She had a sister, Felria of Kitherin, to whom, I guess, the ring should now be given. Did you bury Hrelia?"

"Yes, we buried her with honor. Since you have identified the ring I will see to it that a gravestone is set, if I return there."

Hannah had thought the trouble and darkness of that evening were over. She had felt horror and anger over Hrelia's fate, but it had not struck her heart deeply. There were only three whose fates could do that. Naomi and Jonathan were lost. Barnabas alone was left her, and why should he not return to a village a half-day's walk away? Hannah knew Barnabas too well to think he would speak as he had without reason. "...if I return..." Simple words, but to Hannah, in their context, terrible. She looked up at him, fear gripping her. "Barnabas, why would you not return there?" she asked.

He took both her hands in his and looked intently and lovingly into her face. "Hannah, Beloved," he said softly, "who was the cripple?"

Then she knew. He would go into Cembar. "I must go with you," she said.

"Beloved, Jonathan must not come to this cottage and find it empty. This is not like our trip to buy back the captives of Carrah. I may be gone a long time, and I may need to wander far into places of fear and darkness. But I must go, and you, dear Hannah, though the parting breaks my heart, must stay."

Hannah's eyes filled with tears. It was too hard. Twice he had gone away to war. Each time she had let him go with grief, waited with prayer, and seen him return with joy and great relief. But now there was no war, and he would go alone, and she saw no hope that he would succeed and little hope that he would return. It was too hard. She had loved her growing certainty that Naomi was alive, and the thought that someday, somehow, she would be restored to them. But that had been like dreams of flying. This was like being brought to the edge of a cliff and told to jump. She knew she must let him go. She forced air into her lungs, and said, in a low, controlled voice, "When must you leave, Beloved?"

He had been looking down at their joined hands, but now he raised his head and met her eyes again. "Tomorrow, dear Hannah," he said. "That is why I may not be back to see to Hrelia's gravestone."

"No!" she whispered involuntarily. She could not let him go. Yet she must, and she knew it. The feeling in her heart was certain. She must let him go. But she refused, and gasped out, against her conscience, "Three days, Barnabas, please! Let us have three days!"

He looked at her solemnly. "It is nearly a hopeless errand already, Beloved," he said. "But three days may matter little, after so many weeks. I think the delay will only hurt us more when the time comes, but I am willing. Is it truly your wish that I stay?"

She could not speak, and she still felt she was wrong, but his words comforted her. Surely three days would not mean Naomi's life or death. Hannah nodded, and they stood together and embraced. His arms, tight and strong around her, brought her joy. She wished the moment could last forever. She felt his tears fall lightly on her hair.

*　　　*　　　*

In the pitch-black night, in the hayloft to which Brekon would never come again, Naomi was praying brokenly. "Father, in Glen Carrah I wanted to die, but I had to live. Now I want to live, but I have to die. I do not understand your ways. But my life is yours, and to you I offer it again. I am your weak and foolish child, Father. Please be merciful to me and be near me, for it is very dark and cold, and I am all alone."

She faltered, and prayed no more, feeling too tired and sick to force her reeling thoughts into words with meaning. She gave up the fight to think clearly, and a gentle despair claimed her.

She felt weak and dull, cold and alone. Darkness was closing in on the small, feeble, fading light that was her life. Still, fear touched her only a little. There was real peace at the center of her being; but she was very weak, and her heart ached, and the world was not as it should be. Soft, silent tears slipped from her eyes to wet her cheek and roll down to the blanket beneath her head. She felt very, very sad, but calmly sad: there was no violence or anger in her tears. She passed in and out of feverish unconsciousness. She had no rest from pain or sorrow, but presently another kind of peace came to her: the realization that she had nothing to do but endure. Her choices were all made; her course set; her life utterly outside her own control.

Her thoughts merged into troubled dreams as she sank further from awareness of reality. Naomi, she thought vaguely; her sorrow had something to do with Naomi. "Naomi," she whispered in a fevered dream. "Something else was meant to happen to Naomi, something good. Now it never will. That is why I am crying. It was good, but now it is lost forever. But it is not her fault, Lord; it is not Naomi's fault. She did her best, she gave herself to you. She was not perfect, Father; sometimes she was a wicked girl, but she gave herself to you. Now she is dying, and what you meant for her will never happen. This is very sad. It is worth crying over, so she is crying. But she trusts you, and she knows that you love her, and so she will be well at last."

She felt a hand raise her head, and the rim of a cup was placed against her lips. A light was in her face. "She is going to die," she said. "There is no one to help her; the boy is gone. He did not understand. But it is not his fault. She did not want him to understand. It was the last thing that she could give him. She is dying, and she does not want to die, but all will be well with her at last."

"Naomi," said Brekon, "you're her. You're frightening me, not talking like yourself. It's me, Brekon. I understand more than you think. You won't die here, without seeing your home again, Naomi. I'm giving you my pony, and you can ride him back to Karolan, and if God hears my prayers you'll find Jonathan there too. Maybe you aren't dying; may be you can get well as my father did. Naomi, please to drink what I'm giving you. Naomi, you're frightening me."

Naomi blinked her eyes quickly, and her vision focused painfully into clarity. Her head ached. Brekon's face was very near her; a candle stood a little farther away on a stand. The cup was still against her lips, and the contents smelled strongly of both alcohol and spice. "I am very sick, Brekon," she whispered. "But I am sorry I frightened you. I do not think I can live long enough to get to Karolan, but if you want me to I will try."

"I thank God your talking makes sense again. Now drink what I'm giving you."

She drank. It was warm and pungent, and it did seem to drive away the cold and bring her new strength. It felt like fire in her mouth, and all the way down inside her. The pain of it woke her more fully and cleared her head. "Help me sit up, Brekon," she said. "I thought I had nothing left to do but die as calmly as I could. Now if I am called to struggle on again, I will."

Brekon helped her sit up, and then held the candle close to her face and looked at her curiously. "Do you not want to live, Naomi?" he asked.

Naomi felt too weak to lift her arms, but she realized in her heart that she was not. She did not know how she could possibly get down. She thought of the long ride, through the cold, weak and dizzy as she was with fever. She thought of the roads and ways she did not know, and of the chance of being captured. Did she want to live, to face all this, and not die in the lonely hayloft? She had said, long ago, that if God sent her the adventure she feared she would accept it with trust. The woman who had said that had been whole, well, strong, and happy. Now she was crippled, sick, dizzy, and bereaved. Yet she was still Naomi, and God was still God. "I want to live," she said, and clenched her teeth.

"Good," said Brekon. "Help me knot this rope around you."

The reality of what Brekon was doing came home to her. "I love you, Brekon," she said, "and I thank you from my heart for coming back. But I cannot take the pony that you love, your father's gift. I do not know the roads of Cembar, and I am too sick. I will only lose my way, and your pony, and die far from home. I cannot get back, though I thank you for your loving effort."

"Naomi," said Brekon. "Please to do what I ask."

Her head ached with the effort of saying so much, and she did not know what to do next. She remembered her fevered dreams, and her feeling that something more was meant to come of her life – that it was not God's will for her to die in they hayloft. She was confused. Mechanically, she began to obey Brekon. Her fingers trembled, but she threaded the rope around her legs and arms as best she could, and tied it in front of her. Brekon pulled at the knot. It tightened securely. "I don't understand what you did," he said. "Will it hold you?"

She had tied the only knot she knew for such things. She was too sick to be certain she had tied it correctly. If she had, it would hold her. "I think so, Brekon," she said.

"Then it's time to come down. Here, I will blow out the candle so it can't light the hay on fire."

It was very dark, and she was dizzy. She pulled herself to the little door. The night wind came through it frigidly. Brekon went out, and returned a moment later. Naomi grew too tired to wonder how he dared attempt what he was doing. She would only obey him, now, she thought. She heard him breathing hard beside her. "Naomi," he said, "please to jump out."

She could not jump, of course, but she might be able to slide out and fall. The idea was terrible, but it was what Brekon wanted. She reached out and caught the wooden edge of the doorway. The hard edge beneath her hands gave her a reference point in the darkness, and helped her dizziness. She pulled herself forward, until her head came out through the door and into the icy night air. She could see the ground only very vaguely beneath her. It might have been twice the height of a man down, or a thousand times for all that she could see. She felt very sick. "Are you ready, Brekon?" she asked.

"Yes, Naomi," said Brekon. "I will hold you. Don't be afraid."

She took a deep breath, pulled and pushed herself out as far as she could, and found herself overbalancing and sliding down. She fell an instant through the freezing darkness, wholly disoriented with the fever, almost too tired to feel fear. The ropes came painfully tight across her chest and under her arms, jerking her upright and swinging her hard against the rungs of the ladder. She saw a momentary vision of herself dangling helplessly, with ropes tied around her as haphazardly as around a sack of grain. The ropes bit into her flesh, and the impact with the ladder had bruised her. She was suddenly aware that she was sinking jerkily: Brekon was lowering her. She wondered how he could be strong enough to keep her from falling.

"Naomi," came his voice breathlessly from above her. "Tell me when you see the pony." She was so dizzy that she only sometimes knew which way was above her. The ground beneath her was lost in deep shadow. She had no idea how she could see the pony.

She felt something pulling at her from below. She knew it from the movement of her body, but of course she could feel no touch on her legs. It was a terrifying sensation. But the dusky shape that loomed out of the almost pitch darkness below was somehow reassuring. "Brekon!" she called up hoarsely, "I think your pony is biting me!"

Brekon stopped lowering her at once. A moment later she heard him climbing down the ladder. She was still hanging uncomfortably on the rope. He brushed against her as he passed her, and arrived on the ground. She could hear him talking to the pony in words she did not understand. She felt herself being gently moved, and then she saw that the pony's back was just beneath her, between her legs. If she were only a little lower, she thought, she would be sitting on him.

"Please to untie your knot, Naomi," said Brekon.

Her fingers were weak and trembling, and when she touched the knot it did not seem to her like the one she had tied. It was very tight. She worked at it for a long time. Now and then the pony shifted underneath her, but Brekon held it steady. All the strength seemed to have gone out of her fingers, and she stopped working. She could almost feel Brekon holding his breath. She clenched her teeth and set her hands back on the knot, but she felt hopeless. She felt that her sickness was taking her life moment by moment, killing her simply and irresistibly as she hung there in the dark.

Suddenly she felt the knot slipping beneath her hands. Brekon said something very pointed to his pony, and Naomi fell painfully onto the animal's back. The pony shied, but Brekon hung tightly onto his halter, and he did not throw her.

She could hear Brekon speaking soothingly to him in the darkness.

Before Naomi was aware that Brekon had moved, she felt the reins being pressed into her hands. "Please to hold him still, Naomi," said Brekon. "I have things to keep you safe." She pulled up on the reins as best she could with her trembling hands, hoping the pony would understand. Brekon disappeared into the darkness for a short moment, and, returning, pushed a large bundle of heavy cloth up into Naomi's arms. "It's two cloaks," he said. "Put on the soft one first."

She handed him the reins, and put on the cloaks, afraid at every moment that she would lose her balance and fall off the pony. "Are they both on now?" Brekon asked after she had struggled with them awhile.

"Yes, Brekon," she whispered. "They are very warm. I thank you."

Brekon handed up to her a long strip of cloth that gleamed palely in the darkness. "Please to tie this around you," he said. "Around your shoulders, then crossing in front of you and coming back below your arms. It means fyerilith: no one will touch you."

"A leper?" asked Naomi. "I thank you, Brekon, but I should leave it. If it means I am a leper then I would lie by wearing it."

"Naomi," said Brekon firmly. "Please to do what I say. I don't know what a leper is, but that cloth means fyerilith: no one touches you. You don't want anyone to capture you, so wear it. Please to put it on."

Naomi obeyed him. He handed her a scarf. "Wrap it around your head," he said. "You should see out, but no one will see your face. It is good. You will be safe. Food and water are in bags tied to your saddle. Are you ready to leave?"

"Yes, Brekon," she whispered through the scarf. She wondered how it had happened. It did not seem real to her.

He led the pony out through the trees to a small path that ran along the creek and back to the main road. It was strange to her to see again the road that she had traveled with Brogal, full of hope for freedom and for healing. She had thought of that road during long days in the hayloft, but had not had a hope of reaching it. Now it was so easy, and so free. Brekon, leading the pony, took her in moments the distance she could never have crawled, and the long straight road of Brogal's failed flight was beneath the pony's hooves.

Brekon stopped. "If you die, tell my sister I love her and she is sorely missed in my heart," he said. "To get to Karolan you must go down that road a long way and then turn into the sunrise." He paused, wanting to embrace her. One of her legs was all he could reach, so he hugged it through the cloaks, and held it against his cheek, forgetting she could not feel. "My heart will miss you, Naomi, almost as much, and I'll ache and feel so empty. I love you, and I hurt that you thought I would leave you to die alone."

Naomi took the best grip she could of the reins in one hand, and reached down toward Brekon with the other. She took one of his small hands in hers. "I did not doubt your love, dear Brekon," she whispered hoarsely. "I only thought you did not understand. It was I who did not understand. But that is passed now, Brekon. Now I know that you have given me the most precious thing you have, this pony, and you have rescued me. I thank you with all of my heart. Whether I live four score years, or die tomorrow, I will not forget you. I am sorry to have brought you so much sorrow and so little joy. May God bless your heart. Now go home and wash yourself, and then sleep, and may the angels in your dreams tell you better stories than I ever could."

He clung to her hand. "I do not want stories," he said. "I want you, Naomi. With you I was not an orphan."

"You decided to rescue me, Brekon, and you did, beyond my hope. You cannot take me back now. All I can leave you are my love, my blessing, and my prayers. Those you cannot lose, dear Brekon."

He let go of her hand. "Of course not," he said. "And of course I must let you go, and Grigsy too. Do not forget his name is Grigsy. Now go find Jonathan. Farewell!"

"Farewell, dear Brekon," she croaked. "God bless you and be with you! If my prayers are heard you will be greatly blessed. Selfless love is in your heart. Farewell!"

Then she was riding down the road in the direction she and Brogal had come from so long before, and wondering how it had all happened. She was dizzy, sick, and weak. She felt she had been upheld above her own strength to speak clearly the things she had said in parting from Brekon, and she believed she had said good things, but she could not remember them. She was sick at heart over leaving him, and half her mind confusedly reproached her for taking his pony Grigsy, his father's gift. Her memory was confused, but she felt that she had had no choice. Now and then she remembered that she was probably dying.

Brekon stood alone and small in the middle of the road. Naomi and Grigsy vanished into the starless night very quickly, but Brekon could still hear his pony's footfalls for a long time, in their slow and even pattern, clip clop, clip clop, before they faded out of hearing. He strained his keen young ears to catch the last sounds, and at last there was nothing but silence, and the soft clatter and sigh of the cold wind in the forest. He knelt on the ground and cried soundlessly for a long time. At last he stood and went back toward the mill. Her last phrase rang softly in his mind: "Selfless love is in your heart." Her love and blessing remained with him, even as his sister's did. But there was nothing more.

* * *

Naomi would get back to Glen Carrah, or die trying. Die trying… As the night dragged on and the morning that would never come came at last, that phrase meant more to her than it ever had before. The two words seemed to envelop the whole of her thought, looming large against the haze of delirium. In the hayloft she had been willing to die in peace. Now she had to die trying. In the hayloft she had suffered, but she had not had to fight for anything. Now she had to struggle to think clearly and find the way to Karolan. With the failing remnants of her strength she had to fight to stay in the saddle, and to keep Grigsy moving. Sickness and exhaustion were a never-ending ache, dulled sometimes when she drifted into semi-consciousness, but sharpened whenever she forced herself to think. Yet she would not give up.

Now and then another traveler met her and fled with loathing and fear. She had forgotten why they fled. She did not care. Images flitted at random through her mind, some real, some fevered dreams. She saw Brekon, smiling, parting the hay with his hand, with the morning light behind him. She saw Jonathan, searching for her through a black and barren land with no sun, and then a great light flashed around him, and he fell dead on the ground. She saw her father's face as he parted from her at the door of her home back in Glen Carrah. She saw her mother, as he had often described her, praying in a ray of sunshine in a chapel, where he had seen her first.

She opened her eyes again on the aching light of day. The pony was still walking, and she had not yet fallen off. She felt she had just seen something beautiful and something terrible, some things that were true and some that were false, but she could not disentangle them in her weary mind. She wanted to drink.

She pulled up on her reins. "Stop now, Grigsy," she whispered. "Stop now. Soon again you will have to go." She took the waterskin Brekon had provided for her and raised it to her mouth. The water spilled because she had forgotten to take off her scarf. She sobbed once in weary frustration, but then clenched her teeth and pulled back the scarf. The air that struck her face was bitter cold, but she was able to drink now. She raised the skin in trembling hands, spilling yet a little more, and drank very slowly. The water was good, but cold as ice. She could drink only a swallow at a time. Her hands grew weary from holding up the skin, but at last her thirst was quenched and she leaned forward, exhausted, to rest her aching head on Grigsy's neck. Presently she roused herself to seek for bread in her saddle bags. She tried to eat a bite, but she could not bring herself to swallow. She spat the bread out and lay perfectly still on the pony's neck.

"Father, I am trying to remember something, but I cannot. Help me. Yes, I remember. I thank you. In the hayloft I mourned because I felt my life was not meant to end there. I thought there was to be something else. But what is it, Lord? I beg you to be with me, for I cannot rest now, and I am sick, weary, and far from home. I... I thank you for my freedom, Lord. I trust you that somehow it is a good gift, though it comes with so much suffering. But what is to be the end of this gift, Lord? What is it that was supposed to happen? What one last thing do you intend to make of my life on earth before you let it end? Father, I beg you, do it quickly. I am your child, by your grace. Your child is weary and in pain. Do not abandon her. Do not prolong my distress without reason. Father, I beg you… I trust you. Help me to trust you…"

"Fyerilith! Zrea scanda! Zrea scanda niwa! Fyerilith!" Harsh cries sounded behind her, and a rock struck her between her hunched shoulders. The pony shied. She sat up without thinking where she found the strength, and rode at Grigsy's plodding pace down the road before her.

In the moments when she could think clearly, she remembered that the Norkath commander had led his troops into Cembar on a broad road, well made and straight, running east-west. As she had not crossed it, it must still lie to the north of her, since Brogal had taken her a long way south. Most of the time she could not remember this reasoning, but only the decision she had based on it: to ride north or northeast as best she could until she struck that major road. She tried through her pain and confusion always to choose paths that would aid her goal. But she remembered, now and then, that she had been unconscious and half drowned when the Norkaths started out from Glen Carrah, and that she did not know whether the road she had seen with them would take her back to Karolan or Glen Carrah even if she could find it.

She was very sick. Sometimes she could not find the strength to raise her head to see the sun and guess her direction. The shadows confused her, and she rode blindly on. She was very tired, and there was no one to help or lead her, save God alone. Sometimes she wondered if he walked beside her, guiding her pony's head, leading her toward home. Her faith was unquestioned now, firm beyond wavering. She knew that God was with her. But she was not aware of him, and she felt only her pain. Even if she reached her home by a miracle, it would only be to die on the ashes of Glen Carrah. Was that worth leaving the hayloft for, worth Brekon's sacrifice and labor? Was that worth her present pain? She was too tired to think, and too sick to know.

Though she knew God cared for her, sometimes she wished desperately for some human help. Everyone she saw fled from her with cries of "Fyerilith!" She remembered her father's deep and quiet love. She remembered Hannah's kindness. She thought of Jonathan, the few times in her life she had been sick, coming to her to sit and talk with her, holding her hand, taking her in his arms when she tossed and turned in her bed. Now there was no one to show her love, and she had to fight on alone, through her desperate sickness. She longed for even one person to say her name with love or even kindness, as Brekon had whenever he came to her. "Naomi," she longed to hear just that: "Naomi," not, "Fyerilith," but there was no one to say it.

Night fell moonless and dark upon her lonely struggle in the forest. No wind stirred the trees, but to Naomi the night did not seem still: it was filled with her trembling efforts to stay on Grigsy's back and keep on going in the right direction. Feverish nightmares assailed her. Terrible things moved, she thought, in the dark woods. She clung to her faith in God's love and protection, raising it as a shield to keep delirious terror at bay.

She was still riding on small forest trails, guided now only by the stars. She had almost forgotten the main road that she was seeking. Besides her own exhaustion, she was now aware of Grigsy's. The pony had walked for half a night and a whole day, and now long into a second night, almost without halt. And so long, too, Naomi had fought her weakness and her fever to stay on his back and keep guiding him toward the place she longed to go.

A fire shone painfully bright in her eyes through the trees to her left. She skirted it as best she could by the half-seen trails, having no wish to burst in upon a camp of strangers. The smell of good food came to her, worsening the hollow ache in her stomach. She knew her hunger was only a mockery: she had plenty of food, but could not eat it.

A dark figure, huddled at the edge of the firelight, got up and followed her as she continued past the fire. It moved furtively, but with a clumsy limp. Naomi was aware of it, but from its deformed appearance and the way it seemed to stalk her, she thought it was only another one of her delirious nightmares.

It darted out in front of her and blocked her path. Though she still did not believe in it, she pulled up Grigsy's reins, not wanting to ride it down. It groaned, and straightened slowly. A shiver of icy fear passed through Naomi. She felt she was about to see something dreadful, something that would haunt her forever, whether it was a dream or not. It stood straight up, but still in the tree-shaded starlight she could not make out its features. Long pale hair escaped the hood, but the face was dark: veiled, Naomi thought. The apparition spoke in a hissing whisper. "Fyerilith," it said. The voice was a woman's, as Naomi recognized with a thrill of horror she did not understand. "Fyerilith," it said, "yamrena mreko vrana, hemket fyerilith." Then full realization and increased horror shook Naomi's frame. A woman stood before her, with a swath of white cloth draped around her neck and shoulders and tied oddly across her chest. It was the same symbol Naomi wore herself. The woman was a leper.

Naomi's fear passed as quickly as it had come. She had seen her father, Joseph, give alms to lepers in Karolan. He had been gentle with them, sometimes even touching them, and he had shown no fear. The dreadful disease had never touched him. It had no terror for her now. It was horrible to her to see what the broken world could do to one of God's creatures, but she herself was dying and in pain. Though she was not disfigured as this woman was, she felt a kinship with her, alone in the heartless winter night. Naomi almost laughed, as a further thought struck her. Should she who expects to die of fever before the dawn be afraid of leprosy? She loved the woman in front of her. She would try to bless her.

"I love you, dear fyerilith," she whispered. "You are my companion in suffering and loneliness tonight. I am sorry that I do not know your language or your name. May God bless you. He once reached out to fyeriliths in love, when all others shunned them. I wish I were not so weak, but what I have to give I give you."

Naomi did not take her eyes off the figure in front of her. The woman knelt, slowly and painfully, and raised her cupped hands. Naomi reached one trembling hand back to her saddlebag, and drew out the heavy bag of food that Brekon had given her. She worked feverishly with her weary hands to open the tie of the bag. A good smell of bread and meat and cheese came out when it was open. "Here is food for you," Naomi said, "I would come down to give it, but I could never get back up again."

Naomi guided her pony slowly forward and a little to the side, and held out her arm, with the bag of food in her trembling hand. Her cloaks and her sleeve slid back from her hand as she reached forward, revealing her smooth and youthful skin just at the moment when the leper took her bag.

Naomi saw the woman start suddenly, and then look up at her with grateful awe. "Yethesi fyerilith," the leper breathed, "yetha... yethesi fyerilith."

Naomi understood the look. "Yes, I do not share your affliction, and still I have loved you and sought to aid you," she said. "But I am not worth such adoration. I have done only a little. May God bless you greatly, sister in pain."

Then the darkness was all around Naomi again, but it seemed in her memory that her moments with the leprous woman had been lit by a shaft of starlight. In her confusion she did not know how she had left the woman, or where she had gone. She remembered that the woman had not been able to understand her words, but she was glad she had spoken nonetheless. She did not remember what she had said.

As she rode on, Naomi slowly realized that a change had come to her through her few moments of incomprehensible speech with the leper. God had loved that woman through her. Awareness of his presence, that she had not had all her weary journey, now came to her with power. She felt the love of God, both for herself and for the woman she had left behind in the starlight. It did not lessen her pain, but with overwhelming certainty it told her that all would yet be well.

She felt Grigsy's back tilt beneath her as he started to climb a steep rise in the ground. She leaned forward and held herself from falling off with a frantic effort. Branches brushed past her. Then suddenly she was aware that the ground was flat and smooth beneath Grigsy's hooves, and it glimmered white in the starlight. There was a gap in the forest canopy above her head. She looked to her right, then to her left. She shook her head, sobbed with her weakness and pain, and looked again. Yes. It was real. She was almost sure it was real. She had found the road.

She turned to her right. She wondered whether this was the right choice, and realized that she could not think and could not know. Falling into a dream, she again heard Brekon's steps coming up the ladder to the hayloft. She had been dreaming about an endless, agonizing ride on a pony, she thought – but no, that was real. The hayloft was the dream… or was it? Then, for a moment, her mind cleared and she was certain of reality again. She was riding Grigsy, Brekon's pony, down the road in the direction of Karolan. She was sure that she had turned him the right way, though she did not know how she knew. She sat up and shook the reins to urge him forward. "Home, Grigsy," she whispered, "we are going home!"

Then she felt her strength fading, and somehow she knew that this time there would be no recovery. The world spun around her. Her arms fell limp at her sides, and her hands dropped the reins. "I trust," whispered Naomi. It was much better than dying in the hayloft, she thought. She had fought, and had used the last fragment of her strength, and now she need fight no longer. Jesus her Lord was with her, and she could feel his love. It was much better this way, she thought. She fell from Grigsy's back. The pony and the stars looked down on a gray bundle upon the ground.

Chapter 9

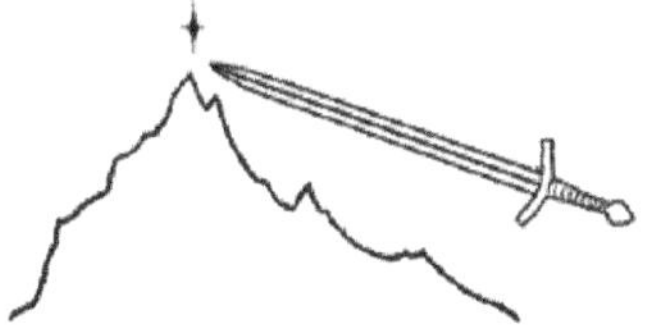

The Search

"I CANNOT SLEEP, DEAR HANNAH," SAID BARNABAS AS THEY lay in bed in the pre-dawn hours of that same night. "Can you?"

"No," said Hannah from the darkness beside him. "No, I have not slept these many hours – and I know that you have lain awake also."

"Dawn is near enough, I think," said Barnabas. "I should leave at once."

"Yes, Beloved. Can you forgive me for delaying you?"

He hugged her close. "I could if I could see your wrong, dear Hannah. I rather see your courage and sacrifice, sending me away after but one day's delay, when you had begged for three."

"I knew that was wrong, dear Barnabas, even when I asked it," she said. "I still reproach myself, though I have repented. And yet, even now I cannot bear to let you go."

"And I cannot bear to leave you, but we both know it must be. Whatever comes, dear Hannah, Beloved, reproach yourself no longer."

Hannah had prepared everything the afternoon before, when she had become convinced in her heart that she must free Barnabas of his promise to wait three days, and must help him depart as soon as he could. A horse, purchased from their neighbor Horntheld, waited by the smithy. Well-packed saddlebags lay ready beside the hearth. Barnabas dressed quickly and warmly, and a few moments' work out in the icy starlight sufficed to saddle the horse.

Barnabas and Hannah embraced in the chill air. He hugged her tightly, rocking her gently in his arms. "I had hoped we had outlived the storms, Beloved," he said. "I had hoped I would never again need to leave you. Alas, that is not how our path is laid, and still we must faithfully follow it. I love you, and will always love you. It will be a mighty shackle that I cannot break, dear Hannah, to return to you. I know that you will pray for me. I may bring her back, dear Hannah. In the grace of God, I may! Do not lose hope."

"I hope," she said through tears. "I hope. I will pray with all my heart. Farewell!"

"Farewell, Beloved! Farewell!" He rode away.

Hannah went in, fell upon the floor, and wept. It had been the shortest and bitterest farewell of their lives, and he was gone. "Forgive me, Father, forgive me," she sobbed. "I held him back, and now it may be too late. And yet my heart is broken because he is gone. What shall I do, what shall I say? Father, do not let him fall. Bring him back to me. Father, it is such a hopeless errand. How can he find her, in a strange land among a people of strange speech? Father, give me hope! Oh Father, let him find her and bring her back."

While she prayed thus, Barnabas rode slowly west with dry eyes but a heart as grief-stricken as hers. The icy wind brought low-scudding clouds that presently blotted out the stars, but the broad, pale road could still be seen. The motion of riding warmed both Barnabas and his horse, and presently he could press forward at a faster pace. Not long after the dreary dawn broke, he crossed the border into Cembar.

In days when this journey had seemed a distant possibility, he had concocted many plans for it. All now seemed feeble and unlikely of success, or else wild and tainted with evil. Yet he must try something. He was well armed, and had a good supply of gold. If he could find a man of Cembar who spoke the language of Karolan, he might set him to search for Naomi, offering a rich reward. Any man of Cembar would, of course, betray him if he could. Barnabas could imagine what was necessary to prevent this. He would have to strike deep fear in the Cembaran's heart. He would have to convince him that he, Barnabas, was a skilled and ruthless warrior, that none would ever get his gold unless they brought him Naomi – and that dire consequences would fall on anyone who failed him or betrayed him.

But Barnabas was weary, and his heart was bereft of hope and strength as it had not been at any time that he could remember. All his plans depended on being watchful for opportunities and dangers alike, and such vigilance was ingrained in his nature – yet now he had to remind himself again and again to keep watch. The future seemed wholly dark. He had left Hannah behind, and he would never see her again. His youth was past, and he no longer had the strength to live as he had lived until now. He had done noble deeds at Dilgarel, at Aaronkal, at Petrag – and on his previous trip to Cembar, with Hannah. But today was different. Today he felt his years, and felt himself too weak to resist the evil that opposed his mission. Today he would fail. And he would die a slave.

Yet he rode on, looking about him carefully, keeping up a watch by force of will. The road was empty and the forest barren. The frozen world seemed dolefully to acknowledge that the winter had been too long. At last he saw motion ahead: a woman and a child, mounted on a single horse, riding toward him along the path. The sight startled him, and as they came on at a gentle trot he seemed to feel his doom approaching. He suppressed an impulse to fly to some hidden dell in the forest. That would be folly, he knew, and would only attract their suspicion, yet still he longed to do it. He reminded himself that nothing about the sight of him betrayed his nationality. As he drew near, he saw that the woman and child were terrified of him in their turn: they saw a broad shouldered, grim-faced man with a sword at his side – perhaps a ruthless outlaw. He nodded curtly to reassure them as he passed, and he wondered at the unreasoning fear he had felt.

He considered it carefully. Suddenly, as if by a shaft of sunlight falling unexpectedly in his mind, he saw that his feeling of inevitable doom was a lie imposed on him by evil. He stopped the horse and turned back toward Karolan, thinking of Hannah's prayers.

"Lord," he said, "you have been with me every time I have gone forth before. You have been my strength and hope, and you have never failed me. The despair I have felt today is a lie. I grasp your truth now as a sword to defeat it. My life is in your hands. Be with me, I ask, because of your love, and grant me success."

He turned forward again with a grim smile. "The knowledge of the truth cannot heal my heartache," he said. "But I grasp the hope I cannot feel, and now I am strong." He rode forward at a good pace, and remembered the strategy of battles, and the joy he had known in his strength, not to kill, but to save. He remembered the desperate retreat to Dilgarel, and the wounded man he had carried. He remembered riding into Aaronkal with Jenn before him in the saddle, and finding Jonathan safe beyond his hope. The forest around him seemed to him again a place for courage, a place for real and honest living, not a nightmare land in which he must despair and die. He had a quest, and would fulfill it, if with his utmost strength he could.

With a hint of exultation now in his heart, Barnabas returned to consider his plans. He must find a man of Cembar who could also speak Karolan. Probably he would need to take him captive temporarily, in order to frighten him and gain time to explain his mission. Barnabas was well aware that such a man, once released, was likely to be a dangerous servant. A Cembaran, motivated by fear of harm and lust for gold, might search for Naomi, but would always be looking for a way to betray Barnabas, capture him as a slave, and claim his gold for nothing. Barnabas knew he would be playing a desperate game with a hostile partner – but as the stake was Naomi's life, he would face the danger willingly. He felt joy in being able to do something for Naomi at last, something to keep the pledge he had made to Joseph as he lay dying. He was glad to fight in righteousness for those he loved, and he rejoiced also in seeing his strength proven. This joy was not wholly humble, but it was very nearly so. Barnabas loved to see what he, God's creature, could do when he trusted his Creator fully.

Yet there were great difficulties with his mission. Months had passed since Naomi had vanished. She might be anywhere in Cembar, in any sort of misery, known by any name. Barnabas knew too little even to guess at her fate. He would have to leave that to the man he captured, threatened, and sent out to seek for her. That meant he needed a clever man with wide knowledge of Cembar and its miserable slaves – and yet one who could easily be cowed by threats and drawn on by greed. He needed a Cembaran with all these characteristics, but most likely he would have to choose his man in a moment by sight alone.

He rode on into the late morning, considering carefully what outward signs might reveal the man he wanted. The forest was very still, with only an occasional breath of wind to stir the upper branches, making a cold, brittle rattle above the broad forest road. Barnabas watched and listened as he rode, with all his vigilance awake. Presently he heard the sound of hoofbeats far away: another single horse, coming toward him. He turned onto a small dirt path that branched off from the road and was sheltered by an earthen bank: a perfect place from which to watch unseen.

The rider came into view. He was a man of about thirty years, dressed well but not richly, riding on a good horse – good, but not as good as Barnabas' own. The man looked very promising. He looked rich enough to own a few slaves, but too poor to turn their management over to others: he must know their language. He was unarmed and looked timid. Not least of his good attributes in Barnabas' eyes was the moderate quality of his horse: if it came to a chase, the black horse from Karolan would easily outpace him.

Yet Barnabas let him pass unchallenged, and did not move until the man was far in the distance and no other hoofbeats sounded on the path. Then Barnabas rode slowly across the road and came to a stop at the ditch that ran beside it.

While waiting for the rider, Barnabas had carefully examined everything around him, and had noticed a gray bundle lying in that ditch. It looked like a crumpled human form, shrouded in a grey cloak. He knew there was not one chance in thousands that it was Naomi, but he had to know: he had to be sure. She could be anywhere. He must be certain, if his search failed, that he had not left her dead beside the Karolan road on the very first day.

He felt foolish as he dismounted beside the gray form. He had given up an excellent chance to capture a Cembaran for this: a futile examination of what was, after all, probably only a bundle of refuse from a nearby farm. Then he knelt down quickly on the frozen mud, suddenly certain it was a human body. He reached out without hesitation and felt through the thick cloaks the flesh and bone of an arm and knee. He turned the shoulders. The body was limp and unresisting beneath his hands, but a scarf and hood covered the face. He took them off swiftly but gently, and Naomi of Carrah lay before him on the frozen mud.

Surprise, terror, and hope struck his heart together. He felt through the tangled cloth of the cloaks to find one of her hands, and felt the wrist for a pulse. He waited, his own heartbeats pounding, but felt nothing. Her hand seemed cold as ice. In despair, he gathered her up in his arms. Again, she was limp, not stiff, as he held her. "Oh Lord, so close," he whispered. "She cannot have been dead long. Oh Lord, oh Father... so close."

He stood there holding her, finally at a loss. She should not be dead. It was wrong, it was desperately wrong, that she should be dead. She felt alive; her eyes were closed; she looked as though she might wake up at any moment. But he had felt no heartbeat. A sudden hope struck him: he imagined that if her hands were cold enough, even frozen, there might be no pulse in her wrist even if she lived. He still stood holding her, knowing he could feel for her breath to learn whether she still had life, but not wanting to do it – preferring to wonder and to hope for one more moment.

She shuddered in his arms. All his thoughts changed in a moment: she was alive, but terribly chilled. At all costs he must get her warm. He ran up on the road, caught his horse's reins with his fingers, and hurried down the forest path that had been his hiding place.

He raced along seeking a place to build a fire. He had not gone far before he found a wide clearing beside the path: a camping place for slave caravans, with a well-used fire ring at its center. He laid Naomi down beside this fire ring, and with a few moments of furious exertion he gathered an enormous pile of brush and dead branches from the forest. He lit it with flint and tinder from his saddle bags.

While the tiny flame licked at the dry twigs, struggling for life, Barnabas sat nearby, panting hard from his violent labor with the logs. He pulled Naomi gently to him, and her head, resting against his chest, rose and fell with his gasping breaths. When at last he had stopped panting, the fire was already burning merrily and giving off noticeable warmth. Barnabas raised a hand to his neck and reverently lifted a loop of string over his head. A slender ring slipped up from under his clothes, and glowed richly gold in the light of the growing fire. He hung the ring around Naomi's neck, dropping it out of sight beneath her cloaks and dress. Then there was nothing more for him to do but wait, until the fire caught and warmed her.

The wonder of it began to touch him. He had found his daughter. She was real in his arms, and even if she were at the edge of death, yet she still lived. Silently but fervently, he prayed over her a prayer of joyful thanks that he had found her alive, and another of tender, deep desire that she should come again to strength and health. He watched her intently, catching every feverish movement and every flickering shade of firelight that passed across her face. Now and then she shifted herself uneasily. Once or twice the rhythm of her shallow, almost imperceptible breathing was broken by a long shuddering breath, and she coughed and seemed about to wake. But she never spoke or opened her eyes.

When the fire was very warm, Barnabas took off the two cloaks she wore, so that they would not shield her from the heat and keep her cold. He saw then that her dress was of good cloth and well made, but unlike any in Karolan or any that he had seen in Cembar. He could not imagine where it had come from, but it concerned him little. He felt her hands: they were warm, and again her wrist had a pulse. He rejoiced. But she did not wake. Often she tossed and turned as he held her. Sometimes she shuddered, and once she spoke. In a painfully hoarse whisper, without opening her eyes, she said, "I trust in God…" Barnabas wept at the words. She was so faithful. She had been tested beyond anything he knew, perhaps even beyond what he could imagine. He feared her body was broken beyond healing. And still her faith was whole.

The fire began to sink down to its coals. Barnabas was uncomfortably hot, and Naomi's brow was beaded with sweat. The warmth of her hands now felt feverish. She was still unconscious. He put her cloaks on her again, thankful for their quality and warmth. He judged that he must move her, sick as she was, for every moment they risked discovery. There could be neither safety nor hope of healing for her until they reached the cottage where Hannah waited with her desperate prayers. Barnabas thought of the hours it would take to ride there. With Naomi before him in the saddle, he was sure to attract more notice than he had riding alone. Yet he would bring her back.

His hand went to his sword hilt. Nothing would stop him now, and it would go desperately hard with anything that tried.

He lifted her gently onto his horse, and then mounted behind her, holding her just as he had held her stricken father when he had fled from Fingar's trap at Aaronkal. "May I bear you to a different fate than Joseph's, hero's daughter," he whispered to her.

He bowed his head to pray: "Father, I thank you that I have found her. Now I ask your help again: may I bring her home, and see her return to health and joy." He raised his sword against the cold gray sky. "To Glen Carrah!" he cried. Sheathing the blade with a ringing clang, he spurred his horse forward to the eastward road.

* * *

Hannah opened her eyes early in the gray dawn. The bed was too big, and she was cold. She had barely slept. The absence of Barnabas was doubly bitter because she had held him back that single day. She knew she had been wrong in this, and her guilt oppressed her. One day after many months could mean nothing – or everything. It was not impossible that the delay would cost Naomi's life and Barnabas' freedom.

She sat up suddenly in bed. "Father, I am sorry," she said. "I beg you to forgive me, and if you will... If you will, please, please, I beg you, I ask you with all my heart, please let him find her. Do not let my sin fall upon Naomi, or Barnabas, whom I love so deeply. Please let her be alive, and bring them both back to me safe and well. Oh Father, they are yours. I know it. They are always yours, not mine... Oh Father... Please do not let him be captured. Please do not let her die."

The kitchen was empty and the fire had dwindled to low coals. A thousand small tasks called out to be done, but Hannah could not bear to stay in the house. Barnabas was far away, on a dangerous mission troubled by her sin. The silence in the cottage seemed tomblike. She put on a thick cloak and hurried out into the dawn twilight.

The snow glimmered white and clean, covering the black ash of the glen. New cottages built on the old foundations dotted the burned village: only a few as yet, but sturdy, and inhabited by people of courage and determination. Smoke curled from their chimneys, ghostly in the faint light. Carrah had been sacked, but it was not annihilated. A cold, fresh wind in Hannah's face helped to wake her. She began to feel a shred of cheerfulness stirring in her heart. But then she followed with her eyes the trodden road toward Cembar, until it disappeared into the shadows of oak trees in the distance.

Barnabas might also vanish, and she might never learn his fate. She might wait out the rest of her life, here, and never see him again. Jonathan, also, might never return… and Naomi was lost already. She fell on her knees on the ground, bowed her head and covered her face.

The sound of hoofbeats came to her through the darkness of her fear and grief. They were already near; she had missed the first sound of them in the distance. She looked up. It was a black horse, coming fast. There were two in the saddle. Eagerly, she climbed the smithy wall and stood there, balancing herself against a corner post, unable to believe her eyes.

"Barnabas!" she cried. "Barnabas, am I awake?"

"Hannah, Beloved!" he called out in answer as he rode up. "It is no dream. Our parting is ended, dear Hannah, and I have found Naomi." He reined in the horse beside her, and she climbed down from the smithy wall. She looked at Naomi and her joy faded. Barnabas, too, looked grim and weary as he dismounted and lifted Naomi down.

Hannah stepped forward, her eyes fixed on Naomi's face. She reached out her hand, and pushed back the brown hair, shorter now than it had been in the days that were gone. Naomi's eyes were closed, and long suffering and patience showed together in her face. Her cheeks were flushed with fever and she trembled as Barnabas held her.

Hannah looked up and met Barnabas' eyes. Deep weariness was in his face, and she knew he had ridden all night long. "Come inside and rest," she said quickly. "Naomi is my charge now."

The little tasks that Hannah had neglected before were now accomplished in a flash. Barnabas had returned, she was forgiven, and Naomi was alive. Nothing was impossible. Naomi was alive, but very sick. She had no time to stop and think or wonder; she must work. She delighted now to labor for Naomi and Barnabas, to be useful and needed. Her heart was full of thanksgiving and faith as she worked, and she had little doubt that Naomi would recover under her care. God would heal her. He must.

She got the fire burning high and warm, and helped Barnabas lay Naomi on a mattress before the hearth. She made Barnabas sit down, and gave him a hot drink. She prepared another for Naomi, knelt down beside her, and raised her head. "Naomi," she said earnestly, "Naomi, wake up. You are thirsty, you must drink. Lord, please let her drink. Naomi, you must drink this." Naomi opened her eyes, but there was no light in them, and Hannah doubted that they saw her. For the first time she felt a chill of fear, but her faith did not waver. Naomi closed her eyes again and raised a trembling hand toward the cup. Hannah gently pushed it back, and tilted up the cup herself. Naomi drank the whole, and did not cough. "Thank God," said Hannah, and laid Naomi's head back on the pillow.

Barnabas' voice came to her, slurred now with his great weariness. "Do you think she will live, Hannah?" he asked.

She looked up at him. "I know she will, dear Barnabas. How long has it been since you slept?"

"I cannot remember, Hannah," he said.

"Come with me," she said. "Trust Naomi to my care." She helped him up, and he followed her gratefully to their bedroom, took off his boots and cloak only, and lay down. She folded their thick blanket over him, and made up their bedroom fire. She kissed him. "You brought her back, dear Barnabas," she said. "Now God will make her well. The spring is coming, Beloved. Our darkness ends. Sleep well."

She went into the other room, knelt at Naomi's side, and wept. She took Naomi's hand in hers, and felt its feverish warmth. She looked up, and prayed. "I cannot tell what the future holds, Lord. But I thank you with all my heart for forgiving me, and giving me a chance to do all that I can to heal Naomi. I ask you to bless her, and heal her, and restore her to life and joy. I appeal now to your love, oh Lord, with all my heart."

*   *   *

It was in the afternoon of the next day that Naomi at last stirred and opened her eyes. Hannah felt her fingers move a little as she held her hand. Naomi looked up into her face. "Where are we?" she asked, her voice a weak, rasping whisper. "Are you in danger here?"

"You are safe, dear child," said Hannah. "We are in Glen Carrah."

"Rest, dear Naomi," said Barnabas, who sat nearby. "Later you will question us and we will answer you; now, rest in the arms of God."

"Yes..." whispered Naomi. "Now is the time to rest. I fought so long, so long... yet also in his care. Do you have water?"

Barnabas followed Hannah's gesture and took a cup of water from the floor beside Naomi's bed. He gently raised her head and held the cup up to her lips, but she drank only a little before she shook her head weakly. He took the cup away and laid her head back down against her pillow.

"No more now," she said. "Now tell me where Jonathan is." Her voice remained a heartrending whisper, but even so they could hear her determination in her words.

"He is alive," said Hannah at last, softly and sadly. "I do not know where he is."

Naomi closed her eyes. "Alive..." she whispered. "He must be searching for me. Father, may no harm come near him, and bring him here soon I pray."

"Dear Naomi, I told him you were dead, for I thought then that you were," said Hannah. "I am sorry."

Naomi shifted her head a little as it lay upon her pillow. "It does not matter," she said. "He will still look for me. I hope he comes here soon."

"So do I, with all my heart," said Hannah.

Naomi opened her eyes and looked up at Hannah. "It is strange that I live," she said. "So often I was sure that I would die. But shall it be for long?"

"I do not know, dear child," said Hannah, tightening her grip on Naomi's hand. "We sent this morning for a physician from Kitherin; he should be here soon. If by any means we can save your life, we will."

Naomi's fingertips caressed the honest calluses of Hannah's hand, and she relaxed against Barnabas' arm behind her. She closed her eyes again and smiled. "It is no great thing," she said. "Though I would like to see Jonathan again, and run –" she smiled again, "as though I could run, now – with him in Glen Carrah, and be his wife. But if I must die, then..." tears came into her closed eyes and trickled down her face. "It is so good," she whispered, "so good to have felt your love for me... and not to die far from here, all alone. But where is my father? I would leave in his mind a different farewell than that I gave him when he went to war, though we did then all the best that we could."

Hannah knelt over her and wept. "It may be that you will live, Naomi. Oh, dear child, you may indeed live. But your father is..."

"He is a hero," said Barnabas, "and without him I and Hannah, and all Karolan, would be dead or slaves. But, dear Naomi, he gave his farewell first. It hangs around your neck now, where I put it when first I found you."

He reached for the piece of twine around her neck, but she shook her head when she felt his hand against her. "It is right that I do this," she said. "I will hold it in my own hand." She drew her right hand out from beneath the blankets covering her, and her fumbling fingers found the string and pulled the ring out from beneath her clothes. She opened her eyes and held it up in the light of fire and candles. It was a simple ring of gold, worn with the years, but still bearing, on the inside, a tiny engraving she had never seen, but of which her father had told her. It was a cross with wild grain thickly growing about its base. Her mother herself had carved it, long ago. It was beautiful: free and lovely, an artwork born of love and intricate, patient labor. She looked at it for a long time, though her hand grew weary.

Finally she let her hand fall back upon her bosom, clasped around the ring. "Alas," she whispered simply. "He died fighting?"

"No," said Barnabas. "He never had to shoot an arrow or raise a sword. He died giving the warning that rescued Karolan from sure disaster."

"There was no better way," whispered Naomi. "He would have wanted it thus. Farewell, Father... we shall... we shall..." suddenly she turned her face away and wept, and the sobs shook her weak frame heartrendingly. Gently displacing Barnabas, Hannah helped Naomi rest her head upon her lap, and now and then she wiped away the shepherdess's tears, just as on the night when Joseph rode away to war.

Chapter 10

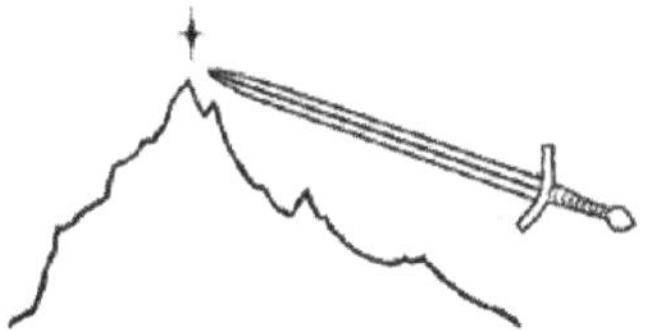

Messenger of Doom

RIDING HARD ACROSS THE DESERT'S FLAT IMMENSITY, leaving a trail of dust behind him, a lone horseman approached Harevan, carrying news that would strike its hearers like a deadly blow. Rangol was watching the desert approaches to the Cloth of Joy, and saw him first. Even while the stranger was far distant, there was something in the sight of him that touched Rangol with fear. He ran out into the desert to meet the rider beyond the last cottages and trees – and the simple greeting Rangol called out was in a tongue unspoken in Norkath, Karolan, Cembar, or the Cloth of Joy.

The rider was raising a spear even as Rangol spoke, and Rangol, likewise, was stringing an arrow in his bow. But they did not fight. The import of Rangol's greeting seemed slowly to dawn upon the stranger, and he cried back words of the same language. Yet while Rangol had spoken haltingly, the stranger's words were clear, confident, and wild. And Rangol, though he only partly understood the reply, knew he had guessed right: The stranger was of the Zarnith race, and had not come to the Cloth of Joy in peace.

"Come to my father, the lord of this place, with your message," Rangol attempted to say. The Zarnith spoke again in words that were beyond Rangol, but he seemed clearly to assent.

Running beside the horse, Rangol led the Zarnith messenger up the forest path to the Gate of Hope. As he went, he called to other sons of Ceramir. Some he called to run with him, while others he sent racing on ahead to warn Mudien. At last they came into the Cloth of Joy.

Mudien was there before the stone house, waiting to receive the messenger. To Rangol's surprise, his father was mounted on a powerful white horse, the greatest they had in the stables at Ceramir. For a moment as the two horsemen faced each other, Rangol studied the contrast.

Mudien wore the well-fitting garments unique to Ceramir. His short gray hair was combed, and peace and authority were in his face. He sat perfectly still upon his proud, flawlessly groomed white stallion. The Zarnith also was still, but there the resemblance ended. His gray-brown horse was incredibly unkempt. Its dusty coat had never seen a brush, and its mane was a matted brown tangle. The short black hair of its rider was almost equally wild, and his clothes were tattered, dusty, and strange. None of Mudien's serenity was mirrored in that fearsome, weather-beaten face, but in the sparkling eyes and the proud, set jaw, Rangol saw courage and a wild vitality.

The Zarnith spoke now at length. His eyes flashed to give emphasis to his clear-cut words. Rangol could make nothing of them, except that they seemed proud, fierce, and almost unbelievably alien. Mudien, however, called for Karlak to bring a writing desk from the house. He asked the Zarnith to repeat himself slowly, and then called down the translation to Karlak, who wrote it out on a parchment:

"Vadshron, Warlord of the Zarnith, will come against you. He can throw his spear through five men. He can run two days and nights without stopping or tiring. We his warriors ride with him, and the number of our thousands is seven score and nineteen. The least of us is stronger than a hunting lion. Together we make the earth shake and a desert gale follows behind us and lifts our banner. Our courage is like the desert: it remains forever. We will destroy you. We will drink your blood and dance on the ashes of your bones. We will drink your water and eat your cattle. We will break your fortresses to piles of stones. You will die and the Wirkriy will eat your ghosts. Tomorrow look up to see the sun when it rises. Ten more times you shall see it, and five, and three, and then we shall come, and you shall see it no more. Look not to the land of the fire, for dust can conquer fire, and shall. Look not to the land of the stone, for dust can grind stone to dust, and shall. Norkath of the fire, and Karolan of the stone: both shall fall before the Zarnith, after you fall."

Rangol reeled beneath the horror of this message, but Mudien seemed wholly unmoved. Imranie appeared from the house carrying a steaming cup, and handed it up to him. He rode nearer to the Zarnith, and held out the cup as to an honored guest. In an almost invisibly quick motion the Zarnith drew a short, curved sword and struck the cup from Mudien's hand. The drink splashed on the ground and the wooden cup was deeply notched by the blade. Mudien's fingers, though the Zarnith sword had passed among them, were unharmed.

The Zarnith raised his sword at the sky and began to sing: the song was wild, fierce, and strange. To Rangol, as he stood with bent bow aimed at the sword-wielding enemy, it seemed an incantation of fear. Mudien, his gruff voice still audible beneath the wailing Zarnith words, called down the translation to Karlak:

Our banner the dust;
Our mother the sky;
Our arrows the death that has wings;
Our father the windblown, hot desert.

None stand before us, none ever.
Before us all enemies fly.
Fly before the Zarnith in despair.
The desert will swallow your bones.

The song finished, the Zarnith messenger wheeled and rode out through the Gate of Hope. Instantly, Mudien dismounted and called to Rangol. "Take this horse and ride with him!" he said. "Let others run alongside you, guarding the messenger as you did before. They are a people who may kill at a whim. See him safe to the desert – see that he rides clean away and does no harm. Then return here for a council."

Paying no attention to the threat posed by the sons of Ceramir, or to the fear of others as he passed by, the Zarnith messenger galloped down to Harevan at a speed Rangol and the white stallion could barely match. Rangol followed the Zarnith through Harevan and out into the desert, letting the fearsome messenger increase his lead as they left the village behind. With a sudden and swift motion the Zarnith turned his horse and threw a spear. Rangol already had an arrow on the string, but he did not shoot. The range was extreme for a spear-throw. He followed the arc of it with his eyes, and did not move as it pierced the sand two paces from his horse's feet. The Zarnith turned again and rode into the southwest until he was only a vanishing black speck against the desert horizon, which was brilliantly lit in that direction by the lowering winter sun.

His heart still pounding despite the calm façade he had tried to show the Zarnith, Rangol dismounted to pick up the spear. There might perhaps be some use in studying and understanding a Zarnith spear, he thought. But then suddenly this and all other things seemed to Rangol to be wholly futile. Vadshron had nearly eight score thousand men. They intended to pillage and raze Ceramir, Norkath, and Karolan. They would. Nothing imaginable could stop them. Rangol remounted his horse and rode back to his father's council.

Evening had already fallen when he reached Ceramir, and the council room was warm with candlelight. Mudien, Imranie, and Eleanor were already there. No one was speaking. The staggering news seemed to have struck dumb the leaders of the Cloth of Joy. At last Imranie spoke. "We have known darkness before," she said, "but this is like the shadow of the end of the world."

Again there was silence. Finally Eleanor said, "It is very strange. I suppose that as far as anyone can tell, this must be the end of everything that any of us have tried to work for on the earth. I mean, of the Cloth of Joy, and Karolan, and of my son's life and reign, and of the lives of everyone who was healed here. And yet I do not feel sad. When I first read Karlak's parchment, I did. I felt sick and horrified. But not now. God loves us. He is with us, here in the Cloth of Joy. Maybe we all will die in the weeks to come. Maybe all the earthly dreams we worked for will be destroyed. But that will not happen if God wants them to be fulfilled. And if God wants us to live, we will not die. Our task is only to live faithfully as the darkness comes. This has always been our task. We are safe, if dawn comes after darkness, and we are safe if it does not. God's love for us is real, more real than the rock walls of Ceramir, and more real than the threat that has come upon us."

Mudien looked at Eleanor with a piercing gaze. She met it for a moment but then looked away without shame. "Many might say what you have said, Princess," he said to her. "But you mean it."

"The Zarnith are very rude, are they not?" said Imranie. "Boastful and without courtesy – to speak of blood and bones, and then dash good spiced wine upon the ground."

Rangol suddenly laughed aloud. A vast host of foes was coming to destroy their world, and yet his mother could criticize their manners. Imranie smiled and laughed too, and even Eleanor and Mudien joined in. Their laughter seemed to roll back the spell of the messenger's fearful words. But Imranie continued after a pause. "I am sad, because I think my children will all die. But if we die, we will die undismayed."

"There will be those who follow God upon the earth even when the true Apocalypse approaches," said Mudien. "They will have only him to cling to, as the world crumbles around them, and he will be enough. It is the same for us. Though all our earthly hopes and works prove futile – even if the Zarnith drink our blood and dance on our burned bones as they have threatened, still God is God, and we are his, and he will keep us."

"But what are we to do?" asked Rangol. "Surely we will fight the Zarnith, futile though such fighting may appear?"

"That is indeed the first question we must answer," said Mudien. "Lady Eleanor; Beloved Imranie, you have prayed for wisdom on this matter, as have I, while Rangol escorted the messenger back to the desert. What, think you, does our Lord want us to do?"

"To fight," said Eleanor. "As is written in the Books of the Travelers, nothing can hinder the Lord from saving, either by many or by few. Let us fight, hopeless though it may seem, and hope for a miracle."

"But for the Zarnith, death means Hell," said Imranie. "It is not so for us. Would God, then, help us slay them, so we can live?"

Rangol sat silent, shocked by his mother's words, but unable immediately to reply to her. It was true: if the Zarnith lived, they might have some chance of learning of Christ and taking him as their Lord – otherwise they were doomed to Hell.

Mudien spoke, and Rangol was startled with how his father's words followed on from his own thoughts. "We must indeed love even the Zarnith," Mudien said. "This does mean seeking to give them the greatest chance to know and love the Lord God. But the grave evil they seek to do here would drive them yet farther away from God. It is not clear that letting them do it unresisted is the true path of love, even for them. It certainly is not the way of love for the weak and children who dwell here, who could not fly on foot across the desert."

"It is clear in the Books of the Travelers that a king or leader is permitted to take up the sword," said Imranie, "though a private person may not do so in vengeance. If you say we should fight, dear husband, I will stand with you as always."

"I do say that," said Mudien. "I have considered flight and surrender, and I see no hope in either. Perhaps there is equally no hope in fighting, but at least thus we shall affirm that the Cloth of Joy is worth dying for."

"Fire, stone, and dust," said Rangol, musing. "In the Zarnith message, the armies of Norkath, Karolan, and the Zarnith themselves were each described by their banner. The stone of the Stone, Sword, and Star was for Karolan, the fire of the Fist and Fire was for Norkath, and the endless dust was for the Zarnith horde. But now we also shall fight, and we have no banner. What is there that can conquer dust?"

"There is wind," said Eleanor. "The great wind off the mountains can sweep dust far away. Let us take the wind as our banner."

"The Zarnith will, of course, send messengers of doom to Karolan and Norkath as they did to us," said Mudien. "That is their way. However, the Zarnith messenger may not reach King Ilohan for weeks. We should send warning to him using Skykag at once."

"I will do that before I sleep," said Eleanor. "He must know at once, of course, though it grieves me to add so heavily to his burdens."

"Indeed," said Mudien, "and there is danger that he – but stay! Suddenly it comes to me. Lady Eleanor, you spoke of wind. Rangol, when the Zarnith come, how would you expect them to assault the Cloth of Joy?"

"Through the Gate of Hope, Father, of course," said Rangol. "The mountain walls might be climbable, but no matter how it is defended the Gate of Hope will be the easiest way into Ceramir."

"In the wildness of their attack the Zarnith might also attempt to scale the cliff walls," said Mudien, "but I agree the Gate of Hope will be our weakness. Suppose, then, that we barricade it with logs – a thick wall of logs piled as high as a tall tree. Suppose that on the day of the assault, God sends us Lady Eleanor's banner: a great wind off the mountains."

"I think the Zarnith will find a wooden wall easy to climb," said Rangol. "As for wind, it blows away dust, not warriors – unless fire…" he saw from his father's expression that he had guessed what was in his mind.

"Fire," said Mudien. "Fire, and wind, and a barricade full of noxious weeds that will make a choking smoke."

"But in the end, the fire will burn down the barricade," said Rangol.

"What of that?" asked Mudien. "If we construct it well, it will burn for many hours. Without fire, as you have said yourself, the barricade will scarcely be an obstacle – and there is no hope without a miracle, in any case. But we must pray for wind."

"Then is our council over?" asked Eleanor. "We have chosen our course, and our main defense."

"Not quite, alas," said Mudien, his face suddenly grim. "One more thing remains to be discussed. As I prayed before our council, and my certainty rose that we must fight, God showed me also another necessity. Tomorrow I will announce to the people what we have chosen – and after that I will leave Ceramir to seek the Zarnith host. I will warn them of the judgment of God. I will speak the words that are given me. I will warn them against assailing us."

There was a stunned silence. "Is it not your gift to remain always in the Cloth of Joy, Father?" asked Rangol.

Imranie answered, though her voice was choked. "No, Rangol," she whispered. "Twice in centuries past, Ceramir has been threatened by a hostile army, and he who then bore the title Mudien has gone out to warn them against making the attack. Once they changed their minds, heeding the warning. The other time they... they did not repent; they killed the Mudien, and an outbreak of plague prevented their attack. But now I had hoped... But I can urge nothing against it." She bowed her head in her hands. "Husband of my soul," she said, "they will kill you without mercy, and I shall be left to face the darkness with only half myself."

Mudien stood, lifted her to her feet and embraced her. "It is only an act of faith, dear Imranie," he said. "As you yourself have reminded us, the Zarnith have value in the sight of God. They must be warned. They may turn back."

In the long silence that followed there seemed nothing to be said. Decisions and plans had been made, and the future was no longer such a blank as it had been. Still, Vadshron's threat seemed almost apocalyptic. Still, the whole world had changed since the morning. Presently Rangol went out in silence; Mudien followed a moment later.

The two women remained, perfectly still, Eleanor sitting and Imranie standing. One of the candles on the table went out, leaving their shadows big and strange upon the darkening walls.

"Do you still think we will all die, dear Imranie?" asked Eleanor.

"When Dradrag came he destroyed the Cloth of Joy, dear Eleanor," she said. "We are not better than those who lived here then. After we are dead Ceramir will be made anew, as it was then. Yet I grieve for all my children, and for the Cloth of Joy. It will be reborn, but I grieve for the good that will die. The new things will be good, but not the same. The same does not return."

Eleanor stood slowly and leaned on her crutches. "All the people we worked to save," she said. "Brint, and all the ones that came before her. They will die just as if we had never seen them if we fall."

The two women walked out of the room and into the darkness of the rest of the house. They parted at the outer door. "I spoke beyond my knowledge," said Imranie. "I truly do not know what may come, though my heart forebodes our doom."

"And I do not know either, dear Imranie," said Eleanor. "We cannot guess his will, only... only..."

Their hands touched in the darkness unexpectedly, and each felt that the other blessed her. Both whispered the same word to finish Eleanor's sentence: "...trust." Then Imranie went to Mudien on what might be their last night together, and Eleanor, after rousing Auria, went with her to the cliffs at the valley's end, and dispatched the great eagle Skykag with a message for Ilohan.

* * *

At dawn, Skykag soared through the open window of the royal bedchamber at Aaronkal, startling Ilohan just as he finished dressing. The king's first thought was that Veril must have arrived already, and the message must have to do with her, but he knew that was impossible. He unwrapped the parchment and read it:

A new Zarnith warlord has arisen, as in the days of Nirolad.
We received his messenger today at Ceramir.
He promised destruction to us, then to Norkath, then Karolan.
He claims the Zarnith will reach Ceramir in nineteen days.
Do not fear for us; God will keep us.
Look to your own people.
The horde of Vadshron the Zarnith is great.
Seven score and nineteen thousands, said the message.
You have, I guess, no more than three score days
Before he reaches the borders of Karolan.
I am sorry that my hand must write such news to you,
But I have no fear either for myself or you.
God is good.

Eleanor, Queen Mother of Karolan.

It was impossible, thought Ilohan, it must be a dream from which he would soon wake. But he was not asleep, and he knew it. He knew also that his mother would never have written as she had if there had been any doubt in her mind that the threat was real.

Perched on the king's table, Skykag preened himself majestically, unaware of the terrible import of the message he had delivered. Ilohan read the parchment again and put it down with a trembling hand.

For a long moment he sat perfectly still. Though his eyes were open, he did not see the eagle, the room, or the growing light. He saw, as clearly as if he stood on one of its great mountain walls, the Cloth of Joy. Its beauty was beyond his understanding; the depth of its goodness more than he could fathom. He could not guess or even imagine its worth.

Far out over the desert he saw a man and woman riding side by side: Veril and Brogal, going where he had sent them, to their deaths. Veril, his beloved, whom he had sent away. Going to Ceramir to die in its ruin. And Eleanor was already there, and there would be no escape. Even Brogal, who had mocked death and captivity so many times, would not laugh before a Zarnith charge.

The vision of the king's imagination swept again over the desert to see the Zarnith, coming, as he had long ago told Jonathan they might: coming again as they had come in the days of Nirolad when the mountains had turned them back. But even then they had razed the Cloth of Joy. Now they planned to sweep eastward around the mountains and destroy Norkath and Karolan. The two nations between them could not now raise a force a quarter Vadshron's strength. There was no hope, even for Karolan. Like the Cembarans long ago, her people would be slaughtered and hunted until only a tiny remnant remained hidden deep in the caves and forests of their desolated land.

"Why are you sitting still?" The thought struck down into his mind, even while it was full of the image of the Zarnith host destroying Karolan. "Would Kindrach have sat still? Would Thomas? Why are you sitting still?" He stood up quickly, then stumbled, and fell down upon his knees. He leaned his elbows on the table, and dropped his head down in his hands. "Darkness..." he said. "I see no light, no hope. I am not Nirolad, not Thomas, not Kindrach, not even Jonathan."

Suddenly he remembered his first moments in the forget-me-not, so vividly that he flung out his arm to feel the space around him and the smooth wood of the table: to know he was not again in that grimy cell of death. He realized that his thoughts had been like the words of Tulbur, mocking him as a weakling. But none of the great kings and heroes of the past could have saved Karolan from a threat like this. Ilohan saw no more hope for Karolan now than he had seen in the forget-me-not. No more. But no less, for then there had been none. And Christ had been with him even there.

King Ilohan sank down away from the table, and lay at full length on the floor. "Father, help us," he whispered. "I have no awareness of Christ's presence now. You have said you will never forsake us. I feel forsaken, but I choose to believe you – or at least to try. I feel drowned in a great flood of tears, the tears of all my people. All that I love will perish, and the hope of Karolan will never rise again."

After lying there lost in darkness for a long time, Ilohan opened his eyes without his conscious choice. The stone floor was smooth, well swept, and lit with cool white light. The air was sweet and clean in his lungs, and less piercingly cold than it had been a week ago. Ilohan stood, walked to the window, and looked out. The land was real, and the sky was bright. On his left the sun kindled the clouds to blinding brightness. The fields of Karolan spread out to the horizon in a vast expanse of white snow, against which trees and hedgerows lifted intricate gray branches. Smoke rose from the chimneys of cottages that were newly rebuilt after Fingar's destruction.

"It is your land, Father," he said. "And my life also belongs to you. Why I stood I do not know, nor do I know why it is that despair did not utterly overwhelm me. But I am standing now. When Nirolad had news such as I have had, he armed his men and marched away to war. God, give me hope, and courage, and send us if you will a miracle such as the world has not known for more years than men can count, since the days when, because you fought for them, one of your people could put to flight a thousand. Fight for us, I pray, Father. But if you will not, then may we nonetheless fight rightly, and die faithfully."

He stared at the south horizon, where the land beneath faded into the thin clouds above. Beyond the veil of those clouds were the great mountains, and beyond that lay Ceramir, where the Zarnith would come with utter destruction in only seventeen days – since Skykag must have taken two days to carry the message. He could call out the knights in training, and ride at their head to Ceramir in that time. But that would be to abandon his people, and if the Children of Ceramir managed to fortify their valley, horsemen would be little needed there. There was another way, beyond the veil of clouds, beyond the dreams and nightmares of Vadshron the Zarnith. King Ilohan sat down to write:

Seven days I shall take to prepare my people for war.
Then I will come to you, by the mountain way.
I will bring a thousand warriors for Ceramir's defense.
Thirteen days ago, I sent Veril back to Ceramir, alas.
I love her. I will marry her if we survive the storm.
I do not see any hope.
If I can die in your defense and Veril's, I will be content.
Ilohan of Karolan.

Ilohan stood and took the sword of Kindrach from the wall. He buckled the sheath to his belt, and drew out the blade to flash the white light of the thinly clouded sky. "The last King of Karolan goes to war," he said.

* * *

"The desert!" said Veril, with wonder in her voice, as she and Brogal rode down the last stretch of the descent from the pass of Luciyr in the morning, and saw, as long before Ilohan and Jonathan had seen, the dry immensity stretched out before them. Brogal felt his heart leap as it always did at the first sight of the vast, barren land beneath the boundless sky. Veril turned to him, and the midmorning sun shone full on her face and hair. "Brogal," she said, "you did not go far out into the desert as you had planned; you could not, in the time you had... What did you do instead?"

"Ah, Veril," he said, his eyes alight with mischief, "that is a secret that should, perhaps, not yet be told. I met a very remarkable person, whom I was not permitted to save. This person was neither sick nor enslaved; a different sort of saving was needed. I had to content myself with asking for a promise, which I received – but I also gave one. The secrets shall be revealed in time, and good things come to light, unless all goes astray."

"I do not think it will," said Veril.

They rode out onto the desert road, and the dry wind seemed warm in their faces after the cold journey through Luciyr in snow. They soon felt lost in the beautiful vastness of mountains and desert, but they rode on at a steady pace. Ever so slowly, new mountains came into view ahead of them, and they knew that though the desert seemed endless, they would cross a part of it at last, and reach their home. They never lacked for water, for Brogal knew every buried stream and trickling spring.

The long journey soothed Veril's sorrow. The endless footfalls of the horses seemed to speak to her of calm, sure patience, that in the end shall cross the desert and reach a land of joy. Sometimes, like a tree in a sudden gust of wind, she was shaken by a moment's fear that she would not make Ilohan a good wife after all, and could not rightly marry him. But Ilohan's own words were held deeply in her heart, and she was not deceived. The path might be long and hard, but she knew her destination. All she needed was the certainty that her choice was right, and though sometimes the desert wind blew back her tears and dried them on her face, she had it.

*　　　*　　　*

In counsel with Benther at Aaronkal, Ilohan had just finished explaining the situation, and his own preliminary plans. The scrap of parchment from Ceramir lay between them on the table. Benther stood and paced back and forth, one hand pressed against his head. "I hope I can advise Your Majesty," he said, "but first I must master my own astonishment. That this should happen again, after so many centuries – and that it should happen to us."

"I, also, could not believe it at first," said Ilohan.

"My head is a little clearer, now," said Benther. "Eleanor told you the Zarnith could reach our border in three score days. I suppose they will come through the mountains at Drantar's Gap?"

"I had not thought of the question," said Ilohan. "There is also a pass at Luciyr."

"There is," said Benther, "but I do not believe a great host of men on horseback could come through it swiftly. You have been there yourself. Am I mistaken?"

"No indeed," said Ilohan, "the horses would have to pass in single file. It would take many days to bring a Zarnith horde through the mountains there."

"Drantar's Gap, then, is a reasonable guess," said Benther. "And that means we must act swiftly. The Gap is a score of days' march from Aaronkal. If we muster the Army of All Karolan at once, and set out when it reaches a score of thousands strong, we will not reach there much ahead of the Zarnith."

"Why do you think it is there that we must face them?" asked Ilohan.

"It is the only place where their movements will be constrained. They will not be able to maneuver around our army for the best position. They must come through the Gap. If my memory serves, it will even be slightly uphill for them, coming from the south, and that may blunt the force of their charge a little."

"We may even be able to raise a wall of felled trees across the Gap," said Ilohan.

"Perhaps," said Benther, "but Drantar's Gap is wide. It cannot be fortified without long labor. Still, it does seem to me much better than meeting the Zarnith on the open plain."

"I agree," said Ilohan. "So we must muster the Army of All Karolan at once. Since we have been talking of Drantar's Gap, which is two week's ride into Norkath, I take it we both agree that an alliance with King Andokar is necessary?"

"Indeed," said Benther. "It will be far better for us to meet the Zarnith at Drantar's Gap than at our own border, where they will be able to maneuver as they please in the open plains. Besides that, Andokar may raise a sizeable force to aid us."

"And it gives us an opportunity to protect Norkath, showing friendship to our former enemies," said Ilohan.

"You speak as Thomas or Kindrach would have spoken, and I commend you," said Benther. "Nevertheless, I must warn Your Majesty that forming an allied army from men who were deadly enemies last autumn will be no easy task."

"No," said Ilohan. "No, it will not be easy. But now another thing occurs to me. By taking our stand at Drantar's Gap, we will abandon the transmontane province of Norkath to the Zarnith."

"There is no help for that," said Benther, "unless Your Majesty would make haste through the Gap, to face the enemy in transmontane Norkath itself. But there the land is flat, and the Zarnith will be as irresistible as the wind. Even apart from that, we could scarcely get there in time."

"The army that marches to Drantar's Gap, then, will not attempt to protect transmontane Norkath," said Ilohan.

"But why does Your Majesty say, 'the army that marches to the Gap'?" asked Benther. "Is not that the only army we shall have?"

"No," said Ilohan. "As I said before, I will take a thousand men and cross the mountains to come to the aid of Ceramir."

Benther again paced to and fro, a hand pressed to his head. "I had forgotten that, Your Majesty," he said at last. "You yourself have been speaking as though you would be in the battle at Drantar's Gap. And indeed, I think you must be. You are the King of Karolan. You must not abandon your people."

King Ilohan stood swiftly. "I have sent Veril to Ceramir – to certain death," he said. "And Eleanor my mother is there also. I must defend them."

"But is it not likelier that you and all your thousand will die in the mountains?" asked Benther.

"I have crossed them before," said Ilohan.

"I know it – yet forgive me, Your Majesty, I understood that you relied quite heavily on Jonathan of Glen Carrah in that crossing. If you try to cross at the head of an army, it is you to whom the others will look for strength. And your journey with Jonathan was perilous, though you accomplished it. And it was in autumn, while this is winter."

Ilohan sat down. "All that is true, Sir Benther," he said. "I and all the thousand may indeed die in the crossing. I must nevertheless attempt it."

"Your Majesty," said Benther, "I am grieved with all my heart to speak thus to you, but as an honest counselor I must say that in doing this I think you betray your people. From your testimony, Ceramir must indeed be wonderful beyond the thoughts of those who have never seen it, and its destruction would be a great calamity. But Veril and the Lady Eleanor can fly from the ruin, and have at least as much chance of life as you will if you attempt the mountains. Your Majesty is King of Karolan, not of Ceramir."

Ilohan stood again, trembling with anger and dismay. He was furious that Benther had dared to rebuke him, but he did not find his advisor's words easy to refute. He knew he would have died in the mountains without Jonathan's superior strength. And Eleanor herself had written of his duty to his people.

"What do my people need from me?" he asked. "Many men are stronger; many are wiser in the strategy of battles. I have never even led an army – it was Jonathan who triumphed at Petrag."

"Your Majesty, I would have said that the knights who were stronger or more skilled in strategy all died in Metherka's charge. Only you and I are left."

"Sir Benther, would you dare to lead the army at Drantar's Gap?"

Benther in his turn leaped to his feet, his face full of anger – or fear; Ilohan was not sure which. "No, Your Majesty!" he shouted. "No, I would not dare! Not for fear of the Zarnith spears – I would fear them no more than straws. But look, Your Majesty, at what you would do to me by making me commander while you went to your death. You would make men say that at last the ambition of Tulbur was fulfilled – that I had sent you off to die so I could claim the crown. You would destroy both me and Karolan."

Silence hung in the room, tense as a bow string, while Benther's impassioned words seemed still to ring in the air. Ilohan found himself breathing hard as though he had been running or climbing. "I see," he said quietly at last. "But is there none who could lead the Army of All Karolan better than I?"

"Your Majesty," said Benther, "your skill as a knight is not the only reason I would have you stay. It is not even the chief reason. You are the King of Karolan, rightful heir of a line that goes back even to Nirolad the Great. The people love you. To them, you are a symbol of hope – hope that Karolan may prosper with justice and with peace, under your benevolent rule and that of your descendents. Yet you have not asked me all this – you have only asked if there is anyone who could lead the Army of All Karolan as well as you. Honesty compels me to give you one name, one who has arisen among the peasants with courage and skill to baffle many knights: Jonathan of Glen Carrah. I say that he could lead the army. I do not say that he could wear the crown."

"Jonathan has disappeared," said Ilohan. "Again and again I have sent to Carrah for news of him, and always the answer is the same. He found his home burned and his beloved slain. He rebuilt his father's house with a heroic effort, and then he vanished."

"I know it," said Sir Benther. "I am sorry."

"Sir Benther, my friend and counselor, I am weary. Perhaps it does not matter what we choose. Even at Drantar's Gap, even if with Andokar we raise an army two score thousands strong, the Zarnith will overwhelm us and destroy us. But one thing at least we have chosen. Let us send messengers to muster the Army of All Karolan at once, and then let us sleep."

Chapter 11

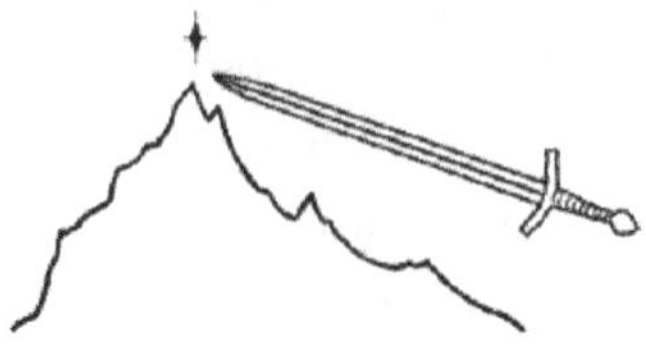

The King and his Dreams

THOUGH ILOHAN WENT TO HIS BED, ONCE THE messengers were sent, he did not find it easy to sleep. His mind was full of turmoil. On the one hand, there were countless things that must be done in order to send a strong army against the Zarnith and yet keep those left behind from starving. On the other hand, it was all most likely futile. He might arm, supply, and organize the army with flawless skill; he might field thousands more soldiers than any King of Karolan before him, and still the host of Vadshron could slaughter them to the last man. Working with haste and wisdom and the authority of royal command, he might ensure that enough grain from northwestern Karolan flowed south and east to feed everyone, down to the last beggar's child – and the grain would only go to the victorious Zarnith, as they feasted in captured Aaronkal and killed women and children for sport.

The knowledge that it was all probably futile did not deter Ilohan from wanting to plan and act as wisely as he could. He found his mind focusing in even on small details, wanting all to be done well – and yet the near-certainty of destruction was always with him. It seemed to split his mind into two parts – a part that planned and worried and considered, and a part that simply stood aghast at what was coming. At last, weariness overtook both halves of his mind, and he slipped into a troubled sleep.

Ilohan had often read of men to whom God sent guidance through a dream – there were several such accounts in the Books of the Travelers. He had always supposed that the dream was like an ordinary dream, only exceptionally vivid, and carrying a clear message. Yet that night something came to him which almost seemed like a message from God, and it was not at all as he had guessed. It did not exactly come in a dream. He had many dreams that night, but they were all vague and confused. None carried any message. But when at last he awoke to the dawn, he knew two things he had not known when he went to sleep. He felt as though he had been told them – but he had no memory of being told. It was as if the knowledge had simply appeared in his mind.

The first item of this strange knowledge was that there was no hope for Karolan unless God sent a miracle, and that therefore all plans should be made with the possibility of a miracle in mind. The second was that he, Ilohan, was going to ride to Glen Carrah to seek for Jonathan. Ilohan was puzzled by this strange pair of ideas. The first, though new to him, did follow almost inevitably from what he had been thinking the night before. The second, however, seemed preposterous. Jonathan was lost. The journey to and from Glen Carrah would take at least four days, which would probably be wholly wasted. And yet, there was a reason to find Jonathan, if he could be found. As Ilohan dressed, his mind was working quickly, not to question the ideas the night had brought, but to fit them into new plans for action.

He hurried down from his bedchamber, and summoned Benther to another counsel over breakfast. Ilohan spoke eagerly and swiftly. "We must prepare as prudently as we can, to fight with all our strength," he said. "And yet, what we should have in our minds is not that we may win by force of arms, but rather that as we work with all the wisdom we can, God may rescue us in some way that is beyond the reach of human wisdom."

"You have hope, now, Your Majesty, when last night you were hopeless," said Benther. "I am glad – but I wonder why you summoned me so urgently. Does your new-found hope change our plans?"

"It changes them but little," said Ilohan, "but it makes them clearer. Last night we left undecided the question of what to do about Ceramir. Today I think I have the answer. I will lead a thousand men over the mountains, as I said before – and I will leave Jonathan of Glen Carrah to command the Army of All Karolan when it marches to Drantar's Gap."

"But... but Your Majesty, as you yourself said last night, Jonathan is lost."

"I believe God intends that I should go to Glen Carrah to seek for him," said Ilohan.

"What if you do not find him?" asked Benther.

"Then we shall have to reconsider our plans," said Ilohan.

"Your Majesty," said Benther, "I do not think the people will accept Jonathan as king in your place."

"They need only accept him as commander of the army," said Ilohan. "From the Battle of Petrag we can see that they are already willing to do so."

"But Your Majesty," said Benther, "we have agreed already that if you attempt the mountains again, you will most likely die. If, then, the miracle you hope for comes at Drantar's Gap, who could succeed you but Jonathan?"

Ilohan was silent. He wanted to say that Benther himself was in the royal succession, but he was afraid to do so after Benther's outburst of the night before. He thought, also, that Benther's fears might not be ill founded: the people might indeed distrust him, connecting him with Tulbur's treachery, if he were made king. Finally Ilohan said simply, "I suppose it will have to be Jonathan, as you say."

"He is not of the line of Thomas, nor any of the kings who preceded him," said Benther. "Also, Your Majesty, though you think yourself but lowly, Jonathan could not be the king to the people of Karolan that you have been, and will be still if you live. If you appoint Jonathan your heir, and go to certain death at Ceramir or in the mountains, your people will feel you have abandoned and betrayed them."

"Sir Benther, I acknowledge your wisdom, but I cannot leave Ceramir unguarded. Nor can I ask any other to lead the army I send to guard it. The Zarnith poem that I followed with Jonathan will not work in reverse – the only hope is to have a guide who has traveled the path himself, as I have. Even if it were not so, I could not send others into such deadly peril unless I went with them."

"You are the King of Karolan," said Benther. "You have heard my counsel, but the choice is yours. Command me, and I will obey."

Ilohan met his eyes. "I thank you, friend," he said. "I will depart for Glen Carrah tomorrow at dawn. In the mean time there is much to plan. We must ensure that whatever happens, grain will continue to be distributed to all who were left hungry by Fingar's war – unless indeed Vadshron utterly destroys Karolan. We must also gather great store of grain and other foods to supply the men of the army. And the thousand who will march with me must have the warmest furs and cloaks that we can find."

"If plans for all that must be set in motion before you leave tomorrow, Your Majesty, we must begin at once and work with great haste far into the night."

"Let us begin," said King Ilohan.

* * *

"Will you carry me outside?" asked Naomi that afternoon in Glen Carrah. Barnabas lifted her gently and carried her out into the cold, bright world. He set her down on a crude yet comfortable chair he had made for her from piled firewood, cushioned with blankets.

"The Glen is still beautiful with the snow," said Naomi.

"Yes," said Hannah, who had followed them out.

"I suppose all my sheep died in the fire," said Naomi.

"Certainly there has been no sign of them," said Barnabas. "I suppose if I had searched the Glen I would have found their burned remains. Jonathan may have, for he did search, I think, long and carefully, looking for some trace of you."

"I have been thinking of Jonathan, of how my love for him has changed," said Naomi.

"What do you mean?" asked Hannah.

"I always wanted him to be happy – I wanted good things for him. I wanted most desperately for him to love God and follow him, so he would be safe from Hell... so he would have joy forever. But I also wanted him for my own – I wanted to marry him and be, myself, a great part of his joy. I thought, 'He must come to love God, so there will be no barrier between us anymore.' But then, believing so many times that I was going to die, I could not hope anymore that I might marry him. I could not hope that he would ever be mine. I could only hope that he might someday be God's."

"You were a loving child, Naomi," said Hannah. "It sounds as though you have grown into a great woman of God."

Naomi laughed – and Hannah rejoiced that she could laugh again. "I am certainly still a child," said Naomi. "If I love God, and Jonathan, better than I used to, it is only because I was forced into it. And I cannot understand the things that have happened to me, nor why I should be here in the sunshine, with a little strength, at least for a little while."

"But you may live, and grow stronger," said Hannah. "The physician may have been mistaken – he said so himself. And Jonathan may return. I believe he will return…" Naomi closed her eyes. Looking at her pale, exhausted face, Hannah felt a spasm of fear for Naomi despite her own hopeful words.

"I still do want Jonathan very much," whispered Naomi. "I think I would give whatever time I have left on earth for one last day with him – even if my death in the evening were to be by a fire like the one that burnt the Glen."

Hannah laid her hand on Naomi's forehead. It was neither feverish nor chilled. "You may stay out here in the sunshine a little longer, dear child," she said. "I will go in to prepare your medicine."

In the comparative darkness of the cottage, Hannah carefully mixed a small spoonful from a bottle the physician had given them into a larger cup of warm water. The medicine did seem to help Naomi, at least a little. Hannah always mixed it with great care because the physician had said that, though in small amounts it was wholesome and good, in larger draughts it was a swift and deadly poison. When Hannah emerged into the bright winter sunshine, Naomi was asleep.

She set the medicine beside her and went a little away to stand with Barnabas looking back at Naomi and beyond to the snowy lanes and fields of the village.

"Is she weakening again, as the man from Kitherin expected?" asked Barnabas.

"I do not know," said Hannah. "She seemed near death when first you brought her here, and she recovered greatly in the first few days. I have seen little change in the five or six days since then. I do not know if she is weakening, but she is certainly not gaining strength – and she has but little."

They were silent together for a long time, and then Hannah spoke with tears in her voice. "I remember something I saw one afternoon, a little before the war. I was drawing water, and a storm was coming from the east. Joseph had taken Naomi to show her some hidden place where she might find safety, and they were just returning from that little journey. I saw them standing together in the sunlight, faithful and beautiful. Dark shadow swept over the world behind them, until they alone were bright. They seemed so lovely and so imperiled that I turned away, so I would not see the shadow take them. My heart was chilled with fear. Oh child, beloved daughter, you were not meant for darkness such as this."

"But the darkness does not rule her," said Barnabas. "She trusts in God, and is grateful. She even has some real measure of contentment, despite her longing for Jonathan."

Hannah looked at the ground and shook her head while her tears dropped upon the snow. "Naomi has grown," she said. "The earth is not her home. She is ready… Alas for our loss… She is ready for the ending of her griefs."

"At least, if she is soon to die, dear Hannah, we have been able to give some peace and comfort to her last days."

"Yes," said Hannah, raising her tear-wet face. "Yes. For that, at least, I am truly and deeply grateful."

* * *

Ilohan and Benther worked frantically all that day in Aaronkal. They sent scores of messengers on many different errands. They pledged vast quantities of the hoarded gold from Petrag to gain the grain, warm clothes, wagons, and other supplies their armies would need. They knew that some of their requests would turn out to be impossible, or would be stubbornly refused, so they worked on alternatives until Ilohan's head ached with the complexity of their plans, and with anxiously imagining all the ways they might fail. They brought out the weapons in the armories of Aaronkal, down to the last dagger, and had them counted and inspected. They sent men to recover swords from the battlefield at Petrag, determined that the men who gathered to fight for Karolan would never again be deprived of the tools of war.

One thought at the back of Ilohan's mind troubled him throughout the exhausting day: the knowledge that Benther believed he had chosen wrong. Benther believed he had no right to cross the mountains to go to Veril's defense. Ilohan could not deny that Benther's reasons had force. The people of Karolan would indeed feel deserted when he left them to go to almost certain death. But the alternative was to desert Veril – and that would be an absolute desertion. He could not send anyone over the mountains in his stead. He could put Jonathan at the head of the Army of All Karolan. Though the people of Karolan might feel deserted, they would not truly be so. Jonathan had already proven himself a commander of astonishing skill. Still, Ilohan wished intensely that he had his friend and advisor's approval in the desperate choice he had made.

As the day drew on toward an evening that would bring no rest, a new idea came to Ilohan that made his disagreement with Benther not less but greater. He had been thinking about the messages, if messages they were, that had come to him in his sleep. The first was that there was no hope of defeating the Zarnith except by a miracle – and that therefore they should make their plans in the hope that God would indeed send a miracle. But that, surely, meant they must not shy away from attempting the impossible, if it was good. And the new idea was something good, and impossible.

Among Ilohan's lovely memories of being in Ceramir, there was one image that was not of the Cloth of Joy at all. On the first day he and Jonathan had spent there, when they climbed the sheet of vines with Karlak, Ilohan had looked out into the desert beyond Harevan. Evening shadow like a soft haze had lain beautifully over everything. He had seen a line of hills to the west, a spur jutting southward from the mountains. These hills had a single gap, through which ran the faint line of the desert road. The irrelevant sight had stuck in his memory. Now, months later, it seemed to stand out with terrible significance. The Zarnith would pass through that gap. At that gap, he could attempt to stop them. If, by a miracle, he succeeded, not only Ceramir but also transmontane Norkath would be saved.

It was not until he and Benther were eating a hasty supper together that Ilohan found time to mention this idea. He began by talking about something very different – that nevertheless was closely connected in his mind.

"Sir Benther," he asked, "what do you know of Dradrag's invasion in the time of Nirolad?"

"Since you ask about an invasion, and I know you are not asking me what every child in Karolan knows, I must assume you are speaking of Cembar," said Benther.

"Yes," said Ilohan, "yes, I am speaking of Cembar – of Nirolad's failure."

"I would not call it his failure," said Benther, "though I do not say I am surprised to hear the son of Kindrach use that word. After Dradrag's Zarnith host was turned back by the mountains of Karolan, he turned westward, as if he would return the way he had come: west along the mountains and then south across the desert to his own land beyond the edge of our knowledge. But he did not return. He sought a new conquest. As is the Zarnith custom, he sent a messenger of doom – to King Yalkos of Cembar. Yalkos appealed to Nirolad for help, and Nirolad refused. Dradrag's host overwhelmed Yalkos and the Cembaran army. The Zarnith easily conquered Cembar. They stayed there for months, devouring the plunder in wild revels. They hunted the surviving Cembarans like animals, and raped, tortured, and slaughtered them without mercy. At last, to the relief of Nirolad and all Karolan, the Zarnith went back south to their distant homeland: they did not sweep eastward into Karolan.

"A few Cembaran survivors emerged from caves and deep forests, and over many years rebuilt their cities and repopulated their land. But they felt that by refusing King Yalkos when he begged for help, Nirolad had handed them over to their merciless foes. Thus the Cembarans swore unending enmity to Karolan, so that to this day they hate us and enslave us when we cross their borders.

"And why would you not call that Nirolad's failure?" asked Ilohan.

"Because Dradrag had such overwhelming force," said Benther. "Even if Nirolad had led a score of thousands to the aid of Cembar, they would likely have been defeated and slaughtered to the last man. Cembar would still have been ravaged. It is even possible that the Zarnith would have ravaged Karolan too, if they realized that the army of Karolan had opposed them and been destroyed. The situation now is different, for Karolan is in dire peril whether we ally ourselves with Norkath or not – and alliance improves our position rather than worsening it."

"But what if there were a part of Norkath that we alone could choose to protect – or not?" asked Ilohan.

"I do not understand Your Majesty," said Benther. "There is no such region. Our stand at Drantar's Gap will protect almost of all of Norkath. The rest, the transmontane province, must simply be evacuated: no action of ours can save it."

"There is a gap in the desert hills west of Ceramir," said Ilohan. "The Zarnith will pass through it as they come up to assail the Cloth of Joy. If I and my thousand oppose them there, and by a miracle defeat them, then transmontane Norkath will be saved, along with the Cloth of Joy."

"But is not Ceramir a steep-sided valley with a narrow entrance called the Gate of Hope?" asked Benther. "Is not this Gate of Hope far more defensible than a mere gap in a line of hills?"

"It is," said Ilohan. "I do not like the idea of standing in the desert gap either. But it seems to me the best course. It seems to me the thing we should do, if we are placing all our hopes in a miracle from God, who said that we must love our enemies."

A wry smile touched Benther's face. "Your Majesty said earlier that Norkath is no longer our enemy," he said. "The enemy now is the Zarnith. Should we, then, go forth unarmed and lay out a feast for them?"

"Such actions might sometimes please God," said Ilohan, "but they are the deeds of saintly monks. I am only a king, who must fight and die in defense of those who wish to live in peace. It is not my calling to try to stop a Zarnith charge with charity alone."

"Dear King Ilohan," said Benther, "I spoke to show an example of folly, and you argued it gravely as though it might have been wisdom. But truly, I see as little hope in the course you wish to choose. You hope to save Veril and your royal mother, the Lady Eleanor. At the Gate of Hope, if it is well fortified, you might possibly succeed – if not in defeating the Zarnith, at least in discouraging them enough that they might leave Ceramir in peace and pass on toward Norkath. But at this desert gap, you and all your thousand will die within a score of heartbeats after the beginning of the fight."

A loud knock came on the door just as Ilohan was about to answer. Instead, he commanded a servant to open the door. A page rushed in. "Forgive me, Your Majesty and Sir Benther," he said, "but a message has just come from King Andokar of Norkath, and the chief of your guards thought it should be brought to you at once."

"He did well, and so have you," said Ilohan. "Give me the message, and go to tell the chief guard what I have said." As the page departed, Ilohan began to read the message aloud:

His Majesty King Andokar of Norkath to His Majesty King Ilohan of Karolan:

I have received your message and I am gathering all the force I can as you have suggested. I consider Your Majesty trustworthy, yet prudence is my duty to my people. I ask for proof, beyond written or spoken word, that the Zarnith truly have returned. If it were in your heart conquer Norkath, while it is weak due to my father's war with Karolan, what better thing could you do than ask me to raise an army and then march away from Karolan? Consider what you have asked of me. Then send me confirmation strong enough to ease my fear.

"Alas!" said Ilohan. "The Zarnith have indeed returned, but I have no proof to send."

Benther looked thoughtful. "I suppose we can be sure it is true?" he said.

"The message from Ceramir?" asked Ilohan. "I could not doubt it, though it said that Vadshron had a thousand thousands. My mother does not lie – and nor does Mudien, who knows the Zarnith tongue and doubtless received the messenger of doom. He can be trusted unto death, and his wisdom is not easily deceived."

"Yet even the wise may sometimes be led astray," said Benther, "as Thomas by my father."

Ilohan looked up to see the shame and grief in Benther's face. "Do not speak thus!" he said. "In my mind you are not his son. It is your folly to use such words to punish yourself for what is forgiven."

"Forgiven only by you, Your Majesty," said Benther calmly. "I cannot forget how I disgraced the knighthood Thomas gave me, siding with... Yet since you ask me to speak differently, Tulbur the Unknighted, who has no son – would I had disowned him sooner! – deceived King Thomas, which shows that even very wise men may sometimes be mistaken. Could not Mudien be so now?"

"Consider what you know, friend," said Ilohan. "Can you think it is so?"

There was a pause, while Benther considered. "No," he said at last. "We had no doubts at first, and there is no reason for them now. A Zarnith came to Ceramir: he wore the Zarnith garb and spoke the Zarnith tongue, and his message was genuine to its fearsome core. Perhaps it lies, but we would be fools not to heed its warning."

"And Andokar's folly will destroy us," said Ilohan bitterly.

"I feared this alliance would not be easy," said Benther, "but there is no reason to give up hope. If you truly do go over the mountains, you must entrust Norkath to me and to Jonathan, and I think that I can shrewdly prevail upon Andokar. The Norkaths will march with us, in the end – whether to death, or costly triumph."

"You are a true friend," said Ilohan, "to me and to Karolan. God grant that you will prevail indeed. Now let us return to our labor."

Ilohan and Benther went their separate ways, giving orders and instructions to scores of people they had summoned to Aaronkal; inspecting weapons; receiving reports; and now and then meeting together to exchange a few words on their progress and further plans. At last, past the middle of the night, the castle was quiet, and they went utterly exhausted to their beds.

Ilohan rose at dawn as planned, and departed for Glen Carrah. By swift messengers, Benther had reserved fresh horses for him at inns along the way. He rode fast and alone, without crown or banner to proclaim his royalty. For most of the day he thought of little but his weariness and haste, but as evening fell and the gibbous moon shone cold and bright from the darkening sky, he remembered the first time he had ridden to Carrah in search of Jonathan. He longed for that simpler time, when the crushing weight of ruling Karolan lay on another's shoulders. Then, shaking off such thoughts, he peered forward into the gathering dusk, and urged his horse to greater speed.

Chapter 12

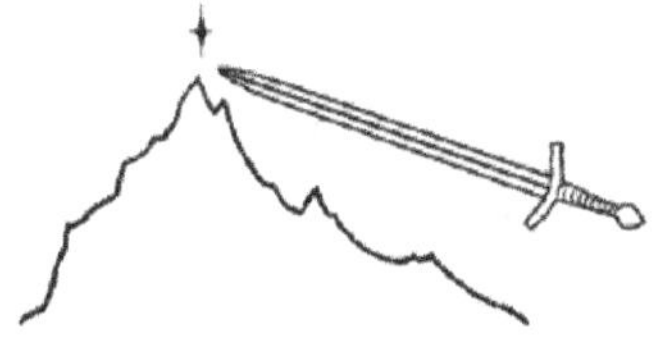

Promise Broken

IT WAS ON THE NEXT AFTERNOON THAT JONATHAN returned to Glen Carrah, and knelt upon the ashes of his joy. Far up on the slope of the glen, where he had dug through snow to the charred soil, he now stood and drew his sword. The patch of black ash that he had cleared of snow lay at his feet. He looked down the broad white sweep of the glen to the few cottages that had been rebuilt far below. The people of Carrah were stubborn, he thought, returning to a joyless place simply because it had been their home. He also might have chosen that course, had he not had another mission: justice.

He looked down at his sword. It was gray, not silver, under the overcast sky. There was no glory about it now, no flashing of the sunlight. There was only the long, well formed blade: simple, strong, and deadly. Justice.

Drantar must die. He was guilty of Naomi's death, and of the death of the other woman, whose body Jonathan had found in the Carratril. He was guilty of ravaging Glen Carrah, and enslaving its women and children. And he was a craven who had refused a just challenge.

But he would not refuse again, when again the justice of the cold sword looked him in the face. Jonathan saw it.

The servants of Drantar, held back by Jonathan's army, formed a circle on the open field in front of the castle. Jonathan faced Drantar with a drawn sword in the center of the circle. Drantar drew his sword, and nodded to him, and the fight began. Drantar raised his sword to parry Jonathan's first attack, but Jonathan could see the blank fear in his eyes. That blade, upraised to block his stroke, would be as useless as a straw. "Naomi died by your hand and the hands of your comrades," he said. "Naomi died, and you did not stand up to save her. Remember how it was. Now for justice."

Drantar, seeing the terrible force of Jonathan's first blow, tried to dodge it and use it against him. Jonathan could see, with perfect, unmoved clarity, that had things been almost imperceptibly different than they were, Drantar would have succeeded and would have killed him. But no tiny difference came to Drantar's aid. One mighty sword-stroke shattered his blade and crushed his skull. He lay at Jonathan's feet, and his blood soaked the frozen ground.

The vision passed, and Jonathan stood, still with the sword drawn in his hand, on the ashes of Glen Carrah. "I rebuilt my father's and my mother's house," he said. "Now I will avenge my beloved's death. Then what? There is nothing left. There is beauty still for me to defend, but she whom my heart loved best was not defended, and I can no longer rise up in joyous courage to defend the rest. My heart beats, my lungs draw air, my arms are strong; is there not life before me? Alas! Once I knew how to live, but now I have lost the power. Fingar, Tulbur, Drantar, do you know what you destroyed? Justice can only kill you, but what you have destroyed was worth so much more than your own lives. For you killed joy, and of what value is life alone, compared with joy? Joy has burned to ashes. I can no longer live – I can only act. Drantar, die, and know that death is less than you deserve. Tulbur, wherever you are, may you find a fate terrible enough to repay your treachery, if such a horror exists in the world of mingled beauty and ugliness that you have darkened."

He sheathed his sword and walked with a strong, steady stride all the way down the glen. At the door of the cottage he had built, he hesitated a moment. Then he knocked.

Barnabas opened the door immediately. They stared into each other's faces for an instant of surprise and recognition, and then Barnabas stepped forward and hugged his son tightly in his strong arms. Yet in that instant, each had read something in the other's eyes. Barnabas saw that his son's intense love of life and beauty was wounded and overlaid with anger. Jonathan saw that his father's joy and thankfulness were beyond all words. Then they embraced, and Barnabas' arms trembled as he held his son. "Thank God!" he said fervently. "Thank God you have come back!"

They parted, and Jonathan saw tears of joy in his father's eyes. "I must tell you at once, Father," he said. "This is not like when we met on the retreat to Petrag. I have done and planned things that will dismay you, and you will no longer be proud to own your son."

"Come in, dear Jonathan," said Barnabas, "whatever you have done, I do most gladly and forever own you as my son. I love you. No act of yours can change that, and if you think it can, you are a fool – a fool whom I still greatly love."

Jonathan found himself pulled into the cottage by his cloak, and the door was shut behind him. The old familiar smells of carved oak, bread, and savory cooking made him feel he had returned to home and peace, even though he did not think the world held either for him anymore. "You do not even know what I have done, Father," he said.

"Of course I do, dear son," said Barnabas. "You have executed vengeance on one who was involved in the burning of Carrah."

Jonathan wavered on his feet, and steadied himself against the doorframe. His father had guessed what was in his heart, and still his love was unbroken. Jonathan had expected his father to be angry; he had expected the ruin of the close friendship they had always had. He reeled under the shock of deep, clear forgiveness and love. "I have not killed anyone yet, Father," he said. "I went to castle Drantar, in Norkath, and challenged Sir Drantar there to single combat because he was among the knights who ravaged Carrah, perhaps even their leader. He refused. I am going back with an army of three hundred men, and this time he will not refuse. Of course I will defeat and kill him."

"Let us speak of this no more, dear Jonathan," said Barnabas. "You know already most of what I might say. I know that no authority I might claim would dissuade you from your purpose. Let me, rather, simply welcome you home."

"But I claim authority that will dissuade you!" A voice that froze Jonathan absolutely still rang clear and strong in the room. "I claim the promise you once gave me, Jonathan, dearest to my heart of all who live," said Naomi. "I claim your promise. Do not go." He turned like one in a daze, and saw her.

Her face was pale, and her lovely hair much shorter than it had been. She sat swathed in blankets in a new chair that reminded Jonathan of those the invalids of Ceramir had used. Her arms, thrust back now to help her sit upright, were painfully thin. But her voice spoke to his heart just as it had long ago before the winter or the war. Her eyes shone with love, and with her certainty that he would do what she had asked.

Jonathan gazed at her, unmoving, as though her words had turned him into stone. His whole life, all his decisions since his hopeless search for her, had been founded on the knowledge that she was dead. Now his whole world changed, and all his choices crumbled, as he looked at her, alive. She had been alive, all the long, hopeless days when he had known her dead. She had been alive. And he had broken his promise to search for her. There was no greater crime. There was nothing he held more sacred than the promises he had given her. He had not kept them. He had failed her.

Her arms gave way, and she fell back on her pillows, coughing. "Jonathan," she said weakly, "Jonathan, why do you not come to me? Oh Jonathan, it has been so long… I thought you were dead, yet still I fought to come back here… to search for you, as though I could search. And you must have thought me dead also, but we both live… Oh God, and must I now die?"

He sat on the edge of her chair, and took her head and shoulders in his arms as he had used to do, whenever she had been sick, in the golden days long gone. She closed her eyes and wept for joy. "You are here now," she whispered. "It does not matter."

But Jonathan was agonized by the depth of his failure, for which he would never forgive himself. He told Naomi the bitter truth without preamble. "Beloved," he said, "I was not searching for you. I had given you up for dead. I beg you, forgive me!"

He saw her shock and dismay, and it shattered his heart. He felt he could flood the Carratril with his tears and still they would not fully express his grief. Yet he only sat there, still and silent as a stone, with the agony all hidden within him. In his arms Naomi did not move. "Naomi, Beloved," he whispered at last, "I wish I had died rather than betraying you! I am sorry. I wish the world had never existed, so that it might not contain the breach of a promise made to one so trusting, so lovely, so deserving of faithfulness. Naomi, Naomi, child of Glen Carrah, beloved of my unworthy heart, my words are weak. I do not ask you to be contented with them. Alas! They are all I have. It was not for lack of love that I betrayed you – I love you! Believe this, yet show me no mercy, for as a coward I fell before despair and I deserve none. Alas! How I love you, yet how unworthy I have made myself of your love!"

He clenched his teeth, cutting off his words. He wanted desperately to hear her speak; to know his sentence from her lips. Yet she said nothing, and her face as he cradled her head in his arms was pale and still. He grew suddenly afraid. "Naomi!" he said earnestly. "Naomi, can you hear me?" She did not move or speak. "Naomi!" he called out louder. "Naomi, please, speak to me!" But she made no response.

Hannah had been sleeping in the bedroom, exhausted from long nights spent caring for Naomi. She woke now with her son's voice ringing in her ears. She got up wearily, telling herself that it had only been a dream. But she knew she must look in the main room of the cottage, from which the voice had seemed to come, before she had a chance of sleeping more. She went softly to the door, and opened it.

He was there, deep grief in his face. In an instant she had embraced him. "Mother, dear Mother," he said, "if only I were a son worthy of you."

"Hush," she said. "Do not speak, now. Only let me hold you. Jonathan, Jonathan, you were lost, and now you are found. Are you worthy of me? When you were born, and for the first time I held you in my arms, were you worthy of me then? Have I ever kept a measure of your worthiness? Or does the rain measure the worthiness of the ground before it falls? You are my son, Jonathan. I love you. Do you not understand what that means?"

Then she released him and met his eyes. "Now tell me what is wrong," she said.

"I think I have killed Naomi," he said in a stifled voice.

Hannah reached past him to feel Naomi's pulse. "Her heart is beating steadily," she said. "Jonathan, you are acting like a fool. What else is wrong?"

"I promised Naomi long ago that if the war separated us I would search for her until I found her. I broke that promise, and when I told her I had, I shocked her so badly that I thought I had killed her. I failed her and betrayed her, Mother."

"What else troubles you?"

"I have made plans to kill Sir Drantar of Norkath as a just revenge for the ravaging of Glen Carrah, and for, as I thought, Naomi's death. Naomi has forbidden me to do this, and long ago I promised her that if ever she forbade me in such a case I would obey her. Naomi believes she is dying, and I am a traitor and a fool. I feel as though a spear has gone through me, and I wish that like Naomi I could fall unconscious from shock. Yet what would that mend? When I awoke all would be the same; I still myself, and Naomi still dying. Now I desperately want to kill something, because I am furiously angry at myself and at fate, which does not exist. And Naomi has forbidden me to kill the one person I have a right and duty to kill. And I am telling you all these terrible things, which must strike you to the heart: you, my loving mother, who have never deserved anything but good at my hands. Alas!"

"Jonathan," said Hannah. "All these weeks I have kept your old room – no, the new room that you rebuilt with bitter labor – as ready to receive you as I could. Go now and sleep in it. You would be spared some of this distress if you knew the love and forgiveness that are in Christ, but you may know them yet. You have said you wished to fall unconscious, and in sleep you can. You will find the world less dark when you awake. I have now no authority to command you, but I have made my request. Sleep, beloved son."

"I am dirty and stained with long travel, Mother," said Jonathan.

"The bed is for none but you, dear Jonathan. How long has it been since you slept in a bed?"

"I do not remember," said Jonathan, and turned at once to obey her. He did not want to try to sleep, as he undressed in the narrow room. He wanted instead to run until he coughed blood and then leap off the highest cliff in the world. Yet he was weary, humbled, and dismayed. His mother's request seemed both harmless and sensible, in contrast to so much that he had done. Also he was fast reaching the level of despair at which the will falters, unable to make further choices since all alike seem hopeless. He lay down and pulled the soft, clean blankets over him, while the straw mattress cradled him beneath. The comfort seemed overwhelming, extravagant, seductive. In moments he was asleep.

Out in the main room Hannah and Barnabas sat near the still-unconscious Naomi. "You did well to send him to bed, Beloved," whispered Barnabas. "But I have no idea what will happen now. At least it is clear what we must do: we must pray until one of them awakes."

"Yes," said Hannah, "but first..." she stopped, biting her lip.

"What, Beloved?" asked Barnabas.

"Dear Barnabas, hold me while I weep!" He embraced her, and held her in his arms while she wept for her joy and her sorrow, her shock and her hope, her son, and her daughter. At last she wiped her eyes, and together they knelt to pray.

* * *

A strange cry fell on Benther's ears, in the fading evening twilight at Aaronkal. He was supervising the unloading of a wagon, but he looked up instantly – and he saw a great eagle soar through the open window of the king's tower room. Benther left the wagon without explanation, and raced through the corridors and stairways of Aaronkal to come at last to Ilohan's bedchamber. Skykag was there, perched on the back of the king's chair, preening his feathers.

Benther unwrapped the parchment from the eagle's talon, and went back into the corridor to read it by the light of a torch:

Your love is great.
I beg you to reconsider your decision.
You cannot save us here – only God can do that.
Do not abandon your people.
I will love and rejoice in you always,
whatever course you choose.
Eleanor, Queen Mother of Karolan.

Benther called a servant to bring strips of meat for the eagle, and then paced up and down while he waited, trying to decide what to do. He had been right to read the message, for it could have been of great and immediate importance. Yet now, what answer could he send? This new message from Eleanor might succeed in persuading Ilohan not to attempt the mountains, but he, Benther, could not presume on the king's decision. However, he must send something – he could not simply let Skykag fly back unburdened. And he doubted that even Eleanor could make Ilohan change his mind. Having fed the eagle, he sat down with quill and parchment. He began, still unsure how he would finish:

I, Benther, write this in the king's absence.
He is away seeking Jonathan to command the army.
His Majesty is determined to come to your aid.
I have tried to dissuade him, but cannot.
Forgive my failure – I have spoken very boldly,
but His Majesty's love and courage are indeed great.
He desires that you should fortify the Gate of Hope,
and also a gap in desert hills to the west,
through which the Zarnith must come.
Sir Benther, Knight of Karolan,
by His Majesty's gracious decree named Fatherless.

Benther surveyed the little manuscript and decided he could not improve it. He had been completely honest, but had written nothing the king would disapprove. He would try again to dissuade Ilohan from taking his stand in the desert gap, but if, as was likely, Ilohan would not listen, the barricade he had asked the people of Ceramir to construct might at least prolong the king's life a few moments. He tied the parchment to Skykag's talon. Not sure what signal the eagle wanted to return to Eleanor, Benther made a gesture like one throwing a spear in the direction of the window. To his surprise, Skykag obeyed instantly with a great sweep of wings, and the eagle's dark silhouette soon faded into the twilit sky, winging swiftly southward toward the great mountains.

*　　　　*　　　　*

Late that night, Hannah sat in a chair near Naomi's bed, watching as she had so many nights before. She knew that Naomi no longer truly needed this, since she had partially recovered, but Hannah did not want her ever to wake without someone nearby to serve her. She rose noiselessly now to tend the fire, following a habit of silence she had formed during these long nights – nights when she watched, and wondered if Naomi were dying – nights when sorrow, goodness, and hope seemed woven together into a thing of breathtaking holiness that broke her heart.

The sudden sound of a door opening seemed to violate the silence, and Jonathan stood beside her. "Has Naomi moved or spoken since last I saw her?" he whispered.

"Yes, she woke at dusk to eat and drink," said Hannah, "after which we helped her to her bed, as you see. She spoke words of forgiveness and love for you, but bade me let you sleep."

Jonathan lay down on the hard floor beside Naomi's mattress, taking care that his dusty clothes did not touch the clean blankets that covered her. Her left hand lay above the blankets, and he gently took it in both his own. He did not sleep again, but he lay perfectly still in a sort of waking dream. His mind wandered strange ways strewn with the wreckage of his life. He remembered falling asleep on the terrible ice plateau of the great mountains, when it was his duty to stay awake to save Ilohan's life and his own. He remembered how Ilohan had dragged him onward, asleep, over the ice. He remembered talking to Ilohan about forgiveness. Forgiveness. Without Naomi's he could not live, and yet he felt she would betray justice by giving it.

He thought of Drantar, lying dead at his feet, his head crushed with the fury of just anger. It had seemed an accomplished thing, already a part of the past. He wondered if he might convince Naomi to let him go, after all. He wondered what the fifteen score men he had asked to gather at Petrag would do if he did not come to lead them.

Then suddenly he realized that none of these things mattered – nothing mattered to him except the fact that Naomi was dying. He knelt beside Rennel's bed at Ceramir, but Naomi lay in it, not Rennel. With all his strength, he could not save her. Few men in all the world could stand against his sword, and his bright courage had stirred the defenders of Petrag to fight as though they were more than men, and yet he could not save her.

Ceramir... Images and feelings from the Cloth of Joy washed over him. Its depth of power and of love awed him: the selfless love of the healers; the joy of the young men; the beauty of the dancing; the clear white light that seemed to rest upon the Lady Eleanor; Mudien's frightening wisdom and authority; Imranie's deep love; Brogal's laughter; the council in the candlelit room...

A hand stirred in his, and a whisper came to his ears, "Jonathan."

He opened his eyes, and remembered where he was. "Naomi," he whispered back. He felt very weary, and strangely at peace. He did not move to rise, but only pressed Naomi's hand in his, marveling that she did not withdraw it.

"Jonathan, I forgive you," she said softly. "I would have said so at first, but I was too weak. I had thought all the time I was lost that you were searching for me, and when you told me you had given me up for dead, it changed the whole world, and I fainted. I did not want to faint – it is only because of my sickness. It did hurt me to know that you stopped searching for me, but not as much as you must have thought. I forgive you completely. Jonathan, I understand what it means to surrender to despair. If I had not known God, I would surely have surrendered myself. I would have let go and died, if I had not known he wanted me to keep on; if I had not known him and his help. And you do not know him, yet..." A bout of coughing interrupted her, after which she was silent for a moment.

Jonathan turned to look at her face as she lay beside him, and saw a tear rolling down her cheek. "I had hoped you would, by now," she said. "However, I have spoken truly, have I not, Jonathan? You have not yet given yourself to God?"

"No, Beloved," he said. "I do not believe God is; I know that men are alone. Alone they fight evil, alone they execute justice, and they guard the beauty of the world, alone."

"If that were true," said Naomi, "I would not be living now. This hand that in reality is warm in yours would be the hand of a frozen corpse – or black ash beneath the snow, yonder in Glen Carrah. And even if I lived, even if there had been no war, we would have no hope."

"I never thought we had any final hope," said Jonathan. "I have always thought that all beautiful things will perish in the end, and that our only victory is to defend them as long as we can, and love them with all our hearts, until they – and we – vanish forever."

"But why fight, why love, if nothing is eternal, Jonathan? You love me now, but according to the physician who has tended me, I will die before the spring – and your heart will break. If, then, you will lose me forever, why love me now? If, when your heart breaks, it breaks without hope, why would you ever stake it on another's life? Why love, when bereavement is inevitable, and brings so much pain?"

"Naomi, dear Naomi, I could never choose but love you! As long as you are Naomi, and I am Jonathan, I must love you. I love you! Love is the most beautiful thing I know in all the world. But it is true, perhaps, that those who love will suffer more than those who do not. That is a great horror and injustice. Perhaps there is no justice in the world, except in the hearts of just men. And if you die, Naomi... If there is a God, and he lets you die, then he is –"

"Do not say it, Jonathan!" She shuddered, and there was desperation in her voice. She was silent for a moment. "I thank God," she whispered, "Jonathan, speak not ill of God before you know him."

"What did you think I was saying, Naomi?"

"You would have said that if God lets me die, he must be evil. My love is wise, Jonathan; wise enough, sometimes, to guess your thoughts."

Jonathan was silent. She had guessed rightly. "Would those words have sentenced me to Hell, Naomi?" he asked.

"Beloved," she whispered, "you are already sentenced to Hell – but no matter what you say, Jesus can lift the sentence if you trust him. Still, some words should not be said, whatever may come of saying them."

"How could God lift a just sentence?" asked Jonathan. "Do you not believe he is the Lord of Justice? How then could he betray it?"

"Beloved," said Naomi, "remember the story, to which, I guess, you have never truly listened. God, in Christ, bent the wrath due us back on himself, and bore it all. So Justice, which you love, met with Mercy, which you do not know, and they were reconciled. So none who trusts him shall face his wrath, yet justice is not denied. It is a mystery from the heart of God. It is our hope and our salvation."

"How can God not be evil if he lets you die?"

"This illness is not very painful," said Naomi. "Perhaps one day I shall simply go to sleep – and wake with my Lord, in Paradise. How is that evil?"

"It is evil to me, left behind in an empty world," said Jonathan.

Her eyes filled with tears. "I am sorry," she said. "I am very, very sorry." A long silence hung in the room. At last she said, "I would die this moment, in any kind of pain imaginable, if it would bring you to God at last. Perhaps something about my death will draw you toward him."

"No, Naomi, Beloved, no!" said Jonathan. "Your death could never be for me anything but an evil. It is only your life that might bring me to God at last – if anything could."

"Maybe you yourself do not understand what my death will do to you, now that you are forbidden to avenge me," said Naomi. "But I do not know... I am very sorry that I must die, and leave you."

"Naomi, perhaps you need not die. While you were still sleeping, I dreamed of Ceramir, which is a place beyond the mountains, to which I came with the prince. Deadly diseases are healed there, and it is a place of great love."

"Do the people of that place worship God?" asked Naomi.

"Never has my disbelief in him been more shaken than when I was there," said Jonathan. "Their faith is like yours, Beloved – and they worship with great joy."

Naomi was shaken by a bout of coughing, and afterwards remained silent for a long time. Her face grew very pale, and her hand in Jonathan's was trembling. "Beloved, speak to me!" he said, alarmed.

"Fear not, Jonathan," she whispered. "I do not think I will faint again. But I am afraid; afraid of another journey, the weariness and pain. I have not told you yet how I was saved from Cembar. I am afraid of having to fight again, when I had thought such battles over. Yet, if God called me, I would attempt it – to obey him, and to bless you, as I have said, at any cost."

Jonathan made no reply, thinking of the road he and Ilohan had traveled. At last Naomi asked, "How many days' journey is it to Ceramir?"

"Twenty days, with a good horse," said Jonathan.

She laughed softly, and spoke in a voice that was calm, happy, and – to Jonathan – terrible. "Do you truly have such hope, Jonathan?" she asked. "I may not live another twenty days even if I stay here in peace."

"You will not go, then, Beloved?" asked Jonathan. "I would ease the journey in every way I could."

There was a long silence. Naomi's lips moved, and Jonathan realized that she was praying. "Jonathan, give me until tomorrow to choose," she whispered at last.

"Yes, Beloved," he said. "Sleep well." He released her hand, and she slept.

Chapter 13

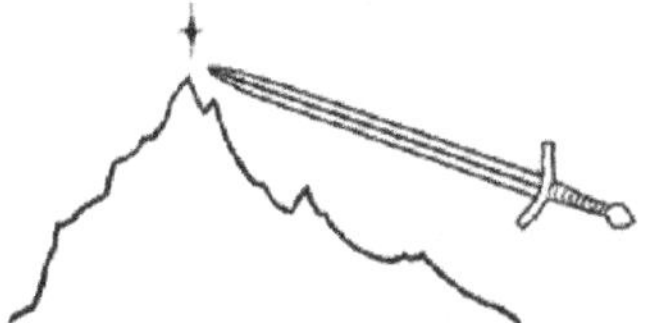

The Second Swordfight

ILOHAN WAS ALREADY RIDING FAST WHEN THE DAY dawned. The brilliant sunrise kindled the snowy, icebound world to something beyond mortal loveliness, but he spared it little notice. Confidence in his dream-borne plans had wholly deserted him. He felt he was a fool. The four or five days spent traveling to and from Carrah would be wholly wasted. Jonathan would not be there, for Naomi's death had broken him forever. Though Ilohan regarded Jonathan as a stronger man in every way than himself, he knew Jonathan was without God, without hope in tragedy. The golden light of prayer would not shine for him in despair's darkness.

So Jonathan was dead. The best friend he had ever known was dead, and he, Ilohan, was wasting precious days on a fool's errand. For a moment he even considered turning back, to save the little time that could still be saved. He would not, having come so far. Yet the thought that perhaps he should made him still more impatient. Ilohan urged his horse forward almost cruelly. The majestic animal, reserved for him by Benther at the last inn, galloped up the stone road at an impressive pace.

Suddenly he saw four bowmen blocking his path, their clothes, faces, and weapons brightly lit by the sun rising behind him. He had been too absorbed in his own anxiety to see them before, and now it was too late to flee. Worry, anger, and despair faded into reckless courage. He drew the sword of Kindrach, spurred his horse to even greater speed, and charged directly toward them.

The archers blanched with terror at his onset. They loosed their arrows, but not one of them aimed true. Ilohan was unharmed, and the horse was upon them.

One of the archers was fitting another arrow to his bow. Ilohan killed him with a single terrible stroke. The other three turned and ran, dropping their bows.

Ilohan reined in his horse and dismounted, his heart pounding. He scanned the trees for any sign of other bowmen, but the wintry forest was empty. The king looked down with regret at the man he had killed. Undoubtedly he had been a scoundrel, a murderer and a thief lying in wait for blood. Still, he had been a man, until the point of Kindrach's sword slashed diagonally across his throat. "He would have shot me in the back had I spared him," said Ilohan, "and even had I had time to consider, I would still have struck him down. I wish that he had fled with his fellows, or else merely been wounded." He dragged the corpse out of the path, broke the four bows with his sword, and swung back into his saddle.

As he rode swiftly on, he thanked God for his rescue from such unexpected peril. The sudden shock had cleared away some of his despondency. He had, after all, no idea what the future might hold. Even the futility of this journey might not be certain. One more hour's ride at his fast pace sufficed to bring Ilohan to the cottage Jonathan had built.

He paused a moment, still astride his horse. Even apart from his mission, he could not look unmoved on this place where tragedy had fallen on his friend. And now, if Jonathan were still alive, he had come not to offer him aid but to ask another great service of him. He dismounted and strode to the cottage door, but the hand he raised to knock was trembling. At the first tap, Jonathan opened instantly.

Ilohan saw his own astonishment mirrored in his friend's eyes. "Your Majesty – Ilohan," stammered Jonathan at last, "I love you as a friend and honor you as my king. I wish I could give you better welcome, but you find me in great distress."

"What is your distress, my friend?" asked Ilohan.

"Naomi..." said Jonathan in a choked voice. "Naomi is dying."

"Dear friend and rescuer," said Ilohan, "I thought she had died many months ago."

Jonathan fell to his knees upon the doorstep with a crash, heedless of the pain it caused him. He looked up at Ilohan with anguish written across his face. "So did I, Your Majesty, so did I, alas! Oh, Ilohan, leave this place! I am no longer worthy to be close to you, much less to be your friend."

Suddenly emboldened, Ilohan pushed through the door and pulled it shut behind him. He grasped Jonathan's shoulders and raised him to his feet. "You have saved my kingdom and my life, dear friend," he said. "How can you now say such things about your worthiness?"

Jonathan spoke in a flood of words: hard, clear-cut, and merciless. "Before I left here with you, I gave Naomi a promise that I would seek and find her if war swept her away. When I returned, I searched Glen Carrah for a day and then despaired. I thought the fire must have killed her. I thought there was no chance that she still lived. I went away. I searched no longer.

Yet she was alive in Cembar – alive and in distress. Thus did I fail her and betray my promise. But this is not all. In Carrah's ruin I found the insignia of Drantar, knight of Norkath. I swore vengeance against him, and even now there waits for me in Petrag a small army I gathered for his destruction. Naomi forbids me now to avenge her, and I obey: one, at least, of my promises shall not be broken. Thus am I struck down by grief, disgraced by treachery, and powerless to do anything good."

"Jonathan, I am deeply sorry for Naomi's illness. I am glad that she forbade you to invade Norkath, for I need Andokar's favor and trust. Yet for the rest, I deny that you are either disgraced or impotent. You are still a mighty warrior and a faithful friend. I have come not to judge or condemn you but to ask your aid – desperately needed aid that you alone can give. As you have heard, a new Zarnith host has arisen, as in the days –"

"The Zarnith!" cried Jonathan, driving one fist into his other palm in a violent gesture. "The Zarnith are coming again? But stay! Why not? Why should there be limits to tragedy or disaster? The Zarnith are coming! By what way?"

"As my messenger told you, by way of Norkath; we expect them to come through Drantar's Gap, after they raze the Cloth of Joy."

Jonathan drew his sword and struck its point down into the wooden floor he had made. "They must not raze the Cloth of Joy," he said, with furious anger in his voice. "Let the earth and heavens perish, rather than the Zarnith ravage the Valley of the Undismayed."

"Did my messenger not come to you, then, calling for the muster of the Army of All Karolan?" asked Ilohan.

"No," said Jonathan.

Then Ilohan remembered that he himself had found the path to Glen Carrah waylaid by brigands. His messenger, he guessed, lay dead beneath the snow somewhere along the road. Thus he himself, unwittingly, had been the first to carry the dire news to Glen Carrah.

"Your Majesty, what is your plan?" Jonathan's voice broke in on his thoughts. "Tell me, in what do you hope I can help you?"

"And sit down by the fire, I beg Your Majesty," said Barnabas, whom Ilohan now realized had for some time been standing nearby, unnoticed. "Urgent though your errand is, I would not have it said that you came to our house and were not even offered the hospitality of a seat."

"I would never speak ill of your hospitality, any more than of your swords," said Ilohan to Barnabas. He sat down near the hearth, and suddenly noticed that Naomi was also there.

She looked at him, and smiled. Her face was thin and pale now – that face that he had thought more beautiful than any other when it was brown with sun and rosy with health and joy. Yet he wondered if she could be as near death as Jonathan had thought. "I have heard all the good you have done for Karolan, Your Majesty," she said, "and I grieve for this new grief and strife that comes upon you – and us all. In what way can Jonathan, whom I love and have wholly forgiven, aid you now?"

"The Zarnith have promised to destroy Ceramir thirteen days hence," said Ilohan. "After that, they pledge destruction to Norkath, and then Karolan. We believe they will come through the mountains at Drantar's Gap, far east of here in Norkath. There the Army of All Karolan, allied with whatever force Andokar of Norkath can raise, will meet them in battle. Jonathan, I want you to lead that army. I will take a smaller force, one thousand men, and cross the mountains to go to Ceramir's defense. If God sends not a miracle, I will die there. If you, Jonathan, triumph and are spared, you will then be King of Karolan."

Jonathan jumped to his feet. "You are the King of Karolan," he said. "You cannot give to me your crown, and go to your death in the mountains. For that is what it will be, Ilohan. Or have you forgotten our journey: the frozen wasteland, the deadly cold, the peaks of terror. You and your thousand will die on the slopes of the Third Mountain."

"Jonathan, you are a hero of Karolan. You are the best leader our army could have at Drantar's Gap. I do not abandon my people in giving you my crown."

"You do abandon them, Your Majesty," said Jonathan. "I cannot take your place. I will not take your crown. Command me as my king, and I will obey you – but I cannot become king in your stead."

"But I must go over the mountains," said Ilohan. "I cannot send anyone else. Besides the perils of the journey itself, there is the hopeless battle at the end. I cannot even defend the Gate of Hope, but must rather take my stand in a gap of the desert hills west of Ceramir. It will be a thousand against eight score times as many, and but for a miracle there will be no hope at all."

"Your Majesty, what could possibly prevent you from taking your stand in the Gate of Hope?" asked Jonathan, aghast. "To fight among the desert hills is greater folly, if possible, than even the mountain crossing itself. Forgive my boldness, but it is true. Surely no place but the Gate of Hope offers a chance to make a strong defense."

"We wrong Naomi by speaking here," said Ilohan softly. "She is weak, and needs to sleep now. Let us go out into the sun."

"No... no," said Naomi, "do not let me drive you away into the cold." Yet her words were blurred by sleep, and Ilohan had seen her nod and then jerk awake during Jonathan's last forceful speech.

"You are very kind, Your Majesty," said Jonathan. "I thank you. Let us indeed go outside."

They went out, into the blinding brightness of the sunlit snow. Jonathan walked swiftly up into the glen. Ilohan was panting a little with the exertion of keeping up when at last the blacksmith stopped and turned. The cottages below looked small and dark, lost in the expanse of white. Jonathan gazed at them for a moment and then turned to Ilohan.

"Why do you propose not to defend the Gate of Hope?" he asked.

"Because I would protect that part of Norkath which lies beyond the mountains, and to do that I must stop the Zarnith entirely at Ceramir. I know there is no hope of victory without God, and he may win a victory as well with a poor defense as with a strong one. Therefore, since the path of mercy and heroism is to defend not Ceramir alone but Norkath also, I choose that path and trust. God's will be done."

Jonathan drew his sword again in a fierce motion, and stabbed it into the icy snow before him. "I wish Norkath destruction!" he said. "And I think you are a fool! I ask your pardon for my bitter words, but I speak them in sincerity. You are my friend and king, but this plan of yours... it does not seem I would be a friend to you by aiding it."

"Eleanor is at Ceramir," said Ilohan. "And so is Veril, whom I love, now, as you love Naomi. You also have seen Ceramir. Can you not understand my folly?"

"But the desert gap – Ilohan, the place to defend Ceramir is the Gate of Hope! Let the Zarnith have transmontane Norkath!"

"But without your aid, how can I defend Ceramir at either place? I cannot leave Benther in command – as he said himself, the people still remember him as Tulbur's son."

"Send Benther over the mountains, then," said Jonathan. "That would be better for your people than going yourself."

"He does not know the way," said Ilohan. "It would be as cruel and useless as killing him with my own hand."

Jonathan slowly pulled his sword from the snow and slid it back into its sheath. For a long time he stood staring out north and east over Karolan with eyes that did not seem to see. "My life is shattered," he said at last. "It does not seem to matter what I do: all paths are misery. Yet here I begin to see my way clear to a sort of choice. Grant me some time, I beg you – grant me until midday."

Ilohan looked into his face, and saw his agony. "The time is precious," he said, "but I will give you what you ask." He went back toward the cottage.

Jonathan turned swiftly and ran. He ran up the glen toward the great mountains. He ran with all the force of his anger, agony, and despair. He ran as if he would wear out his lungs and heart and die, sooner than stop. And yet, when his breath was a gasping pant, and the iron taste of blood was strong in his mouth; when he had run like the wind more than half way up the glen, he did stop. He fell facedown in the snow and lay there sobbing and panting.

There was no reason to run. He could escape nothing. His savage treatment of his body did not ease the guilt of his soul. Naomi was dying, and he could not save her. There was no hope, no comfort: the world was vicious and ugly and he himself a traitor. The beauty of the world, if it had ever been more than an illusion, was all doomed in the end. Though some beauty would long outlast him, with Naomi's death his power of knowing or loving it would perish. If there was any good left in the world it would not be good to him.

For a moment, he felt as dead as the ashes under him. Merely going on living seemed beyond his power. Then, for no reason that was clear to him, he stood. Slowly he drew his sword once more, and slowly he forced it down into the snow at his feet. He stepped back a few paces and looked at it, the blade that he had wielded at Petrag, with which he had defeated so many men since then, proving to them that he was Karolan's hero. That blade stood for courage and strength, and yet as he stood looking at it, he thought himself a coward and a weakling. He had been thinking that he could not live, that, from where he was, he could find no way to go on. How could that be? That was a thing a man ought never to say. He must go on. Once, near this very place, he had surrendered to despair in his search for Naomi. He must never do that again. Never.

The agony of his decision was terrible. Nothing in his desire answered the call of his will, that he must and would go on. He looked at the sword. It was thrust down through the snow, into the ash beneath. That was how the decision seemed to him: a sword thrust through the ashes of his life, agonizing, but strong. Strong as the ash could not be, sharp and hard, inescapable and irrevocable. He shut out of his mind the possibility of turning back. He strode swiftly up to the sword, pulled it out of the ground in passing, and sheathed it as he went on down the glen.

* * *

The king stood outside the cottage, and watched Jonathan come. He could see his swift, determined stride, and knew the decision was made. Yet he did not know what Jonathan had chosen. Ilohan thought of Naomi, dying behind him in the cottage. He remembered the morning below the Cliffs of Doom, when Jonathan had raised his shining sword to the sky, with adventure-joy bright in his face. That joy was gone now, and that desire blighted. The hope that had upheld them both on their impossible journey across the mountains was dead.

Jonathan came before him, and knelt. "I need no homage, Jonathan," said Ilohan. "Not from you, who fought the Battle of Petrag and opened the forget-me-not."

"Your Majesty," said Jonathan, rising, "I must lead your thousand across the mountains. You must retain the crown, and command at Drantar's Gap. This simple change answers all objections."

"I cannot let you go to your death on my behalf," said Ilohan.

"I expected you to say that," said Jonathan. "I challenge you to a friendly match with swords."

"What is the stake?" asked Ilohan, though he had already guessed.

"The privilege of death," said Jonathan. "The winner will lead your hopeless march to Ceramir. The loser will be king."

"I refuse," said Ilohan.

"Then I will take Naomi to Ceramir through Luciyr, and we will die together on our hopeless journey," said Jonathan.

"Hopeless indeed," said Ilohan, "as Ceramir will be destroyed before you reach it, and you will encounter the Zarnith in the desert."

"To prevent it, you must simply accept my challenge, and defeat me."

"I have made the decision I thought right," said Ilohan. "I cannot stake it on a sword match."

"Are you certain beyond doubt that you are right?" asked Jonathan.

Dead silence fell. The king felt that he could not breathe. Benther had vehemently opposed his decision – even Eleanor's message had said, "Look to your own people." Was he certain?

"Every reason is against it," continued Jonathan. "I am much stronger than you, and far more likely to come alive through the mountains. I cannot take Karolan's throne. You are a king such as I could never be, and your people need you as the darkness comes. But my decision has cut through my despair. I can wield my voice like a torch and my courage like a sword. I will lead the thousand men over the mountains to Ceramir."

"I cannot let you go to your death," said Ilohan.

"You are wrong," said Jonathan. "You cannot keep me from death. Have you forgotten that all my paths from here are hopeless? Save one: the path to your throne, and that I will not take unless you accept my challenge and prevail."

"I bear Kindrach's sword," said Ilohan. "It can cut through tempered iron."

"I do not fear that," said Jonathan. "I am content to let it be your advantage."

Ilohan closed his eyes in the white sunlight. The strangeness of it overwhelmed him: that he must fight for the privilege of casting away his crown. But there seemed no other way. God must simply grant him victory, and that was all. "Jonathan, I accept," he said.

They went to a place far up beside the Carratril where the ground was flat. Though a glaze of ice covered the snow, their feet crunched through it and did not slip. It was a good place. They stood still a moment, facing each other with swords drawn. Jonathan thought for an instant of the fight with Drantar that he had planned. That would have been against his greatest enemy on earth, save Tulbur. This was against his greatest friend.

Ilohan gazed at the great mountains, the unconquerable stone. There was something terrible about those white peaks, but at least they could not be overwhelmed by the darkness that threatened to swallow Karolan. He took a deep breath, turned to Jonathan, and said, "Let it begin!"

The swords gleamed in the sun, blinding beauty of bright metal against the spotless snow. Again and again the blades met: glancing blows, each probing the other's strength and skill. Each watched with eagle eyes for an opening.

Jonathan fought with the strength of his decision, and the cold control he had forced down on his despair. Ilohan fought with fierce desire for victory, born of his love for Jonathan and his longing to fight in Ceramir's defense. Ilohan attacked most often, using all the subtlety of swordsmanship that his knightly training had taught him. But always Jonathan parried. His defense was like a wall of iron.

Whenever Jonathan did attack, Ilohan reeled back before his force. Always he recovered himself, but each time he felt that it was only the sword of Kindrach that saved him. He knew that Jonathan was holding back, lest excessive force should shatter his blade. Ilohan knew that if Jonathan's sword had been like

Kindrach's, the blacksmith would swiftly have overpowered him.

The battle went on for breathless moments of flashing blades, dazzling snow, clashing, clanging, jarred hands and desperate focus. The victory was balanced on a knife edge. If the intense concentration of either wavered for an instant, the fight would be lost. And the stake was so high…

"I must save him," thought Jonathan. "Perhaps I can do one act of true honor and heroism before the darkness comes. Ilohan, your life is not broken as mine is: your life shall be saved!"

"Best of friends, true heart broken," thought Ilohan. "You are stronger than I, yet by the grace of God I shall defeat you, and who knows what the courage that held Petrag may do at Drantar's Gap? For Naomi's recovery, Jonathan, for a miracle from beyond the confines of the world! Oh, may you not make but one small mistake?"

Jonathan did make a mistake. He slipped on the trampled snow, and went down on one knee to dodge Ilohan's stroke. To parry the king's next blow, Jonathan had to use force he doubted his blade would bear. The clang was deafening, and the terrible jar bruised his calloused hands. A spark, visible even in the bright daylight, was struck out from the clashing blades. But Jonathan's sword did not break. He leaped to his feet and attacked, with more force than he had dared to use before, and Ilohan gave ground in dismay. But the king's defense held, and the battle went on, and still neither could gain an advantage.

Their weariness grew, and their control was less sure. A time came when Ilohan knew that he could no longer be sure of stopping his sword if Jonathan ever failed to parry. He might wound his friend, or even kill him, through his weakness and exhaustion. Jonathan saw this fear in his eyes. "Fight on, dear Ilohan," he said. "Stop for an instant and I will disarm you. Fear not: I shall never fail to parry."

Ilohan fought on. The stakes were too high to stop, and even in his weariness his strength and his control were great. He would not hurt his friend: he must save him.

The end came suddenly. Jonathan attacked hard, thrusting toward Ilohan's body, and the king parried with desperate force, his sword held awkwardly close to his chest. The point of Jonathan's sword snapped off with a deafening crack and another brilliant spark. As if unaware that his sword was damaged, Jonathan struck even harder. With cruelly jarred hands, Ilohan instantly raised his sword to block the blow.

Even as his broken sword came toward the king's, Jonathan was envisioning the immediate future of the fight. He let go all caution, and staked his victory on this one stroke, turning the blade unexpectedly to increase his force and weaken Ilohan's leverage. It happened just as Jonathan had expected. His own sword burst into shattered fragments, but Kindrach's sword was smashed from Ilohan's aching hands. It spun in the air, flashing the white sunlight, and landed flat on the snow several paces away. Ilohan staggered toward it.

Jonathan was weary, panting, and off balance from his final lunge, but he was still a runner. His hands had barely touched the snow to stop his fall before he was racing toward the sword. He reached it a pace ahead of Ilohan and snatched it up without breaking his stride. He let the tremendous speed he had gathered fade over a few more steps, and then he turned around and fell to his knees, gasping for breath.

Ilohan of Karolan walked toward him across the snow. He, too, panted hard, and he wavered on his feet. He had lost. He looked down at his shock-numbed hands, marveling that they were empty – or else that they, too, had not been ripped off by the blow that had torn away Kindrach's sword. The last part of the fight had seemed to him like a flash of lightning: there and gone in a moment, but lingering in dazzled vision with a terrible, jagged shape that no man could alter. He tried to remember what he had done, and could not: he could only remember that he had fought with all his strength, and there had been a crash that still rang in his ears, and then he had had no sword. "How can it be, Father?" he said as he stumbled over the snow. "How can it be? What shall I do now?"

Then he raised his eyes and saw Jonathan. He was kneeling upright now. His hands, still trembling with weariness, were held palm upward before him. The sword of Kindrach lay across them, gleaming in the light of the snow and sun. The bitter joy of the hopeless victory was in his face.

"Take back your sword, Your Majesty," he said. "I will die at Ceramir, and the Zarnith will still come on. You will fight at Drantar's Gap and live to stop them. All is as it must now be."

Ilohan reached out his hand for the hilt of the sword, moving as if in a daze. Then suddenly he drew back. "I will not take it, friend," he said. "The sword of Kindrach I give to you. Your strength is greater, and your need will be more desperate."

Jonathan remained kneeling, as still as stone, for a long moment. Then a flash of joy lit his face for a fleeting instant, swiftly swallowed by his iron despair. "Ilohan, my friend, I thank you," he said. "This gift would bring me great joy, if my heart could still hold joy. I have longed in vain to make such a sword, and I delighted to wield it at Luciyr. It will cut down the Zarnith like straw."

"Stand, Jonathan, hero of Karolan," said Ilohan, "and ask me for anything else your heart desires."

"My only remaining desire, Your Majesty, is that in the midst of this ruinous world, Naomi should have your aid in doing whatever she thinks right to do, before she dies."

*   *   *

When they came to the cottage, Naomi was awake. Jonathan fell to his knees beside her, and took her hand in his. He felt that nothing mattered except her. She alone was still and calm, while the reeling world splintered around her. Even his triumph over Ilohan, even the duty he had won, were lost in that irrelevant outer chaos. Only his dying beloved, and himself, anchored by her hand, were clear and meaningful.

"You and the king spoke of Ceramir's destruction," she said softly. "That was the place you wanted to take me, was it not?"

"It was, Beloved, alas."

Her eyes filled with tears. "I am sorry that even that hope has failed you," she said. "But Jonathan, Beloved, I want you to know I would have gone there. I would have borne the journey, and struggled still to live, for love of you. That was my decision." She coughed weakly.

It was not until that moment that Jonathan realized how meaningless was the favor he had asked of Ilohan. Even if somehow Ceramir were saved, there was no way to get Naomi there. If he sent her through Luciyr, she would encounter the Zarnith in the desert, as Ilohan had said. If he sent her through Cembar, those who carried her would be enslaved, and she would be left to die.

"What has the king asked you to do?" asked Naomi.

"Beloved, he asked me to succeed him, to take his crown and lead the Army of All Karolan against the Zarnith. He intended, himself, to cross the mountains to defend Ceramir."

"You would be a great leader for the army, even as you were at Petrag... Barnabas has told me of that. But surely you cannot accept King Ilohan's crown?"

"I cannot, Beloved. And it is only his courage and heroism that make him dare the mountains – I know he could not live to cross them. I saw the perils of that journey when I crossed them with him before the war. I have won from him the privilege of going to Ceramir in his stead. He will lead the Army of All Karolan. He will retain the crown. I will take a thousand men across the mountains to fight for Ceramir – unless you use again the privilege of my promise, to prevent it."

"Why must you go over the mountains, Jonathan?"

"For the same reason that forced us before: it is the fastest way, and there is no time."

"You say that the king would die if he tried to cross the mountains. Will not you?"

"I am much stronger than King Ilohan, Beloved," said Jonathan. "I will come to Ceramir alive."

"And then?" asked Naomi.

"Beloved, the Zarnith are nearly eight score thousand strong."

"So you will die at Ceramir," said Naomi. "You will fight heroically, as at Petrag, but this time you will die."

Still nothing seemed real to Jonathan except Naomi. He was vaguely aware that Ilohan, Barnabas, and Hannah were all now in the room, but they were part of the outer world. Only Naomi mattered – Naomi with her hopeless silence and her gleaming tears.

"I cannot forbid you from this mission," she whispered at last. "But Jonathan, what do you want to do with me?"

The way she had framed her whispered words, as though she were some possession he must dispose of, opened a deep well of grief within him – and yet he smiled at her. "King Ilohan granted me anything I wanted, Beloved," he said. "I asked that he would enable you to do whatever you thought best, for the rest of your days."

"But what do you want me to do, Jonathan?"

"Naomi, Beloved," he said. "I want your life to be preserved and your sickness healed. I would have you seek these things, just as you have chosen, even though there is no real hope. I would have you ask Ilohan for trustworthy men to guard and carry you, and I would have them take you to Ceramir by the pass at Luciyr. If you evade the Zarnith in the desert, and Ceramir is not destroyed, and you survive to reach it, then I believe you will be healed. Those are three unlikely chances, and the journey will bring you pain. Yet, Beloved, with deep sorrow in my heart, that is what I want you to do."

She closed her eyes, and for a long time made no answer, until Jonathan wondered if she had fallen asleep. Then she opened her eyes, and her face was transformed with happiness. "Beloved," she said, "I know now what I want."

"What do you want, dear Naomi?"

"I want to come with you over the mountains."

"Naomi, it will kill you. You do not understand. The mountain way does not belong to this earth; it is of the frozen sky, meant for stars and angels, not for men. The very sight of it is terrible, and I, at the height of my strength, could scarcely find breath in that air. You will not last two days upon that journey."

"I believe you," said Naomi, "but, then, I will die in your arms."

"But Naomi, your life, your beautiful life. Will you throw away your life?"

"I do not throw it away in making this choice," she said. "I spend it. Death to me is the gate of Heaven. I think words will be given me as I approach it – words I in turn can give to you. Maybe through my eyes you will see, just for one moment, what will change your course forever."

He knew then that she had overcome him. Even before these last reasons, he had understood her. In her place his desire would have been the same – not to be parted from her, even if staying beside her meant his death. She was right to choose that over the impossible hope he had offered. But still he fought against her choice of certain death, even as he had fought what seemed a hopeless fight at Petrag. "I will take you with me," he said, "but in the air of the high mountains it is hard to speak for the labor of drawing breath. Grant me, then, this one comfort, Beloved. Grant that if a time comes when you can no longer speak, I may send you back to Karolan with trustworthy men. By then you will have already spoken any words that might open to me the gate of Heaven, and I, as I go on, may hold some fragment of hope that you reached the lowlands alive, and are being carried eastward toward Luciyr."

"When, probably, I will have died within the first ten score paces of the journey down," said Naomi, smiling. "You are very stubborn, Jonathan my beloved. I grant your request."

There was a short silence, and then the door opened, and Jonathan was aware again of the world beyond him and Naomi as real and significant. King Ilohan was returning; Jonathan had not even realized he had been away. "I have purchased the best horse in Carrah for Jonathan to ride as we start for Aaronkal," said Ilohan. "We must go on the wings of the wind, for in three days Jonathan's thousand must be ready to march from Petrag."

Jonathan had not thought of going to Aaronkal, but now, as he stood, he saw strong reasons to do it. He could choose how his thousand were selected from the assembled Army of All Karolan, and on the way to Petrag he could test them. "Your Majesty," he said, "Naomi's desire is to come with me over the mountains. I have told her this will certainly mean her death, but she will not be dissuaded. This, then, is my request: let ten men of my army be laid under your royal command to carry Naomi to Ceramir, deeming this, not fighting, as their primary mission."

"I understand, though I grieve for you both," said Ilohan. "I will do all that you desire. For the present, Naomi can be carried to Petrag to await your coming."

Jonathan turned to her. "Forgive me, Beloved, for leaving you for those three days," he said. "Yet truly I see no other way. You cannot ride to Aaronkal on swift horses, traveling day and night, as I and the king must do."

"No, I see that, dear Jonathan," she said. "Three days of life I have in me at least, and I will be glad to wait for you in Petrag, where you fought the great battle."

"You are worthy of Jonathan, Shepherdess of Glen Carrah," said King Ilohan. "Alas for both your fates."

"They are not yet settled," said Naomi. "But now, dear Jonathan, you and the king must leave at once."

"Let me, first, find men to carry you to Petrag," said the king to Naomi.

"I will undertake that, Your Majesty," said Barnabas. "I know the men of Carrah well – and she is my daughter."

Naomi looked up at him, and smiled.

Chapter 14

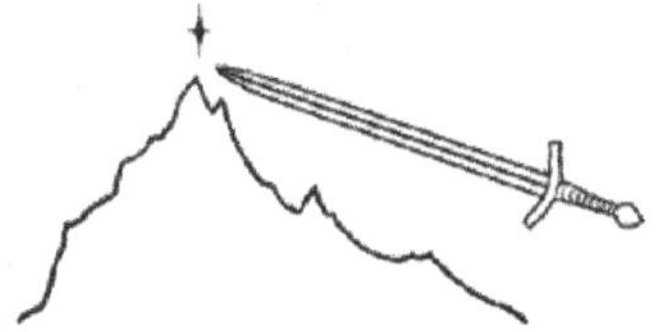

To Guard the Cloth of Joy

MUDIEN WAS GONE, AND ALL IN CERAMIR KNEW OF THEIR desperate plight. The Children of Ceramir, who had stood so long, in laughter, love, and courage, seemed almost to be dismayed. Though the buds of spring gleamed like unpolished rubies on the trees, a shadow hung over the valley and no one laughed.

Imranie and Eleanor together upheld the Cloth of Joy. Imranie was the mother of Ceramir, and like the presence of any good mother, her presence comforted her children. "I do not know what will happen," she would say, "but I know that God is good." Her love and faith somehow encouraged the hearts even of those who had no hope that Ceramir would escape destruction. But Eleanor had hope, and the darkness through which she had passed made her hope shine like a star upon the earth.

The people of Ceramir and Harevan worked every day and long into each cold and weary night. Men carried the goods and possessions of the people of Harevan up through the Gate of Hope and into the shelter of the great rock walls of Ceramir. They built new cabins beneath the mighty trees of the Cloth of

Joy, to house the refugees of Harevan. They sawed great trees in the outlands of Ceramir to bar the Gate of Hope. They even piled boulders on the mountain walls, in case the Zarnith in their fury attacked that way too.

Many longed for Brogal, but he was gone. He was not there to come running through the woods, mocking disaster, to attempt the impossible with a smile, or to lighten weary work with laughter undismayed. Yet Eleanor came among them now and then on her crutches, fearless when the great trees crashed. She would speak of the love and might of God, who, if he chose, would turn back the largest army the world had ever known before some scores of archers and a barrier of trees. She believed so utterly in the love of God that even those whose faith was weak stood in awe of her and wondered if she might be right. She said that though the destruction of all that they knew loomed above them, there was nothing for them to fear. She said that before the power of God Vadshron and all his host were nothing. Even those who disbelieved her words took heart.

Many of the women and children of Ceramir, including Imranie herself, covered their mouths with cloth and their hands with gloves, and gathered from the woods of the outlands all the noxious weeds and bushes that they could find. Their backs ached with the work, and the vapor and dust of the foul plants burned their eyes and lungs. Yet they carried on, and when Eleanor knelt beside them, and with them pulled up the poisonous weeds, she spoke to them softly of the victory of God, and said that whether they fell or triumphed they were safe. Tears shone in some eyes then that were not brought there by the stinging vapor of the plants. Those who had no hope of their own remembered that Eleanor hoped, and took heart. Her vision seemed to reach beyond the confines of the world, and above the shadow of their doom.

Besides the endless work of preparing the defense, many other tasks had to be done in Ceramir. Some tended the children who were too young to take part in the long labor. Others cooked vast quantities of food in the kitchens of the stone house. Still others made arrows for the great bows of the sons of Ceramir. And some, under the guidance of Karlak son of Mudien, took on the bitterest task of all: they used the healing skill of Ceramir as it had never been used before, to take poison from the noxious plants, and refine it until arrows tipped with it were fearsome messengers of death. And among all of them Eleanor and Imranie walked, bringing hope and comfort, and the surety of the love of God.

Over the whole of the Cloth of Joy there was a sense of love and labor. There were no slackers in the long work of defense. Though the shadow of their doom was heavy upon them all, though they were weary and their hope wavered, and they who had so long seemed safe and full of joy teetered on the edge of black despair, still they did not fall. Still they were the Undismayed. And they were faithful.

* * *

Yet even Eleanor was not wholly free from the shadow. She was often able to entrust Ilohan and Veril to God, and let her thoughts be held from anxiety by her works of love and service in Ceramir. But fear would strike her at odd moments. She would envision the terrible mountain journey – the deadly path that Ilohan might dare a second time, for love of her and Veril. She would wonder how it was that he had sent Veril away. She would fear that Ilohan would not succeed, as Kindrach had, in balancing love with duty.

It was worse on the morning Skykag brought her Benther's message. She showed it to Imranie, and they stood beside the lake discussing it.

"He will certainly come, now," said Eleanor. "He will attempt that impossible journey again, in the winter. If I had been wise enough to foresee it, I might never have sent the first warning."

"You had to send it," said Imranie. "You gave Karolan weeks longer to prepare than if the Zarnith messenger of doom had been their first warning. Even apart from that, keeping your own dire peril a secret could have been no true act of love for Ilohan."

"I know it," said Eleanor. "I thank you." They stood silent a while in the now-dead grass upon the shore. Great thick clouds of mist rose off the warm lake, and the bare branches of the trees above it dripped with condensation.

"I have thought, sometimes, that it might be through Ilohan and his thousand that God will save us," said Eleanor. "But at this moment, I feel it will be a miracle if any of them survive the journey."

"I wonder why he wants us to fortify the gap between those hills, out in the desert," said Imranie.

"He cannot intend to make a stand there," said Eleanor. "Perhaps it is for some kind of feint. That heartens me – the thought that he is already making detailed plans for the defense here. It means he truly does expect to lead it, to survive the mountains. The mention of Jonathan is also cause for joy. He proved a great leader at Petrag, and setting him over the Army of All Karolan is the best thing Ilohan could do, other than leading it himself. Yet still, how will the people fight, knowing their king has likely gone to his death?"

Several young girls were playing at the edge of the lake, and one of them now ran up to Eleanor, embraced her as best she could, and looked up at her with shining eyes. "The eagle has come to you again, Ella!" said the girl. "Inli just told me she had seen him. Does it mean your son, the king, is coming to save us?"

"The message did say he would come, little fern," said Eleanor.

"I knew he would!" said the child. "Now we will be safe, and the horde of bad men cannot come and kill us. But you look sad. Are you afraid your son will die fighting?"

Eleanor knelt painfully, laid down her crutches, and embraced the girl. "I have been afraid, little fern," she said.

"But you are praying for him again, are you not, Ella?"

"Yes, I am."

"Then you have nothing to fear. The bad king, Vardshon, will die just like the other one, and your son will be safe. Wasn't the other bad king squished like a spider? This one will be too, or maybe your son will kill him with his bright sword. He does have a bright sword, does he not?"

"Yes," said Eleanor, smiling at her. "Yes, he does. I thank you for bringing me joy."

"But surely I cannot bring you joy, Lady Ella. That is what you give all the people of Ceramir: you bring them joy, so that they do not mind so much to pull up the bad weeds and pile them, and so they are not so afraid of the bad men who are coming. I pulled up some of the weeds myself, and they made my eyes burn and I coughed, but I did it. See my hands." She held her small hands out to Lady Eleanor, palms up, and they were a little blistered by the gloves that she had worn. "What do we want the bad weeds for, Ella? To make the bad men's eyes burn, and make them cough? They will still be able to fight, will they not? It will only make them fiercer than ever."

"Some things you need not know, little fern, but this much I will tell you. Mudien told us all to pray for a wind from the mountains when the bad men come. If God sends the wind, then we will build a fire across the water at the Gate of Hope, and throw the bad weeds on the fire, and the smoke will blow into the faces of the bad men when they try to attack. The smoke will be very bad, and they will cough and not be able to see, and then Rangol and other men, maybe even your father, will stand behind the fire and shoot them with arrows."

"Oh, Ella, I do not think they will need to do that. The Gate of Hope will look so terrible, and the smoke will hurt them so much, I do not think they will dare to come up to it. And what men would be fools enough to try to run through a fire? It would burn them."

Eleanor smiled at the girl's childish mixture of wisdom, hope, and misunderstanding. She was envisioning a few hundred men perhaps, Eleanor thought, with evil scowls on their faces, trying to run up through a fire. A little child of Ceramir could have no understanding of the fierceness and determination of the Zarnith host, nor of its vast numbers. Yet, as the girl embraced her once again and then went back to playing by the misty water, Eleanor's thoughts ran different paths – paths of renewed hope. She compared the young man who with a thousand soldiers would try to resist the Zarnith host to the young woman who had once tried to escape on foot a company of mounted knights determined to kill her. Then still other thoughts came to her, and she saw a Zarnith spear through her heart, and the gates of Heaven flung open to her in the staggering welcome of Christ. All the sorrow of the world, and her own marred-ness and evil, would fall from her at his welcome, and, safe forever in the boundless glory of his love, she would meet Kindrach and Ilohan as they were meant to be.

* * *

The sixth day of the muster at Aaronkal dawned clear and cool, with a hope of spring in the air. Snow faded from the ground, and icicles dripped on the trees. By midmorning, hundreds of women and children from surrounding villages joined the soldiers on the field, for word had gone out that the king would address the people. Rumors said he had arrived only that morning from Glen Carrah – and that Jonathan, the hero of Petrag, was with him.

For the most part the people were quiet and afraid, knowing the dire danger that threatened them. Yet as they looked around at their land, burgeoning now with the hope of spring, it seemed impossible that the Zarnith could blight that promise. Some, however, remembered farms that had seemed just as lovely and inviolable before the Norkaths came, that now were ashes.

The king appeared on the steps of Aaronkal, and a cheer broke forth from the gathered crowd. The sun was bright on his face, and his crown flashed its light. He wore a crimson robe and a gleaming sword. A waiting silence fell, while the spring wind sang high and free through the treetops, and the blue banners of Karolan shone in the sun.

Ilohan looked out over the sea of faces before him. The wintry sun, not yet risen high, shone brightly behind them. The light on their hair haloed them, but left their faces deep in shade. "Valiance and sorrow," he thought, looking at them. "Light upon upraised heads; worn faces shadowed and unseen. It is good that Jonathan conquered, that now I shall not leave them. Yet alas for Veril, whom I cannot defend, and Jonathan, who will die in my place. And this great host looks to me for salvation, when I cannot save even my beloved or my closest friend."

"Lord Christ," he prayed silently, "you alone are the Savior. Save us now. To you I give myself... my people... even Veril and Jonathan. May my words now be wise and pleasing in your sight." He raised his hand, and the trumpeters on the battlements of Aaronkal blew a clear blast, the signal for his speech to begin.

"People of Karolan!" he cried, loud enough to be heard even to the edges of the crowd. "The Zarnith are coming again, as they came in the time of Nirolad. Vadshron the Zarnith, however, remembers Dradrag's failure all those centuries ago. He knows already that no man can conquer stone. He will not try to lead his host over the great mountains. Nor will Vadshron destroy the land of Cembar, as Dradrag did after the mountains turned him back. Vadshron's host is even greater than Dradrag's was, for it numbers seven score and nineteen thousands of mounted Zarnith warriors. His plan is this: to destroy first Ceramir, then Norkath, and then Karolan." The king gestured to the beautiful land around them, trembling and sparkling on the threshold of spring.

"Karolan," he said. "This is our land, the land of our fathers and mothers, and the land of our children. Though we may march with little hope, still we must march to defend it, if we are men. Yet to where shall we march? Of Ceramir most of you know nothing. It is a valley of joy and healing, where dwell both Eleanor, Queen Mother of Karolan, and Veril, who, if she and I are spared, will be your queen. But Vadshron intends to destroy it only eleven days hence, and no army we can send would reach it in time, except by going over the mountains. That only Jonathan of Carrah and I have done, of all the living, and our journey was terrible, and that was not in winter.

"Norkath, I know, many of you would be glad to see destroyed. We can imagine that the Zarnith will execute on it a just revenge for what Fingar did to us. Against such thoughts we must consider the fact that Fingar is dead, and King Andokar is a friend to Karolan. We must also remember the words of Christ, that we should forgive those who wrong us, and love even our enemies.

"Then there is Karolan, our home, defended through all the centuries from Nirolad to now – defended at Petrag, at fearful cost, by many of you who are here today. I am your king, the King of Karolan. It is your land, and you are its people. Karolan, at least, we must defend.

"If we defend only Karolan, we will meet the Zarnith at our own border, after they have ravaged Norkath – for of course Andokar, with his army decimated through Fingar's brutal folly at Petrag, will not be able to stand against them. Much of our border is rich and fertile – and flat, like the desert plains from which the Zarnith come. There is nothing there to hamper their devastating charge, which, it is said, has never in history been broken. Vadshron can choose where to invade us – can split his vast horde into separate armies to evade us and begin the rape of Karolan even without a battle. If there were no other way, of course we would fight the Zarnith even at such cruel disadvantage. But Sir Benther and I believe a far more prudent choice is offered us.

"Vadshron must cross the mountains, just as surely as Dradrag did. He will cross them in the east, where we can be sure they will not stop him – but they will hamper him. The first eastern pass, Luciyr, offers no passage to an army of horsemen. The second, Drantar's Gap, deep in the land of Norkath, is wide and easy. There, we believe, Vadshron will cross the line of the mountains. Oakwoods and high stone hills will constrain him in the valley. His host will have to charge uphill. And we – Karolan and Andokar allied together – will face him with whatever fortifications we can raise before he comes.

"I do not say we shall triumph. Even at Drantar's Gap the Zarnith can still charge. Even at Drantar's Gap they shall outnumber us five or six to one. If we triumph, I believe it will only be through a mighty act of God. But God may indeed act for us. In going to Drantar's Gap, we will show kindness to our former foes, even as Christ commanded. And if we do fall, at least there will be fewer Zarnith to destroy our homes, rape our wives, and kill our children. At least we will leave, for those few of our people who survive, a heritage of heroic mercy. When they emerge, as the Cembarans did after Dradrag's time, they will not look to the past with bitterness but with wonder. Our blood, even if we fail, may yet yield a harvest of peace and courage for children we will never see.

The king paused, and the crowd cheered. Wholehearted acclamation burst from the uncounted thousands of Karolan. The barren woods rang with it, and even in the thick-walled armories of Aaronkal the sound could be heard. With deep gratitude, Ilohan realized that his words had done just what he had hoped. But he was not yet finished.

He raised his hand again, and the gathered thousands quieted. "Ceramir still remains," he said. "Though Dradrag the Zarnith could not cross the mountains, they can be crossed. In nine days I and Jonathan of Glen Carrah went from Ceramir to Aaronkal – and today eleven still remain before the time Vadshron has set for the destruction of Ceramir. A thousand soldiers, I deem, Karolan should spare for the defense of that valley of joy. For love of Veril and Lady Eleanor, I longed to lead that force myself – but I have been shown that in doing so I would abandon you, my people, my first duty. In boldness and great love another has come forth to lead. In a moment he shall address you.

"But first, hear my words concerning this mission. There shall be no compulsion. If less than a thousand are willing, less than a thousand the force shall be. Let all who would volunteer understand what they are doing. There is no hope here, only heroism. The mountains themselves may slay you all. There is no word that they have ever before been crossed in winter – and though spring now is near, the cold will be bitter beyond your dreams. If you do reach Ceramir, in the battle you will be outnumbered eight score to one. But for an act of God, there is not the slightest hope. But God may act. He may work great salvation for this valley that so honors his name. There can be no certainty. This course is for those who would be heroes among heroes – who would go to find either a miracle, or death. Now I will let the leader of this venture speak. People of Karolan, here is Jonathan of Glen Carrah, who led you at Petrag.

The great assembly had cheered loudly before, to honor the king and his words. But now all who were sitting leaped to their feet, and the storm of sound that broke forth from them seemed to shake the walls of Aaronkal. The long months of that winter, combined with his strange disappearance, had sufficed already to make Jonathan almost a figure of legend. That he had returned now, to attempt the impossible again in a dark hour, made thousands in the great assembly feel that victory was sure. And it was not only for Jonathan that they cheered, but for King Ilohan also – their king who had gone alone and disguised to Glen Carrah, and somehow brought back this hero who had been lost.

Jonathan raised his hand to quiet the cheering. "I will speak only a little," he said. "His Majesty has said all that is needful. I hope that some fifteen score of you are from the army I gathered to invade Norkath – I hope you all knew, when King Ilohan's messenger came to Petrag, where your true course lay." There were scattered cheers at this: the little army at Petrag had indeed broken up when the king's messenger brought word of the Zarnith.

Jonathan continued, "To all who are inclined to follow me over the mountains, I say this: Do not go that you may be remembered as heroes. There is no certainty than any shall be left alive to remember. Neither would I have you go in the hope of a miracle. I have no such hope. I believe we will be killed to the last man. If you go, go for heroism, for honor, justice, and courage alone. We will die. We will not be remembered. But we can know, as we attempt this desperate thing, who we are. We can know that we are heroes despair cannot break – that we have courage to fight, with hope or without it, as long as any of us can hold a sword.

"Now I have words that will be better to hear. We will cross the mountains – at least, the greater part of us will. Only a few will die on the way. We will make a journey only two have made since the days of Dradrag. We will walk a land of ice far up in the bitter sky – a land few mortals have ever beheld. We will see it and live – until the battle at our journey's end.

"I have said only a few will die in the mountain crossing. At the king's word, let all who would follow me gather at the south end of the field. We shall run on foot from there to the battlefield of Petrag. Only those who reach it before me may follow me across the mountains. If only five score pass this test, then with only five score I will march. The rest must return to Aaronkal. Thus mercilessly and through pain will I sort out those strong enough to challenge the mountains – the mountains that have no mercy.

It was still before midday when Ilohan and Jonathan met to say farewell, near the great crowd of volunteers. There had been nearly two thousand, but Jonathan assured Ilohan that no more than a thousand would pass the test: the clothes and supplies the king and Benther had already dispatched to Petrag would be sufficient. Each burdened only with a sword and a small bundle of food and water for the day, the volunteers waited to start the grueling race to Petrag.

"I have found ten good men willing to carry Naomi," said Ilohan. "I laid on them my royal command to carry her wherever you desire, and to hold that as their primary duty. They will ride behind you with the last supply wagons."

"I thank you," said Jonathan.

"I am sending you to your death," said Ilohan. His steady, almost cold voice did not hide from Jonathan the immense effort he was making not to show his distress before the crowd.

"You are sending me to a more honorable death than I would have found for myself," said Jonathan, "in a time when all roads lead to death."

"Unless God sends a miracle," said Ilohan. "Do not forget my words about the desert gap, dear friend."

"There are no miracles," said Jonathan. "But I will not forget."

"Farewell then," said the king. They hugged each other and then parted. A trumpet sounded: the beginning of the race. Jonathan turned to run to the mountains, and did not look back.

* * *

At dusk Jonathan stood below the mouth of Petrag, where the rolling hills' fertility faded into the rocky soil of the valley. The race was not finished, and already it had been grueling even for him. His legs ached and his lungs were sore. He searched the groups of running men who hurried past him for a particular sort of man – one who had come so far and fast not because of his strength, but because he had driven himself nearly to death. Whenever Jonathan saw such a man, he ran alongside him and commanded him to return to Aaronkal. He had no mercy. Several times, when the man did not immediately obey him, Jonathan threw him down hard upon the stony ground. These men got up to begin limping back toward Aaronkal, weeping. Jonathan wanted men who would be willing, when the time came, to drive themselves to death – but none for whom that time came in the lowlands after only one day's run. At last Jonathan decided that all the men strong enough to survive the mountains had already gone past. He turned southward to run up into Petrag himself.

Night fell cold and clear. The moon was waxing toward its full, but it would be long before it rose high enough to shine into the deep valley. Its glow lit up the sky, but that glow, together with the starlight, was all that illuminated the valley floor. The darkness made the race dangerous, and some men's ankles were sprained upon the stones. They would limp back to Aaronkal, aided by others. Even Jonathan could not see well enough in the faint light to avoid slipping occasionally, but his powerful legs absorbed missteps without taking harm. He did not pity the injured, nor those who lost their place in his army by cautiously slowing down and falling behind him. All these would have been marked for death in the mountains from the journey's beginning. In the Army of All Karolan they could fight bravely and win honor.

At last, when the moon had long been shining into the valley, Jonathan reached the battlefield. The men he had allowed to reach there ahead of him sat or lay about on the stone, exhausted, looking ghostly or corpselike in the moonlight. But a little farther up the valley he heard sounds and saw motion: people, mostly women it seemed, were hard at work at something. Forcing his own sore limbs to move, he ran up there. As he approached, he saw that they were setting up what seemed a whole village worth of tents. One man came forward to meet him, and in a moment he recognized his father.

"Welcome, Son!" said Barnabas. "These tents are for your army. They were stored at Castle Byinkal until a messenger from the king came there late this afternoon. We met him and heard the news that you would all be coming to the battlefield on foot. Riders from Aaronkal, together with women of Petrag and some of the garrison from Byinkal, have been hard at work moving the tents here to be ready for you. Naomi and your mother were given the first tent. I have helped in the labor since then, but much remains to be done."

"I will soon alter that," said Jonathan. He ran back down to the battlefield. "Men of Karolan!" he cried, his voice strong and warm against the chilly night. "You have run far, but the journey is still ahead. Now is no time to rest! Yonder, only a little up the valley, women labor to set up the tents where you will sleep. Go now and aid them, and swiftly we shall all have warm shelter."

The more Jonathan saw of the preparations, the better he was pleased. All, he guessed, was owing to the wise efforts of Benther during Ilohan's absence. Besides the tents there was an ample supply of blankets, fur cloaks, and rope. There were also smoked meat, and cheese, and skins already filled with fresh, clean water. As he was investigating this, Jonathan was called away by the arrival of the last supply wagons from Aaronkal. They carried fresh bread, bows and arrows, even more warm clothes and blankets – and, as Ilohan had promised, ten men who had pledged to carry Naomi wherever Jonathan would command them.

When all the wagons were unloaded, and all the men divided into tents, Jonathan went to the one, a little apart, where Naomi slept. There was no sound from within. Hannah, he guessed, was still awake there, but he would not speak to her lest he disturb Naomi. He gathered a blanket close about him, and sat down on a stone near the tent. He remained there motionless while the moon sank toward the western cliffs and vanished. He could feel again the temptation to surrender to despair. Naomi was dying. Nothing in the world mattered. Why should he do anything, much less this thing that he had chosen to do – this hopeless journey that would hasten Naomi's death and cost him such meaningless, agonizing effort? But he had already answered that question back in Glen Carrah. He would go on because true men did not despair. He would go on because he had made his choice: the sword blade piercing though the ash.

He rose silently, reasonlessly, and walked down toward the battlefield. Moonlight gilded the high cliff walls. Broken stones shifted beneath his feet. The night was clean and open, and the cold wind that hissed and moaned over the jagged rocks seemed only to intensify the silence. Jonathan remembered another night here, when all that was silence and beauty now had been horror and noise – when men had struggled on through weariness as desperate as any that now lay ahead on the mountain way. He remembered the hellish firelight and the rock slippery with blood, the cries of the dying and the courage of those who fought until the dawn. Suddenly the memory of that horror, which the men of Karolan had faced and vanquished, kindled like a raging fire in his heart. That victory must endure. The Zarnith would herd women and children into this valley and slaughter them. Their blood would run down to join the blood of those who had fought for their lives and their freedom in the Battle of Petrag. The Zarnith must be turned back. He knew it was impossible, he knew Vadshron would conquer them, but against all that impossibility his anger burned more fiercely than the flames of Glen Carrah, and he was glad he was going to die in battle. He strode back up to the tents, found one with room for him, flung himself down there, and slept.

Back in the tent Jonathan had left, Barnabas stirred a little as he lay near Hannah. "Are you sleeping?" he asked her.

"No," she said, with no sound of sleep in her voice.

"Do you have any hope?" he asked her.

"I do not know," she whispered. "I suppose there is none, truly. Naomi will die in the mountains, and you and Jonathan will die at Ceramir, and Karolan will fall. Have you any hope yourself?"

"No," said Barnabas. "I had thought you might."

"In the end we will be saved, Beloved."

"You know that I did not speak of that hope, dear Hannah."

"Yes, I know. I am sorry. Yet..."

"What is it, Hannah?"

"I know that I can find no reason to hope...yet I hope all the same. I said once that this spring would bring good things. I think so still, though I cannot say why. Naomi may survive.

Vadshron may fall ill and change his purpose. I cannot know. I am afraid. And yet… dear Barnabas, I hope!"

"I am glad," he said. "I love you. When we were young together I loved you, and I hoped that you would love and bless me. The years have been hard, Beloved, but your love and blessing, and your aid and comfort have been more – immeasurably more – than I dreamed or hoped. Remember this… remember it, whatever comes."

"I will. And you also, Beloved, remember…"

"What would you have me remember, dear Hannah?"

"Remember that, when she was young, Hannah of Tremilin loved you and gave you her hand in marriage, and left what had been her home. Remember that all the days of her life she loved you. The joy and goodness of being your companion, your beloved, through the long years of following God together was more than she could ever deserve. Remember that you have helped her follow him, and that she honors and loves you, and will forever."

They held each other close in the darkness, and together they slipped into sleep.

*   *   *

Far out in the desert west and south of Aaronkal, Mudien had at last come upon the trail of the Zarnith host, and found their camp. He had slept in a hidden place near it, and awakened at dawn to enter the camp and seek an audience with Vadshron.

He sat very upright in the saddle as he rode past the outer guards. Arrows whistled past him, and a few spears flew with deadly force close by his body, but he did not react. He might be killed at any moment, but he knew his best chance of surviving to speak with Vadshron lay in a show of absolute confidence and indifference to threats. He heard wild insults shouted at him. He tried to fix his mind on interpreting them, straining to remember long ago lessons from his Zarnith friend. He was able to determine that he had been called a glowworm (myrklagi), a dead cactus (shlixlanred), a corpse animated by an evil spirit (antrifru wyrkranigok), and a windblown grain of horse's dung (floshkik whyflaiah). At last, to his surprise, the shouts and threats diminished. It seemed his calm, determined courage had indeed won the respect of the Zarnith host.

The scale of the camp awed him. Its ragged tents seemed to stretch out forever. He could not count the men, but he easily believed Vadshron's boast that there were almost eight score thousands. The motion of horses and men raised a constant haze of dust, gilded now by the rising sun. The stench of unwashed men and horses came to him strong and harsh. He passed through several circles of guards, armed with ever more imposing weapons. A guard of the last circle commanded him to dismount, and then, leading his horse, he approached a large tent strikingly painted with six red bands. The flap was pulled aside, and a man came out.

The calm gray eyes of Mudien of Ceramir met the wild black ones of the Zarnith lord, and they stood, face to face, for a long moment without speaking. Mudien was tall, and Vadshron was no taller. The Zarnith lord wore garments of dust brown cloth, little different from the clothes of his warriors except for the belt of burnished gold at his waist. But Vadshron's matchless strength showed clearly in his bare, superbly muscular arms and his powerfully poised legs. The whole man seemed bursting with life, restless energy, and ferocious determination. Even his long black hair – long as the Zarnith permitted only the warlord's hair to be – seemed to participate in his wild vitality. Mudien knew that the lordship of the Zarnith was decided by a contest of strength, but even this had not prepared him for the actual appearance of the Zarnith lord. He found himself glorying in the splendid creation that was the body of this man, even while he abhorred and feared the decisions of the warlord's will.

Gesturing fiercely with the spear in his right hand, Vadshron began to speak. His voice was harsh and his eyes alight with his challenge, as though all the wildness of the desert was in them: "Zy thrond meredkor jok whythak jel. Zy thrond lo Arnith sk'shre jan bonthor sra thraiah shoosha. Zy thrond nograk vronkor zyk, nag jel. Zy thrond nykra zyn nogral, f'nograk zyn fooshdinkor yk nogralfookd! Fo zonsha yk naralagonka, mydoroka, sagakagon Vadshron Gonk Zarnith?"

In the midst of this speech he took his stout wooden spear in both hands and broke it over his knee with terrifying force. He took the end that still bore the head, and broke it again in the same way, splinters flying after the loud crack of splitting wood. He retained in his hand the final piece – the piece to which the spearhead was still attached.

The words came slowly to Mudien, as he used all his strength of will to dredge them up from his memory while reeling from the warlord's intimidating display of strength. The Zarnith word order was strange, but after a few heartbeats of work that seemed to take ages he thought he understood. The Zarnith lord had said, "I can leap once over nine horses. I can run two days in the desert without ever being weary. I can kill five men with one spear throw. I can break my spear with my hands, and with the little broken piece in my left hand throw and kill you! What is your business with the mighty, the ferocious, the undefeatable in battle, Vadshron, Warlord of the Zarnith?"

Mudien prayed in thought and then spoke, slowly and clearly, and the Zarnith words he wanted came. "I am Mudien, from Ceramir. You have heard that Ceramir is like Paradise, and you want it for your own. I tell you, if you come to the Gate of Hope and ask us, we will bring out to you everything we have to spare. We have much to spare. But if you come against us to destroy us, you will offend the One Who Is, whom you do not know, because he loves us. It is he who made the desert and the stars, and you, and he can destroy you if you displease him. I warn you: turn back while there is yet time, for no man can stand against his anger. I warn you: we are even now asking his help against you, and if he hears us you will charge to your own destruction."

Mudien paused a moment, searching for words that would form an authentic Zarnith curse to express his warning. "The gate of Paradise will become to you the gate of Hell. The Gate of Hope will be the Gate of Fear. Your charge will falter as a horse dies for want of water. Your strength will leave you and children will shout over you in triumph. You will reach out to destroy the place of love, and it will become to you a place of destruction. The rocks, the air, the trees: all will slay you. You will say, 'We thought to win joy, but instead, here is fear and horror. Deadly things we know not have come upon us out of Hell. We must have angered Nagryn, warlord of the fiends, for the fiends have come among us to slay us by thousands.' But in truth you are against One greater than Nagryn. You will come against the Undismayed, and your survivors will turn back, dismayed. Terror shall fall upon you, and terror shall never leave you, for the Valley beloved of the One Who Is cannot be taken without his will."

Mudien stood perfectly still, astonished at some of the things he had said, yet glad that the words had come. His warning was given. Death had no power over him.

Vadshron turned his back on Mudien contemptuously and picked up a bow and an arrow from beside the tent. In one fluid motion he swung around, drew back the arrow, and shot, aiming for Mudien's heart. But at that instant another man, suddenly emerging from the tent, leaped at him with a cry. The arrow was slightly deflected, transfixing Mudien's right arm rather than his chest. A sword seemed to appear instantly in Vadshron's hand. The two Zarnith fought in a flurry of movements Mudien's eyes could not follow, and then Vadshron stood alone with a beheaded corpse at his feet. The head rolled face up, and Mudien saw that it was the Zarnith he had cared for in Ceramir, who had taught him the language and given him the poem of the Mountain Way.

Mudien knelt stiffly, dizzy with pain, blood streaming down his arm. Gently he touched the hair of the man he had known and loved. Ignoring Vadshron, he dragged the body toward him, put the head back in its place, and composed the legs and arms so that the body had some dignity. He stood up and looked Vadshron in the eyes. "So dies a hero," he said in Zarnith.

"So dies a traitor," yelled Vadshron, and leaped forward to discompose the body with his bloody sword. Mudien reached out and stopped the blade with his own right hand, making no sign of pain as it cut him. The blood from his two wounds ran down his arm to mingle with the blood of the dead Zarnith on the ground. Vadshron suddenly laughed and struck Mudien a stinging blow across the face with the flat of his sword. "You are dead, grub worm of Ceramir. Vadshron the mighty kills always with one arrow, so you are dead. He struck Mudien hard again, across the other side of the face, spat in Mudien's face, and then stood still, watching him with contempt from the utter security of his strength.

Mudien gave no sign of pain as he broke the shaft of the arrow and pulled it forward out of his arm. He bound up his wounds with strips of white cloth from his saddlebags, pleased to see that no tendons in his hand had been cut. He lifted the body of the dead Zarnith onto his horse and then mounted himself, carrying the head. He turned his back on Vadshron and rode away, marveling at what seemed to have happened: the warlord's own arrogant boast – that he could always kill a foe with one arrow – had secured his life. It did not secure him from harassment, however. Shouted curses and insults were flung at him from all directions as he rode out, and dozens of arrows came terrifyingly close. Nonetheless, it seemed that no Zarnith wanted to take the responsibility of killing one who had come forth alive from the warlord's presence. Mudien passed the outermost guards and rode out into the free desert.

He rode on for a long time, still looking only ahead, and holding his body perfectly upright despite the dizzying, throbbing pain he felt. When at last he looked back the Zarnith camp was invisible and there was no sign of pursuit. He rode on, knowing that he would be racing the Zarnith back to Ceramir now. They would travel at the speed of the slowest in their mighty host, and he knew that even carrying the body of the dead Zarnith his horse could outpace them. Still, he would wait until evening before he stopped. Then he would find a hidden, waterless place, where the Zarnith would never come, and bury the body of his friend.

Chapter 15

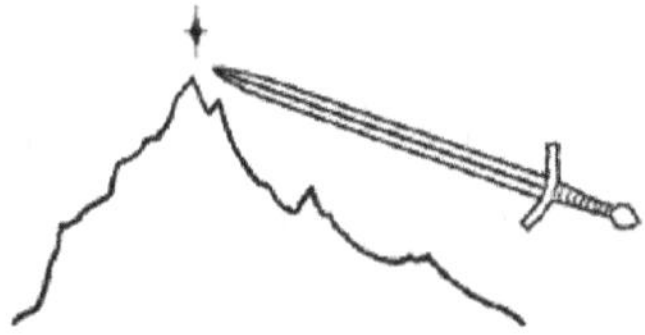

Parting Beyond the World

IN THE HIGH FOOTHILLS ABOVE PETRAG, JONATHAN URGED his army forward at a swift pace. He had let the men rest and eat until midmorning in Petrag, but after that had ordered them to march. So far he had not regretted the decision. Sir Benther's meticulous preparations had allowed them to pack in less than an hour. The strong men Jonathan had chosen for his army seemed to have recovered well from the grueling race he had used to select them.

He did begin to worry, however, as afternoon faded toward evening in the sparse pinewoods. He had hoped, at least, to camp that night in the last rocky valley before the great chasm – if not at the edge of the chasm itself. However, there was as yet no sign of either landmark. The distance now seemed longer to him than it had when he and Ilohan had walked it together, bounding along almost giddy with delight after their escape from the great mountains.

He pushed on at the fastest pace he thought the men would hold. The army had stretched out into a line nearly half a thousand paces long, while treading the narrow path through thicker pinewoods that morning. Now, although the pines were giving way to stone and they could have marched in a more compact formation, Jonathan found his army was still strung out over a long distance. Those in the rear were evidently not hurrying as he could wish them too – but he did not want to run back and urge them to greater speed, lest those in the front should go astray without his guidance.

Finally, when the moon was already shining brightly through thin clouds, they came upon the place Jonathan was seeking – a shallow valley of barren stone, now covered in icy snow pierced here and there by a few stunted pine trees. High and far off to the south he could just make out the broader white gleam of the vast ice fields that lay on this side of the great chasm. He led on a little way into the valley, and then turned to address the foremost of his men.

"Men of Karolan, you have done well," he called, trying to make his voice again a thing that would bring strength and warmth to those who heard. "Already we are far above the last farms and dwellings of our land. I had hoped today to reach the great chasm, beyond which the mountains begin in earnest – but it still lies an hour's march ahead, and some of your comrades are lagging. The time has not yet come to push on regardless of weariness, to the bitter edge of strength and life. We will camp in this valley, and tomorrow we will cross the chasm and challenge the mountains in earnest. Now, all of you, begin making camp. Stake the tents down well against the wind. Eat only after your tent is pitched. Pass on my orders to others as they arrive – I go now to urge the stragglers on."

He turned and began running down the line of men, surefooted and fearless in the moonlight, though no joy was in his heart. He called out encouragement to the men, mixed increasingly with rebukes as he came to those who had lagged the farthest behind.

And yet this was not his main purpose in running back. At the end of the line he found two strong horses. On one of them rode Barnabas, with Naomi before him in the saddle. On the other rode Hannah, alone. Barnabas reined in his horse as Jonathan approached. "There are no men behind us, my son," he said. "All day I have watched to see that we passed no stragglers, just as you asked."

"I thank you, Father," said Jonathan. "We are now very near our camp. May I carry Naomi there?"

"Yes, dear Jonathan," said Naomi in a low voice, "yes, you may certainly carry her."

He reached up and took her down into his arms. "I am glad to find you awake, Beloved," he said. "But Naomi, you are trembling with cold."

"It is only the wind," she said. "Once in the tent I shall be warm – indeed, I am already warmer now that you hold me."

The moon shone out through a sudden break in the clouds, and Jonathan seemed to see the glimmer of tears on her pale face. "Are you very unhappy, Beloved?" he asked.

"Not now," she said, raising a hand to her eyes. "Not now, when I am in your arms."

"I am sorry I have been so little with you," he said. "I could wish that we were back in Glen Carrah, and I had no task but watching at your bedside."

"I could wish that, too," she whispered, "but in many ways it was impossible. I would not have had you neglect Karolan or the king in their need, for the sake of staying more with me."

"I love you far more than Karolan or the king, Beloved," he said. "It is only that I tried to do what was just and honorable."

"I know," she said. "I did not forbid you. I do not wish you had made a different choice. But now, dear Jonathan, why do I feel your tears falling upon me?"

"Only because you are so beautiful, Beloved," he said.

"My hair is shortened, I am scarred with fire and gaunt with sickness, and the moon is behind a cloud," said Naomi.

"You are beautiful," he whispered, and could say no more. Tears choked him, and he did not say what was in his heart: that she rang true always, that she was faithful and loving; that these things had always given her greater beauty than her lovely face and form, and that this beauty seemed to shine more clearly than ever now. He did not say that her life had never seemed to him more precious, and that he knew she would die the next day on the Third Mountain.

Instead, she broke the long silence by saying, "Dear Jonathan, will Hannah die because of me?"

"Not because of you, Beloved," said Jonathan. "To tell you why will make me speak of things that break my heart."

"You mean that I will die of cold and harsh air before she does, and then you will send her back down with my body?" asked Naomi. Jonathan said nothing, but his arms tightened around her. He had been horrified to find, only that morning, that his parents intended to accompany him. Their love for him, like Naomi's, would bring about their death in the mountains, and he could not dissuade them. Yet his mother would turn back with Naomi's corpse, and thus she might survive. His father would stay with him and die. To Jonathan these new griefs were only further cracks in a life already shattered – a life that had been shattered when he found he had betrayed Naomi, and again when he had learned that she was dying. She would still be dying, even if she did not attempt to cross the mountains. And if Barnabas stayed with the Army of All Karolan, he would still die – in battle at Drantar's Gap. Jonathan remembered his own words when Ilohan first mentioned the coming of the Zarnith: why should there be limits to tragedy or disaster?

Naomi had fallen asleep in his arms, but she woke as he laid her down in his mother's tent. "Are you warm enough, Beloved?" he asked when he saw her eyes open.

Painful coughing wracked her, and when it subsided she was shivering. "I was warm enough while you carried me, dear Jonathan," she said hoarsely. "But the ground here is chill."

"The tent is pitched on ice, child," said Hannah. "But here, I will wrap more blankets around you. Here is a leather one, to keep you from the damp."

Naomi spoke to Jonathan from the thick blankets that wrapped her still-shivering form. "Remember that you are not to blame," she said. "The evils of this journey come from the Zarnith." He gazed at her from the depths of his grief, wanting to speak longer with her, but not knowing what to say. Her trembling quieted, she smiled at him, and then slipped into sleep.

* * *

Jonathan roused his army in the darkness before dawn, and before the sun had risen clear of the mountains they were already gathered at the edge of the great chasm. Jonathan climbed a hillock of rock and ice. The soft dawn colors in the eastern sky set off the harsh contours of ice and rock below. The immense chasm and the staggering mountains beyond it dwarfed the thousand men drawn up on its edge like ants.

"Men of Karolan," called Jonathan, "behold the challenge you undertook at Aaronkal! Before you is a crack that drops into immeasurable black depths, crossed by a bridge so strange and frail that those who first reported this route said it had been made by demons.

"But the crack and bridge are easy. The mountain beyond it is what you should fear. High up on its western flank there is a pass – the highest pass of our journey. Some of you will die there. You will collapse from the harshness of the air, and perish from the cold. But those who live to descend from that pass will most likely complete the journey, long and bitter though it still remains.

"I say now to all of you, and especially to those who lagged behind yesterday: there is still time to turn back. You have now seen the chasm, the bridge, and the great mountain. You could not have imagined these back at Aaronkal. If, now, you do not wish to challenge them, turn and go back to the Army of All Karolan. Neither I, nor the king, nor any other man of wisdom will despise you. But if you cross this bridge with me, there will be no turning back. I shall expect every one of you to follow me across the mountains – or spend his last strength and then die in the attempt. I shall expect you to remain in a close formation, where one may help another. You must not lag behind or suffer others to do so. If I give a command, I shall expect you instantly to attempt obedience, no matter how impossible or how great your weariness. The mountains have no mercy, and I shall have none. Let all who will not cross the mountains now begin the journey back to Aaronkal.

Jonathan waited long in the mountain silence. No one moved. "I commend your courage!" said Jonathan. "Beyond the mountains stands Ceramir, the Cloth of Joy, a place of healing for all who come there – and more than healing. Happy are those who ever see it; happier still those who live there in innocence and joy. There dwells Eleanor, Queen Mother of Karolan, and Veril, King Ilohan's intended bride, and perhaps half a thousand others. Vadshron would leave nothing but the ashes of their bones."

Jonathan let his words fade away into the vastness, waking only weak and distant echoes, like the vanishing of beauty into ghosts and ashes. Then he raised his voice like a trumpet call – the voice that had called men at Petrag to fight until the dawn. "Men of Karolan, we shall defend them!" he cried. "With heroism unsurpassed in the tales of all the ages, we will march, and we will fight. At the gates of Ceramir the Zarnith will meet fury such as they have never seen before, and they will wade in their own blood before they spill the last of ours. No man who fights in the last defense of Karolan at Drantar's Gap will do more to save his land than we, for every Zarnith we strike down at Ceramir is one who will never advance against our homes. Now, for Ceramir and Karolan, for courage and heroism, for King Ilohan – we will cross the mountains!"

And cheers rang out in the icy air – but not like the cheers of the great host at Aaronkal. There the people had merely praised the king and Jonathan, confident that those two could lead and save them. Now, the thousand who followed Jonathan roared out their determination to make his words come true by their own effort and agony. They would be heroes. They would cross the mountains.

*   *   *

In the outlands of Ceramir, Auria took off her gloves for the fifteenth time that day, pushed back her hair from her face, and tied it behind her with a piece of cord. Her hair was damp with sweat, cold though it was. She did not grudge the bitter labor, but weariness and fear wore at her. The work seemed endless and meaningless. They might strip out every last noxious leaf in the outlands of Ceramir, and still it would not stop the Zarnith. She wondered how she would die. Remembering the words of the Zarnith messenger, she shuddered with horror.

"Sister!" She looked up in sudden happiness at the hearty cry. "Sister, what ails the Cloth of Joy?"

"Brogal!" she cried, and ran to the edge of the river. Veril and Brogal, both mounted, had reined in their horses just across the stream from her.

"Dear Auria!" he said. "God give you joy. Your life brings joy to many." A hint of laughter came into his eyes. "But will you not swim the stream to greet us?"

She stood still and looked at her brother. He did not know that Ceramir was doomed. He did not know that this was no time for laughter, or for the happy abandon with which they had climbed trees and swum rivers when they were children together.

"A great shadow is upon us, Brogal," she said.

He was suddenly serious. "I know, Auria," he said. "We have passed through Harevan already. But will you not swim the stream to meet us?"

Then she suddenly understood what she could hardly believe she had forgotten. Even if the world were ending tomorrow, laughter and hope would still be in Brogal's heart. With that same mischievous twinkle in his eyes, he would still have asked her to swim the stream. She leaped in fully clothed and swam it.

Brogal dismounted and embraced her, wet though she was, and so did Veril.

"You should not let Brogal persuade you to such things," said Veril. "Not now, when your heart is greatly troubled."

"But less troubled with your coming, both of you!" said Auria. "How I love you! Yet–" her joy faded, "yet perhaps I should wish you far, far away. The Zarnith will be here in nine days. They said… they said they would destroy us, and drink our blood and dance upon the ashes of our bones. They said we would die and the Wirkriy would eat our ghosts. Vadshron is their leader's name; he has seven score and nineteen thousands of followers. And Father… Father has gone alone to warn him of the wrath of God."

Veril and Brogal were silent for a moment. Tears formed in Auria's eyes and ran down her cheeks. Veril hugged her again, suddenly, and held her tight. "Has Eleanor sent Skykag to the king?" she whispered. "Has he offered help?"

"Yes," said Auria, trying to speak through her tears. "He comes with a thousand warriors, over the mountains. Yet what are a thousand, when Vadshron has nearly eight score times as many?"

Veril released Auria suddenly. Fear and horror were in her face. "Over the mountains…" whispered Veril. "A thousand men… Ilohan… If I have brought you to this, I would with all my heart that you had never seen me! Oh Father… how can this be… Father, I love the king so much. Yet when have I ever brought him anything but harm?"

"It is a pity I did not go wandering out in the desert, as I had thought to do," said Brogal.

Veril looked at him in astonishment. "The Zarnith would have found and killed you," she said. "Thank God you did not go!"

"Ah," said Brogal, "you do not think I could have turned back eight score thousands? Perhaps I could have told them we all had the plague. Though indeed, knowing nothing of their language would have made it harder."

Auria smiled through her tears, but Veril said, "Dear Brogal, you would jest with even the warlord if you found him. Would that we could all laugh... But King Ilohan... Alas!" Veril covered her face, fell to her knees on the path, and burst into tears.

Brogal gently raised her to her feet and pried her hands away from her face. "Dear sister, I do not jest now," he said. "Ilohan is free, and whatever comes of his decision you will not be to blame for it. And who can say what may come? The world is new with each new dawn, and we can never guess what the day will bring. Perhaps a thousand thousands of angels will ring the Cloth of Joy with flaming swords. I have always wanted to see God's army go out to battle. Have not you? Ah, Auria, you are shivering. Take my horse. I will run beside you up through the Gate of Hope, and you must warm and dry yourself at a fire within."

They went up the path and through the Gate of Hope, Veril and Auria riding, and Brogal running beside them. Soon they were sitting by a hearth in the stone house of the Cloth of Joy. The news that Veril and Brogal had returned spread rapidly through Ceramir. Children flocked to Veril, rapturous in their delight at her return. She would have liked them to stay away, and leave her to take in peace the shock of this strange homecoming. But she would not refuse them, and so she knelt among them and spoke to them, comforting them and answering their floods of questions as best she could.

"Yes, the king has a great castle. Yes, he is coming to help us. No, he does not have more soldiers than the Zarnith. Yes, he is very strong, and so are his soldiers. Yes, I am afraid of the Zarnith. I do not know if they will kill us, but if they do Christ will still save us if we trust him. Yes, Christ is stronger than the Zarnith. Yes, he could defeat them all. No, I am not sure he will. I do not know – he does not always do as we expect. If we die, we will be with him, in a place that is far better than here.

Yes, I am sure it is better than here. No, I am not sure what it is like. I know the best part about it is being with God. Think of the joy you have in being with Ella or Imranie or Brogal, and then think how all their goodness and delight comes from God, and he is far more wonderful than they are. No, I am not sure the Zarnith will kill us. God might save us. Children, run away from me now, for here is Imranie, and I want to greet her."

Veril rose and ran into her mother's arms. Imranie hugged her and held her tight. "Dear Veril," she said, "you have been gone so long, and yet because of our danger I hoped you would not come. But I – and Ceramir – have deeply missed you! And now there are no safe places in the world."

"Karolan is not safe either, then, Mother?"

"No, dear child. Vadshron has vowed to conquer Ceramir, Norkath, and Karolan. From all I hear it will be a miracle from God if he does not."

"A miracle… And Karolan too… But Mother, our God is the Lord of miracles."

"May he bless you, daughter. Perhaps there is hope. Eleanor has some, but I… your father is gone, and I am left to lead alone. I trust God, but I think we shall fall. He may bless our death as well as our life. I know he will bless us in whatever he sends us."

Eleanor came to them, seeming to lean more heavily than usual on her crutches. "I love you deeply, and you have been sorely missed," she said to Veril, "yet I grieve at your return."

Veril went to her and they embraced. "Veril, dear Veril," she said, "Ilohan told me you were coming, yet he loved you. What dark miscounsel took him, that he sent you away?"

"None but his own, Lady Eleanor," said Veril. "It is only that he loves me greatly, but does not understand my love for him. He would spare me the grief and weariness of the throne.

He does not understand that a life of serving with him, even in sorrow and pain, would be the most joyful life I could live."

Veril looked into Eleanor's eyes, as they stood face to face. Lady Eleanor was very beautiful, she thought, despite her weariness and sorrow. Her eyes were full of love and faith, but sadness was in them too. "I understand," Eleanor whispered. "I am sorry. Can you forgive him?"

"I already have," said Veril softly. "I forgave him at that very moment. And he did not leave me without hope. It is Vadshron who would do that."

Brogal stood. "Vadshron will die," he said. "I have not yet been without pity, but for him I have none. Let him heed my father's warning. For if he comes against the Cloth of Joy, he will come without excuse, and find a fear beyond his greatest fear."

All in the room were silent for a long moment. No one had ever before heard Brogal say such a thing. Imranie wondered if it was wrong to speak as he had. But Auria stood at last in the silence. "I am glad Brogal is home," she said.

* * *

Watching his men march up the vast fields of gleaming snow, Jonathan concluded that their slow progress the day before had only been due to the brutal race he had led them from Aaronkal to Petrag. Now, with that ordeal two days in the past, their natural strength and endurance had returned to them. Some even laughed, or spoke exultantly as they looked down. The mountain slope had already hidden the great chasm from their view, and the forests of Karolan had vanished into a soft gray-blue haze. By their own strength and choice, the warriors of Karolan had already climbed into an alien world of rock and ice, where grass and forests became a fading memory. Jonathan knew the time would come when his men would cower before the brutality of this new world, when they would shake their fists at its unyielding mountains and long for the scent of wood smoke or the feel of grass. For now, though, they merely exulted in having reached it – and that was good. He called a brief halt for food and water, and, forgetting these things himself, went to the stretcher that was carried in the midst of the army.

Naomi lay there, pale and gasping for breath. Even though he had expected this, he was shocked at how quickly her condition had worsened – while the strong, healthy men he had just been watching seemed hardly yet to feel the effects of the mountain air. Wordlessly but with great gentleness, he gathered her up out of the stretcher and held her in his arms. She coughed hard, and then spoke in a whisper. "A thousand men acclaim you as a hero, Jonathan. They speak well. All goes as you would wish it?"

"The journey is going well, Beloved," said Jonathan. "But what is that to me? You are dying."

"We both knew I would die today, dear Jonathan," she whispered. "I am not afraid of that. When death is upon me, I will send for you, and you can hold me in your arms."

He lifted her higher, and buried his face in the blankets that covered her. She raised a trembling hand, and touched his tangled hair. "They see me as a hero, Beloved," he whispered, his face now close to hers. "They will see me thus until the end. But you see me as I truly am, and from you I will hide nothing. All my courage is like the thin white snow of Glen Carrah, with only ashes underneath. I fear the Jonathan you loved is already dead. I have betrayed you, and sought vengeance while I had still a chance to save you – as if I would have cared whether

Drantar lived or died, if you were safe and well! And now you are dying, in following me. I feel as if I have stabbed you with my own hands, and even as you bleed to death in my arms, you still love me. I look for anything that can shine light into my darkness, and I find nothing."

"Even I cannot?" she whispered.

"Naomi, you were the sun! With your setting, all else is darkening, and I have no heart to see the lamps. Even they will soon be extinguished."

"I am not dead yet, Jonathan," she said in her heartbreaking whisper. "Yet I can see death coming, and it shall be like the letting go of a great weight carried far too long, or like a frightened child who climbed a tree too high, yet feels at last her father's arms take hold of her to bring her safely down. What would be your thoughts of death, if it came near you? What were they when it came near you on your adventures?"

"Desperation and anger, Beloved, even as I feel now at seeing you draw near it. How could it be otherwise? It is evil."

"Its evil has been turned against itself," she whispered. "It is a conquered foe. It has lost its sting. Now it is the end of a weary journey, and the coming home."

"Home is lost," said Jonathan. "I lost it the day I left you, tears and courage together in your eyes, in Glen Carrah before its ruin. I lost it, and I lost it forever."

Coughing shook Naomi again. At last, recovering herself, she whispered, "Home is not lost, Jonathan. It is we who were lost; wanderers on earth, far from home. Now I am going there at last. You cannot follow me unless you follow Christ. He waits for you. I love you more than I can say, but his love is greater. He is the beloved Savior, the healer of the world. But if you fly from him... Jonathan... Beloved of my soul... Choice is the most terrible of all his gifts. He may let you fly. Do not cling to your pride, to your faith that holds for you no hope. There is hope, Jonathan. Do not turn away from it!"

He looked down into her eyes, not listening to her words, feeling no hope but only agony.

"Jonathan!" she cried, and her voice, though it cracked, was not a whisper. "Jonathan, do not leave me!" She coughed hard after the effort of speaking, and licked bloody froth away from the corners of her mouth. "Please do not leave me," she whispered. "I am in light – light that only brightens after death. Do not go into darkness."

"Naomi!" he said, speaking softly, though his grief-stricken heart wanted to cry out with a mighty voice. "Naomi, do not you leave me!"

"I have no more choice," she whispered. "When I could, I always chose to live. But it is you who have... you who have the choice now, Jonathan."

*   *   *

Sunset on the Third Mountain flung up a sheet of deep violet in the east and north, while far to the west over Cembar a sullen red line glowed under a black bank of cloud. A wind shrieked over the icy slope, biting cruelly at any exposed skin. Combined with that wind, and the wild landscape all around, the colors in the sky seemed apocalyptic. As he urged his men onward, Jonathan thought of the hail of stars he had seen with Ilohan, and of the staggering destruction that Vadshron now threatened. The light faded; the sunset colors grew even deeper and wilder – and it was then, under that sky, that Naomi's summons came to him.

Instantly calling a halt, he raced back through the close-gathered ranks of his army. He bent over Naomi's stretcher and lifted her up. He could scarcely see her face, so shrouded was she in blankets, but the sound of her labored breathing seemed to fill his whole world. In his arms he could feel her struggle to draw each breath.

"Beloved," he said, and could say no more. As the wind whipped the beautiful word away, it sounded in his ears like the essence of desolation. But now, astonishingly, with great effort, Naomi was speaking to him. She spoke in a harsh whisper, gasping for breath between words.

"You... must not... seek God... to find me," she said. "God... only God... not me." A dreadful paroxysm of coughing shook her. Afterward she could only gasp for long moments, but at last she spoke again. "Dying... but death is... not the end. Love... of God... beyond all. Yet Jonathan... even my love... stronger... stronger... than death. Love... stronger... than death. God... only... God... not... me."

She coughed dreadfully again. Afterwards she could not seem to breathe. Her stiffly-held form relaxed in Jonathan's arms. "Naomi!" he cried. "Naomi, breathe, wake – speak to me!" After a terrible moment she did begin breathing again, the same labored breaths as before, but she was no longer conscious.

Jonathan laid her back in the stretcher and turned to the men who carried it. "Take her down!" he cried. "Take her back down to the Luciyr Road! Hurry!"

He stood back from the stretcher. Forms were busy about it, including his father and mother. There was some talk, some exchanging of clothes and supplies. None of it made sense to Jonathan. His mother came and embraced him. He held her tightly, remembering that he would never see her again, but he did not hear what she said to him, and he said nothing in return. None of it seemed real. He wondered at the length of time they were taking to obey his orders. Then at last, with haste that comforted him a little, the bearers began going down the mountain. His mother followed them. She had not been able to hold the uphill pace, he remembered, and had been carried herself since midday – but now she was hastening down on her own feet, easily keeping pace with those who carried Naomi. He marveled dully at her strength.

Then he was running to the head of the army, shouting out some words of courage and strength, urging his men on through the moonlight and the bitter wind. He had forgotten why he was doing it. He could not remember any reason to do anything. Only his will, holding to the decision he had made back in Carrah, forced him on through his stupefying grief.

Chapter 16

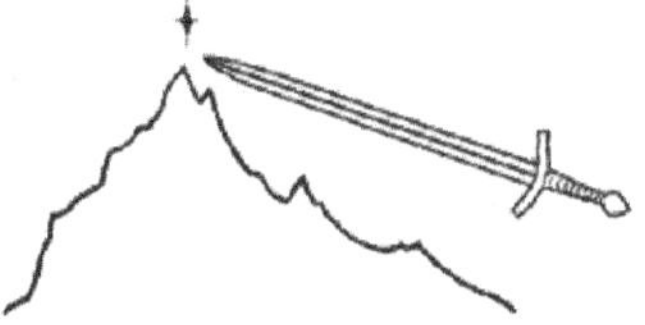

In Hannah's Hands

HANNAH AWOKE AT MIDDAY WITH A FEELING OF SICK sorrow in her heart. She let her weary memory think back as she slowly came awake. She remembered the previous day, crossing the chasm at dawn with Jonathan's army. She remembered how the ropes were frayed and the bridge was slippery with ice, and no bottom could be seen to the haunting, nightmare crack. She remembered that men had turned pale and wept and trembled, and that Jonathan had urged them on with reckless courage, ordering the steadiest and boldest to carry some of the others, until at last they were all across, and not one fell.

She remembered the grueling climb into the mountains, and how Naomi's breathing had grown worse and worse until at last she had sent one of the men who carried her to fetch Jonathan, saying she was about to die. Jonathan had given orders that she should be carried down as quickly as possible, in the hope of saving her life. Hannah, of course, had gone with her. Thus, in one terrible moment, Hannah had parted both from Jonathan – who had said nothing – and from Barnabas. She would never see either again on earth.

She remembered Barnabas' last words to her. "Alas, Beloved, another parting," he had said. "Yet this, I believe, shall be the last. When next I see you, it will be where there is no more parting."

"Still I wish I could come with you, even to die, like Naomi," she had replied.

"She may rally when you get to kinder air, and then she will need you," said Barnabas. "I curse Vadshron for parting us, beloved Hannah, but truly I see no other way."

"There is none, dear Barnabas," she had said. "You must go with Jonathan, as we said before, and I… I must leave you."

"If Naomi rallies, try to take her through Luciyr to Ceramir," said Barnabas. "Hide from the Zarnith by staying near the mountains, where they will not come. If she dies, bury her near Abigail's grave in Carrah, and then go to the mines of Petrag. You will be as safe there as anywhere when the Zarnith come, and there is much good that you can do."

Then Hannah and the men assigned to carry Naomi had begun hurrying down the terrible, icy mountainside, desperately trying to reach kinder air before Naomi died. They had come all the way back down, and camped at dawn, terribly exhausted, on the rock outcrop at the edge of the gorge. Hannah shook herself fully awake. That, of course, was where she was now. She lay in a low tent, wrapped in blankets, beside Naomi. She could hear Naomi's labored breathing: she was still alive! Hannah leaned over her and pulled the covers gently away from her face.

"Naomi," whispered Hannah. "Naomi, we are going to Ceramir."

Naomi opened her eyes, but they were clouded with pain, and did not seem to see Hannah. "The most terrible gift," whispered Naomi. "Choose light… You must, you must… but you are leaving me again, and I must… I must… I will let you go." Heartbreaking sobs shook her frame, and she coughed hard.

"You are delirious, Naomi," whispered Hannah, gently smoothing back her hair and massaging her shoulders. "It is only Hannah. I am taking you to the Cloth of Joy, to be healed."

"No one can heal me," said Naomi. "And he is still in darkness."

Hannah was sick with worry at Naomi's delirium, but she forced down her fear, and lifted her up and embraced her. "I love you, Naomi," she said. "And I love Jonathan. I would give my life for you. Now you should sleep." Hannah laid Naomi back down, and spread the covers over her. She lay still, except for her labored breathing.

Hannah put on her shoes and her cloak, and went out into the cold. The third mountain rose before her in immeasurable slopes of ice and rock. She threw back her head to look at its distant peak, gilded with white fire against the deep blue sky, with the blinding sun only a little above it. She scanned its awesome flanks for any sign of Jonathan and his army, and saw nothing. They were gone. The only one she could serve now was Naomi.

She considered what she must do. The Luciyr Road passed above Petrag – she remembered crossing it two days before. Yet she did not know how to reach Luciyr, and she knew even less about the second leg of the journey, through the desert. She would take Naomi to the mines of Petrag. They would have maps there, and people who could tell her about the journey, at least as far as Luciyr. Naomi might recover a little in the comfort and warmth of the miners' rock city. Then they would take the Luciyr Road in haste. For now, she must rouse the men who would carry Naomi. They might reach the mines of Petrag that evening, if they made haste.

In a few moments Hannah had woken the men, who had slept in two tents near hers and Naomi's. They grumbled about being sore and weary, but they seemed to accept Hannah's reasoning that they must hurry to reach Petrag that day, and they could all rest once they reached it. They began a hasty breakfast in the piercing cold.

One man, young and golden haired, approached Hannah timidly. "My Lady…" he began. Hannah turned, smiling at the title he had given her.

"What is it?" she asked him.

"I did not understand, when I volunteered for the king's service in this… I did not understand that we were doomed. But if Karolan is to be destroyed and my old mother back there killed or enslaved, or whatever it is they will do to her, I do not want to be hiding in rocks in the desert. I want to fight them. I want to die fighting with the king."

Hannah was silent for a long moment. "Did the king not explain the state of things to you when he asked you to be a bearer for Naomi?" she asked.

"Yes, he did. But somehow it did not get into my head that all Karolan was doomed."

"But you promised the king that you would do what he asked, if you could?"

"Yes, my Lady. I did. I will keep that promise, too, if you do not release me from it."

Hannah looked at him pityingly. "I am sorry," she said. "If we can get horses at Petrag, I will release you. But if not, I will need all your strength for the long road to Ceramir. In that case, to obey the king, you must remain with me."

"I thank you, my Lady," he said. "I am content."

"May God bless your faithfulness," said Hannah, smiling at him. She turned away, and at that moment her eye was caught by a strange motion at the edge of the rock outcrop. An instant later, the air was full of wild cries – and of arrows. She saw four men killed before her eyes. Bewildered and panic stricken, she ran for Naomi's tent calling out her name.

The blond young man followed her. "You cannot save her!" he cried. "You must fly this instant!" She would have resisted still, but he caught and lifted her, and began to run toward the side of the outcrop. He had almost reached it when he gave a great cry and fell. Hannah tumbled with him off the outcrop and fell down upon a jagged ledge. The young man was dead, shot through with many arrows. One had come all the way through him and wounded Hannah in the back. Besides that, she was dazed and bruised by the fall.

Through her dizziness and pain, Hannah heard unfamiliar voices, and realized suddenly that she had been taken for dead. She tried to stay as limp and motionless as a corpse, as men clambered down to the ledge and dragged her roughly back onto the outcrop. They laid her on a pile of bodies – the bodies of the men who had carried Naomi. Her back was soaked with their blood, and her hands were warm and sticky with it.

She heard many heavy footsteps. "Good shooting," said a harsh, deep voice. "But now to business. Karolan is in a bad state. You would think, with nearly all the men off to war, that things would be good for us, but no. Women have crossbows and are scared and watchful, always ready to use them. Korfin and his crew found that out last week – a good haul, but three dead and a girl escaped to give the alarm. King's messengers are on all the roads, very brave and hasty and armed with swords. We lost Melfor five days ago to one of them – who rode down, if you please, four archers without a hint of fear.

"So Karolan is disappointing, for the present. This army out of Petrag is another matter. They're trying to cross the mountains, mark my words. Heltin and his lads are already shadowing them. There's a rich haul to be made from the clothes and weapons of those who freeze to death – and if that turns out to be all of them, we can make the Free Bows a force to frighten even kings. It's a dangerous game, though. If they give up and turn back in good order, they could wipe us out.

"Meanwhile, we need to think what to do about these Zarnith. We'll keep out of their way, of course – but we'll come behind them. They'll burn and pillage, but they won't take everything. What's left in their tracks will be ours. So that makes it obvious. We cross the mountains by the Dark Way, and hole up there a little east of Brightshadow. After the Zarnith go past, we follow them all the way to Norkath.

The harsh voice stopped. Hannah could hear the movements of many men around her. "What about Heltin?" asked a voice.

"You've just volunteered to take ten men and wait for him here, Korfin," said the first voice. "If the army from Petrag comes first, forget Heltin and bolt to the Dark Way."

"But Karolan is full of lonely women," said a third voice. "They don't all have crossbows. Why must we leave now? Why the Dark Way?" There were murmurs of agreement with this all around."

"I see," said the harsh voice. "Some of you think I don't lead well. Some of you would like to be Bowlord yourselves, perhaps. Well, let's crown this heap of bodies – and don't forget three of them were my kill alone." Hannah heard him come very near her. He leaned into her field of vision. She tried hard to keep her eyes glazed and fixed, but even so she saw him clearly. He had a huge head and a shaggy beard. Thick gold wire was twined in a crude circlet through his thick black hair. Yet in his hand gleamed a jewel of astonishing beauty. Hannah had to force herself not to turn her eyes toward it. It was a tremendous sapphire, flawlessly cut. It seemed to catch the light of sun and sky and concentrate them into a breathtaking flame – a blue-white star captured from heaven, languishing now in the Bowlord's hand.

"I'll just set it here," said the Bowlord. To Hannah's astonishment and fear, he placed the stone upon her chest. "The jewel of jewels for a dead hag's adornment," he laughed. His feet scraped the stone as he stood back. "Now!" he said, his voice a roar of challenge. "Is any man stronger than the Bowlord? Will any man take from me the Sapphire of Vykadrak, and the mastery of the Free Bows?"

Dead silence reigned for a long moment. At last it was broken, not by an answer from the assembled men, but by a hoarse woman's voice crying out, and then a series of dreadful coughs. Hannah heard running feet and ripping cloth. "A girl!" said a voice. "Sickly now, but must have been beautiful once."

The Bowlord turned and ran toward the tent. "We have no time for girls, sickly or not!" he said. "Cut her throat, to remove temptation."

Hannah never remembered making her decision or getting to her feet, but somehow it was made, and she was running to the edge of the chasm with the jewel in her hand, astonished that her battered body served her so well. The brigands shouted behind her, and an arrow passed her, but then she stood on the dizzying edge, and the Sapphire of Mount Vykadrak flashed blue fire in her hand. "Stop!" she cried. "Lay down your arms or I throw it away!"

"Obey!" roared the Bowlord. "She speaks the truth!"

She stood looking at them for a long moment, she as frozen as they. "If you harm the girl, I throw it into the chasm!" she cried. She prayed frantically, wondering what on earth she could do, if anything, to save Naomi and herself. Even if the brigands left them alone now, they would still die – at least Naomi would. Escaping from the brigands would not be enough – she had to force them to help her. "What is the Dark Way?" she asked. There was no answer.

"You do not understand me," said Hannah. "Everyone I loved has gone to death, except this girl. I care nothing for my life or your jewel. I must save her if I can. I am pledged to take her to a valley called Ceramir, beyond the mountains. If you do not tell me of the Dark Way, I will leap into the chasm with your sapphire." She stepped even closer to the edge, so that her foot shoved bits of gravel over.

"Your Ceramir is the valley we call Brightshadow," said the Bowlord. "For us it is a place of death. The Dark Way is a secret path under the mountains to the southern desert."

"Can you take me and the girl on this Dark Way?" she asked. "Can you bring us to Ceramir?"

The Bowlord burst into raucous laughter. "I can," he said, "but I would rather rip you into little shreds to feed to pigeons. How long will you stand there with my sapphire?"

"No longer," said Hannah, a wild yet possible plan suddenly coming to her. The rock face below her was terrifyingly exposed, but it was not sheer; there were ledges she could grip. Below her on the right was the bridge. She slid the sapphire into a pocket of her clothes and instantly began climbing down. She heard the brigands' cries of rage above her, and knew they would soon have her if she did not reach the bridge. She could feel blood trickling down her back beneath her clothes. Her head ached, and she felt weak. Yet she was climbing, climbing for Naomi's life.

She came to the bridge and started across it. Ten paces out, she turned to face the brigands now hurrying toward her. She was trembling with the tension and terror of what she was doing, and sweating with exertion despite the cold. She held the sapphire out over the rope rail of the bridge, to make it absolutely clear that if they shot her, the jewel would fall even though her body might not.

"I will hide your sapphire on the other side, and return to you," she shouted. "Bring me and the girl alive to Brightshadow, and I will tell you where it is hidden. Touch her, or seek to follow me now, and it is lost forever."

"I will torture you until you speak," said the Bowlord. "I will torture you until you wish you had never been born!"

In her desperation a new idea came to Hannah. Hidden under her clothes was the bottle of medicine for Naomi. God, she believed, had forbidden suicide – but she could threaten it. Fumbling in her clothes with her left hand, she drew out the bottle. "Here I have a swift and deadly poison," she said. "Remember I care nothing for my life. Touch me or the girl, frighten me with torture again, and I shall drink it dry and die with my secret. Take heed!" She replaced the bottle and continued across the terrible bridge, still holding the sapphire out above the abyss. She reached the other side, and sank to her knees trembling and panting.

When she was a little recovered, she began to seek a hiding place. Anywhere in the rocky desolation surrounding her might suffice, but she knew the brigands were still watching her across the chasm. She needed a place they would not see, a place they would never find without help – but also a place she could easily remember and describe.

She was weary. She had crossed the bridge as though she had no fear, but the terror of the missing planks, the bottomless chasm, and the icy wind remained with her even as she knelt upon the solid stone. She was afraid, and alone. She doubted herself fiercely. Her plan was foolish, she thought. She had abandoned Naomi. When she came back – if she could get back across that terrible bridge without falling – she would find the brigands had raped and killed Naomi. They would expose her bluff about the poison, and torture her until she told them where the sapphire was hidden. She was tired and lonely, and Barnabas and Jonathan were going to their deaths. Their farewell had been so brief, their last farewell…

"I hope." The words came back to her as she knelt, despairing, on the cold rock. She had said, "I hope," when it had seemed that she alone could truly say it. And now what right had she to let go the hope that God had given her? "There is still hope," she said in a low voice, instantly borne away on the wind.

She stood. She was tired, and her back ached dully, but her eyes and her mind were clear. And the right way to hide the sapphire was suddenly obvious to her. The blue jewel must be hidden in blue ice – frozen invisibly into a solid chunk. And there, not far away, was the vast bank of ice at the chasm edge – the ice that Jonathan had been able to see by moonlight from their camp far below.

Hannah walked steeply uphill with the chasm on her right. The ice when she reached it was hard as rock beneath her feet, and though she slipped and fell once at first, soon she was walking on with cautious grace. Presently she looked back, and the distance she had come surprised her. Through the vastness of clear air, she could see the narrow strand of the bridge spanning the chasm. She could not, at this distance, make out any brigands either on the bridge or the rock outcrop. She guessed that they could not see her either.

Happy in the knowledge that she could no longer be watched, she began looking for a good place to hide the sapphire. The strange shapes of the ice bewildered her, until she could not imagine ever remembering them well enough to describe a hiding place. Seeking to understand the broader structure of the ice, she went toward the chasm – and stopped short one step from the cliff edge. Dully she had imagined that the ice must end in a cliff, but the reality still shocked her. The ice fell away in a sheer, vertical face, making no ledge where it met the rock, which dropped sheer in its turn into inky blackness. The view of vertical ice and rock vanishing into the bottomless abyss was terrifying, dizzying. It was easy to imagine what it would be like to fall, insignificant as a windblown leaf in that terrible immensity. The wind would roar in her ears, she thought, and the cliff would seem to fly past, until she vanished into that impenetrable blackness. She supposed anyone who fell died in the end, in shattered ruin on some invisible floor of stone or ice. It was hard not to imagine, instead, that they fell forever into an infinite void.

Hannah wavered on her feet and stepped back. She knelt on the ice, out of view of the black abyss. To calm herself, she let her eyes wander the bright snow of the Third Mountain, which towered up beyond the chasm. It was then that she saw them.

Five black figures, dwarfed by the mountain to the stature of ants, were making their way slowly along its lowest slope. She gazed at them with glazed eyes for a long moment. They seemed unreal; tiny and far away. Any sound they made vanished in the vast mountain silence, so that they seemed people of a world without sound, separated from her world by an impassible gulf. Then she breathed in softly and deeply, and stood. Sound could not cross the gulf, but vision could. Those five men had been sent there to watch her. She looked behind her, wondering if watchers had also been sent across the bridge, in defiance of her ultimatum. She scanned the ice all around her very carefully, but saw no one.

She walked away from the cliff edge. The men across the chasm were below her, and so in doing this she went out of their sight. She went on a good way, wanting them to lose all knowledge of her whereabouts.

Her eyes were caught by a band of slightly different color in the ice immediately ahead. She wondered idly what it was, but she knew nothing of crevasses, and walked on it without fear.

She cried out as the snow broke under her and she fell. In an instant the terrible irony of hiding the sapphire and her own corpse forever at the bottom of a pit flashed through her mind. Then she landed painfully on her back, and realized that she had not fallen far, and had landed on hard-packed snow, unhurt. She lay there a moment, getting her breath, thanking God for her escape. Then she rose and climbed out, cutting a foothold in the ice using a small wood-carving knife she had carried since leaving Carrah. It was only when she stood again on the surface, looking at the shadowed hole she had made, that it occurred to her to hide the sapphire in a crevasse.

The crevasse into which she had fallen ran on into a larger one, partially unroofed. That crack, in turn, formed part of a whole network of crevasses, some with snow-roofs intact, and some open to the air. Hannah walked all around this network, climbing every little hummock she could find to get a better view. The pattern of cracks was chaotic, yet somehow harmonious – like the tangled ivy on a stone. She would remember it.

Looking back, she saw that her feet had left little mark on the hard ice. The place where she had fallen into the crevasse, however, was obvious: she must not hide the jewel anywhere near there. She found a place where a crevasse with a hard ice floor offered a sort of stairway down under a solid snow roof. Taking great care to leave no marks, she passed down into the alien world beneath the ice.

She could see clearly, once her eyes adapted, by the faint blue light that filtered through the snow. Some of the crevasses had floors of hard-packed snow, while others vanished into blackness. She explored the strange labyrinth, testing every step of the floor with a careful leading foot, even climbing along some of the unfloored crevasses by means of ice boulders she found firmly wedged in them. Often she retraced her steps, wanting to memorize the pattern from below just as she had from above. At last she selected a place. Deep in one narrow crevasse, a slow stream flowed over an ice floor. Where that crevasse joined a wider one, the water cascaded into a black pit. There was no way to reach that small crevasse without climbing over the pit. Besides that, there was the uninviting, frigid stream, which would also obliterate any traces she might leave. Hannah removed her shoes to keep them dry. Barefoot in the bitter cold, trying not to think about the blackness below, she climbed from one wedged boulder to another until at last she could step into the inaccessible crevasse from which the stream fell. Far back, where the crevasse was so narrow she could barely squeeze through, and so dark that she could scarcely see, she found a large, solid ice boulder wedged at her head level.

Again, she took the knife from her belt. She bored a hole into the boulder, as deep as the knife would go, carefully catching the ice-shavings in her cloak. She took the incomparable sapphire from her pocket, and without sparing it even a glance she forced it to the back of her hole. She gathered the shavings in her hands, breathed on them to make them wet, and crammed them into the hole. They would freeze again into solid, contiguous ice. She hurried back down the stream and up the wedged boulders. Gratefully she plunged her numbed feet back into wool stockings and shoes.

She threaded her way unerringly through the labyrinth, and emerged into the daylight. She hurried up toward the cliff edge, looking all around to see that she was unobserved. When she reached the edge, she again saw ant-like figures on the slope of the Third Mountain. She walked about in their view for a while, kneeling now and then to feign interest in a particular part of the ice. Then at last she started back to the bridge. It was done. She had hidden the Sapphire of Mount Vykadrak where no one would find it without her aid, though they searched for a thousand years. Now she only had to get back to Naomi, and to whatever fate awaited them both.

When she reached the bridge, the sun was already far down behind the mountains, and the shadow of the great peaks was dark and cold upon her. The wind that always blew along the chasm was howling now, and the bridge was swaying horribly. Now and then fragments of ice cracked off the ropes or planks, and flew away in the wild wind.

Hannah wondered how she had ever crossed that bridge. She remembered that she was Hannah of Glen Carrah, a humble blacksmith's wife, herself a worker in wood and leather. She was no heroine, no queen. In her weariness, all that she had done that day suddenly seemed a dream. She was Hannah of Glen Carrah; she could not do such things. She could not cross that bridge.

"...it fell because Mer was true while her world broke around her. I know another woman who was as faithful."

She seemed to hear Barnabas' voice saying those words of high praise to her now, to encourage her in her need. And her own answer, too, she remembered: "The slab fell because God willed it so. And for that reason also four children and one woman were saved, of all of Glen Carrah."

"So it is," said Hannah. "It is done by his power, to his praise. But we are foolish if we think he cannot use our feeble faith, even while our world is breaking, to accomplish things beyond our dreams."

Then suddenly she felt sick, because she must cross the bridge. It was possible, it was necessary; there was no escape. "Naomi," she said. "Naomi lies on the other side of that bridge, at the mercy of terrible men, protected only by their greed. If they give their sapphire up for lost, she is lost... And whatever happens she is sick and cold and frightened and alone. I will go to her."

She put her first foot on the bridge, and could feel the tremors and shakes of the whole structure, in the gale of wind that now blew down the mighty crack. "Father, help me," she said. Trembling, she took another step.

She walked on, thinking only of the planks before her feet and the ropes in each of her hands, until she got about thirty paces out. Then the terror of her position struck her again. She was only thirty paces away from the solid rock, but a journey of many days elsewhere might well be less perilous than that little distance. Below her was the blackness of the abyss. She wondered if the souls of those who fell into that could ever rise to Heaven. The wind wailed, and worried the bridge like a dog with its bone. Far up ahead of her a plank blew loose and fell, flying down and away in the icy wind: no sound of impact ever heard. "Father, I trust you, and I love Naomi, and this fear is only foolishness," she said.

Then she went on, slowly, carefully, considering each step before she made it, moving with cautious grace. Soon she was at the center of the bridge, where the wind was as its worst, and the gusts changed her balance unpredictably. Several times her feet slipped and she was saved from falling only by her death-grip on the hand ropes. She remembered that she had crossed with only one hand on a rope before, holding out the sapphire in the other. She calmly accepted the fact that she had been stronger then, and went on. At last the swaying decreased. Her face, numbed by the wind, began again to derive some warmth from her furred hood. Then her feet were on the blessed solid rock, and she had crossed the gulf.

One dark, wild figure came to meet her in the deepening dusk. She could still see a dim gleam of gold in his hair. She felt she ought to challenge him, but her voice when she spoke trembled. "I have hidden the Sapphire of Mount Vykadrak," she said. "If you bring the girl and myself to the valley of Brightshadow, unharmed and unmolested, I will tell you where it is, and you will easily find it. Without my guidance you will seek in vain, though you search for a thousand years."

The hulking figure of the brigand-king turned his back on Hannah and addressed his unseen followers. "Fools and simpletons," he roared. "She has come back, as I foretold – and you would have raped or slain the girl! This hag has courage and wisdom. She will keep her pledge – I hear it in her voice. Yes, it smarts to be thus bested by a woman, but it is only thanks to our strength and boldness that we can do as she asks. None but we can tread the Dark Way. We shall do it now, and the hag and girl will be but added baggage. In the end, we shall regain the sapphire – and the bows and swords of the army from Petrag shall be ours also."

"I say she never hid it at all!" cried a voice. "Strip her and search her, and if she has it, kill her. What if we do all she asks, and she just walks away without–" The man's speech was cut short by an agonized cry. Almost without changing his stance, the Bowlord had thrown a knife that took him through the heart. Now he was drawing another from his belt.

"Are there any other questions?" asked the Bowlord. "The hag will, in the end, trade the sapphire for her life. If she does not, or we find it without her, we will tear her to shreds. For the present, we set out at dawn to take her and the girl on the Dark Way. Have the watchers returned? Good. Let them remain with Korfin and search for the sapphire until Heltin returns. Korfin, if the sapphire is found, do your best to overtake us on the Dark Way. We wouldn't want the hag to escape her just reward."

Only the wind spoke in the falling night. Hannah shuddered at the Bowlord's cruelty and hatred, but was thankful that she seemed to have won his respect. She went to Naomi's tent. The fabric had been slashed open. Naomi was lying in a strange position inside. Her hands were ice cold, but her body was warm and she seemed to breathe easier than she had that morning. She was somewhere between sleep and delirium, but somehow Hannah made her drink a little without choking. Hannah herself was ravenously hungry, but after taking only a little food she found herself unable to eat more. She tied a blanket across the tears in the tent, shifted Naomi into a more comfortable-looking posture, and lay down beside her. She slept fitfully, her hand always on the bottle of poison, alert to any sounds around the tent.

Chapter 17

Fainting Before Murderers

AS THAT SAME NIGHT FELL HIGH UP ON THE THIRD Mountain, Jonathan could feel his army's courage faltering. Thus far the men had done well. A few hours after Naomi's departure he had allowed them to sleep, huddled together in tents on the bitter mountainside. Even he himself had slipped into a black unconsciousness shot through with nightmares. He had awakened in the icy dawn and struggled out of his tent. Golden clouds had shone achingly bright in the east, even while cold stars still gleamed above – and he had roused his men at once to eat quickly and break camp by sunrise.

All that day they had climbed higher, and the alien majesty of the mountain world had pressed upon them. The mountains struck at the very foundation of their life: their breath itself. Even the strongest now panted and wheezed in the harsh, cold air. Every hour they climbed it grew worse. Men who at first had exulted in the strange world to which their strength had brought them now gazed round as if watching for the attack of a ruthless foe. The mountains were killing them slowly, snuffing out their lives with unbreathable air and with the vast weight of awe – with their immeasurable size and their savage grandeur.

Now the day was ending and icy darkness was coming on the world. Exhausted men lagged behind the main army, losing the tight formation Jonathan had commanded. Sometimes a man would slip, and crawl for a little before struggling again to his feet. Others cowered down to shut out the sight of the mountains and the sky. Jonathan did not scorn them, for he and Ilohan had felt that terror, and even now it touched him. He knew they had left behind the only world where they could live. But in his despair over Naomi, Jonathan had lost fear along with hope. The mountains' terror could do no more than brush his thoughts, locked as they were in the iron of his despair – and his decision.

He forced the men on, not slowing the pace for those who lagged. Sometimes he dragged stragglers bodily up the mountainside, until for pure shame they found strength to keep onward and keep up. Iron determination seemed to give him inexhaustible strength. He seemed to his men more than human: a merciless, tireless archangel, leading them where mortals could not go – leading them up to die in a frozen world above the stars.

In reality Jonathan was weary, though he did not allow himself to show the slightest sign of it. The state of his men worried him. He guessed that even if they held their pace all night without sleep, they would not reach the pass until late the next day. If they slept here, on the other hand, they would die of cold. For a moment he let his mind consider the futility of it all. This was not his mission, not a mission to defend Naomi or avenge her. Naomi was lost forever. This was Ilohan's mission. And whether it succeeded or failed, there was no hope. All that he had ever loved would perish. Ceramir would fall. He and his father would die defending it. Ilohan would be routed at Drantar's Gap and Karolan would fall. The citadel of Aaronkal would be captured; Luciyr and the ashes of Carrah would be overrun. Somewhere in the chaos, Zarnith warriors would hunt down his mother and kill her without mercy… Inevitable loss, regardless of what he did in the present crisis.

Crunch, crunch, the sound of his footsteps on the snow. He was still climbing. A man slipped and began crawling not far away. Jonathan ran to him and heaved him up. He had said to himself that this was not his mission, but that was a lie, he knew. It was his, for he had won it from Ilohan. He had nothing else. So he would succeed. No hope beckoned him forward – but his choice, his word given to the king, and his own merciless determination drove him on. He renewed his decision to keep on, no matter what it cost him. And the men of his army marveled once again at his courage and strength.

He pushed on through the moonlit night. Sometimes he would walk behind, attending to the stragglers. Some he rebuked with blistering diatribes until their shame and anger drove them to greater effort. Some were truly near the edge of their strength – and he commanded stronger men to aid them.

At other times Jonathan went to the head of his army and called back words of courage and strength for all. Though he paused now and then to gasp for breath, still his voice came warm and strong through the bitter air. He gave the longest of these speeches when the near-full moon had just passed the zenith, and it seemed the night would last forever. "The Zarnith are coming," he cried. "King Ilohan conceived this mission, and we accepted it. We must fulfill it now or be forsworn. We are the strong – we are those who crossed the chasm. We cannot now turn back with honor. We cannot turn back and still hold up our heads. But even if we had the choice, would we return? Those back in Karolan can choose to hide in caves, to see their homes ravaged and overrun, to be hunted down at last or slain by hunger. Or they can choose to die as heroes in the last defense at Drantar's Gap, where they will see the King of Karolan and the royal banner fall forever. But we – we will face Vadshron's first mighty charge; we before all others will bring death to those who come to kill our land. We will die as heroes defending Queen Mother Eleanor, and the maiden Veril, who in happier days King Ilohan chose to carry on his line.

"The terror of the mountains weighs on us now, and we feel the agony of our weary journey. The choice now seems less clear than it once did. But back in Karolan, if you could return there, you would find it ever clearer, until regret for your returning seemed to blot out the sun. I know of what I speak. To surrender to despair, to falter in the chosen task – there is no greater agony or shame. So onward! The mountains terrify? We defy them! The cold chills us? Our courage shall warm us! The air is harsh? We breathe it yet! Our bodies fail us? They are slaves that must obey our will!

"Men of Karolan; heroes, warriors, dauntless travelers! It is not peace or victory or even fame to which we go, only glory. None but the Zarnith may be left to remember our valiance. Let us make them remember it indeed! Let us cross the mountains and come to Ceramir with strength beyond Vadshron's dreams!

As the glowing words faded from the air, Jonathan trudged on through the darkness, thinking how worthless he now considered the glory he had spoken of. Yet, worthless as it was, it was the only thing he could still win.

The age-long night went on as before, with Jonathan sometimes in the rear, encouraging the stragglers; sometimes in the front, calling back his speeches of undying courage; and sometimes at the side, alone, wrapped in the darkness of his hopeless thoughts. The night went on, and Jonathan led five score and a thousand men, and they followed him to the edge of their strength and beyond. The mountain dawn broke over them with its unearthly splendor, and still they followed him. They followed him through air that made them gasp for breath even when resting. They followed him through a land so strange and high that they felt even the stars must have been left below, in the blue haze that covered Karolan. The cold grew so intense that they felt they must also have climbed beyond the sun, and they marveled to see it, still above them, blindingly bright but cold as a winter star. They followed Jonathan, though they wavered on their feet, though strange visions flocked against the closed lids of their eyes when they blinked. At last, with the sun still high above the peaks of ice, they reached the pass: the Pass Among the Stars. They fell in heaps upon the barren snow, gasping for breath, overwhelmed by what they had done.

But even then Jonathan gave them no mercy. To rest at that pass was death. Though he himself was almost too weary to stand, he called them up with ruthless words. Only the strongest rose. Jonathan looked down off the far side of the pass. It fell away far more steeply than the northward face they had just climbed – he could remember now how he and Ilohan had struggled there, using both hands and feet to finish the climb. But the snow was deeper now: few rocks protruded from it. Jonathan grasped a fallen man by his clothes and dragged him off the brink. The man slid and tumbled at an alarming speed, but at last, scores of paces down, he came to a stop and staggered drunkenly to his feet. Jonathan did the same with another of the men who had not risen at his command. Soon the others who remained on their feet were doing the same. Dozens of exhausted men found themselves tumbling ignominiously down the mountainside. Others staggered up to escape this fate.

But many remained in crumpled heaps at the pass. Of those who were flung down, not all got to their feet. They slid widely varying distances, and thus were scattered over the mountainside. Jonathan turned and scanned those who were still standing at the pass. Among them he saw Barnabas, gasping, hunched forward with his hands on his knees, but determined not to collapse.

"Father," cried Jonathan, "take the men on this side and go down – go down and gather together those I send to you. Men of Karolan, obey this man as you would me until I come to you."

Barnabas staggered down the far side of the pass, together with the several scores of men Jonathan had indicated. Jonathan and those who remained with him continued flinging the fallen down from the pass. The labor was an agony. Many who had reached the pass standing collapsed after sliding one or two of their comrades down. Some of these struggled up again; others had to be slid down themselves. Jonathan himself neared collapse. The bright snow seemed to pulsate and waver before his eyes. His breath came in great gasps, and the iron taste of blood was stronger in his mouth than he ever remembered it before. The air was torturing him, making things impossible that would have been easy for him down in the world of men. But he would not collapse. To his men he must remain the tireless leader, immune to human frailty, giving orders with authority and wisdom to the last.

He gazed around the pass with his dazed vision. It was empty of fallen men. Those who had worked with him were starting down toward Barnabas. He followed them – the last to leave the Pass Among the Stars.

Jonathan's vision cleared as he trudged down from the deadly pass, to where Barnabas had gathered most of the army together into ordered ranks. There were black heaps beside those ranks, however: the men who had not risen when they were slid down from the pass. Jonathan knelt beside one of them. The man was not dead, any more than Ilohan had been when he collapsed at the Pass Among the Stars. Ripping blankets and rope out of the man's own pack, Jonathan wrapped him up and knotted the rope around the blankets. He left a loop free by which the man could be pulled.

"Men of Karolan," said Jonathan. "Thus we can drag our companions, and not abandon them. Do now as I have done." The men obeyed, moving clumsily in their exhaustion. None questioned Jonathan's implication that for those who had not collapsed, there was still to be no rest.

"Now," said Jonathan when the work was done, "it is death to camp this high. We must descend. But fear not! We shall rest soon." Dazed with fatigue, the men followed him. The strongest of the strong, brave men who had taken the task on themselves, dragged the fallen. Jonathan, of course, took one of them. The unconscious, blanket-shrouded figure continually slid ahead of him on the steep slope, sometimes yanking him so hard that he fell and slid several paces down himself. The others found their burdens equally difficult. Despite this, they could descend far faster than they had climbed – and Jonathan urged them on at the swiftest pace he thought they could endure.

At last, as the sun sank over the western peaks and then was covered by thick, fast flying cloud, they reached a flat shoulder far down the great mountain. They halted and stood dazed, reeling on their feet. Jonathan felt weariness like a crushing burden across his shoulders, depriving him of the strength to raise his head or take another step. He did raise his head, however, to gaze at the lowering clouds. Their import slowly dawned on him.

"Pitch the tents!" he cried. "A storm is coming. Work quickly!" Before they were finished the storm struck. Wind howled out of the east, laden with blinding snow. Jonathan kept working, setting up one tent single-handedly. He called out into the gale, and men came crowding to the tent – a dozen where it was meant to house six, but at least they would be warm. Jonathan found another tent and pitched it too, alone. He cried out again for men to occupy it. None answered. There had been some stragglers as they came down, he knew – some who still needed shelter. They had vanished into the snow-filled night, and did not heed or hear his call. He realized that he had no certainty himself of finding another tent in the blind night, and that if he slept alone he would freeze. At that moment he heard cries out in the darkness, and answered them as loudly as he could. Four men came, dragging six more who had collapsed. Jonathan helped them all into the tent and then crumpled to the floor among them. Sleep beckoned him like a promise of paradise. Rejecting it, he crawled to the door and staggered to his feet.

"Stay here, Jonathan," said a voice.

"But other men are lost out in the snow," he said. Someone grabbed his shoulders and pulled him back down onto the tent floor. He ordered himself desperately to get up, but his body would not obey. His thoughts merged into a shadowy dream –

and then deep sleep descended, and even the will of Jonathan of Glen Carrah could not hold it back. Barnabas slept beside him, having saved his life.

* * *

Rain fell hard over Aaronkal, sheeting down with the gusts of an easterly wind. The wild spring night held promise for plants and flowers, but it was cheerless for the men of the great army gathered before the castle. Benther and the king sloshed on foot through the sodden camp. They ordered bonfires kindled hot and high so that the drenching rain could not extinguish them. Many of the tents were waterproof, but some were not, and dripping men gathered round the roaring fires.

When Benther and King Ilohan went back into the castle, they found the lower halls full of wet people crowding up to the wide hearths. They passed these by, and continued up to a council room, which also boasted a good fire. They crowded near it just like the soldiers and peasants below. The king took off his cloak and crown, and squeezed water from his dripping hair. "The wind blows hard," he said.

"Still Andokar will not give us leave to cross his border," said Benther.

"May we not forget our hopelessness even for a moment?" asked Ilohan. "The rains of spring water the earth, and the greatest army Karolan has ever known gathers before the gate."

"We may forget our problems, Your Majesty, but did we not come here to discuss them?" asked Benther.

Ilohan became grave. "It is true," he said. "I rejoiced like a child in the rain and the greatness of our army, but laughter will not win our battles. We should have marched today, had

Andokar been wiser. Alas. The Zarnith will have Drantar's Gap before they clash swords with a single defender. With the hills of Norkath rolling down before them to the fertile plains, they will be as unstoppable as the sunrise."

"I see as little hope as Your Majesty," said Benther, "but we must try something."

The king drew his sword, and laid it down on the table before him. "Though all the flowers of Karolan will be trampled at last, let us see to it that there are fewer feet to trample them than Vadshron dreams," he said. "We will march tomorrow for the border, and wait there until Andokar beckons us across."

"To where on the border would Your Majesty march?" asked Benther.

"To the castle of Felrin in the hills," said King Ilohan.

"That leaves Aaronkal and the heartland of Karolan open to Norkath assault," said Benther.

Ilohan hesitated a moment. "Curse Andokar for a viler traitor even than the Unknighted if he attempts it," he said at last. "Yet I do not alter my choice."

"My own thought confirms Your Majesty's decision," said Benther. "We have no leisure to fear anyone but Vadshron. What do you expect of the future?"

"What do you mean, Sir Benther?" asked Ilohan. "I expect the destruction of my life and all that I love on earth. I hope for a miracle from the hand of God to prevent this. What else can I say?"

"What do you expect will cause Andokar to believe in the Zarnith and let us cross the border?" asked Benther.

King Ilohan gazed for a long time into the red coals of the fire. "He may receive a messenger of doom," he said at last. "If not, the Zarnith will come without warning upon his southern villages. When the first fugitives come flying north with their tales of merciless destruction, he will believe."

"Then it will be too late, Your Majesty."

"It has always been too late," said King Ilohan.

"So we will march south and east to the border," said Benther, "leaving the heart of Karolan unprotected from Norkath invasion. We will wait there for a summons from Andokar which we know will come too late. And this, we both agree, is the best plan we can make. I could almost laugh, if the jest were not so bitter."

"At least there may be some bitterness in it for the Zarnith also," said Ilohan. "And Andokar will not invade us. He has been acting like a fool, but he is no scoundrel."

Both were silent for a moment. The sound of rain and thunder came faint and distant through the thick walls of the castle, and the fire flickered in a draught. The decision they had just made seemed to Ilohan like a door slammed shut behind him, leaving him in another world. He would lead the Army of All Karolan out to fight its last battle, and from tomorrow until the end he would live in the war camp, traveling ever farther from a homeland he would never see again. "You have chosen as Prince Kindrach would," said Benther.

Then sudden bitterness came upon Ilohan, and he said, "Prince Kindrach would not have left the defense of his beloved to another."

"Prince Kindrach would not have deserted his people," said Benther.

"Let us speak no more of this," said Ilohan.

"Very well, Your Majesty. We march tomorrow. Now, is there anything else to discuss?"

"There is the ancient legend you mentioned to me," said Ilohan. "I have spoken with the sages, and even read some of the records myself. It is haunting."

"The legend concerning the third charge of the Zarnith?" asked Benther.

"Yes," said Ilohan. "If, in open battle, their first and second charges are broken, the third charge will be different. The legends speak of a mighty power, full of dread, that comes to aid the Zarnith."

"Is it not said that no one in history has broken a Zarnith charge?" asked Benther.

"It is," said Ilohan.

"Then the thing of which this legend speaks has never happened," said Benther. "But even if the records said it had, why should we believe them? Is it not just such a story as the Zarnith might spread abroad to strike fear into their foes?"

"I hope it is only that," said Ilohan. "You hearten me, and I thank you. You may go now, and may God bless your sleep."

Benther bowed and went out. Ilohan sat alone for a long time. He had forbidden Benther to try to comfort him any more concerning Veril, but she was never far from his thoughts. He longed for her most painfully now, but he felt that in letting Jonathan take his place he had deserted her. He had given Jonathan a message for her, on that terrible morning. The memory was shrouded in sorrow, and he was not sure of all that he had written – but he knew he had asked her to flee the Zarnith, with Brogal if he were willing. He supposed that there might be some such flight of the last remnant of the Cloth of Joy, but he did not know if Veril would go with them. She might choose to die with her people: with Lady Eleanor, and the children, and others who could not fly. Even if she did try to escape, how could she? If she went east, the Zarnith would find her; north, and she would die in the mountains; west, and she would be enslaved in Cembar. South there was only the desert. She could not escape.

The king nodded in his chair, and woke suddenly to see that the ashes of the fire were gray, and he was cold, and the white light of early morning came dimly down the chimney. He stood. "Alas, day comes, and I have slept ill and have no strength," he said.

"Father," he prayed, "even now, in my weakness and my folly, be with me and be my strength – not for any worthiness of mine, but because of your great love." Then he walked a little stiffly to the door, opened it in a swift motion, and went out to meet the day.

* * *

Hannah awoke in a darkness that was filled with thunder. She and Naomi were together in a stretcher, and the tight cloth around her head prevented her from seeing out. She wondered how long she had been asleep. The motion of the stretcher as it was carried had changed greatly from what she remembered before. She was furious with herself for sleeping so long: the brigands could have stolen the bottle of poison that was her frail defense against torture. She felt for it under her clothes and found it intact – and kept her hand clasped round it.

Hannah felt that it must be well past dawn – but they were far underground. The Dark Way was called so for good reason. She remembered the previous day's swift journey. The brigands had gone east along the great chasm, and descended by a narrow ledge into a smaller crack that joined it. At the beginning Hannah had refused to be blindfolded and carried, but on that tortuous path she had not been able to keep up with the Bowlord and his followers, burdened though they were with Naomi. They had put Hannah in the stretcher too, added more bearers, and, astonishingly, continued onward as fast as before. The wide cloth of the stretcher had sagged down under the combined weight, cutting off Hannah's view almost as a blindfold would have done. She could still remember, however, the glimpse she had caught of the dark, rugged stone shutting out the sky when they entered the Dark Way in earnest.

But now – what was happening now? The thunder had become very loud, and for some moments the stretcher had been swaying and swinging very strangely. It was impossible that they were still being carried over land – more likely they were hanging from ropes. She wondered what new danger or treachery that could mean.

Suddenly the stretcher tilted steeply, and Hannah heard men out in the blackness shouting with urgency and dismay. She grasped Naomi tightly as they slid together toward the end of the stretcher. Her feet emerged from the cloth into frigid air. Still holding desperately to Naomi, Hannah got her head free of the cloth and out into the icy darkness. She blinked, trying to make sense of what she saw around her. The stretcher was still swaying and bouncing oddly, and the thunderous roar filled her ears. High above her in the cavernous blackness were some yellow torches, moving erratically, shining on men who seemed to be frantically working on some difficult task that involved ropes. The torchlight also shone fitfully on vertical black rock above their heads. Much closer to her there was a strange continuous movement that she could not understand. It was as if white feathers were falling fast, with now and then among them something that inexplicably glinted or flashed.

Suddenly she understood. It was a waterfall, a great waterfall in a cavernous space beneath the mountains. The brigands were lifting her and Naomi up beside it on a long rope. Panic clutched at her heart as she pictured what must be below them: a nightmare plunge into thunderous darkness. She lay back in the stretcher and tried to wedge herself and Naomi in as tightly as possible. Ropes groaned and popped in the darkness around her, but she did not feel much motion. Hannah wondered what the men were doing. She wondered whether she truly was hanging in space over a mighty waterfall in a cave beneath the mountains. Perhaps it was all a nightmare – perhaps she would wake up to see Barnabas sleeping soundly beside her in Glen Carrah.

A rope snapped with a crack – she heard the flying end of it whistle past – and the stretcher jolted beneath her. She screamed as she and Naomi slid out into the freezing blackness. But rather than plunging with the water into an awful pit, she found that they were sliding swiftly over steeply tilted wood planking. They struck something soft, and stopped. The thing they had struck moved a little and groaned with the voice of a man. The planking swayed horribly beneath them. Hannah felt sick with fear, and the blackness and uncertainty of everything oppressed her.

With a sudden change in perspective, she thought of the man in front of her. She knew from the sound of his groans that he was badly injured. Their sliding into him could not have done that; it had to have been something much worse that had already happened. The wood around her and Naomi had a comforting curvature that suggested they were not about to fall off. Hannah shifted her weight, preparing to crawl down and see if she could do anything for the injured man. She hesitated, fighting her fear and her disinclination to show the ruthless brigands any mercy. Just then another rope snapped, and the world turned upside down. Hannah found herself and Naomi draped over a stout wooden beam, swaying crazily. There was no question now that what lay below them was the roaring black void. Hannah held Naomi and herself against the beam with a desperate strength that made the wood dig painfully into their ribs.

From above came a sound of heavy things shifting and thudding against wood. A voice roared, "Heave!" just above her head. The world turned upside down again, and Hannah and Naomi fell back onto the planking. The groaning man was nowhere to be found. Hannah lay still, breathing hard. The wood beneath her was still rocking and steeply tilted, yet she reveled in the solidness of it: a floor between her and the void.

When she had lain there a while, she noticed that torchlight now illuminated her surroundings. She raised her head and saw that she was lying on the bottom of a long, narrow boat with beams across it for seats and footrests, and oars hung beside them. The man who held the torch was just placing a large hook with a rope attached to it under one of the beams. He jammed it firmly and then called again, "Heave!" The boat came level again. There was a whizzing in the air and a loud bang as another hook with a rope attached landed on the bottom of the boat. It, too, was forced strongly into a beam, and then the ropes groaned even above the roar of the waterfall, and the boat began to rise. Hannah pulled Naomi back into the stretcher, which lay on the bottom of the boat just in front of them, and pulled the heavy cloth over them both. She held Naomi in her arms, closed her eyes against the torch-lit darkness, and prayed. Soon the boat began grinding and scraping against rock. Hannah could hear men yelling and working hard around it. Then there was a splash and a different grinding sound, followed by the sound of swift water rushing underneath. They had reached the top of the waterfall.

Hannah heard shouted orders, and then felt the boat rock as men clambered into it. A rhythmic pattern of sound and motion told her that the boat was now underway. Hannah guessed that the Bowlord's men were pulling it upstream along a swift and narrow channel.

Suddenly Hannah felt Naomi shift in her arms. "Where are we, Hannah?" she whispered faintly. Hannah's heart filled with surprise and delight. Naomi had not been conscious since the morning they were captured by the Bowlord, and now she sounded not only conscious but clearheaded.

"In the care of God," said Hannah.

"I remember – there…" Naomi said a good deal more, but in such a low whisper that it was lost in the rushing of water beneath the keel. Hannah moved her ear nearer Naomi's mouth. "Say it again, child," she said. "I could not hear you over the noise of the river."

"I remember there were many evil men," said Naomi. "And I saw you lying on a heap of bodies, and I screamed…" Naomi panted for breath, tired even by the small effort of speaking in a whisper. "…unless it was all a dream… No, I think it was not. Are we captives, or – no, it cannot be that we are dead. Are we captives?"

"No, child, we are not captives. But I hid a sapphire, a treasure of these men, in a place where they cannot find it without my help. I have promised to tell them where it is, if they bring us to the other side of the mountains. They are carrying us now, by their own secret way. It goes under the mountains, through caves and cracks I think, so it will not go up into the harsh air that you cannot breathe. They will take us to the Cloth of Joy."

"I remember... I remember..." Naomi shuddered. "...no, it must have been an evil dream."

"Tell me, child, if it would ease you."

"In my dream you... you left me, and evil men came and gathered around me... they looked down on me as I lay twisted on the ground. I had no strength to move... I was afraid and prayed. I sank into darkness, and I was afraid. There is so much darkness."

"You are in the hands of God, Naomi, and he will keep you," said Hannah.

"Was it a dream, Hannah?" whispered Naomi, and Hannah could feel her body tense in her arms as she said it.

"No, child. I did leave you, but not without protecting you as best I could. And I returned to you when I had hidden the sapphire. My chance to hide it was the gift God gave us to rescue us from the power of these men. It put them in my power instead."

Once more Naomi trembled and stiffened in Hannah's arms. "Hannah..." she whispered. "They wanted to rape me. They stood around me and mocked me... and said that as soon as I slept they would... Hannah, I have slept! Have they done it?"

"Though they had you would be innocent, and, in my eyes and the eyes of Jonathan, pure! But Naomi, dear child," Hannah held her tightly, "they did not. Oh child, in that time greed and pride, black sins though they are, stood over you and protected you like angels, for they were stronger than lust. No, the men of the brigand Bowlord did not touch you. I commanded that they must not, on pain of the sapphire's eternal loss. I would have known, child, if they had."

"Oh Father," said Naomi, "Father, I thank you! And I thank you, Hannah. You have cared for me so well. You have been to me... a mother..." Her whisper was weakening, and it seemed to Hannah that she could feel her sinking back toward darkness and delirium in her arms. Her body relaxed, and her speech slurred. "Are we going to look for Jonathan?" she breathed.

"Yes, child," said Hannah.

And Naomi slept.

But Hannah wondered on for a long time, forgetting that she was being taken up a swift, icy river under the vast mountains of Karolan. It must have been terrible for Naomi, she thought, to be sick and helpless, sinking toward delirium with the brigands taunting her. And yet, Hannah guessed that even then God had given her some measure of peace as she prayed.

"I thank you, Father," said Hannah. "I also was afraid for her, and yet you protected her, and now we may even reach the Cloth of Joy, because of your great power and love. Guard and keep us still as you have kept us up to now… watch over Barnabas and Jonathan, Lord God, and by your great power defend them and the Cloth of Joy… and turn the Zarnith back, dismayed."

Then Hannah was silent, and despite her hopeful words the darkness oppressed her. Their position seemed to her almost absurdly insecure: alone in the hands of unfriendly men, on a dangerous path of which they knew nothing. Their destination would be sacked and utterly destroyed before they reached it. They were… they were… "In the hands of God," said Hannah to herself. She rested in him in the darkness, and she turned her thoughts to calm and lovely things. She remembered watching sunsets with Barnabas when they were young together. She remembered Jonathan as a young child, her pride and joy, before she knew he would not share her faith. She remembered the wet gray morning when Barnabas rode home from King Thomas's invasion, and she ran out into his arms, and they stood there holding one another while the rain fell around them. The darkness and peril were real, but so was the goodness of the past… and the love of God.

Chapter 18

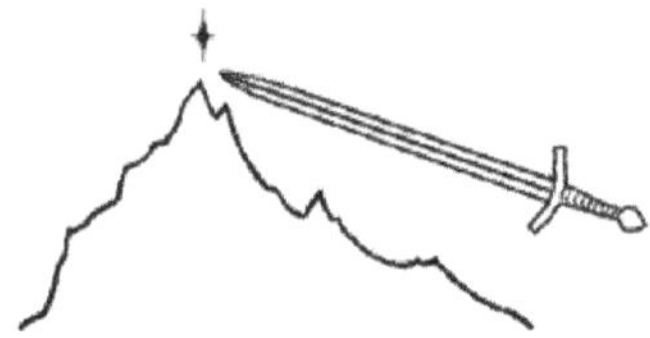

The Tireless Commander

THE KING HAD COMMANDED A BLAST OF TRUMPETS, AND all possible finery and glory, for the last march of the Army of All Karolan. As at all times through Karolan's history, the army consisted not of professional soldiers but simply of all the men of Karolan who dared muster to the king's banner. But the people loved and trusted Ilohan as they had not other kings, and he had hidden nothing from them of the direness of the threat. And so a greater host had gathered to his banner than had ever assembled for any other king in the history of Karolan: a score of thousands, and nine thousand more. Every man of them bore a bright sword, sharp and strong. Ilohan had salvaged the weapons from Petrag, emptied the armories of every castle in the land, and asked each man to bring whatever sword he had. There was no treachery this time. This time the brave men who had gathered to defend their land were armed with the power to do it.

The night's drenching rain had given way to a gray morning. Soft mist cloaked the land, but it was not very cold. Only the deepest drifts of snow remained, now slushy and melting fast. The air was full of a smell that promised spring. It did not seem like a time to march for war. Many men thought more of plowing and planting than of the battle and death to which they marched. Ilohan, mounted regally on a great horse at the head of the army, wished for sunshine and blue sky as a setting for the brave banners and trumpets. Yet this way, he thought, had its goodness also. Through the light mist of a spring day, under a blanket of soft gray cloud, the last march of Karolan would begin as in a dream.

The king lifted his standard and swung it forward in the still air. The banner briefly unfurled, and the diamond star glimmered faintly even without the sun. Blast upon blast of trumpets sounded from every part of the army and even from the battlements of Aaronkal. King Ilohan's sword sang from its sheath, and he raised it high. With a noise like a rushing wind, a score and nine thousands of other blades were similarly drawn and raised throughout the great host. "Men of Karolan," called the king in a voice that all could hear, "choices and perplexities all past, let us cast our hope on the grace of God, and march to war." The king rode forward, with the knights-in-training clad in full armor around him, and behind them came the vast host of brave men from every common walk of life, who were the backbone of Karolan's army in her every war. The banners hung limply in the wet, still air, but the forest echoed and reechoed with clashing thunder as the king and all his host re-sheathed their blades.

Old men and women and children lined the path the army took, awed by its might and splendor. Some wept, and some cheered. Some only stood still, trying in vain to grasp the incredible thing that was happening: the great army, composed of their husbands, brothers, sons, and fathers, was for their sake marching to certain doom – doom that would swallow them all. But then, spreading from the king and his knights backwards, in a great wave of song, the anthem of Karolan roared into the still, misty air. The men marched at a good pace, the supply wagons creaked and jolted along behind their teams of strong horses, the forest rang with the war song, and not all the tears of those who watched were tears of grief.

*　　　　　*　　　　　*

Dim, yellow light, seeping through briefly opened eyelids, connecting at first with the dim memories of many nightmares. "Where am I?" A cold, high hissing sound, and a heavy smell of the breath of many men. Jonathan opened his eyes again. The light was still yellow, but now a slanting line divided his field of vision: half of it was dark. "Where am I? I must get up, that much I know… But why?" Someone groaned and shifted in his sleep. Jonathan raised his head and looked round at the sleeping bodies that crowded the tent. The knowledge of where he was and what he must do came flooding back. He did not gasp in despair as he remembered, for despair had not left him even in sleep – and now he merely remembered the causes of his agony and grief. He stood slowly and silently, his aching muscles wracked with pain. Jonathan stretched painstakingly, easing and loosening the limbs he had used with such unsparing ruthlessness. The crowded men had made the tent blessedly warm.

He went to the opening of the tent and pulled aside the flap. The piercing light of the mountain sun struck full in his face, dazzling and blinding him. He stepped out, squinting painfully. The icy air stung his face and burned in his lungs. His eyes began to adjust to the brilliance of sun on snow, and he looked around.

The sun was lowering over the western peaks: he had slept all night and far into the next day. The tents of Karolan were scattered haphazardly about, each partially buried in its own snowdrift. It had been an easterly gale, so the drifts were on that side: piled up over half the height of each tent. On the west, where, conveniently, the opening of Jonathan's own tent was located, the snow was only a handbreadth deep. The wind still blew the powdery snow in shifting patterns around the tents, making the hissing sound to which Jonathan had awakened. The slanting division between dim yellow light and blackness that he had noticed had been, of course, simply the line of the snow drift that was piled up against his tent.

Jonathan climbed a little way above the flat space on which they had camped to get a better view. He gathered his fur cloak closer around him against the cold. There seemed to be enough tents to account for most of his men. Some had perished in the storm, he knew, but perhaps not very many. He turned and looked the other way. They had come more than halfway down the Third Mountain. It towered above them now, blotting out the northern sky. Its western flank shone with the dazzling light of sun on snow, while in the east it was deeply shadowed. The sun-gilded slope that led up to the Pass Among the Stars looked fully as remote as its name implied. Though he had stood there himself only yesterday, the sight of it made Jonathan feel the idea that men could walk there and live was as fanciful as the wildest ancient legends.

He turned his gaze to the south, toward Ceramir. The high, mountain-ringed expanse of strangely sculpted ice that the Zarnith had called the 'white wildness' seemed to stretch out forever from the foot of the Third Mountain. The mountains beyond the plain might as well have been beyond the sky, so inaccessible did they look. Yet as he stared at them intently,

Jonathan did recognize one as the peak that marked the pass he and Ilohan had taken above the Cliffs of Doom. So he knew where to lead his army, if any of his men would ever awake.

He strode down to a tent, not the one he had slept in, and drew aside the flap. It was filled with sleeping men, but one, a young man dressed in a warm cloak, was standing up drinking from a water-skin. The man turned and looked at him, and Jonathan recognized one of those he had initially gathered for the invasion of Norkath. Adoration shone from the young man's face, and Jonathan realized that to this man, perhaps two years younger than himself, he was as much a hero as Nirolad. It was dreadful, he thought, that a despairing promise-breaker such as himself should be admired so. Before Jonathan could speak, the young man said, "When do we march, Sir?"

Jonathan could not bring himself to correct the false title. "As soon as we can," said Jonathan. "But I fear the men will be hard to rouse."

The young man smiled. "I have a trumpet," he said. "May I sound it?"

Jonathan, in his turn, looked in astonished admiration at the man who had brought a trumpet over the Pass Among the Stars. "I would have thought it a worthless burden on such a journey," he said, "but now, indeed, it may be the very thing that can help us. Come with me into the center of the camp, and blow the greatest blast you can."

They went out together into the dazzlingly bright, piercingly cold afternoon, and the young man blew a mighty blast in the icy air – a valiant sound that stirred even Jonathan's heart with some echo of hope or joy. All through the camp men rose up in wonder and staggered out of their tents. And Jonathan found again words of blazing courage, words like the ones that had called the defenders of Petrag to fight until the dawn. Before the sunset the camp was struck, and the weary men were marching onward. Sixteen bodies had been found beneath the snow, and perhaps a score of others had vanished in the storm. They were mourned, but the loss to the fighting force was small.

Far away, Heltin the brigand and his men came back to the Wirkriy-bridge and made their report to those fruitlessly searching for the sapphire there: the army from Petrag had marched too fast for them and perished in the storm, higher than they dared go even to strip the bodies.

* * *

Hannah came awake in total darkness, angry at herself for sleeping so deeply. Beyond the clammy tent she could hear the underground river rushing by. She thought this was the second camp they had made on the Dark Way, but it was hard for her to remember. Time here passed undivided by the lights of heaven. She tried not to sleep either in the camps or in the stretcher, fearing always that a brigand would steal her poison – after which they could break her by torture, find the sapphire, and do with her and Naomi whatever they pleased. Sleepless anxiety had blurred her thought and weakened her – until at last sleep overcame her. And what had wakened her now?

She could hear no sound but the river. The camp was certainly not stirring yet. But something had roused her. There was the sound of exhaled breath in the blackness just above her, within an arms' reach of her face. "She is still asleep," breathed a man's voice in the faintest possible whisper. Hannah realized in horror that the slight weight across her chest that she had been feeling without noticing it for the last few moments was a man's arm and hand. She could see no hope at all. Even if she had really intended to commit suicide, if she reached for the bottle now he would know where it was, and would easily overpower her. Yet somehow she remained relaxed and still. The man's action seemed somehow uncertain: she was at his mercy, the bottle was his for the taking, and yet he made no move.

"Be careful, Vrag," came another whisper from outside the tent.

"Why?" breathed the man who appeared to be called Vrag. "Will not the Bowlord honor us for this?"

"He has not commanded it," whispered the man beyond the tent.

"It will free him of the shame of obeying this old hag," said Vrag.

"Vrag, have you ever tortured anyone?" asked the other man.

"No," said Vrag, "but I am eager to try it."

"I won't deny it's a real pleasure," whispered the man outside, "but it's best if it's not for anything important. It won't be as easy as you think, especially here in the dark, with, you might say, not all the tools of the trade available. People can be shockingly stubborn – and then suddenly die when you least expect it. The Bowlord is set on getting that sapphire back. As for this hag... we know already that she's stronger and more crafty than she looks."

"And even being caught near her... and if she wakes..." breathed Vrag. There came a sudden sound of another tent being opened, and feet crunching on gravel. Vrag's arm was instantly withdrawn from her chest, and Hannah heard the flap of the tent close as he quietly stood – outside. She lay awake, breathing hard, for what seemed like hours – until at last the camp awakened for another march.

She ate and drank what was brought her, staying well apart from the men, as usual. Naomi woke to semi-consciousness and drank a little. When Hannah noticed with surprise that the men were dragging their boat far up onto the black stream's banks, rather than preparing to launch it, she asked the Bowlord if she could be allowed to walk rather than being carried in the stretcher. He laughed loudly. "Your feet will never take you where we're going today, hag," he said.

Hours later she could acknowledge that he had certainly been right. The men were climbing what seemed an endless pile of boulders at a great pace in the torchlight. Six at a time struggled with the stretcher that bore her and Naomi – and yet they were never dropped or injured on the jagged stones.

As the interminable march went on, always upward, the air grew colder. Hannah heard the men breathing harder, almost gasping now, especially those who carried the stretcher. And not they alone: Naomi also began to struggle for breath, just as she had on the lower slopes of the Third Mountain. Hannah could only listen. If even this underground path rose too high for Naomi to breathe, there was simply no hope at all. Naomi would never survive long enough to go back and around via Luciyr now, even if Hannah could somehow convince the Bowlord to take such a course.

At last the path stopped ascending. The bearers laid the stretcher on the ground and lay around it panting and groaning from their exertion. Naomi was breathing very fast, in short, painful gasps. It seemed to Hannah that Naomi was growing more and more tired, that merely breathing had become hard labor for her – and that at any moment it might grow hard beyond her strength. While Hannah bowed over her, watching every moment of the unconscious girl's struggle for breath, she was dimly aware that the Bowlord was giving a speech. He was congratulating his men on the good climb, and explaining that they could camp where they were – assuring them that on the next day the trail would descend into warmer and better air.

This last fact woke Hannah suddenly to the significance of the speech. She leaped to her feet and confronted the Bowlord face to face. "The air is not good here!" she said. "It is too harsh for my daughter. Look at her – she cannot breathe. We cannot rest here. We must go down – far down, into better air – before we camp."

"So she speaks who has been carried all the way!" said the Bowlord loudly. "We must go down now – we cannot rest – lest her whorish brat gasp out its last somewhere under the peak of Nifdiyarag. But let me see." He went over to where Naomi lay, and stared at her contemptuously with his hands on his knees.

Knowing that she might be exposing herself to the theft of her poison, Hannah knelt beside Naomi's head, almost at the Bowlord's feet. One of her hands gently went through Naomi's hair as she gasped for life. "If she dies, you will never find the sapphire," said Hannah calmly.

"Then if she dies," said the Bowlord, "I will torture you to death. Have you ever seen anyone being tortured?" He drew a knife, which flashed cruelly in the torchlight.

Hannah stood and met his eyes, her hands clasped behind her. "I told you I did not value my life," she said. "How certain can you be that the torture will indeed break me? But if you do what I ask in this: if you hurry on to better air now, and for the rest of the journey press forward at what seems to me a good pace, doing neither me nor my daughter any harm, I will give you the sapphire's hiding place even if she dies. I will give it you if you have done all that you could to carry her through in time, and if you bring me and her dead body safe to the valley of Brightshadow."

"And if I do not do all this?" asked the Bowlord.

Hannah turned suddenly and ran up to the top of a great, hard-edged boulder at the edge of the torchlight. She drew out the bottle of poison and lifted it up. "Behold!" she said. "I do not value my life! Yet for you, my life is the Sapphire of the Free Bows, to be bought with a little more walking in the dark. It is true that I was carried, but I am an old woman – a hag, you have called me. Do you have the strength of men?"

"May a whore's death pull you down to burn in Hell!" shouted the Bowlord. "If you will walk, and let your brat alone be carried, I will now order the descent."

Moments later they were hastening onward and down. Hannah was hard pressed to keep up on the rugged, boulder-strewn trail, but she did it – breathing almost as painfully as Naomi was, and praying that their swift march might save her life.

* * *

Jonathan drove his men and himself across the white wildness almost without rest. After waking on the slopes of the third mountain, he had marched them all night and all the next day. At evening he had allowed them some hours of rest, but at the rising of the bright gibbous moon, he had roused them again with a trumpet blast.

He himself felt a slave, forced on beyond his strength, helpless in the merciless grip of his will. His will, holding to the decision he had made in Carrah, sometimes seemed a hostile force external to himself. Its power frightened him. It would drive him on through exhaustion and relentless pain to an end without hope. Yet in moments of clearer vision he remembered what he had said to his men: there was no other choice. Surrendering to despair was unthinkable. Arriving at Ceramir too late would be worse than not coming at all. It was not the decision he had made that was destroying him, but the circumstances that had made that choice the only honorable one. In such moments his anger burned, and his determination hardened even more. He would conquer the great mountains. The Zarnith would turn back in terror before his vast anger – before the iron courage of his despair.

Jonathan's men felt as they had before: that he was more than human; that he was an archangel with courage like a flame and determination stronger than stone. Those who had longed to march with the Hero of Petrag found him all that they had dreamed and more – but pain drowned their awe as he led them on mercilessly.

Jonathan had more reasons than merely haste for allowing only that one small rest in the white wildness. Ever since his return to Carrah, nightmares had plagued him. Now they had grown terrible, pressing in on him even when he dozed for only a moment during one of their brief halts for food. He had to use all his force of will to hide their effect on him, and he had become terrified of sleep. So he pushed on relentlessly, and his men thought he had no weakness. Even Barnabas did not guess that he was having nightmares.

* * *

In the afternoon of the day after they reached the Norkath border, Benther and Ilohan sat together on a hill to the south of the main camp of Karolan. The king had just been reading a message from Andokar, but now his eyes gazed past it to the soft winter landscape spread out below. Thousands of tents and campfires dotted the brown meadowlands near the border castle of Felrin. Here and there among the tents stood gray, leafless trees: sparse outliers of the thicker forests that lay to the north, nearer Aaronkal. Felrin was a minor castle in the hills south of Dilgarel. It was a strange place for the greatest army in Karolan's history to cross the border into Norkath. But then, Ilohan thought, the times were strange – strange and dire. Many things would now be done that had never been done before. Yet the land seemed so soft and kind: winter on the edge of spring in the border hills, with the smell of wood smoke borne to him on the soft breeze. It was hard for Ilohan to believe in the Zarnith, and for a moment he could not blame Andokar. Surely they would not come to such a place as this, this ground unbloodied, this air unshaken with the sounds of battle. Surely this peace was inviolate. But so some had thought before Fingar came to Aaronkal. The threat was real. Ilohan himself might doubt Vadshron's reality on a soft afternoon at spring's dawning, but nonetheless Vadshron would come, and lay waste this land with fire and horror, and even now Andokar would not let the Army of All Karolan cross his border.

"As you have read, he is coming to meet us with eight thousand men," said Benther, breaking into Ilohan's reverie. "He will camp across the border from us, and attack if Your Majesty so much as lets the nose of one soldier into Norkath.

"Shall we cross the border and march for Drantar's Gap before he reaches us?" asked Ilohan. "He might then chase us until the first news of Vadshron came, when he would see that we were not the threat."

"It seems he had thought we might do that," said Benther. "Our spies say he has divided his army in two halves, one marching straight here from Guldorak, and another traveling south, seemingly intending to cut us off from Drantar's Gap. If we cross the border against his will and march for the Gap, we will be waylaid by four thousand Norkath warriors before we reach it."

"Alas," said the king. "Is there no end to his distrust? He knows we could rout his army and raze Norkath to scorched soil. He sees that we do not strike, yet still he will not trust us. He must have his small force on his border to oppose our great one. We could march now, and crush his four thousand that oppose our way to Drantar's Gap, but that is not the course of a true knight. In any case we can afford no losses either to his troops or ours."

There was a long silence, as the wind fluttered the parchment in Ilohan's hand. At last the king called for a scribe, and began dictating a message. "To His Majesty Andokar of Norkath, from Ilohan, King of Karolan: greetings. We are grieved at your lack of trust, and assure you that we design no ill upon your sovereign realm of Norkath. However, we affirm and protest that our warning of a Zarnith invasion is most real and urgent, and that, for the preservation of your people and your crown, you must permit us to enter your land, and you must march with us to Drantar's Gap to meet the foe, gathering with haste all the force that you can. We can say no more; your doom and ours draws nigh, and your distrust may seal it. Consider our character and that of our fathers, Prince Kindrach and King Thomas, and judge rightly whether it is likely that we will betray you now."

"Addendum:" said Benther. "We commend your spies, who have relayed to you our intended destination within a day of our march. They are all the more to be praised because we have not yet determined who they are."

King Ilohan smiled grimly at the grim jest. "Thousands knew our counsel before we marched," he said. "A few, at least, rode swift horses to Guldorak. But Andokar must know we know this, and Karolan too has her spies. Send the message as it is. And pray God sends him yet a change of heart."

* * *

A man rode through the deserted village of Harevan and onward up the dirt path toward the Gate of Hope. He rode with his left hand only, while bloody bandages swathed his right hand and his shoulder. His horse was dusty and tired with long days of hard riding, but he himself sat upright in the saddle, uncowed by weariness and pain. For a while he saw no one, and it seemed to him as if some evil had already cursed the Cloth of Joy, leaving it barren and empty of its children. At last, far up ahead, he saw a single figure clothed in brown, kneeling on the path to pluck up something that grew beside it. The figure straightened slowly and wearily at the sound of his horse's hooves, and turned toward him.

But then he knew her, and she, though she did not believe her eyes, knew him. She stood like a statue in the center of the path, as he approached her and dismounted. Even then she stood a moment longer, not moving or speaking. Then she simply wept without making a sound, smiling through her tears. Her smile was warm, bright joy, like the sun on Eden, as full of surprise as Eve, newly wakened, must have been when God brought her to Adam for the first time. But he stepped forward and embraced her, scorning the pain of his wounded arm. "Imranie, dear Imranie," he said, "I have returned, and though the Zarnith come by thousands my heart is light. We have proved faithful, you and I, and by the help of God we shall be faithful to the end. Dear Imranie, we face the end together, in the Valley of the Undismayed."

"They did not kill you," she whispered, held in his arms. "They did not kill you. Mudien, we have lived as a people without the sun, or a tree without its trunk. I have felt old and alone, though my children said I gave them strength and joy."

"You did," he said, "and I spoke with Vadshron and lived. We each alone have done what we were called to do, by the help of God, but it is together that we have joy."

"This is right," she said. "This is right. Let us go up together through the Gate of Hope."

They stepped a little apart, she being careful of his wounded arm, and then they turned and walked side by side up the path. Imranie led the weary horse. The news spread swiftly that Mudien had returned beyond hope. When they came to the Gate of Hope, there was a great crowd already waiting for them within.

They passed through the last remaining slot in the great barricade of hoary, interlocking trees that had been built across the Gate of Hope. Leaving that ugly wall behind them, they came to the bank of the warm lake where all was beautiful, in free and lovely order. Sweet mist curled around their legs as they walked hand in hand along the shore, and the gathered Children of Ceramir watched them in wonder. Then, at some unseen signal, all the people began to sing. The song had been made hastily by Rangol and Eleanor, but it rang out clear and beautiful, sung by the children of Ceramir with all their hearts.

Praise for a servant's returning
Rescued from death by his Lord.

Praise for our hope newly burning,
Praise for the foe's cheated sword.

Praise for the first light of dawning
Now in the darkness we fear,
Praise that, though our grave is yawning,
God's strength to rescue is near.

Foe that has boasted his dread might
Now sees our leader go free,
Thus at the start of our dark night,
New hope of dawning we see.

Praise for the hope in the darkness,
Praise for the dawn that shall come,
Praise for God's might and his goodness,
Praise him; let his will be done.

Into the darkness go singing,
Our life and our death in God's hand,
Trust as our battle cry ringing:
Evil is founded on sand.

Mudien stood with the Children of the Cloth of Joy all around him, and the wonder of his return sank into his mind. He had gone away to die. He had been as sure that he would die as that the Zarnith would assail Ceramir – and yet he had not died. The past was beyond his understanding, wise and stern leader though he was. The future he would not even try to guess. He let Imranie and Karlak and a crowd of young children lead him into the stone house, tend his wounds and put him to bed. He sank into a deep sleep, while around him the long labor of the defense continued. Yet each felt Mudien's presence as a shield and guide, heartening them and giving them a stern but not grim determination to do their best. The work was long and hard, and the miracle they would need to save them seemed very far away. But Mudien had returned beyond their hope.

* * *

"I cannot keep myself strong much longer, Father," said Jonathan to Barnabas in the late afternoon. Barnabas sat on a slab of ice, weary beyond any weariness he remembered, even at Dilgarel. Jonathan stood near him; they were a little apart from the others.

In two nights and two days of swift marching, with only a single halt for sleep, they had crossed the icy plain and arrived at the ascent to the final pass – the one the Zarnith had called the Pass Beneath the Stars. Both Karolan behind and Ceramir ahead seemed fables to nearly all the men. The reality was this, this other world between the blue-black sky and the aching whiteness of the tortured ice. The reality was this, where each night exposed them unshielded to the heavens' staggering beauty – the stars that knew nothing of the woes of earth. This was the only world, this world that drew forth their awe and wonder even while it slew them. They would never climb the last mountain wall or go through the Pass Beneath the Stars. They would never descend to a land where the sky was soft and water ran free beneath a kindly sun. In their desperate weariness, the world where men could live seemed a fantasy. Yet some clung to the underlying knowledge that it was not. They trusted in Jonathan, believing that, impossible though it seemed, he would lead them back to the living world. Some even remembered that back in that world they intended to die, facing the largest army in all history.

And Jonathan felt the crushing burden of their trust. He had led a thousand men to do what they had felt was impossible, and they expected him to lead them to the end. But it was too much for him. "I am breaking," he said to his father, his quiet words a desperate cry for help. "I do not know what to do."

Barnabas sat on the ice, his head bowed. His eyes would not focus on the dazzling ground before him. "This is what I have wanted," he said to himself. "Lord God, now Jonathan has nowhere to turn but to you. And yet... Alas, I do not know what to say."

"You do not want me to say anything about God," he said. It was a statement, not a question.

"No," said Jonathan simply. Barnabas knew that some great turmoil lay behind that single syllable, that Jonathan said it alone for fear that he should say much more – but what that much more would have been Barnabas could not guess.

"I am weary," said Barnabas.

"I know, Father," said Jonathan. "I am sorry. But things go very ill with me, and I do not know what may happen. The men all think I have no weakness."

"They trust you. But you have no stronger one to trust. All your life God has offered you help. Now – "

"Father," cried Jonathan – he forced down his voice that the men might not hear – "Father, say your great words, tell me what God offers me – what good is that to me? I do not believe any of it. I am where I am, and I am at the end of my strength, asking for your help. Have you any to give me? Or will you withhold it because of my crimes?"

Weary as he was Barnabas leapt to his feet and gripped Jonathan's shoulders in his two strong hands. His eyes as he looked into his son's face were blazing. "Jonathan," he said, "if you have forgotten what I told you when you came back to Glen Carrah, remember now. If you have forgotten what love means, remember now. Nothing you could do would break my love, or change my intent to do you good." He stood facing his son for a long moment, and then his grip on his shoulders weakened and he sat back down upon the ice. "I am weary," he said. "The things I wish to say you will not listen to. Yet I would ask you this: what did Naomi say to you, when – "

Jonathan made a violent motion. "Do not speak of that," he said.

"Remember what she said, then; do not speak of it to me. Remember that she is trying to get to Ceramir. If the Zarnith die by a plague, or choose to pass by the Cloth of Joy, and in ten days Naomi comes there, alive but dying, would you have her hear that when you dared the great mountains the second time they proved too much for you, and you died with all your men? Would you have her hear that though she wait for you a score of years, you will not come for her?"

Jonathan trembled violently. "I know I must go on," he said. "But I do not think I can. I am breaking, Father, breaking. Do you understand me?"

"Rest, beloved son," said Barnabas. "It is now afternoon. Order the tents pitched, and sleep, you and all your men, until tomorrow's dawn."

"There is no time," said Jonathan. "Who can say how much time we shall need to climb down the Cliffs of Doom? And…and…" but he could not bring himself to speak of his nightmares, to confess the fact that he was afraid to sleep.

"I am weary, Jonathan," said Barnabas. "If rest does not heal you, nothing can, save him of whom you would not speak. If you fall, your men fall with you, and if by resting for a night you can regain your hold on life, that night is well spent though time is precious. If you fall we shall never reach the Cliffs of Doom. If you rest, we may not come too late – and we can descend in haste."

"You have not seen the Cliffs of Doom, Father. Already we are late. And we lost some of our rope-bearers in the storm. All is evil; the very air and sky hate us, and there is no hope."

Suddenly Jonathan found that he was running, on legs that felt numb and strange, to the head of the army. In a ringing voice like that which had once echoed from the walls of Petrag, he called the men forward to climb the last mountain and reach the Pass Beneath the Stars. They groaned, and looked up with weary eyes, but they saw the figure of Jonathan above them standing straight in the white sunlight from the west – and they followed him.

They followed him up among the broken black boulders and the white ice, with the glare of sun on snow dazzling their aching eyes. They followed him doggedly, in awe at his tireless strength and his relentless determination.

Jonathan marched at the head of the army, to the men its fearless leader, to himself the broken wreck of a man, ready to collapse at any moment. When he closed his eyes for an instant the nightmares came crowding in. To try to hold them back he did repeat to himself Naomi's whispered words at their final parting. He knew them by heart. "You must not seek God to find me," she had tried to say. "God, only God, not me. I am dying, but death is not the end. The love of God is beyond all. Yet Jonathan, even my love is stronger than death. Love is stronger than death. God, only God, not me."

It was strange that she had spoken thus, so insistent that he seek God rather than her. Truly she had loved God – loved him more than her own life, more than she loved Jonathan himself –

more than anything. Her whole life had been devoted to God: devoted to a phantom with no real existence.

She had died believing that God would give her endless joy – and believing, too, that Jonathan would yet come to the same faith. She had died hoping in vain for herself and for him, for endless joy... It was a mighty folly. He had loved her, and even loved in her the faith he did not share. Now he saw how it separated her from him. Earlier on the third mountain she had spoken of Heaven as light, and Hell as darkness. She had begged him not to leave her by going into Hell, not to separate himself from her eternally. But it was her faith itself that was the real separation, the chasm that had always divided them. Now in their darkness it yawned deeply. She had hoped, but he despaired. He was almost angry with her for her relentless hope.

And yet he loved her! With all of his being, he loved all of hers – even her stubborn hope, even her blazing, self-abandoning devotion to a God who did not exist. There was no part of her that he did not love: her life was wholly precious to him in every way. He would never have sought to change her. He would have died for her a thousand times.

But it was she who had died. Certainly she was dead – she had been within moments of death when he left her. She must have died on that terrible mountain. She was dead. He wondered what had become of her body. He pictured her as a frozen corpse, shallowly buried beneath the snow, cold, cold... He knew corpses were nothing; the man or woman was not in them. The man or woman was dead, destroyed, gone forever. And yet it was hard to think that it did not matter what happened to the body. To Naomi's corpse... "Naomi, Beloved..." She was dead. Nightmares came upon him thick and fast, even as he walked, eyes open, in the dazzling light of the mountain sun on ice.

He was desperately tired, and his nightmares reached out claws of fear to destroy everything: his mind, his heart, his soul, his being... He was unsure of everything save his pain as he reeled beneath their power. He was dizzy, and his breath came hard in the icy air, and he knew his men must expect him to call them forward with another great speech of courage and glory, but he could not. They had been climbing for a long, long time – it seemed to him as long as an age of history. His men must need encouragement, but he could not give it. He could not... He was not sure any of it was real; he was not sure he himself was real now; how could he...

He noticed suddenly that the ground beneath him was flat, and that the light had dimmed – unless it was merely that his eyes were failing him. But he looked to his right and saw the terrible, unearthly glow of a mountain sunset behind the western peaks. Night was coming, night with its terrors, and he was deathly tired upon the Pass Beneath the Stars... His men must need encouragement. His men must expect him to call them forward again...

"Jonathan, Jonathan!" A man was beside him; it was his father. "Jonathan," said Barnabas, "you must allow the men a rest at the nearest place where they can. I am telling you this, and I do not speak beyond the truth. They have given you all they have. The weaker will drive themselves to death or fall behind and freeze if they do not rest. The strongest are desperately tired. I, your father, say this. Let us reach the Cliffs of Doom late – the men must rest, or die."

"You must call them forward..." Jonathan's own thought mocked him. "You must call them forward, they cannot rest here..."

"Men of Karolan, you are the strongest of the strong and the bravest of the brave!" Scores of faces were upturned to his with sudden hope and wonder. He felt once again that he was being killed slowly by the merciless grip of his will. "Men of Karolan, we have done together what Dradrag could not do with all his thousands. This is the last pass – now it is only down into Ceramir. We have conquered stone! Follow me with the last of your strength, and the greatest of your mighty courage, and we shall come down soon to a shoulder of the mountain, where we may rest!" He ran forward across the pass, and began descending the terribly steep far side. And the men followed him.

It was an agony. To Jonathan the mountains were only half-real, and he walked with aching steps through a nightmare world. Nothing was constant but his grief and pain, and the shadow of fear that hung over him. The descent seemed to take ages of the world.

And then there came again a time when he found again that the ice was flat beneath his feet. He walked on for aching moments, forgetting what this meant, and then suddenly there was nothing beneath his feet and he was sliding on very steep, hard ice. He landed after a fall of only twice his height, at the bottom of a steep sided valley with a flat floor. It was a huge crevasse that had filled with the snow of many years. It was flat, and sheltered from the wind: it was the perfect place to camp.

"Men of Karolan, come down and pitch your tents in this valley!" he cried. The dark forms of his men came down the valley wall in the twilight, many falling uncontrolled and crumpling when they landed. Some of these groaned and did not get up. He must call them up again, and order them to put the tents up well and warmly, or they would die in the cold.

But the nightmares came upon him with more strength than ever before, with a depth of horror of which he would never speak, and he could not.

"You must," said his thought in the horrible darkness.

"I cannot," he said.

"You must."

Then his hand went to his sword. "I will," he said.

He went to the nearest of the men who had fallen, and helped him up. Some men nearby were pitching a tent, and Jonathan ordered the man to help them. The man obeyed him.

Jonathan turned around and scanned the starlit valley for others who needed his help. He was like a beast turning at bay, looking to see what forces the vicious world had mustered against him, what tasks beyond his strength he must attempt. There were many. Men were lying on the ground. Others were going in to sleep in tents only half pitched, that would not keep them warm. It was too much; it was much more than he could do. Nightmares raged around him: he was at the edge of a delirium filled with horror.

"I will not break," he said in a voice that seemed to him small and faint, lost in the howling darkness.

"You will not break. You will not break. Jonathan of Carrah, you will not break."

His father was beside him, and had clasped his hand. That hand, and those words, served as one solid reference point in his howling darkness, and steadied him, and he went to work.

The men got up quickly when he called them, and roused others. When he put his own hands to a tent they were joined by scores of others. The tents were pitched sturdily and well, eight score of them in the starlit darkness, filling a long stretch of the small, sheltering valley. He stared through the darkness to see if any men remained who were not safely in a tent, and he realized he could not tell. He must walk the rows of tents to make sure. But he was so tired, so tired... And horror engulfed him on every side. He fell down upon the snow, and did not rise.

A dark figure came away from the shadow of the valley wall. It stooped, and slowly straightened, holding Jonathan in its arms. And Barnabas looked down upon the face of his son in the starlight. He felt Jonathan's body tremble, even as his own arms trembled with the effort of holding him up. He stood there long, trying to pray, trying to think and lay a hand upon his thoughts. But he could not; deep love and deep grief were in his heart, and his body and mind were exhausted. He carried his son into a tent, laid him down and covered him with a blanket, and then lay down to sleep himself.

Barnabas slept dreamlessly and quietly, his trust in God. Jonathan at his side slept a sleep full of nightmares and horror, and often jerked or groaned in his sleep. But at last a deeper rest claimed him, and he sank below the realm of nightmares as below the waves of a black lake. A kind of peace came over his face as he slept, and his merely physical exhaustion was healed.

Chapter 19

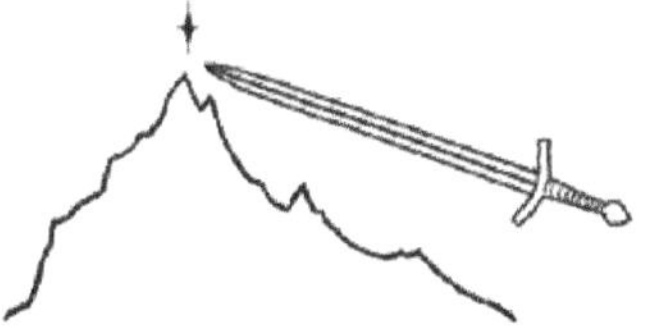

The Shadow on the Cliffs of Doom

AS EVENING FELL THE NEXT DAY, AND THE UNEARTHLY violet shadow rose high in the eastern sky, Jonathan and his army came down the last slope of the mountain above the Cliffs of Doom. A short walk across icy stone would bring them to the cliff edge.

The long rest of the night before had brought new life and hope to the men. In the cold wind that wailed up to them from the cliffs some even caught a faint hint of the smells of the living earth. The sight of the icy peaks that had struck fear into the hearts of Jonathan and Ilohan at the top of the Cliffs of Doom was not so terrible to men who had gone through the Pass Among the Stars, and were now headed back toward the world where they could live. They had seen things wilder and more strange. They had been higher up in the frozen sky, and nearer the bright, unfeeling stars. Yet the peaks that towered above the Cliffs of Doom were still terrible: steep and jagged, standing out black against the twilight while night swept westward through the unearthly sky. Some of the men looked back in fear, wondering how they could have come through those mountains. A few wondered if they had not: if the mountains had indeed killed them; if they wandered now as homeless ghosts, lost forever between frozen rock and frozen sky, far from the kindly world of men.

Jonathan walked in a short reprieve from agony. His mind simply refused to think of anything that would hurt too much, and his nightmares, for this short time, could not reach him. He marched at the head of his army with Barnabas beside him. Yet he still had no hope.

"I think I can see the edge of the Cliffs of Doom," said Barnabas, looking far ahead in the dusk.

"Yes," said Jonathan. "We will reach them before the darkness is complete."

"How shall we descend?" asked Barnabas.

"As I said before, we have lost some rope," said Jonathan. "We still have, I think, at least three times enough to hang down to the base of the cliffs. We must lay it out and knot it together. The difficulty is that no one is strong enough to climb all the way down without rest – and the rope cannot hold more than about ten men at a time. It could take us days to get everyone down. Some may not be able to climb a bare rope at all."

"You could tie knots in the rope, for handholds and footholds," said Barnabas.

Jonathan considered for a moment. "That is a very good idea, Father," he said. "It will take time to tie the knots, and it will reduce the length of the rope, but I think it would be well worthwhile. Men could then climb faster, and go longer without rest… yet it will still take a long time – more time than we have."

Then they spoke no more, for they had come to the brink of the Cliffs of Doom. They had come to the edge of the world. They looked off into a vast, dim gulf, seemingly filled with nothing but shadows, until far away in the east below them, small mountains reared their dusky silhouettes against the fading sky.

Jonathan stood for a long a moment, still as a statue in the twilight. The men gathered and murmured behind him, wondering what he would do next. But he was thinking of the frail ropes they would cast out into that shadowy void, and of ordering men to climb down them. He remembered his and Ilohan's exhaustion when last he had stood here. "We will come to Ceramir too late," he muttered. "We will die. So goes the world."

Turning then to his men, he raised his voice again in bold authority. "Set down your packs," he said, "and bring out whatever rope you have!"

While the bustle of obedience began behind him, Jonathan saw a shadow move in the dusk at the cliff edge: a shadow that he had thought a stone. His hand went to his sword.

"Peace, valiant friend," said a voice. "I have long expected your coming, though you are not the one I expected."

"Who are you?" asked Jonathan.

"Ah," said the voice. There was a laugh in the darkness, clear and undismayed. "Who am I?" The shadowy figure lay down on the boulder where it had been standing, and laid its head back to look at the brightening stars. "Who am I? Let that question stand. Perhaps I would not answer, now; perhaps I cannot. Who can say? Yet I think that now I know your name – which is not the same as knowing who you are. You have come a weary journey with little hope, Jonathan of Glen Carrah. Yet though hope is hard to find in these days, and seems foolish, maybe it is not."

"How do you know me?" asked Jonathan, his hand still on his sword.

"Once," the clear, strong laugh sounded again in the darkness, "I improved your opinion of churchmen."

The world seemed to spin around Jonathan as he recognized the voice and manner of speaking. And suddenly he felt that a small green plant had sprouted in the barren desert of his hopelessness – a plant that grew there undismayed by the approaching sands that soon would stifle it. "Brogal," said Jonathan, "how did you come here?"

Brogal stood. "Come with me, leader of Karolan's army," he said. So Jonathan followed him, climbing over the boulders at the edge of the Cliffs of Doom, while the men of the army, catching up their half-opened packs, came wondering behind. Soon they came to a place that Jonathan recognized. He and Ilohan had reached the top there, long ago it seemed: a single winter ago, in another age of the world. Brogal crouched near a boulder at the edge of the cliff, and disappeared. Jonathan went to the place and looked down. Feelings and thoughts he could not grasp assailed him; he opened his mouth but did not speak. For there, stretching down until it disappeared into the darkness far below, was a rope ladder. It was wide, with good rungs and huge, thick ropes. Brogal looked up at him, and laughed.

*　　　　*　　　　*

In the Army of All Karolan, encamped on the Norkath border, uncertainty troubled almost every man. Andokar had camped just across the border with nine thousand men, and he steadfastly refused to grant Karolan permission to cross. Benther and the king posted many guards to watch ceaselessly for any unexpected movement in what it was hard not to think of as an enemy army. Spies and assassins were a constant concern. At Benther's insistence, Ilohan had reluctantly appointed a personal bodyguard of five men. He was also very careful of everything he ate or drank; again yielding to Benther's caution.

Ilohan had frequently invited Andokar to meet with him, insisting that the Zarnith threat to Norkath was real and the Karolan threat perceived by Andokar was not. Yet his invitations were always refused. Andokar would not believe that Karolan, Norkath's long enemy, was now insistently offering her help. This undeserved lack of trust wore at Ilohan. It was losing them even the feeble hope a stand at Drantar's Gap might have offered.

Today he sat alone in his tent, save for the guards at the door. He thought of Veril and of Ceramir – and of Jonathan, Naomi, and Glen Carrah. So much had been destroyed. So much more was now doomed before the Zarnith. Only two days now remained before the date the Zarnith had set for the destruction of Ceramir. Ilohan rose, trying to turn his mind from thoughts that brought nothing but pain. Followed by his bodyguard, he went out into the afternoon. He would go among his men, and try to encourage them and lift their hope. But how could he, with no hope of his own to offer?

He remembered the forget-me-not. He no longer had the blessed feeling of closeness to Christ, nor the wondrous power of prayer, that had come to him in that death cell. Then he had had nothing to do but pray until he died; now he was responsible for choices that could mean life or death, justice or injustice, for scores of thousands. Yet this could not mean that he was beyond the reach of God's comfort. He must not cease to pray only because he was less aware now of God's closeness. The reality did not change with his perceptions.

"Lord Christ," he said, "may I lead these people well, as long as I am their leader. May my leading draw them close to you, and may they follow you wholeheartedly. We march to death, Lord; may we be among those who live, even though they die. I pray for the souls of my people, for every one – but especially for Jonathan. Lord God, I pray for Jonathan's soul. I pray for him, and… I pray for our rescue."

He realized that he had prayed for the impossible; the absolutely impossible. It was just as though he had asked God to make the sun rise in the west. And yet he had spoken those words; "I pray for our rescue," without noticing their impossibility as he said them. His faith, perhaps, was deeper than he knew. From somewhere, hope had come into his heart. Maybe it was not to be disappointed.

He found that he had been standing absolutely still for a long moment in the wintry sunshine. He stirred himself. He would go among his men and do what he could.

* * *

Late on that same afternoon, Jonathan led his army into Ceramir. They had spent much of the night climbing down the rope ladder, three score at a time. Then Jonathan had wanted them to push on to Ceramir without sleep – and they had followed him with joy. Trees had greeted them like heralds of paradise. The sweet air of the living world filled their lungs. Forgetting their weariness, they pushed on through their exhaustion and reached the descent to the Cloth of Joy at sunset.

Men were weeping as they came down the last steep descent, following switchbacks hewn out of the cliff that backed the Valley of the Undismayed. Warm air with a blessed touch of moisture came up to them from the valley below. There were smells, too: smells like that of hay and kindly lowland trees. The twilight was falling soft and blue, without a vast violet shadow in the east or colors of terrible intensity in the west. The men of Jonathan's army at last believed they had passed through the mountains and were returning, exhausted to the very edge of their strength, to the lands of life. The twilit valley embraced them with a gentleness and comfort that almost broke their hearts. Few remembered that they had come here to die, but Jonathan did not forget.

Jonathan had known, from the first sight of Brogal's rope ladder, that they would indeed reach Ceramir in time. The hopeless battle with the Zarnith had changed from a hazy fable to a reality that he must face and plan for. This last stage of the journey had given him long hours to consider his plan, and he had come to a new decision – a strange compound of his loyalty to Ilohan and his own despair. He had decided that if the people of Ceramir had indeed barricaded the gap out in the desert, as he knew Benther had asked them to, he would lead a third of his men out to make a stand there. The rest could fight under the command of Barnabas and Mudien.

Jonathan did not forget that he had rejected such a plan as utter folly when Ilohan first mentioned it. But he also could not forget that Ilohan, in almost his last words to him, had asked him to remember the desert gap. He found himself drawn to it now. If he fought in Ceramir he would die trapped, bottled up in a valley from which there could be no fleeing. He would die with the Cloth of Joy being raped and ravaged around him. But in the desert he could fight Vadshron as he had fought Fingar: in open battle at a long barricade. He would die heroically and swiftly, with Ceramir yet unspoiled behind him. He would never see its ruin, the death throes of its beauty. And he would die granting the wish of his friend and king.

It was with this decision in his heart that Jonathan led his army at last onto the fields of the Cloth of Joy. They were received with a tremendous welcome – all prepared thanks to Brogal and the others who had labored on the ladder, who had returned early to herald their coming. Cheerful bonfires beckoned men across stubble fields. Beside each fire, Children of Ceramir handed out hot drinks and steaming pots of savory food. Others called weary men to put aside their burdens, while scores of willing hands set up the tents. But Auria found Jonathan and called him to the stone house. He followed her across the unplanted fields, under the great trees, and past the misty lake: places well known to him and yet strange now, because they were all imperiled, and because he had come from the mountains, and because he had not slept. At last they came to the stone house of Ceramir, all welcoming and warmly lit.

Eleanor stood at the door with a candle in her hand. "Welcome, Jonathan of Carrah," she said. "I thank you for the life of my son."

Bitterness rose within Jonathan at her words: he had not saved Ilohan's life but only delayed his death, and he deserved no thanks for what he had done. Her words seemed to mock him because of the bitter truths she did not know: the truths of his broken promise and his broken life. Yet he could not answer her with frank and harsh rejection of her thanks, as he had first intended. The words would not come, not while she stood there at the door with her candle, with a look on her face that he could never describe. Purity and goodness clothed her as surely as did the long white dress she wore. "Welcome," she said again. "Come within, if you will."

He did, and followed her into an inner room where sat Brogal, Imranie, Rangol, and Mudien about a table. He had seen the room before; it was where the council had been held so long ago, when Ilohan chose to dare the mountains.

"Welcome, Jonathan of Karolan," said Mudien. "May the blessing of God be upon you. Your courage is great. Brogal has brought us word of what you have done. I know that you must be weary, yet I would know a few more things from you before you sleep."

A chair was set ready for Eleanor, and she took it; another stood empty for Jonathan, but he remained standing. "What shall I say?" he asked.

"We have guessed that the Zarnith will make for Drantar's Gap," said Mudien. "Is that where King Ilohan intends to lead the Army of All Karolan?"

"Yes," said Jonathan.

"Does he believe he can reach it before the Zarnith?"

"The time is close," said Jonathan. "He is unsure."

"The king will certainly have left Aaronkal by now?" asked Mudien.

"Yes," said Jonathan.

"What are your own plans?" asked Mudien.

"Have you barricaded the desert gap according to the request Sir Benther relayed from King Ilohan?" asked Jonathan.

"We have," said Mudien, "though we did not understand the reason. The barricade is frail, but it does span the whole gap."

"Then I will divide my army in two parts," said Jonathan. "One third of the men I will command, at the desert gap of which the king spoke. The rest I will leave in my father's command and in yours, to defend the Cloth of Joy. You may take council with my father concerning your strategy for the last defense."

Eleanor stood suddenly. "Jonathan, that is folly! We thought the barricade could only be a feint, not a place where men would truly stand. What confusion took my son, that he would suggest it?"

"He wanted to protect transmontane Norkath," said Jonathan. "He said it was the true course, the course God would be most willing to bless with a miracle. He said there was no hope without a miracle, whatever course we chose."

Jonathan saw Eleanor's shocked expression suddenly change to one of joy. "Have you, then, pledged yourself to God?" she asked.

"No," said Jonathan – and just as in his conversation with Barnabas before the Pass Beneath the Stars, he said no more.

"The barricade is frail," said Mudien, "and the Zarnith will outnumber you nearly half a thousand to one."

Jonathan met Mudien's gaze for a long moment without speaking. At last he said, "I wish to leave the council, and to ride with Brogal to spy upon the Zarnith host where they are encamped."

Brogal stood eagerly. "I will gladly go with you, Jonathan," he said.

"Brogal tells me you have been two days without rest," said Imranie. "You should sleep yourself, and let another go with Brogal – yet I would ask you to speak with Veril and Eleanor before you sleep."

Mudien looked at Jonathan again. "As Imranie has said, you should not go without rest," he said. "Will you accept my authority in this?"

"No," said Jonathan.

But Imranie rose, and went with quiet footsteps to the door. Jonathan looked at her. She did not truly bar his way, and there was no command or arrogance in her face. Yet because of her he did not leave the room, though Mudien's authority could not keep him.

"I ask you to speak to Veril," she said. "I claim no right to command you, and I understand neither your suffering nor your power. But, Jonathan of Glen Carrah, I love my daughter, and I beg you to tell her before you go whatever you will of King Ilohan her beloved."

Jonathan looked at her: Imranie, wife of Mudien, mother of the Cloth of Joy. Her dress was brown, her hair gray. There were wrinkles in the skin of her face, and her hands were brown and rough from long labor. She was not tall or stately, yet she seemed to him as she stood there more than a queen. What more he could not say, and he was weary and did not wish to speak to Veril or Eleanor. Yet he did not refuse her.

A few moments later he was in another room, gathered around a cheerful hearth with Veril, Eleanor, and Imranie. They all sat in chairs pulled close to the fire, but he remained standing. "The king gave me this message for Veril," he said, and pulled a crumpled parchment from a pocket of his clothes.

Veril touched the parchment very gently, almost reverently, and slowly she unfolded it. Then she sat absolutely still, her lips parted a little, seeing and knowing nothing but the words she was reading. Sorrow and happiness were together in her face, but at the last sorrow won out. She looked up at Jonathan with a question in her eyes. "What does he mean by his weakness?" she asked.

"I never read it," said Jonathan. "What does he say about it?"

Veril read the message aloud, very softly: "I thought that in sending you away I protected you, giving you yet one more chance to choose a shielded life in Ceramir if you would. Alas! Unknowingly I sent you to your death. And because of my weakness and my crown, I have not been able even to come to die in your defense. If Ceramir falls, I beg you, go with Brogal and such others as may escape. Follow him in whatever path he thinks the wisest, whether over the mountains or into Cembar. Do this, I beg you, so that when I fall in battle I may hope that somewhere far behind my battle line you are still safe and free. It may be that you will marry another and raise children in hiding, for the rebuilding of our world. In spite of everything, believe that I love you." It seemed to Jonathan that the girl's soft, low voice filled the whole world as she read. The love she shared with Ilohan was as deep and wondrous as Naomi's love – and equally doomed now in the ruin of the world. Jonathan forced his weary mind to remember the question that she had asked. She had asked what Ilohan had meant by his weakness.

"Ilohan wanted to give me the crown," he said. "He wanted to come and defend you. But I could not accept the crown. I challenged him to a friendly match with swords, to decide the issue, because there was no other way. I defeated him, and so saved his life, for a little while. I defend you in his place. He calls it weakness that he was conquered by me, but he is strong."

All now seemed futile and worthless to Jonathan: his victory over Ilohan, and everything else that he or any other had ever accomplished. He had fallen out of the realm of hope and purpose, into ashes and emptiness. Yet, like a drowning man reaching up his hand into the air for one last time, he tried from the depths of his own despair to comfort Veril with words spoken as if there were still hope. "Ilohan loves you, Veril," he said. "If you doubt his love because he has not come, cease doubting. Go wherever your heart leads you."

Veril stood and ran to Jonathan. She took his calloused hands in hers, and tried almost frantically to move them, but he held them rigidly at his sides. "You have saved him from dying for me," she said, tears coming into her eyes, "But now I am the cause of your death instead!"

He was desperately weary and bewildered. He searched frantically through his mind for some comfort for her, and suddenly he considered her a little child, and spoke to her as he might have to a child. "You are not the cause of my death," he said, pushing her gently away. "Do not be foolish." He thought that, like a child, she would believe him. She let go his hands, and hardly knowing what he did he turned and left the room.

Veril stood looking after him, unmoving, her hands still lifted as she had lifted them to hold Jonathan's. Then she turned and sat down on the hearth, her head bowed, her grief too deep for tears. King Ilohan had not come, but another had, to die for her. She would never see Ilohan again, but she would have laid at her door the blood of another man, a man who did not love her, a strange hero whose pain terrified her. She felt his anguish, but did not understand it, and it was a nightmare to her.

She started suddenly, and then realized that Lady Eleanor had sat beside her and put an arm around her. "Jonathan is not yours to care for," said Eleanor. "Others will have that task, so do not be troubled about him. Believe what he has said, for he does not lie."

"But why did he come here, Ella, except to save Ilohan, and why did Ilohan need to be saved, except because of me?"

"Because of the Zarnith, child. Because of the evil in the world. But more than only that, Veril. Ilohan and Jonathan know, as Kindrach knew, that part of love's power has always been its willingness to die. Grieve over death, but do not blame yourself for the terrible strength of love. It is one of the signs of God's triumph. Selfless love cannot be turned to evil, nor does it die with lovers' deaths. It comes from God, and has his blessing, and the goodness of it lasts forever. Earth is not your home, Veril, nor Ilohan's, and it is not the home of your love."

"But Jonathan..."

"Have peace concerning Jonathan," said Eleanor. "He is not your charge, dear child."

Eleanor stood and slowly left the room, leaning heavily on her crutches. Veril slid close to her mother, who had also sat upon the hearth. Imranie wrapped her arms around her, and held her close. Veril felt her mother's love as a more powerful thing now than she ever had before: it was tried and proven by the greatness of her need.

But Imranie, as Veril leaned against her, thought, "I am so poor a mother that another has had to speak words of comfort for my child, while I stood by with nothing to say to her. Ah, Veril, if only you could see the depth of my love for you, maybe it would bring you some comfort – but how can that be, when it is of no use?" Veril drifted to sleep in her mother's arms. Imranie sat there for a long time, praying for all her children.

Chapter 20

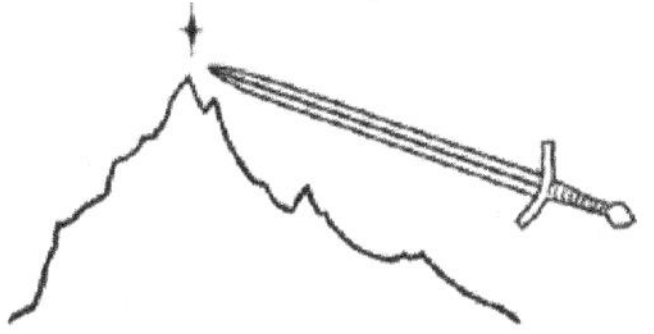

Under an Iron Sky

IN THE FAINT MOONLIGHT A LITTLE WHILE BEFORE DAWN, when it seemed to Jonathan that beyond doubt the night would go on forever, Brogal suddenly reined in his galloping horse with a word of caution. A glow stood in the sky ahead of them, but they were not riding east. It was the light of fire, not dawn.

Jonathan, so weary that the whole world seemed a dream, felt it took them ages to creep up on the Zarnith encampment. Yet the dawn did not overtake them, and at last they walked their horses softly down a rocky gully, and peered from behind a boulder at the camp of Vadshron the Warlord.

A pall of dust and smoke hung over it, veiling the stars. The lurid light of thousands of campfires, burning strangely bright for such a late hour, made the sky glow with a strange, dead light, not like any of the natural lights of stars, moon, or sun, twilight or dawn or full blue day. It was like the glow of iron, Jonathan thought, when it is drawn out of a fire and the red-hot brightness of it dwindles to a pale, dying light before fading to blackness. The Zarnith had turned the sky to iron.

"By the smell, they have roasted some of the cattle that were with them and had a grand feast," said Brogal, "and that also explains why there are so many fires." His voice startled Jonathan, for he had forgotten that he was not alone. "They are less than a day's ride from Ceramir," continued Brogal, "yet according to their messenger of doom they will not attack until the day after tomorrow. In any case it is not likely that they would have feasted so heavily if they intended to attack tomorrow. They will bide their time until they are ready. But they must have a weakness."

"Yes," said Jonathan, forcing himself to think through his weariness and his nightmares. His iron will must still hold his faltering mind and body to their task, and he must learn whatever he could about this army. Then he would return to Ceramir to sleep, one last time. He stared at the Zarnith host, trying to think of what he should notice or look for. But in that moment, despite his efforts, he did not see Vadshron's camp with the eyes of a military commander. He saw it with the eyes of a dreamer – the eyes of one who had once passionately exulted in the beauty of the world, and who even now was deeply aware of its ugliness. He saw a ragged circle of red stars spread out on the plain: a wheel of fire, evilly mocking the stars of heaven which were lost in the haze above it. Its vastness oppressed him: it was too big to take in, and there were too many fires, thousands of them. Something twisted lurked in the very shape of the pattern; there was something not as it should be in its deepest essence… a monster below the world… but he was slipping into nightmares again. He looked at the haze above the great army, and saw in it a single star. It did not seem to him a hopeful omen. It seemed instead an unfaithful star, as though by some dark treachery to its brethren in the heavens it had gained the right to pierce the cloud that shut them out – and yet, it shone through only as a pallid ghost of itself… It was not the morning star.

"I want to go down into the army," said Brogal.

Jonathan shook himself. He must not let his thoughts wander so. "Yes," he said to Brogal, his voice seeming to belong to someone else as he searched for words, "but will they not have guards?"

"They will, I think," said Brogal, "but take this, and do not touch the tips of the arrows."

Brogal gave him a small crossbow, which he easily loaded without the crank. He looked down in consternation at the childish weapon, and the small arrows that fitted it. "They are poisoned," Brogal explained.

They crept down among boulders and through shallow gullies. Brogal moved soundlessly and swiftly, with enjoyment obvious in his face whenever it caught the eerie glow of the sky. Jonathan followed after him more clumsily, fighting hard to remain careful and alert. Yet it was he, more grimly and intently focused than Brogal, who saw the first guard.

The guard stood by a low fire well beyond the outer ring of the camp. A great bow was in his hands. Their path lay right past him; indeed, it was surprising that he had not already seen them. Jonathan stopped Brogal with a hand, and pointed silently to the enemy. Brogal calmly aimed, and shot him in the chest. Jonathan shot also, but his arrow missed, ricocheting off the boulder behind the guard. The guard put both hands to his chest, staggered, and fell without a sound. Brogal continued unconcernedly down the gully, and Jonathan, not knowing what else to do, followed him. When they came near the fallen guard, Brogal astonished Jonathan by leaving the gully and running over to the body, silent as a shadow. He returned with both their arrows. "We will do well not to let them know that we are men," he said. "It is better that they think we are demons."

"Have you ever killed before?" asked Jonathan.

"No," said Brogal calmly. "But these have ridden for Ceramir's destruction. They have been warned and have not heeded the warning, and they have not given us leisure for mercy. I love mercy. But where it cannot be I will not cling to a pretence of it, destroying what I love."

Four more times they saw a guard, but always before he saw them – so Brogal and Jonathan lived, and the guards died. One gave a loud cry as he fell, and Jonathan tensed for a hopeless flight, but no one woke. They crept up the gully until it ended, actually within the outer ring of fires. Then, walking silently as ghosts, but feeling dreadfully exposed beneath that glowing sky, they made their way toward the center of the camp. The tents were not packed close together, and the Zarnith, after their feast, slept well. Now and then a tethered horse looked up at them, and then Brogal would speak to it in soothing yet Zarnith-sounding words that seemed to calm it almost instantly.

They came suddenly within view of the camp's central hub. Scores of guards ringed it, and again Jonathan thought they must surely have been seen. But Brogal slipped silently behind a tent and knelt upon the ground. "We must go back, and we have learned nothing," breathed Jonathan, kneeling beside him and using the faintest of whispers. "If only we could have seen what is at the hub of the wheel – I mean the center of the camp."

"So to you it seemed a wheel also," said Brogal, looking at him intently and speaking in what Jonathan thought a very loud whisper. "And the center of the wheel is its most important point: break that, and the wheel is broken. What is at the center, I wonder? Vadshron? I would shoot Vadshron if I could."

Brogal took out his terrifyingly sharp knife and cut a hole in the wall of the tent. He went inside, leaving Jonathan in shock, sure that Brogal's foolhardiness would cost both their lives. He felt a vague anger at the prospect of being killed before the battle, after all the work he had done to get here in time to fight in it. But though he considered himself about to die, he felt little sense of loss or fear: he was too tired. When Brogal reappeared at the opening and beckoned him inside, he followed in a daze. Brogal threaded his way carefully between the sleeping forms of seven Zarnith. To Jonathan they seemed very strong warriors, but almost incredibly careless of comfort, cleanliness, or beauty. The tent stank strongly of their unwashed bodies. At the far side of the tent, Brogal gestured to two small holes he had made in the fabric, just big enough for a man's two eyes to stare out.

Jonathan put his face to the rough cloth and stared long and hard. At first all that he saw confused him. Scores of Zarnith guards stood in a curved line that he guessed encircled the center of the camp. All of them stood very straight and looked alert and dangerous, with great bows in their hands and spears stuck into the ground beside them. Behind this formidable cordon, however, there seemed to be nothing but a large herd of animals: some sheep and horses, a few cows, and others which he did not recognize. Trying to see past these, Jonathan at last made a satisfying discovery. Behind the sleeping animals, a ring of huge wagons formed the true center of the camp. Hundreds of warriors stood leaning against them, each armed with an axe – and each seeming subtly different from the Zarnith guards. Jonathan wondered if they were Zarnith at all, rather than mercenaries or slaves from another people. He withdrew his gaze and looked at Brogal in the dimness of the tent.

"Vadshron is inside that ring of wagons," whispered Brogal. "I want to go and find him."

"Do not be a fool," breathed Jonathan.

"I will not," said Brogal. "I know that some things cannot be. Now let us return to Ceramir."

He tiptoed across the tent and slipped out the hole he had cut. He led Jonathan back along the way they had come. They passed out of the camp like ghosts, silent beneath the hellish sky, unnoticed by man or beast. They arrived at their own horses so soon that Jonathan could hardly believe it. He felt it must be a trap of the earth, lengthening and shortening to confuse them and hand them over to their enemies.

But Brogal knew the horses had stayed where he had left them because he had told them to, and they loved him. As he and Jonathan mounted and set off to the northeast, the first gray light of dawn showed itself ahead and to their right. It was the true, faithful light of heaven, Brogal thought, putting to shame the Zarnith fires and the evilly glowing haze as dawns always put to shame the lights of men. As the light brightened, Brogal looked back at Jonathan. Jonathan's eyes were glazed, and grief and pain were heavily written on his face, but his hand was sternly clenched upon his reins. Brogal saw a desperately weary man, haunted, going to his doom without a hope or a cause, yet holding his course with an iron will that gave neither him nor others any mercy. Yet that will could break the mind and body it controlled, and thus defeat itself. Jonathan was near the breaking point, Brogal thought. They must reach the Cloth of Joy – and sleep – before it was too late. "The long war with evil is not hopeless, brother in arms," said Brogal. "Do not heed appearances when you are weary and have borne so much. We are riding now for a citadel of love undismayed."

Brogal spoke the words with a hint of mirth, despite their grim night's work and their dire peril. He cried aloud to Merya in the cold morning, and she obeyed his will, her speed like wind and her hooves like thunder, while Jonathan's steed beside her matched her pace.

"Love undismayed..." That phrase stuck in Jonathan's weary mind: the one thing there that was not born of nightmare. "Love undismayed." He clung to those words, and they led him to the thought of Naomi. Yes, her love was undismayed, undismayed in the face of everything that had befallen him and her, undismayed even in the face of his betrayal of her. No. Her love had been like that, but now she was dead. And despite her last words, her love was not stronger than death. Like every other part of her, it had vanished forever from the world. "She is dead. She is dead. I betrayed her trust, and she is dead." He rode on, his face set like a stone. But below his outward calm his grief was so great that it swallowed all the sick darkness of his nightmares, and seemed to swallow his whole being, so that the desert landscape dimmed before his eyes. His horse followed Merya by its own will, for Jonathan no longer guided it. At length he became too weary to feel the full intensity of his grief, and his mind turned from it to a sort of aching gray dullness, and in that state he arrived at the Cloth of Joy.

* * *

He must have dismounted and walked somewhere, for after a while he found that he was no longer on a horse, but in a dark room on a bed. The aching dullness of his mind had receded, and he found himself instead in a dreamlike state. His great sorrow remained, but it loomed over him like a vast thundercloud that dropped no rain: in his dream world neither it nor anything else could touch him. Yet he knew he was not really asleep. He knew an act of his will could tear the veil aside and bring him to full alertness – and full despair. Instead he let himself remain in a half-dream, and therefore only half heartbroken.

He stood and wandered through the silent rooms and out the great front door. It was strange to him that it was night, for he did not realize he had slept for many hours. None seemed to be awake in all the Cloth of Joy. It was as unguarded as a sleeping child, alone in a wild place. He wondered if the Zarnith had already come with some great curse and slain all the others, leaving him to wander alone and hopeless in a place of death. Then he heard the sound of sobbing, and he saw a woman sitting by the lake with a sleeping child between her knees. The night was windless and still. The only sound in the Valley of the Undismayed was the sound of tears: this mother weeping for her child, because the coming day would bring its death. It seemed to Jonathan that the joy of Ceramir was broken.

The woman did not notice him. He stripped off his clothes and slipped gently into the warm lake, naked, fearing no eyes and caring for nothing. He swam just as he had swum after Rennel's death. His grief then had merely brought him anger and a little uneasiness about the future. Now it threatened to undo both his body and his mind, and there was no shadow of a hope. Yet as he swam, even now, the mere repetition of the motion became a sort of comfort, and his dreamlike state still shielded him from the full grief of Naomi's death, Ceramir's coming destruction, and the utter failure of his life.

He had come over the mountains to fight and die in defense of Ceramir. He would certainly do that. Yet as he swam, without ever doubting that he would do it, he idly wondered why. The warm water and the dream-world were kind. He could simply stay there and let the Zarnith come and kill him if they would. Yet he would not – he would get out and do what he had come to do. Justice and honor required it. But what were justice and honor, and why had he followed them at such cost? Certainly not because they would lead to happiness: he had never expected them to do that, and they had not. They were supposed to be things that ought simply to be followed, no matter what. No other reason was needed. But why had he believed that? Had justice and honor any more reality than God? Naomi had died serving her God, even as he himself was going to die serving justice and honor. Was his faith any less foolish than hers? But it did not matter. He would do as he had chosen. He had chosen out of love for Ilohan, out of loyalty to honor and justice. Honor and justice, and even love, seemed meaningless to him now – but then his own life also seemed meaningless. He had vowed one nothing to those other nothings, and the vow would be kept.

A song formed itself in his mind as it had so long before. It seemed to him a mockery of that earlier time, when he had thought he knew what grief was. Yet he was lost and reeling, and the words seemed to join themselves together without his will. He was astonished that the words had real meaning, born as they were out of his bewildered mind and heart. The song eased him a little by its clear statement of his grief, his despair, and his choice – just as a sick man, who has long guessed his fate, might be eased when told clearly that he is dying:

Long have I fought, but in all have won nothing;
False, weak, I lie in the dust.
Reft of my loved one, without cause or hoping –

Dying, because die I must.

Long, dark and bitter has been my last struggle,
Yet from its grief and its pain
Shall come no triumph, and no clear bright morning:
Shall come no justice or gain.

Honor leads onward in fight that is hopeless;
All who dare follow will die.
Yet till now honor has had all my trusting.
Can I turn back now, and fly?

No! That were darkness, and death even deeper.
Once more I raise my cold sword.
All I have lost, and gained nothing for payment;
Here shall death sever my cord.

Meaningless, hopeless, the world holds no comfort;
Caught twixt despair and despair!
Faithless defender of good that shall perish,
Cut off from all that was fair.

Was ever goodness, or was it but vapor?
Had I some reason to die?
Hopeless, yet I will defend what I wish was;
Perish beneath an iron sky!

Yes, so it was. The Zarnith had turned the sky to iron, and beneath it he would die. There was no hope, no reason to fight, no justice or honor, nothing that would last. It all perished; it all mocked; it was all meaningless. He dragged himself out of the lake, shivering in the cold. He dressed himself quickly and went into the house, glad now of the fires that, though all burnt down to glowing coals, gave forth vast amounts of heat. He wrapped himself in a blanket and lay down in the bed from which he had arisen. Sleep came swiftly upon him, strong and deep, from a far off place.

* * *

When he awoke it was early dawn, and a hand was shaking his shoulder. So deeply had he been asleep that awareness of that hand came to him even before he remembered his despair. It was a sturdy, calloused hand, steady but not cruel in its grip. It was the hand of a man who could be trusted, who would not rouse a sleeper without good cause.

Jonathan sat up, and it was his father who had woken him, and he remembered. He remembered that today he would go out to fight the Zarnith with a small band of men, and that he would die with them in the desert. The iron control of his will flooded back to him fast and strong, and though it brought intense pain, he desired it. For one moment only he hovered on the edge of asking himself again why he should fight. But he knew he had no answer, and he pushed the question away. There were choices to be made and things to be done. "How long do we have?" he asked his father.

"Not long," said Barnabas. "Rangol's scouts say the vanguard of the Zarnith will reach the gates of Ceramir a little after midday."

Jonathan stood. He would have been alarmed, if his despair had not been so deep that no bad news could darken it. "I will face them at the gap in the hills, as I told Mudien," he said. "We must hurry."

Barnabas looked his son in the face, and for a moment the older blacksmith felt that time stood still. The sun had not yet cleared the eastward mountains, but the whole sky in that direction was filled with dawn light, pouring soft and fresh upon Jonathan's head. He was young and strong, and his long sleep and swim had given him nearly a full recovery from the terrible journey. He was a young man, capable of deep joy and great love.

"And his love is great," thought his father as he looked at him. "His love is great, for Naomi and for Ilohan, though it has been blocked and marred and brought him grief, because of the evil of the world and his hopelessness. But his hopelessness is true, because he is without God. And the joy that once shone in his eyes and brought me joy is broken. And he is my son, and I love him. He has no hope. I have not led him to the love of Christ, the stay and center of my life..."

That was Barnabas' greatest grief, on this morning of apocalyptic disaster. For a moment he was tempted to draw his sword swiftly and wound Jonathan, so that he could not go out to die. That would keep him in Ceramir, which might hold out against the Zarnith a few hours longer. But he knew he must not do it; he must let him go. Barnabas closed his eyes, and his hand slipped away from his hilt. "Father, forgive me," he prayed silently. "Only you can save him."

"Let us go now and rouse our men," said Barnabas aloud.

The woods of Ceramir were almost unbelievably fresh and lovely. Mist floated off the lake and lay in forest hollows, gracing the bare branches with shining drops of dew. Soft cool color filled the clear sky. Tiny buds waiting to burst forth into full-blown spring lent a hint of red and gold to the gray trees, and birds flitted about singing songs of hope.

When Jonathan and Barnabas reached the camp of Karolan, the men were already awake. Many of the Children of Ceramir, including Veril and Auria, were serving them hot food and drink. "Wait until they have done eating," said Barnabas, "and then call them to battle. We may ourselves eat, and discuss our plans."

They sat down on a log at the edge of the woods, and food was brought to them; steaming plates of meat and eggs and root vegetables. Jonathan did not notice the one who brought them, but Barnabas did, and the sight of her stayed in his memory. Her face was pale and still, with eyes that seemed to plead humbly for something. He could not imagine her either laughing or singing, but there was not the air of shrinking in her manner that he would have expected to go with such pleading eyes. "She is between darkness that once claimed her, body and soul, and light which would have her now," he thought, "and her darkness was so great that she can hardly believe in the light. Gradually her eyes are opening to it. But this world is moving from light to darkness, if the Zarnith are to have their will, and they would break her before her sunrise comes. There is great reason to defend this place, where healing such as hers is possible."

"There is little need to plan my battle," Jonathan's voice interrupted his father's thoughts.

"There are a few choices to make," said Barnabas. "You must decide whether to hide yourselves behind the barricade and attempt to surprise the Zarnith, or whether you will challenge them to charge with a banner. You must decide how you will attack them when they come."

Yes, Jonathan thought, there were those things to decide, and others: what to say to his men, how to choose those who would die with him, and how to lead them. He was suddenly weary with the choices. But he pushed his weariness aside, and thought hard. The Zarnith would see the barricade. That alone might be enough to make them charge, so attempting to ambush them was likely futile. In any case, he did not want to do that. He wanted to defy the Zarnith and provoke their charge – the legendary charge that could never be broken. If all the horses in their front rank were suddenly transfixed with arrows, would the charge remain unbreakable? He would see.

Jonathan walked with a swift stride up through the stubble fields. He climbed a rock that sat in the midst of the camp of Karolan: some splinter off the great mountains that had long ago fallen out here in the soil. All around him in the mist, men looked up expectantly, some still with bread in their hands.

He had done this many times before, but this time was different. In this peaceful place it seemed strange and impossible to give a great speech about death with honor and courage without hope. He wondered if he had ever known what courage or honor meant, if they meant anything at all. But he must speak; the men were looking at him expectantly from every side, waiting for his blazing encouragement and call to arms.

"Men of Karolan," he said, in a clear voice that reached every ear in the listening army, "you have come a long road, with great courage, and today is the culmination of your adventure. It was the will of King Ilohan that I lead you out to the gap in the desert hills just west of here. Yet he laid me under no command regarding this. I will not lead all of you out to the desert. The mountain walls of Ceramir make it a great fortress, and that fortress must have defenders. Yet King Ilohan is a great king, merciful and kind, a mighty warrior loved by his people. I do not wish to neglect his desire. Thus I intend to march out with fifteen score of you – if so many will follow me

– to the desert gap. We will fly the banners of Karolan without fear, and the Zarnith will charge as they have not since the days of Dradrag. Their horde will cover the land, and their arrows fill the sky. We will kill as many as we can, but we will all die, for against such a host we have no hope at all. Those who do not march with me will stay in Ceramir, to fight in its final defense under the command of my father Barnabas, and of Mudien Lord of the Cloth of Joy, who are both wise and mighty men. To neither army can I promise any hope. Both roads are roads of courage, for you have all long ago left the roads of cowards behind. Who will march with me?"

*　　　　*　　　　*

In the darkness below the mountains, Hannah sat beside a dwindling fire. Only she was awake: the brigands lay asleep all around her. Naomi, still alive, lay wrapped in blankets, with her head on Hannah's lap. She was dreadfully thin, and the firelight played strangely over the hollows of her cheeks and her closed eyes. Hannah feared every day that she would die, and with every new awakening she was surprised and thankful to find her alive. Yet she felt sick herself – sick with her fear, and her helplessness, and the intensity of her love for Naomi. She wondered what these days were doing to Naomi, what scars they were leaving on her body and mind that might not be healed even if by a miracle her life were saved.

The darkness seemed to arch over Hannah like some vast presence of brooding evil. She leaned over Naomi as though to protect her from it. "Aye, protect her now," the darkness seemed to say. "It is because of your crime that she is here, dying, weak, alone. Already she has gone beyond recovery, and her mind is broken. But she would have been well if

Barnabas had found her a day earlier. You held him back. You have slain her. Protect her now, now that it is too late."

Hannah felt herself stained by that past sin, that selfish clinging to Barnabas, that cowardly shrinking from pain. Because of it Naomi would die, and she herself would die. Beyond her death there loomed the greater calamity of Hell that she deserved. Under the brooding, malignant darkness – the darkness in which she had so long striven alone for Naomi's life – Hannah's usual common sense and humble hope deserted her, and she was all alone, cringing in her guilt and fear.

"What a place for Naomi to die!" thought Hannah, with shame and horror deeper than words can describe, "And I have brought her here." The darkness was cold and vast. Hannah was sitting on coarse, cold sand, damp from the new underground river they were following. The roof and walls of the cave arched far away in the black void, and legions of evil things with eyes that saw in the dark might be watching there, gawking at the poor humans that had stumbled in there to die according to their pleasure. In the darkness the roar of far-off water might be the mirthless laughter of fiends, and the groans, booms, and rumbles that sometimes came to Hannah's ears might be monstrous forms moving about with evil intent.

"And you are fit to be their prey," said the darkness to Hannah. "But Naomi is not, and yet they will have her too, because of you. Cower over her, do! It will not save – "

"I trust," said Hannah aloud, cutting off the voice of the darkness.

No triumphant vindication came to her heart. No blazing shaft of white light parted the darkness. She was still afraid, still sick with grief and shame and guilt. Still the darkness towered above her and gloated over her, and she felt powerless. But there were her own two words, spoken aloud, heard in the echoing cavern: I trust. And that was her answer. She trusted God to be who she knew he was, to forgive her and redeem her as he had promised. She trusted Christ, who had borne the darkness and the guilt for her, faced it all, died beneath it, and then broken it all forever when he came back to life. He loved her; he was her Rescuer and her Redeemer.

Hannah said no more words, gave no bold challenges to the darkness that still seemed a vast, malignant thing bending over her. But gradually her trust spread through her being, and she knew that God had forgiven her. The darkness lied, but Christ her Lord was true. She clung to him, and had nothing else. She closed her eyes and felt as though she were swirling in a black whirlpool, but yet she was not afraid. She opened her eyes and looked down at Naomi's face in the firelight, and it was full of peace. For a while it seemed to Hannah that the darkness did not exist, that the whole world was just as large as the circle of the dying fire, and Naomi's peace filled it. They were not afraid. They were not in danger. They were loved, and that was all she needed to know. Naomi breathed quietly. "Father," said Hannah, "I have thought she would die so many times. You kept her through the high places when she could not breathe, and still she lives. Father, bring her back to health and strength, and joy... Father, you know what is in my heart... I cannot say it..."

She wept quietly, and later on when the Bowlord and his men woke up they found her still leaning over Naomi, asleep. They did not steal the poison and wake Hannah with torture. They loaded her and Naomi roughly into the stretcher, covered them with blankets, and carried them to the boat in which they were now traveling. They knew, though Hannah did not, that half a day more of grueling travel would bring them to the desert not far from the valley they called Brightshadow.

Chapter 21

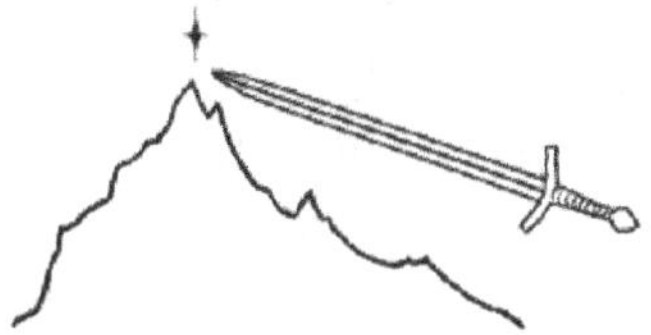

A Score and Five

"I SEE THE SPEARS," CRIED JONATHAN'S WATCHMAN IN A voice that rang all up and down the barricade between the desert hills.

Jonathan leaped up on a great tree trunk that formed the top of the barricade near him, and stood there looking out into the west. The morning sun cast his long shadow on the pale desert rock before him, and in its light everything looked sharp and clear, right to the distant horizon. That horizon stood out bright against the sky behind it, which would remain a dusky blue until the sun rose higher to brighten it. Jonathan had to look a moment before he saw the Zarnith, but once noticed they were obvious. They darkened a wide stretch of the bright horizon, and dust billowed up from them in a pale cloud before the dull blue of the sky. Jonathan could see no spears yet, only that dark mass on the desert and that brown-white cloud in the sky. Still he marveled at the number of men and horses that must be coming.

He jumped down from the barricade, and looked up and down its length at his men, one third of those he had led from Petrag, widely spaced now across the long barricade. He wondered why they had come. So many had been willing that he had had to turn some away. Why would men die for justice and honor, why would they stand firm with courage when there was no hope? He did not know. Yet here they were, and here he was, and they would stand.

The banner of Karolan shone against the blue sky just above him. It had no wind to unfurl it, but still it was beautiful. He thought of leaping up next to it, of standing there and holding it aloft, of giving his men one more great speech of courage and glory. He looked up and down the line, and saw them all resolute and calm, their bows in their hands and their swords ready. "No," he thought, "I have given my last speech, and I do not know why I am here. They have more courage than I, and I have already told them all that they must do. Now it is only to wait."

The waiting seemed intolerable, but he bore it by thinking only about how he would fight, not about death or despair or Naomi's loss. As the waiting drew to its end, it seemed to have passed too quickly. Jonathan's heart beat fast. Something in him wanted desperately to cling to life despite the pain it had brought him. But then his fear went down in burning rage against death, and he was determined to fight as he had never fought before.

The Zarnith horde changed form as it came toward them. The very desert and sky seemed to wait in dreadful silence. The men behind the barricade looked at one another without speaking. Thoughts flew through their minds that they could not put into words and would never have time to say. They saw the Zarnith horsemen come together in ranks, half a thousand riders abreast, filling the gap between the desert hills. Their motion changed and became faster: the Zarnith had begun to gallop. A moment after the men of Karolan saw this, they began to hear its sound, like distant thunder. The earth beneath them was trembling. It was a Zarnith charge, a legendary terror for years without count. The Karolans stood to meet it, stretched so thin across the barricade that each man could not reach out his hand and touch his neighbor. Some would have laughed, had the awe and terror of it been less great.

The thunderous roar of the charge filled the air, gathering force at every moment, as though it would at last grow loud enough to rend the shaking earth. The men of Karolan stood firm. Suddenly a new sound came to them, even louder than the deep thunder of the hooves: a screaming wail that yet possessed some horrible wild music, eerie beyond words. Some felt it carried a dreadful curse to pierce their impotent defenses and slay their hearts and minds. It was the Zarnith war song, sung by seven score and nineteen thousands, and even Jonathan was unprepared for its terror.

Despite the sound of the charge and the screaming of the song, its words somehow came through with fearful clarity. Only Jonathan of all the men had been told its meaning, but few failed to understand its import. Fearsome, dire, and merciless it sounded, and fearsome, dire, and merciless it was:

Lo skiera skacal whyethree
Lo hrethri ska yeen yohilee
Lon ikrok ska neer red whython
Lo hrado scha Arnith thraigon

Korak srad astrailo, srad thraiah
Astrailon thro fooshgorn whyflaiah
Whyfra strai sko Zarnith sgearoth
Scha Arnith fo hreon druboth

The song's screaming power stabbed the ears of the men of Karolan, while the earth shook beneath their feet. Jonathan repeated to himself the translation Ilohan had given, long ago, at the first sight of this desert:

Our banner the dust;
Our mother the sky;
Our arrows the death that has wings;
Our father the windblown, hot desert.

None stand before us, none ever.
Before us all enemies fly.
Fly before the Children of the Desert in despair.
The Desert will swallow your bones.

The song ended and the men of Karolan breathed easier for a moment, though the Zarnith drew ever closer. Then at last the battle began with yet another sound: this time one that was familiar as well as strange. All the men of Karolan had heard the swift, shrill whisper of an arrow drawn and shot. But now that sound was multiplied a hundred thousand fold. A fierce, high wail filled the air: the terrible wild song of the Zarnith bows. The arrows leaped up in dark clouds from the charging horde, and fell upon the barricade like hail.

The air around them now filled with flying death, the Karolans huddled behind tree trunks and wooden planks, trying to shut their ears against the wail of the arrows leaping up and the vicious, splintering cracks of them coming down. It was a terrible time. From their hiding places many of the men could not get a view of the Zarnith, to tell how close they were. Jonathan's orders were to draw bow when the Zarnith vanguard came within three score paces of the barricade, and shoot into the horses' hearts when they came within fifteen paces. The arrows would come straight and fast, striking with terrible force, bringing down the whole front rank of the Zarnith. The next rank of horses would slam into them as they went down, and then crash in terrible ruin before the Karolan barricade. The mighty force of the Zarnith charge, the charge that had never broken in history, would be turned against itself.

But the men could not carry out this plan if they could not see the Zarnith coming. The thunder of the charge filled their ears and seemed to numb their minds, and their hands holding their great bows hung limp. Rather than preparing to shoot the Zarnith, they waited for the shattering impact of the Zarnith charge. It seemed to them that they and their barricade would be trampled into the dust, until nothing remained of them but a faint red stain on the path of the Zarnith: their blood and entrails pounded into the desert sand.

"Draw!" thundered Jonathan. Not all heard him over the thunder of hooves, but those who could see the enemy were already fitting arrows to their bowstrings. Others saw this and imitated them: in a few heartbeats all bows were drawn. Behind the barricade there was a sense of grim joy; they would get to fight after all. This was it. This was the end. Soon they would be dead heroes, but, if any were left to remember, it was the deeds of these moments that they would tell of in their songs.

The sound of the Zarnith bows ceased abruptly; the Zarnith vanguard was too close and they would not shoot their own. The men of Karolan stood up to aim. The thunder of the charge filled their ears. "Hold!"' cried Jonathan, seeing some over-eager to shoot. The Zarnith were coming on. Their horses were lathered, their wild hair blew in the wind, they were reaching for their spears. The earth and the barricade shook with their galloping. The Karolans desperately wanted to shoot; the bows trembled in their hands because the earth trembled beneath their feet. "Hold," said Jonathan. The Zarnith were coming on. The Zarnith were fifteen paces away, seeming twice the height of normal men, two heartbeats from shattering impact with the barricade, leveling their spears to throw. "Shoot!" cried Jonathan in a voice like thunder.

The Karolan arrows advanced too fast for sight. The front rank of horses screamed, reared, and crashed to the ground with deafening noise. The chaos was staggering, overwhelming. Some of the Karolan warriors merely stared at it, open mouthed, unable to do anything. Others drew and shot too fast to aim, with breathless, frantic effort. For a moment everything seemed to go as Jonathan had hoped. The Zarnith behind crashed into those in front of them with terrible force. Men were thrown into the air, horses were torn limb from limb, the air was full of shouts and screams and the cracks of breaking bone. Many of the Zarnith riders had managed to jump clear of the wreck. Some were stunned or crippled, but the rest charged the Karolan barricade on foot, throwing their spears with terrible force, and drawing their serrated red swords as they came.

The Karolans shot many of them, but the Zarnith spears splintered wood planking and burst through shields, and many Karolans fell before them. Some of the Zarnith swordsmen reached the barricade, and the fighting was brutal there. Jonathan, after deflecting two spears with the sword of Kindrach, had to fight three Zarnith at once as he stood on a large tree trunk in the barricade. His blood was hot within him, and he felt the battle was going well. The Zarnith fell back before him in terror, and he shattered their weapons and killed them with terrible sword-strokes. Their blood stained the ground beneath the trunk on which he stood, but before their bodies even hit the ground he was looking up again, sword ready, to meet whatever was coming next in the fight. Only moments could matter now, one by one as they came, moments of fighting with all his force and all his thought.

But even as he fought furiously he became aware that all was lost. For the strength of the Zarnith charge was ever that it could not be broken: that, no matter what, it would go on. And this was no legend. The warriors of Vadshron knew what to do almost without thought, and their horses obeyed them as their own bodies. They had been taught since childhood that one thing was more important than all else: the charge must not break. It did not.

The ground was littered with fallen horses, writhing and groaning in their death throes: a barricade of bodies to throw the charge into disarray. But as Jonathan looked up in fleeting instants of the fight, he saw the new ranks of Zarnith riders come – riders who had had just the heartbeat of warning they needed. They did not slow; they hardly even turned. Wounded horses reared and screamed around them, and yet somehow they came through, utterly unscathed, without a hint of stumbling or injury. The men of Karolan were already fighting hand to hand at the barricade. No arrows came to answer the new ranks of Zarnith riders, and their spears flew straight and fast and hard.

The spears killed many, sometimes after splintering through planks and shelters that had seemed secure. An instant later the riders reached the barricade.

They leaped it where they could, and where they could not they rammed it, killing their horses and sometimes themselves in a terrifying effort to crack it by force of speed. The Karolans who could still fight stood up to meet them, slashing or stabbing at horses and men as they went by. But now the Zarnith had become an irresistible flood, coming over the barricade by thousands. Some still threw spears at the defenders with terrible force, or spent their horses and themselves trying to shatter and trample some part of the barricade that was still standing – but many simply went by. The barricade was broken, and no miracle had come. The Zarnith could look ahead to Ceramir, and to the wide empty lands between them and defenseless Norkath.

Still Jonathan stood upon his tree trunk amid the flood, and fought as he had never fought before. Spears glanced harmlessly from the blade of his sword. He leaped aside from a horse as it came at him, and slashed off its foreleg with a mighty blow. Before the rider could leave his saddle Jonathan had split his head, and then turned to meet his next foe. The barricade trembled and the tree trunk shifted beneath him as the defenses were shattered, but still he held his place, and took down another horseman.

But the next horse came while he was fighting another enemy on foot, and though he slew that man, he lost his chance to jump out of the horse's path. He raised the sword of Kindrach in a lightning motion and plunged it into the horse's heart. But he had transfixed the horse in the midst of a leap, and it still threatened to crush him. Its speed carried him up and over the barricade, still clinging to the hilt of his sword, even while he tried with all his strength to push the animal sideways and down. Finding purchase for his feet on the stone at the last moment, he succeeded. Alone, he threw down that horse and crushed its rider beneath it: the greatest feat of strength he had ever performed. Jonathan recovered his sword, gasping and trembling from the effort, and turned to face the battle again.

The horse's leap had taken him to a place where a low wooden wall still gave some protection – but not much. Even as he turned, a horse was leaping over it. The rider's sword-stroke missed him, but the horse struck him a glancing blow that threw him forcefully to the ground. He had managed to wound the horse as he fell, but there was no time to think of that. Instantly he was on his feet again, trying to regain his tree trunk. His left shoulder did not seem to work quite properly after the fall. He saw splinters spray from the top of the low wall, and then suddenly he was on the ground again. Something had grabbed his right thigh and thrown him down. Blood was flowing all around him. He realized dully that he had been speared. Just as he tried to get to his feet, a horse struck the low wood wall before him and brought the whole structure crashing down on his head. Darkness swallowed him, a darkness filled with thunder.

The darkness did not last long, but it ended with only a narrow slit of light, and the consciousness of tremendous pain. His head was oddly clear, and his mind very focused on the battle. He must get up and keep fighting. He pushed himself up and the wood above him cracked, two large pieces parting to let him through. His sword was still in his hand. He stood, gasping and dizzy with the pain in his thigh. He looked down, and the spear was still sticking into his leg, but it seemed partly to have worked loose. In sudden rage he struck at the spear with Kindrach's sword, slashing away from his body, turning the blade to catch the wooden shaft and pull it out. The world seemed to fill with pain. He found himself falling, but he clung to consciousness with an iron grip. He was lying on splintered wood, still bleeding from his thigh, but the spear had come out.

He stood. The Zarnith were no longer coming over the barricade, and it was oddly quiet. Yet he did hear a distant sound of shouts, the creaking of wood, and the cracking of whips. He looked to the west to try to find some explanation of this, and he saw no Zarnith riders at all; the entire host had passed over the barricade and gone on toward Ceramir. But he did see the wagons that he and Brogal had noticed on their spying journey. They were huge, and there were scores upon scores of them. Each was guarded by a small contingent of warriors marching on foot, armed with axes. There were at least a score of horses to each wagon, but even with so many they did not go forward at more than a walking pace. He must attack them, of course, even if it were utterly hopeless: he had chosen to fight to the end, and he would. Yet he stood staring at them a moment first, while the blood ran down his leg.

They were wagons... the wagons he and Brogal had seen... the wagons at the hub of the wheel. Jonathan realized that he was faint, and must not let his thoughts wander – and yet perhaps there had been something in them. "Break the hub," Brogal had said, "and the wheel is broken." These wagons had been that hub. One particular type caught his attention. Their sides were made not of wood planks but of some variegated dark material that bulged out through frames of massive wooden beams. About a third of the Zarnith wagons were like this – different from any other wagons Jonathan had ever seen. Suddenly he guessed what they carried. It was these he must attack, without hope... yet if only he had known earlier, if only he had understood... Were any alive to follow him now?

He climbed up on the shattered remains of his tree trunk. "Men of Karolan," he cried, "stand up and fight!"

And men stood. They were a wounded, bloody remnant, no more than two score men, and they dragged themselves out of the wreckage unable to believe their ears. Some were a long way down the barricade from Jonathan, and had a pain-filled journey to reach him. Yet when they looked at him, standing there on the log, they came to him and gathered round in wonder. He pointed with his great sword. "Those are the water wagons of the Zarnith," he said. "Destroy them, and though they capture Ceramir, they will die of thirst in their own desert, and never reach Karolan or Norkath."

The nearest wagon was almost upon them now. "Men of Karolan," cried Jonathan, "we fight with all our strength, and at the end of our strength we fight still. For King Ilohan! For Karolan! For justice, for honor, for glory! Charge!"

And they charged. They ran, marveling that their limbs obeyed their will. They felt a strange glory in fighting now as wounded survivors of the unbreakable charge – as those who should already have been dead, and who now ran toward death, not victory. As Jonathan ran he said between his breaths, in a low voice, "For justice, for honor, for glory. For hope, for joy, for love, for beauty. For Ceramir, for Naomi, for Heaven, for God, for all that would make life worth living if only it existed. Charge." This was the end. When he stopped running now he would die. His ruthlessly driven mind and body would at last cease from their long struggle. This was the end, the last losing fight in a long, bitter war – a war fought for things that had never existed.

They reached the first wagon, and to their surprise the ten axe-wielding warriors fled in terror. The wagon's size awed them. The fabric that contained the water seemed to be many-layered leather, bulging out within a framework of huge wooden beams. The enormous, iron-bound wheels stood above their heads, and the score of powerful horses pulled the wagon along at a good pace. Jonathan, followed by four others, leaped up on the lowest beams. They slashed the leather with wide sword-strokes. Water gushed out in huge torrents, throwing them forcefully from the wagon. The horses lurched forward with the sudden reduction of their load. The men picked themselves up, bruised, soaked, and gasping, from the drenched ground. "Now on!" said Jonathan. "There are many more!"

The men were at the end of their strength, weak from loss of blood, and wracked with pain. Still they forced themselves to run up to wagon after wagon. Each time, the guards ran in terror. At the risk of being crushed by the great, slow turning wheels, the men of Karolan clambered onto the beams and slashed the leather. The Zarnith host's life-giving water came rushing out, throwing the Karolans to the ground with bruising force – except in the case of wagons that had already been drunk dry. Of these they found three, and each was a blessed relief.

One by one, the men of Karolan died of wounds and exhaustion. Some simply collapsed on the desert ground never to rise. The rush of escaping water cast two down under the wheels of one wagon, where the still-vast weight of the emptied wagon crushed them. Jonathan led his dwindling band mercilessly onward, though he himself saw strange hazes shimmer in his vision, and wondered if he had the strength to raise his sword for one more stroke. They had now slashed a score and four of the great wagons, but fourteen of them had died, and there were many wagons left.

A large force of men with axes came suddenly into sight from behind the next wagon: the guards who had fled before had gathered together and now turned at bay. Jonathan looked back at his men, and saw that though they stood at the edge of death, their courage was not broken. Without speaking he turned and raised his sword for the charge, but he did not look at it. In his mind he pictured the blade cold and gray, bereft of glory in the meaningless world.

The men of Karolan saw Jonathan's sword flash brilliantly in the morning sun as he ran forward to the hopeless fight. They followed him, and they fought. They were wounded, bruised, hopeless, and weary, yet still they fought. The axe men drew back in terror from their first onslaught. The men of Karolan reached the wagon, and used it as moving cover on one side while they fought their last stand.

One by one the Karolans fell, hacked brutally beneath the heavy blades of their enemies. When only Jonathan and five others were left, their foes tried to force them beneath the wheels of the wagon, and one man was crushed this way. But Jonathan heard his scream, and thought how they had not yet destroyed this wagon. A last rage kindled in him against death, and against these enemies who would kill him, and against the wagon that had crushed his companion. He fought with terrible ferocity, as though he were not wounded – as though he were not even weary. Heads and axe-hafts cracked before his mighty sword, and for one fleeting moment his enemies fell back again in terror. In the instant of respite he struck at the wagon wheel with the hardest sword-stroke he had ever given. He put into that blow all his strength of will and muscle, down to its last dregs, with nothing held back, no caution, no fear, no hope. Any sword but Kindrach's would have shattered before that fearsome impact, but Kindrach's held. There was a deafening crash and a painfully bright flash of light. The sword that had once been Eleanor's dowry rebounded fiercely and fell from Jonathan's numbed, bruised hands, ringing like a bell struck by a madman. But the great iron wheel rim, thicker and broader than a man's two hands placed together, was broken.

The sturdy wood beneath it groaned with the weight of water it suddenly had to bear alone, and broke with a crack like thunder. The horses reared and whinnied as the wagon ceased rolling.

The whole attack on the wheel had taken perhaps two heartbeats in that desperate fight, yet when Jonathan turned to face his enemies again, his last remaining companions were dead. The axe men rushed at him, shouting. His sword lay on the ground at his feet, and his jarred hands would not obey his will. He saw an axe stroke coming down toward his head. He raised his left hand to block the haft below the blade. Terrible pain shot through him as both hand and arm were broken. Yet at this cost he had diverted the blow; the blade went on his left and did not touch him. He was still weaponless amid a surging rush of enemies.

A man whose axe he had broken earlier drew a dagger and stabbed him in the back, below his left shoulder. The blade went deep, up to the very hilt, and then broke off with a crack. Jonathan fell to his knees. He felt no pain, but he knew it was over. He could not fight with this wound: he was dying now. He heard the man's yell of triumph, as if from a long way away. An instant later it turned into a scream of terror, echoed by many voices: the wagon was tilting over with groans and cracks as its frame broke against the desert stone. A haze was in Jonathan's eyes, but through it he saw the sword of Kindrach and a shadow falling across the ground before him. He caught the sword up swiftly in his right hand, and swung it high above his head. He felt it cutting something, and then a great weight of rushing water pushed him down. There was a loud crash and many screams, and cold darkness enveloped him. A strange, disconnected thought flitted through his mind: "A score and five is not enough." Then the greatest strength of his iron will could no longer hold his thought, and darkness took him wholly.

Chapter 22

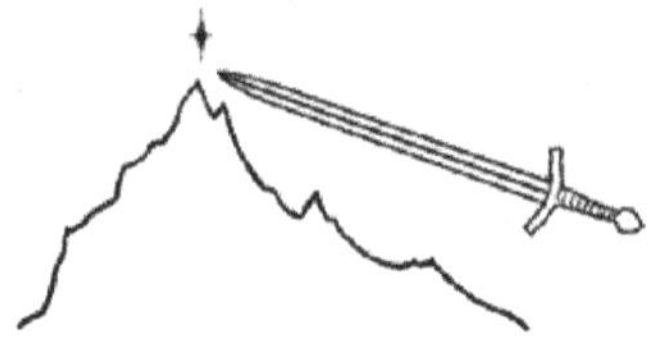

Waiting for Wind

KING ILOHAN STOOD IN HIS TENT ON THE NORKATH border, with Benther at his side. Before them on a table lay the body of a Zarnith messenger of doom, killed at Aaronkal two days before. Guards from there had brought his body to the king, and carried news also of his deeds. He had ridden openly and slowly through the nearby villages to the gate of Aaronkal, and a considerable crowd had followed him there. He had thrown down two tokens on the steps of the castle, and made a thunderous and incomprehensible speech in the Zarnith tongue. He had ended by throwing his spear into the crowd, where it killed a child. A guard had shot him dead even as he was raising his second spear. The exact message he had brought could not be known, but the tokens showed his intent clearly enough. One was a huge bundle of miniature Zarnith swords, seven score and nineteen, tied with a rope. The other was a piece of ivory engraved with a symbol of the sunrise, a score and sixteen times. Above the last sunrise a crude parody of the Stone, Sword, and Star had been engraved, and above that a human skull. "A score and sixteen days, and then they come with seven score and nineteen thousands, and it is death to Karolan," said Benther, examining it. "I suppose that is when they intend to reach Aaronkal."

The king said nothing; he was looking at the face of the dead Zarnith. His final spear, the one he had not thrown, lay beneath his body, and the hand that would have thrown it was gray and cold at his side. His dead face was set in ferocity, his teeth bared. "They were to be at Ceramir today," said Ilohan. "And they have no mercy."

Benther was silent. The king's eyes, still looking at the dead face, no longer saw it. His thoughts were far away, with Veril. He would have given anything he had ever had to be with her, to defend her, even without hope. Eleanor was there too – and Imranie and Mudien and Auria and Brogal... And the Zarnith threw spears into crowds and killed children, and he was not there to defend Veril.

Benther knew what he was thinking, and tried to comfort him. "You stayed with your people, Your Majesty," he said.

Ilohan turned on him with anger in his eyes, but then the flame went out and there was nothing but deep, deep pain. "Forgive me, Sir Benther," he said. "I thank you for your attempts to comfort me. But all my plans go astray, and there is no hope... At Aaronkal, a score and sixteen days from two days ago... That means... At Drantar's Gap in about fourteen days, or sixteen at the most. And we could scarcely reach it in a score. They will be through the gap; they will be on the plains of eastern Norkath. Unstoppable as the wind..."

There was a long silence. The morning sun shone on the outside of the tent, but the air was cold and still. The dead Zarnith had a strong smell, not yet of decay but of a life without washing, and of strange oils that the Karolans did not know. It seemed to Benther as he stood there like the smell of despair.

He wanted to advise Ilohan to order the dead messenger buried, now that they had both examined the body, but despair pressed on him until he felt that to speak would be like lifting a heavy weight. Then a sound of far-off shouting reached his ears, and Benther sprang to the entrance of the tent with his sword drawn. He saw that a Norkath warrior was making his way through the camp of Karolan, escorted anxiously by many Karolan guards with drawn swords. He appeared unarmed, but the Karolans did not trust the appearance. He came toward the king's tent, and Benther halted him at a distance of about five paces.

"What is your business?" asked Benther. "And how did you get past the guards at the camp's edge?"

"I beg your mercy if we have done wrong, Sir," said one of the Karolans escorting him, "but he came to the edge of the camp claiming he had a message for King Ilohan. We thought it best to escort him here rather than turning him back, for we guessed the tale was true. He wears the livery of one of Andokar of Norkath's own servants."

"And did you leave your guard posts unfilled, then?" asked Benther sharply.

The man turned pale. "Sir, we did," he said.

Benther advanced slowly until his sword point was a handbreadth from the Norkath messenger's throat. It trembled there, gleaming in the sunshine. "If you draw any weapon, or seek to fly," said Benther, "I will kill you." Then, without taking his eyes off the messenger, he said, "Guards of Karolan, get back to your posts with all speed!" They hurried off, and he was left alone with the Norkath.

"Have you a message for the king?" he asked.

"I do."

"Spoken, or written?"

"Written."

"Lay it on the ground, and leave the camp," said Benther. "I will present it to His Majesty."

"I was told to see it in His Majesty's own hand," said the messenger, "and to present it with the hope that my master's former distrust of His Majesty may be pardoned, and that my master's army and His Majesty's may yet march together in peace."

"Those are welcome words, though they come too late and I know not whether to trust them," said the king, coming forth now from the tent. "Sir Benther, I thank you for your vigilance, but I would not have you hold this messenger under threat any longer. If he is an assassin, he will have to be skillful indeed to kill me now, and my death would not much lessen our hopes. Do not sheath your sword, but remove it from his neck, and I will receive the message from his hand."

"I do this unwillingly," said Benther. "Does Your Majesty command me?"

"I do," said Ilohan. "I would welcome this man with courtesy now, though he has come from those who have doomed our hopes, and may have my death in his heart."

Benther lowered his sword, and the messenger stepped forward wordlessly to give Ilohan a piece of parchment. Ilohan took it carefully in his left hand, while his sword gleamed in his right, but the messenger made no suspicious movements, and the parchment was innocently what it seemed. Ilohan stepped back, broke the seal, and read, "His Majesty King Andokar of Norkath to His Majesty King Ilohan of Karolan: Forgive me, if you ever can, for my distrust of you. The Zarnith messenger of doom reached me last night, to my loss. I march at noon. If I have not bred in you undying hatred, I beg you to follow me as quickly as you may."

"What did the message say, Your Majesty?" asked Benther, alarmed at the shock in Ilohan's face.

The king stirred instantly. "Sir Benther," he said, "call the men to break camp at once. We march at noon for Drantar's Gap."

*   *   *

"Jonathan and his army have fallen, and the Zarnith are coming," they told her. "They have split their host into three. It seems they will attack not only the Gate of Hope but also the mountain walls themselves on both the east and west." Eleanor knew she ought to mount her horse and go back, but still she stood staring dully at the bare ground where her roses had bloomed the day Ilohan and Jonathan came to her. The cottage behind her was empty, its wall blackened as if by fire, its doors broken and hanging on their hinges. Rangol and others had done this the day before. They hoped that what looked burnt and ravaged already the Zarnith might not burn to the ground, and so the rebuilding – if it ever came – would be less hard.

Auria was suddenly beside her, with her youth and warmth, standing straight and leaning on no crutches. "It is time to go into Ceramir and close the gate, Lady Eleanor," said Auria gently. "Your flowers will bloom again."

Still Eleanor stood looking at the ground, leaning heavily upon her crutches. She thought of Jonathan, and all the men who had died with him. She remembered Kindrach. "He also stood alone, to protect me, and he also died before his time," she thought. "Why must it be so, why must love kill the lovers? I tried to comfort Veril, but now the words I spoke to her seem hollow. Alas, my Lord, I who have taught others do not know, and I who have thought to strengthen others am weak. The darkness is coming, and Jonathan has died for me and my son – when it would have been better that we, or I at least, had died for him that he might yet come to you."

"You should not have come with us, dear Eleanor," said Auria.

"I know," said Eleanor. Her cottage, where she had grown flowers and brought children joy, seemed to her a symbol of the new life God had given her after her great darkness had passed. Seeing the cottage now ruined, she was brought closer to the darkness. She wondered if ever again children would come eagerly to her door, and laugh to hear her stories.

"Yet I had to come, Auria," she said. "I thought he might have listened to me."

Auria, Brogal, and Eleanor had come down to look for a young orphan boy who had run from the Cloth of Joy that morning. Their frantic search had at last found him, weeping beside his mother's grave, knowing the Zarnith would soon desecrate it. Brogal was now carrying him back to Ceramir. Eleanor thought of the child's grief, one drop in a sea of tears that would be shed over the deeds of the Zarnith. Now they were advancing on the beloved Cloth of Joy, that had been to so many a star of refuge and hope amid the weary world. "And shall we fall, Lord?" she asked in thought. "Shall we fall, indeed? Who can see any hope of our standing?"

Then she raised her eyes from the dirt, as though she had been told to do so, and she looked up the valley of the outlands toward the hidden Gate of Hope, and then higher and higher to the great peak of Dilfandokir, a sheer and mighty sentinel to the northwest of the Valley of the Undismayed. The majestic, snow-crowned peak caught the morning sun and glowed white against the clear blue sky. It would never be conquered or razed by Vadshron and his host.

"So with my children, bought with the blood of my Son," she seemed to hear whispered in a voice only her heart could catch. "They also are beyond the reach of evil, high in my love, from which nothing can bring them down. You have nothing to fear."

"But what of my roses? What of little fern, and Auria here beside me, their bodies so full of life and health? What of Ceramir? Is it nothing to you if evil destroys it and all its defenders? Do you care nothing for mortal good and beauty?"

"Not a sparrow can fall to the ground for which I do not care."

"But what of Jonathan, my Lord – forgive me; I rest in your grace and dare to ask such things."

"Rest in my grace."

"I will, my Lord! Oh, help me!"

"Ella, Ella, please, you must come! Why do you stand so still and strange?" Auria spoke with fear in her voice, lapsing in her urgency into what she had called the Lady Eleanor long ago when she herself had been a child.

"I will come; forgive me, Auria," said Eleanor. "In a daydream I thought God himself was speaking to me, answering the questions I asked in prayer. It is arrogant; I should not let myself think he would speak to me."

"Why should he not?" asked Auria. "Hurry! The Zarnith are coming. I will help you onto your horse."

Side by side they galloped up the forest path, Auria with her vitality and springtime youth somehow undimmed despite the threat of imminent death; Eleanor with her soul reeling from the things she had heard and prayed, and her faith burning with renewed intensity that she knew was from God. They squeezed through the last opening in the barricade. With relief, Rangol and other men cut ropes above the barricade, and great tree trunks surrounded by thorns and noxious weeds crashed down to fill the gap.

* * *

"They are coming," said Barnabas, high upon the eastern mountain wall of Ceramir. He waited there with twelve score warriors of Karolan, sent up in haste to meet one part of Vadshron's unexpected three-pronged attack. The gray cliff dropped sheer below him, to the desert plain. Far away the horizon met the blue sky, and all was bright and vast beneath the midday sun. The desert road was a faint white ribbon stretching away to lose itself in the immensity. But the vastness of the sky and desert did not dwarf the host of foes that came galloping across that plain, with the white dust billowing up in great clouds from behind them. They seemed to fill the desert as they swept toward the feet of the cliffs that guarded Ceramir.

"They are coming," said Rangol, high on the western mountain wall, seeing a similar host thundering across the desert plain toward him. He looked along the ridge that he would defend to the death. Great piles of boulders were ready to be thrown down on the attackers. Each of his fifteen-score men had a sword and bow, and a great quiver of poisoned arrows. Rangol again gazed out at the Zarnith horde. He imagined them storming up the steep cliff below him. It was a hard climb, but even if the Zarnith fell and died by thousands, there would still be tens of thousands more. "They will destroy us," he thought. "They will fling us back into the valley, and sweep down upon the Cloth of Joy... God, help us!" The prayer sounded hollow to him, and for the first time he considered it possible that he was neither a brave man nor a faithful one.

"They are coming," said Mudien, behind the barricade at the Gate of Hope, hearing the sound of the Zarnith crashing brutally through the lovely woods beyond the gate. "They are coming, and there is no wind." Even the watchmen on the mountainside above the barricade could not yet see the enemy through the thick forest – though they could see innumerable birds rising from the treetops, crying in alarm. It was eerie: the noise of their foes' coming filled the earth, but they could see nothing. And of the wind they had hoped and prayed for there was no sign.

Brogal stood with several other men on the lakeshore near the barricade. Torches blazed and smoked in their hands. The noxious weeds that the Children of Ceramir had collected with so much painful labor were piled high throughout the barricade, ready to make smoke: thick, choking, and terrible, if only they were lit. But there was no wind.

Eleanor stood near Brogal and Mudien beside the lake. An army of half a thousand, both Karolans and men of Harevan and Ceramir, was gathered behind them. "We dare not light the barricade," said Mudien. "We will only choke ourselves. God has not favored us with wind, and we must do without it."

"I do not believe God will withhold his help from us in this war," said Eleanor. "The wind will come. May we not light the barricade, as an act of faith?"

Brogal looked from Mudien to Eleanor. In his father's face he saw the faithful servant leader he had always known, seeming more faithful and more noble than ever in this desperate time. He might almost have worshiped his father, standing there, had he not believed so deeply that all good comes from God, and that he alone is worthy of worship. And his father's words were wisdom.

But when he looked at Lady Eleanor he wondered if he had ever seen her before. He forgot utterly that she was lame, and wondered if she alone of everyone in Ceramir could walk. Faith clothed her like a garment made of light; it rested upon her face and shone in her eyes. It was faith unstained by pride and unshadowed by fear. "She alone," he thought; "she alone in this moment is truly among the undismayed." But he did not throw the torch. The sound of the Zarnith drew closer. There was not a breath of air stirring in the valley, and the sky above was flawless blue.

"We have prayed most fervently, with hearts his love made pure, for wind this day," said Eleanor. "Surely he will not withhold it. The barricade should be lit."

"He does not always do as we think he must," said Mudien. "He is ever free not to grant the things we ask. We should not light the barricade."

And Brogal looked from one to the other again, and again he did not throw the torch.

The Zarnith began their war song. All three of their advancing armies began to sing at once, and so it seemed the Cloth of Joy was surrounded by the screaming, wild song. Its purpose was to terrify and curse and kill, and none who heard it failed to understand that much at least. It echoed off the sheer mountains behind Ceramir, so that some looked back to see if by some marvel the Zarnith were attacking from that way too. Brogal was among these, but he saw only the gray cliffs. His heart was beating fast.

"Friends," said Lady Eleanor, in a clear and joyful voice. "Look not that way. Look up."

Brogal looked up, and in the sky that had been clear only moments before there was a streamer of cloud blown back from one of the mountain peaks, a sign of great wind high in the air. It was beautiful, ethereal and pure against the deep blue of the sky. "The banner of the Cloth of Joy," cried Brogal, "the wind from the great mountains! Behold its herald: an icetrail from the peak of Dilfandokir unfurls above us!"

Mudien saw it, and then looked Lady Eleanor straight in the eyes. She met his gaze unwaveringly. "I would not gainsay your will, Sir," she said quietly. "Yet in my heart I find no trace of doubt that God will bring us the victory today, and that he will give to us the wind we asked of him. I beg you, permit the barricade to be lit."

But before Mudien could speak there was a roaring rush in the air. Brogal had thrown his torch as hard as he could into the very center of the barricade. Fire blossomed there. Still no wind stirred. The other torchbearers looked anxiously at Mudien. But he said, "It is done! Light the barricade!" He turned to Eleanor. "Lady, your faith is greater than my own. Whatever comes this day; if I never again speak to the princess whose healing was among my greatest tasks and greatest joys, remember that my last words to you commended you. Your faith is bright even if this day proves you wrong. Now go into the house with all speed, for a moment hence the arrows will begin falling."

Eleanor obeyed him, and Imranie rose to meet her. Eleanor sat down beside her, and wept. Her tears came fast, and Imranie embraced her and held her close. "What is it, child?" she asked.

Eleanor cried all the more. "It is just everything," she said. "The tale of my life is so much more than I can grasp, so much more than I deserve or could imagine. My brokenness… and then the healing you and Mudien gave me, long ago... and Ilohan... and now this... Have I made the defenders of Ceramir light a barricade that will stifle them and then burn away to let the Zarnith through?"

"It was God who healed you, Eleanor," said Imranie. "Surely I had nothing to do with it. And were you wrong to make them light the fire? Look."

She looked, and a bird's feather on the ground outside the window lifted a little and blew toward the Gate of Hope, and the first hint of breeze caressed her tear-wet cheek.

Chapter 23

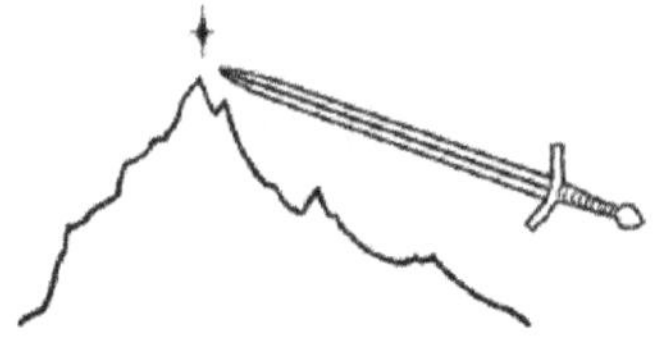

The Song of the Storm

LIKE HAIL, LIKE RAIN, LIKE SOME DEADLY CLOUDBURST AT the world's end, the arrows of the Zarnith came. In their wooden shelters behind the barricade, the defenders shuddered in awe. The arrows easily cleared the cliff walls above the Gate of Hope. No man or woman left unshielded in the lower part of the valley could have lasted long. The smoke of the barricade grew slowly, and drifted out the Gate of Hope in the light breeze, but enough remained behind to sting the throats of the defenders. They looked high up above the barricade, to where the watchmen of Ceramir huddled in arrow-shelters precariously anchored to the stone. Through the hail of arrows, they saw each watchman raise a single gold flag: enemy in sight.

The arrows came so thick that the ground was covered with their flying shadows, and the deadly hail seemed even to dim the sun. They multiplied by thousands on the shores of the lake, points buried in the mud and feathered shafts upward like fast growing, evil flowers. Thousands more washed in rafts down the stream to lodge against the smoking barricade. They splintered out the fury of their flight on the stone roof of the house, and stuck quivering by hundreds in the trunks and branches of the trees. The defenders dared not even look through the arrow slots in their shelters, for the Zarnith shafts came so thick that they seemed to find out every crack.

The watchmen raised one red flag beside the gold: enemy can be shot through the barricade. "Draw and shoot!" ordered Mudien. "This is the time of decision. God has given us the wind. He calls us now to courage. Lay down your fear of death."

The men obeyed, risking death by an arrow through their own arrow slots, shooting the long, poisoned shafts of Ceramir as fast as they could. Skillfully made loopholes had been built into the barricade, marked on the inside but concealed without. The defenders now shot through these hidden channels, their arrows flying straight, fast, and deadly. The Zarnith were taken wholly by surprise, as the arrows came from what seemed a solid wall of logs. Roars of pain and rage came to the defenders' ears. The hail of Zarnith arrows intensified. One of the watchmen on the cliffs was struck, and fell screaming to his death on the rocks just inside the Gate of Hope. The others raised a second red flag: assault gathering upon the barricade.

The barricade was not yet fully aflame, and the wind was not strong. Mudien thought the Zarnith might well scale it now, with their courage and strength and utter disregard for life. Thousands might come over in a flood to seal the doom of the Cloth of Joy. Brogal left his shelter and his bow in reckless folly, and ran through the hail of arrows. Miraculously, he reached the cliff just east of the Gate of Hope, and climbed high and fast to take the fallen watchman's place. Mudien saw him reach the doubtful safety of the arrow shelter with a feeling of deep relief. He turned from watching his son to survey his soldiers, but he gave them no command. Already they were shooting as fast as they could, and there was nothing more to be done.

From his lofty vantage point Brogal looked out over the outlands of Ceramir. The Zarnith filled the forest. Their arrows leaped up in sheets like upward rain, and they roared as they charged the barricade. But thick black smoke was already billowing off of it. Hundreds of Zarnith reached the barricade and began to climb, only to fall back well below the top. The straight-flying arrows of Ceramir were deadly, and the choking smoke stole both breath and sight so that even hardened warriors faltered, fell, and died.

But some did reach the top. Brogal raised a third red flag: barricade surmounted, Zarnith in Ceramir.

Mudien saw it, and saw too the enemies as they leaped down from the flaming barricade, roaring with rage. The Zarnith arrows ceased falling as though at a single word. "Out swords! Leave your shelters!" commanded Mudien. "Fight as the men of God did long ago, for apart from him we have no hope."

The defenders left their shelters and walked where a moment before it would have been death to walk. The Zarnith came against them by scores, burned, enraged, and bent on slaughter. The defenders of the Undismayed, with Mudien at their head, stood their ground until the mud was red with blood. But still the Zarnith came, and Brogal saw that the stream below the Gate of Hope was choked with their burned bodies. Still they threw themselves upon the flaming barricade, and their corpses formed a partial shield against the flames for new waves of Zarnith. Mudien and those with him could not hold out forever. "Lord Christ, we have no hope," said Brogal. "Save us by your might."

He remembered the precautions Rangol had insisted on: that there must be a way to reinforce the barricade if the great trees that formed its structure burned away. Huge tree trunks were held by ropes out of the flames, ready to come down across the Gate of Hope above the barricade if the ropes were cut. Swiftly Brogal climbed down into the choking smoke and began slashing at the ropes with his knife. Tree trunks weighing more than scores of men crashed down upon the barricade, and sparks went up in smoking towers to blow down against the Zarnith.

Brogal was blinded and oppressed by heat and smoke. His thought measured his life in heartbeats, and in an instant's wild decision he threw himself from the cliffside. He fell through cool air, and opened his burning eyes to see water below him. He would just miss the rocks, he thought.

There was a terrific splash, and he went deep. He struck the bottom, but not hard. The power of the current swept him away, and his lungs sucked against his closed lips, begging for air. He found himself pinned by the power of the current against a lattice of wooden beams. He remembered that he himself was the reason for this: he had insisted that they make some underwater barrier lest the Zarnith try to swim under the barricade. He struggled along the grating to an eddy near shore where the current was less strong, and then struck out away from the barrier with all his force. He came up an instant later, gasping for air almost beneath the barricade. He pulled himself out of the water and staggered away from the deadly smoke.

Mudien gripped his arm. "Son," he said. "You have saved the Cloth of Joy."

Brogal looked around, and saw that no Zarnith were left in Ceramir alive, and no more were coming over the barricade. Some of the defenders had been killed or wounded, but many remained whole. "Praise God," he gasped, "but it is not saved yet! Father, you must restart the archery!"

The surviving watchmen were showing two red flags, and Mudien saw that Brogal was right. He ordered the defenders back into their shelters, and then turned to tell his son to seek shelter in the house. But Brogal was running for the cliffs again, to regain his earlier post as a watchman. With a swift, fervent prayer for Brogal's safety, Mudien ran to a shelter himself and then gave the word to begin shooting.

Brogal regained his previous lookout. Peering down, he saw that indeed Ceramir was still imperiled. The Zarnith had uprooted trees and were rushing forward to lean them up against the barricade as makeshift ladders. They came now with the same wild, self-abandoning ferocity as before, but now with a better plan born of increased respect for their foes. Brogal saw the arrows leap up faster than his eyes could follow, ending the respite from archery that had begun when the first Zarnith successfully scaled the barricade. He guessed that Vadshron or some other commander must have realized that no Zarnith were left alive in Ceramir, and that the archery would continue until the barricade again was scaled.

The Zarnith now swarmed against the barricade, roaring. Scores of them leaned whole trees up against it with staggering displays of strength, and hundreds more scrambled up through the brutal smoke and poisoned archery. It seemed to Brogal that the Cloth of Joy was doomed: that from this second assault there could be no recovery.

* * *

Barnabas, laying down before God his agony over Jonathan, led his army with what skill he could. He had never led before in battle, and he had not Jonathan's wild, contagious courage, but he was a veteran of Dilgarel and Petrag, with the wisdom of many years of life. He knew how to lead men to fight bravely and calmly to the end. Though spread out desperately thin over half a thousand paces of cliff top, his army had thus far managed to hold back the overwhelming Zarnith host. His men had fought well, and he was pleased with them – and they knew it. They fought on with good courage, a little hope, and much bright-burning determination.

At the beginning of the battle the Zarnith had launched a storm of arrows at Barnabas' army, just as they had at the Gate of Hope – but the cliffs here were so much higher that no arrow could reach their tops with deadly force. Many had fallen back down among the Zarnith host. No more had come. Thus Barnabas and his men fought without fear of enemy arrows, and their task would have been easy save that the enemy outnumbered them so overwhelmingly.

As it was they lived on the edge of disaster. The Zarnith climbed up by thousands, with spears strapped to their backs and red serrated swords at their belts. If they once gained the edge – and every time they killed even one defender, a gap opened that might permit this – moments later they would have a thousand men upon the cliff top, and the end would come. Barnabas and his soldiers kept this fate at bay, chiefly using the long poisoned arrows of Ceramir. They made every shaft count, shooting from close range at the climbers nearest the ridge. Each Zarnith they struck knocked others down to their deaths as he fell – and the Karolans shot almost as fast as they could draw bow. Still, the Zarnith could well afford their loss. Still they came by scores and thousands, sometimes singing snatches of the Zarnith war song, sometimes climbing up with silent ferocity and terrifying, agile speed. Some, even as they fell to their deaths, would pull out their spears and throw them with terrible force. One Karolan was killed this way, taken through the heart by an enemy who had intentionally leaped to his death to buy one instant when he could throw his spear.

Every man of the defenders knew what would happen if the Zarnith ever got even a handful of men upon the ridge. Every moment they were nearly there – yet every moment the Karolans fought on with ceaseless vigilance, and held the ridge.

Barnabas peered over a cliff edge with a great bow in his hands. Though the wind was chilly, he did not feel it. Sweat ran into his eyes and blurred his vision. To his left, he saw a company of Zarnith climbing a new rope, anchored somehow within twice a man's height of the cliff edge. And it was not hard climbing above their anchor. The Karolan defender at that point did not see them. "Look down at that rope!" shouted Barnabas.

The defender turned at the cry, and shot the first Zarnith through the heart. He slumped against the rope and then fell without a scream, but he fell alone. The others were climbing on, enraged. The Karolan shot three more arrows, in quick succession, and killed five Zarnith with them. More were coming fast, untroubled by the dead men who had fallen past them. Barnabas looked away from the dangerous battle around that rope, to the stretch of cliff directly below him. A Zarnith warrior was there, climbing alone, already perilously close. Barnabas could see the man's face clearly. There was no ferocity in it, only determination. His face was darkened by the sun, and weathered like leather by wind and sand. His muscles stood out on his bare arms. He reached fingers hard with calluses into cracks in the rock and pulled himself up with grace and power. In his weather-beaten face his eyes were black and bright, youthful and daring, but not cruel.

"He might be Jonathan, if Jonathan had lived as he has lived," thought Barnabas. "How can this world be so evil, that I must kill him? How can I kill him?" But the next instant the man was falling down the cliff with Barnabas' arrow through his chest, his right hand frozen in the act of reaching for a spear. His body broke in a red splash on the rocks far below, amid hordes of his comrades that were pressing on to climb the cliffs themselves, but Barnabas was already looking elsewhere. A troop of two score Zarnith climbers was hastening up a crack not far away, and Barnabas' first shaft took their leader and five others with him. The tears of pity that had gleamed for a moment in Barnabas' eyes had not blurred the sharpness of his aim, and his face was set like stone.

* * *

Brogal reached for his third red flag, as he watched the Zarnith come near the top of the barricade. They would come over it any moment, he knew, and then after a short and desperate fight the Cloth of Joy would fall. Below him Mudien and the others still huddled beneath the staggering hail of Zarnith archery. Three arrows had brushed Brogal's head as he looked out the small hole in his lookout shelter, and of the two red flags he held one was ripped to ribbons by a Zarnith shaft. It was in his mind, when the barricade was breached, to run to Veril and offer to take her over the mountains to Karolan, but he knew that even if she were willing to try they would not succeed. He was not Jonathan. There was no hope. All that he loved would die before the sunset. "Father, we shall all see your face before the night," said Brogal. "May we die worthy of your name. My blood runs hot, but there is nothing to do. I want to laugh, but I cannot. Father, I am yours; always yours, whatever comes."

His hair blew wildly in the wind, and though they would destroy all that he loved his heart lifted a little with wild exultation in the fierce courage of the Zarnith host. The wind seemed to be rising, cold and strong. He liked that wind, the wild, free wind...

He froze suddenly in a listening stillness. He had heard screams among the Zarnith. Screams of dismay, he thought, not exultation. He thought fast and looked intently, trying to understand what had happened. Then in an instant he leaped up and stood, utterly exposed to Zarnith archery, on the top of his wooden lookout shelter. Two red flags and one gold in his hand blew furiously in the wind, and the Zarnith greeted him with roars of rage and thousands of arrows. Still he stood there, while the arrows soared up toward him. They were caught in the mighty wind and swept away to fall among those who had shot them. As long as that wind blew there could be no archery against the Cloth of Joy. Brogal laughed aloud, and roared his defiance to the Zarnith far below: "Come in battle against the valley loved by God, and wonder not if death is all your reward!"

* * *

Eleanor and Imranie sat by the shuttered window. The room was full of people, desperately afraid. Wounded men groaned on the beds. It seemed dark, though a fire was on the hearth and some light came through the chinks around the window shutters. The warm brook, alone unaffected by the siege of Ceramir, chattered to itself as it ran across the floor.

"What do you see, Auria?" asked Eleanor. She was in a chair below the window, but Auria sat on the window ledge with her arms around her knees, holding herself into the small space so that she could see out a knothole in the shutter.

"No more arrows are falling, my Lady," she said. "When they stopped before it was because some Zarnith had come over the barricade, but now, I think, it is not so. I do not see any Zarnith coming over. Father and the men with him are still shooting arrows through the barricade; the Zarnith must still be attacking it with all their force. Can you hear their roars? It is terrible! Ah – Oh, what is it?"

"What is it?" asked dozens of voices, terrified by the terror in Auria's voice.

"The light is darkened," said Auria, climbing down from the window and seeking her mother like a frightened child. "It is dark, and the wind blows hard. Oh, what is it?"

It was growing dark. All who waited in that fear-filled room could see that less light was coming through the chinks around the shutters. The terror was so great that some began to weep with stifled hysteria. They had thought the Zarnith might come and kill them all, but could they also put out the light of day?

Chill wind blew through the chinks of the windows. Eleanor rose in the fast-falling darkness, and stood straight despite her crutches. Her white dress seemed almost to glow in the dimness, and all eyes were on her. "Fear not," she said, "for the day and the sun belong to God, and so do we. Trust in him."

A crash that seemed loud enough to break the rock beneath their feet fell on them from the unseen sky. Children screamed, and Auria dropped her head in her hands. Eleanor stood silent, her face pale – but Imranie said, in a calm, natural voice, "Fear not, children. It is thunder."

Eleanor raised her eyes to the heavens, feeling she could see them very well despite the stone roof above her. "It has come," she said. "It has come. Oh, Father, you have given it. It has come." A lightning flash followed almost instantly by another crash of thunder lit up her face, and few who saw her in that moment could ever forget the sight.

*   *   *

Dark clouds carried on the mighty wind swallowed the sun. Mudien and his men still doggedly shot their arrows through the gaps in the barricade, though they wondered at the clouds and the great crashes of thunder. The Zarnith would be over at any moment, they knew. Though the arrows seemed to have stopped, they dared not yet leave their cover. The barricade seemed to glow brighter in the shadow of the dark clouds, but the Zarnith were still climbing it.

One of them reached the summit, only to fall back on the Zarnith side with an arrow in his belly. The defenders gave a ragged cheer at this, but it showed them how close they were to losing the barricade again. This time they would not recover it.

A great sound, not thunder but a sustained roar, began above them and behind them. It seemed to fill the sky. Mudien left his cramped shelter and stood unprotected. He looked up to see the tall trees waving wildly and bowing in the wind. "Defenders out of shelter!" he cried above the roar. "We have prayed for wind, and God has sent it! Arrows will reach us no longer. Yet keep up your archery, for the wind blows arrows, not men." Even as he spoke the wind reached the ground, and he spread his arms in its wild power.

The trees of Ceramir bowed before the gale, and sang a song that no man could ever forget. It seemed to come from everywhere: a steady, mighty roar. Men thought that not only the trees but also the air, the clouds, the whole vast volume of sky, were singing of wild freedom and of measureless, endless power. It seemed to fill the whole world, and reach into men's hearts with a wild but steadfast courage. It was loud, loud and strong, filled with the mountains' vastness and the unending patience of the mighty trees. If any other sound had grown so loud, men might have wanted to cover their ears against it, but this they wanted all the more to hear, for its very power was beautiful. In time of peace it might have frightened them, but now, with all their fear centered on the Zarnith, the wind brought them only a wild exultant joy.

The barricade glowed like a furnace when the bellows are pumped. Roaring flames blew out nearly horizontal in the wind. Thick black smoke, filled with sparks and windblown coals, streamed out from the Gate of Hope. The heat of the fire was so great that it reached warm rays even back against the wind, comforting the defenders amid the coldness of the coming storm.

But to the Zarnith the heat was not comforting. From his lookout Brogal saw them fall back, their screams faint as the wind swept them away. Their makeshift ladders burst into flames all in a moment, and blew back from the barricade to crash in ashen ruin in the stream or in blazing coals upon the ground. Every warrior climbing the barricade died, and again the river was choked with their scorched bodies. Thousands of Zarnith even back in the woods now collapsed on the ground, holding their hands across their eyes, writhing in pain, coughing and gasping with the noxious smoke in their lungs. Some even turned to fly – and died on the merciless spears of those behind them. Vadshron's battle was not going as he had planned, but he was not beaten yet. The Zarnith had but one law for those who fled when the warlord had not called retreat. Brogal lowered the two red flags in his hand, and only the gold remained: enemy in sight.

* * *

On the western mountain wall, Rangol's army was disintegrating. He was used to leading a score or so of young men, who knew him well and knew well how to fight, and to them he was an excellent leader. Yet now he had fifteen score soldiers, some husbands and fathers from Harevan, and some untrained warriors from Karolan who were longing for Jonathan. He did not have Barnabas' experience or Mudien's authority, or Jonathan's relentless, contagious courage. He could not hold the army together.

He prayed frantically, and thought and worked with all his strength. He had succeeded at many things throughout his life, but at this, the most desperately important thing he had ever attempted, he was failing. The Zarnith attacked with dogged intensity, crowding so many climbers on the cliff that the weaker ones were pushed off to their deaths. Rangol had deployed his archers sensibly, but they did not fight as he knew they should, and he did not know how to command them. Dozens had been killed, and they were wasting arrows. The wind made aiming difficult. Some of the men from Harevan, insufficiently dressed, were now shivering uncontrollably from the cold.

The mighty wind was not wholly a disadvantage, however. More than one Zarnith warrior, as he attained the ridge and staggered to his feet, suddenly toppled backward with a scream – blown off by the startling force of the wind, to die in shattered ruin far below. Rain and hail began to fall, together with the wind. Rangol was pleased, hoping it would make the rocks too slippery for the climbers. It intensified to a blinding, chilling downpour. Lightning was frequent, and terrible thunder-crashes seemed to shake the whole valley. Shivering defenders aimed dripping arrows through the rain, and missed half-seen Zarnith struggling up the cliff – and drew again, and missed again, and were killed suddenly by spears they had never seen coming. Rangol ran, risking his life in several ways, along the edge of the rain-soaked cliff, trying to lead his men to fight with prudence and determination to the end. But he had not won their trust, and his cries were lost in the storm. He stumbled on an unseen ledge and fell hard, and no one came to help him.

The Zarnith broke the line. In an instant there were five score of them on the cliff, spreading out in both directions and killing the defenders with their deadly spears.

Rangol struggled to his feet, climbed a rise upon the ridge, and saw them. He saw them kill one of his men and fling the body heedlessly out toward the desert. Other defenders were flying from them. Other Zarnith were hurriedly climbing to reach the cliff edge they controlled. Rangol stood still a moment, frozen. He remembered words of the Zarnith language that he had learned long ago from Mudien his father – probably futile words, but at least words he could say. He took a deep breath, and in a mighty voice he cried out, "Brat'hronk lo zeera sradmeeg, ilstald thrond Nami Gonk Yeen Yohilee!" The Zarnith heard and understood: "Come no further into our valley, unless you would try to conquer the holy and terrible Warlord of the Heavens!"

"We are untouched by fear!" they roared back in Zarnith. "We will drink your blood and the blood of your father!" Abandoning the pursuit of other men, they ran toward Rangol together to strike him down.

To reach him they had to climb a steep portion of the ridge, almost a low cliff. At this place they crowded together, the ones behind reaching its foot before the first ones had finished climbing. One of them, cresting the cliff, raised his serrated sword toward Rangol in a gesture of brutal contempt – and in that instant the lightning struck him.

They heard the awesome crash of that thunderbolt down in the stone house, and far on the other side of the valley where Barnabas led. All marked it as one of the greatest thunder-cracks even of that terrific storm. The cliff side where the bolt had struck exploded, throwing rock fragments high into the air. Not a single one of the Zarnith warriors on the ridge survived. The lightning had leaped down among them, scorched them, scattered their bodies, and shattered the very rock on which they climbed with terrible force. Rangol was deafened and knocked backwards on the ground. The lightning bolt had seared across his vision as a blinding column of blue-white light. It stayed there, pulsing in his dazzled eyes, for long moments.

Even before it faded he leaped to his feet and ran to the edge of the cliff. Zarnith were still upon its lower reaches in great numbers, but none were climbing higher for the moment. Rangol ran along the long stretch of cliff he had to defend, seeking out the defenders who were still alive, and calling them to be ready for the Zarnith to renew their attack. "It may be that God himself fights for us, and if so we have hope," he said. "Yet we must be faithful, and fight to the end whether he chooses to rescue us or no. His aid in this our battle means that we may yet triumph, not that we need not fight." Rangol arrayed his surviving warriors once more across the cliff, more widely spaced than before, but leaving no place utterly undefended.

The Zarnith down below shouted insults and even shot arrows at those on the cliff, who had refused to climb higher since the terrible lightning bolt. They began climbing again at last, and Rangol and his men continued their desperate defense.

* * *

On the eastern ridge the men of Barnabas' army still stood their ground. They were running out of arrows, and Barnabas had ordered them to keep those they had left for some last defense, and use the boulders and rocks that had been piled along the cliff edge. The rain and hail hindered the Zarnith. It drenched and slicked the stone on which they climbed, and it pelted stingingly in their eyes as they raised their spears to throw. The defenders, with their backs to the wind, could see much more clearly. Their rocks flew straight and fast when they threw them, and the Zarnith – blinded, shivering, and clinging desperately to slippery stone – fell before them by scores and hundreds.

Wild thoughts came into Barnabas' head that they might hold out forever this way, that his scores of men might defeat Vadshron's scores of thousands, and that when morning came the Zarnith bodies might be heaped at the bottom of the cliff while Ceramir was still safe. But he knew these thoughts were only dreams. The storm could not last forever, and even before it ended they would run out of boulders and stones and shoot their last arrows. Then the Zarnith would come by thousands over the edge of the cliff. There would be a short and hopeless fight with swords upon the ridge, each man all alone in a host of foes, and then the end. All of them would die, and the Cloth of Joy would fall. Yet even before that Barnabas guessed that the defense at the Gate of Hope would be overwhelmed, and he and his men would find themselves attacked from both sides while below them the ravaging of Ceramir went on apace.

These thoughts distressed him even while he fought furiously, hurling boulders far down the cliff to strike with devastating accuracy and force. His men also were fighting splendidly around him, and the awesome storm might have been sent to aid them. Yet all this was still not enough. It only prolonged their agony, showing them what hope might have been theirs if only they had had more arrows and more men, or if the Zarnith had not had such overwhelming numbers and such ferocious, reckless courage. Jonathan was dead, and Naomi was dead, and Hannah was lost, and Jenn was lost, and Karolan would fall. His men, who were fighting now with such selfless, blazing courage, would die in spite of it, and the Zarnith would drink their blood.

"Father, why?" his heart cried even as he heaved down an enormous rock upon a group of Zarnith who were coming up a rope. "Why must we fight like this, so well, so faithfully, and yet without hope?"

Then he thought no more of such things, because four Zarnith had actually reached the ridge on his left and come across to kill him, while others were climbing quickly up from below. The first spear from those upon the ridge missed him and sailed off into space over the cliff edge. The second glanced off his sword as he ran toward them. He reached the leading Zarnith before a third spear could fly, and a swordfight of a few heartbeats left him victorious. As soon as their companion fell, two of the remaining Zarnith launched spears at Barnabas with terrible force. He saw their hands go back to throw, and in a lighting motion that strained his muscles to their limit he heaved the dead Zarnith up between himself and the spears. He threw the body down with two spears stuck through it and sprang over it to kill the two Zarnith before they could draw either their swords or another spear. He turned to face the one remaining warrior, wondering why he had not speared him. The Zarnith lay dead upon the stone with an arrow in his back. Barnabas looked up, and a man from Ceramir, standing a little way away upon the cliff edge, saluted him. A longbow was in the soldier's hand: he had judged it time to use one of their hoarded arrows. Barnabas returned the salute and ran back to his own station. Zarnith were on a rope there within a spear's length of the cliff edge, but Barnabas instantly tipped down a heavy, angular boulder on them. They fell with the sickening crunch of breaking bone.

A momentary lull came in the fighting, and in the brief respite desponding thoughts again troubled Barnabas. But now he did not think quite as he had before, and with shame and contrition he prayed again. "Father, I know that you can save us if you will. But even if you do not, my trust and my worship are yours forever."

The desperate fight went on.

Chapter 24

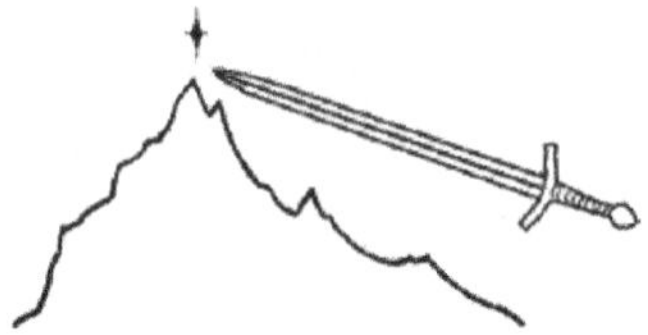

They Do Not Fly from Men

HANNAH STOOD IN THE LIGHT OF DAY. SHE SPREAD HER arms and tilted up her face to the sun, drinking it in like one long thirsty who at last finds water. She had not known how desperately she missed the sun, down in the dark cracks and stream-cut canyons beneath the mountains, whose unseen roofs of rock or ice shut out the light of day. She felt that with the light around her she could see everything more clearly, not only her surroundings but the truths about her life.

She gazed in wonder at the scene before her: a sunlit rock face split by a wide crack, through which a swift stream rushed out and fell to sink into the desert sand. It was beautiful, and the crashing, daylight roar of the waterfall was music to her ears after days spent with the cold dark sounds of water echoing and gurgling under the mountains. Hannah marveled at the brigands' strength and ingenuity, for they had brought her and Naomi down that waterfall. After days of travel in a second boat, down a swift and narrow underground stream, they had at last found themselves rushing down a dark canyon that opened on bright day – and the waterfall. At just the right moment, men had leaped from the boat onto precarious ledges on the canyon walls, and fastened ropes there to keep the boat from going down the fall. They had carefully let out the ropes until the boat's long, narrow bow protruded about two paces beyond the top of the falls. The current had rushed under the hull with an angry sound, but had not been able to sweep the boat away, nor tip it forward. The brigands had lowered Hannah and Naomi from the bow. Hannah had been terrified that the stretcher would swing back into the waterfall, but the brigands had been too clever for that, and Hannah and Naomi had come to rest on the sand – the desert on the far side of the mountains – in safety.

Now Hannah stood in the light and waited, while the brigands pulled the boat a little way back up the dark swift river, to some hidden mooring place where they would leave it until the time came for some of them to traverse the Dark Way in the opposite direction. Though they had offered her plenty of food throughout the journey, she had not been able to eat much – and of course she had slept little, in fear of them. Through the lightless days she had known the ceaseless pain of Naomi's illness, and fear and guilt had stalked her like wild beasts only temporarily kept at bay. All these things had taken their toll on her, and as she stood in the blessed warmth of the sun she felt weary to the bone. But the Bowlord must not see her weakness. She must defeat him in a desperate game of threat and counter threat, the sapphire against her life and Naomi's. "Lord, help me," she prayed.

The Bowlord and his followers were coming back now, nimbly descending ropes beside the waterfall. He came up and faced her. "I have brought you safe through the mountains, and the girl lives," he said, "Tell me where the sapphire is, and I will let you go alive to cursed Brightshadow."

"I cannot walk there, carrying my daughter," said Hannah. "You must take me there, as you promised."

"We never go there – except some few now and again who are ill or wounded – and they do not return to us."

"Nevertheless you must take me there now, or your sapphire is lost to you forever," said Hannah.

The Bowlord cursed viciously. He turned to some of his followers and muttered orders to them that Hannah could not hear. They went off swiftly and vanished behind a spur of the mountains. Hannah stepped back from the Bowlord uneasily, remembering the horrible moments when two of his men, thinking her asleep, had discussed the difficulty of torturing her. Perhaps here they had the tools – and the light – to do to her everything they wished. She put her hand on the bottle of poison beneath her cloak. Yet when the men returned after a long wait, they brought not implements of torture but a large, raw-boned brown horse.

The Bowlord turned to Hannah. She was shocked to see that he had a loaded crossbow in his hands. "If you will now tell me where the sapphire is hidden," he said, "I will give you this horse to carry you and your brat to the valley of Brightshadow. Neither I nor any of my men will take you there. If you refuse this offer, I swear I will kill you where you stand."

The knowledge of what she had to do came like an inspiration to her, and though she trembled at it she did not hesitate. "Bowlord," she said, "I know that you want to kill me. You want to break your bargain; you want both the sapphire and my life, and if I slip you will indeed take both. But I want to keep both my life and my promise, and I will, for I am your match. With my knife I will scratch out a map for you upon a piece of wood or leather – but not such a map as will lead you to the sapphire without further aid. Then you must put the girl on the horse, and come with me, alone, out into the desert away from your men. You must give me a loaded crossbow, like the one you yourself now carry. I will stand by the horse, and you will stand ten paces away. I will explain the map and tell you how to find the sapphire, and if I do not you may shoot me. But if I suspect that you are about to try to trap or kill me, I will shoot you. When I have finished telling you how to find the sapphire, you will walk back to your men, and I will ride away on my horse."

"No," said the Bowlord, "you will shoot me as soon as my back is turned."

"You suspect me of a heart like your own," said Hannah. "But you may walk backwards, with the crossbow aimed at me, until you are out of bowshot. Then I will turn and ride away, and you will have nothing more to fear."

"I will walk backwards," said the Bowlord, sneering, "and my aim will shift with my walking, and maybe I will trip, while you, unmoving, keep a steady aim at my heart."

Hannah had not foreseen this objection, but the answer came into her mind, again as if by inspiration. She smiled. "I see how it is, then, Bowlord," she said. "Though Bowlord be your name, you fear that an old woman weak with weariness and hunger may have a steadier hand on a bow than you. So I shall die, knowing you feared me, but the Sapphire of Mount Vykadrak is lost to you forever."

*　　　*　　　*

Brogal stood on the roof of his lookout shelter, and saw the Zarnith regrouping for another assault. Though they sought to destroy all that he loved, he felt a strange admiration for the courage and determination with which they fought, even after all their deadly repulses. He had not seen Vadshron, but he guessed that the warlord was here, before the Gate of Hope, leading the largest of the three Zarnith armies that assailed the Cloth of Joy. He seemed to see the great commander's ruthless authority in this new attack on the Gate of Hope. Vadshron had been repulsed so far, but he had not pushed to the utmost his warriors' strength and ferocious loyalty. Now he would. He had lost thousands, but his army was so vast that a thousand was a small thing to him, and the honor of the Zarnith was pledged to take the Cloth of Joy.

Waves of Zarnith warriors leaped into the stream to try to go underwater past the barricade. Thousands more divided themselves into two groups and ran up toward Ceramir, one on each side of the river. They did not try to assail the deadly barricade this time, but rather the cliffs on either side of it. Though the cliffs rose very high and sheer on either side of the Gate of Hope, they might perhaps be climbable – unlike the flaming barricade.

Black smoke, noxious and laced with glowing coals, billowed out from the barricade. Even where the Zarnith were now climbing it touched them now and then as the wild wind blew it to and fro. Brogal thought it impossible that the Zarnith could climb through that smoke. Then he saw them do it. Many fell, but others came on, swords at their belts, bows and spears strapped to their backs. They climbed clear of the worst smoke and heat and flying coals.

Brogal leaped back inside the lookout shelter, and held out three red flags for the defenders far below. He climbed down with reckless speed to the warm lake, before the Zarnith came in spear range of his shelter. He swam the river just in front of the barricade to reach Mudien, stood beside his father and told him of the new Zarnith strategy.

Mudien looked up into the blinding rain. He was soaked through in it, and cold. The torrential rainfall had caused the lake to rise until it flooded the whole lower valley, knee deep where he stood. The steep cliff sides on either side of the Gate of Hope, around which the Zarnith would come, loomed misty and obscure through the storm. Mudien had shot a bow with his men at the worst times of the fighting. His wounds had re-opened, and blood trickled down his arm, reddening his clothes and mingling with the rain that soaked him.

Gray silhouettes of men appeared on the cliff edges, and arrows fell among the defenders. Mudien's commands rang out through the storm. Long arrows of Ceramir soared up through the rain and hail, and Zarnith bodies fell upon the blazing pyre of the barricade.

Brogal took his father's bow and joined the defense. The Zarnith came to the ridges above the Gate of Hope by scores, rained down arrows on the defenders, and then climbed or leaped down into the Cloth of Joy. Most of them were half-blinded by smoke, and scores fell down to their deaths. Many of their arrows went wide, but there were always more arrows and more Zarnith to come. Wounded defenders fell and drowned in the rising water. Veril, Auria, and Imranie began rushing out from the stone house whenever a man fell, to carry him back and save him from this fate.

The heads of Zarnith swimmers appeared in the stream inside the Gate of Hope. Brogal could not believe what he was seeing: he knew the river below the barricade was walled off with a lattice of sturdy saplings. "They have sawed the grating!" shouted Mudien. "Defenders, shoot the swimmers! They must not reach the shore."

"We are lost," said Brogal, even as he shot at them as fast as he could draw bow. "There are too many of them."

"The time is not yet come to say those words," said Mudien. And Brogal was silent, shooting the Zarnith swimmers with no laughter in his heart. The water slowed the arrows, so that poison rather than wounds killed those who were hit. It was terrible to see them writhe and then sink as they were slain by what they thought a minor wound. And there were more Zarnith, both in the water and on the cliffs above, than the defenders could shoot. And they had few arrows left.

*　　　*　　　*

The rain fell harder, and the wind blew stronger. Large hail was carried now in the screaming gale. The trees of Ceramir roared louder. Small branches tore off them and flew high and far, some of them going out above the Gate of Hope to fall among the Zarnith. On the east and west ridges the men led by Rangol and Barnabas huddled between boulders and the cliff to escape the merciless wind and hail, and fought as best they could. Many strong Zarnith warriors lost their grip on the rock and fell before the force of the wind and hail alone.

Down in the valley the water rose fast and cold, as the influx of icy rain overwhelmed the warm water of the springs. It flooded the stone house knee deep, and then waist deep. Eleanor and Imranie did their best to keep peace and hope shining in the darkness of the crowded refuge, but the people were terrified. Mothers took their smaller children on their shoulders and in their arms, while the older ones shivered in water that was up to their chests or shoulders.

There were brave children in that room, standing still with eyes wide with fear, silent because they knew their parents could do nothing for them that they had not already done. There were frantic tears, and there was fear that mounted wave on wave like a cold flood deeper and more deadly than the water. There were hands held and prayers spoken in voices that trembled and then were held steady for the sake of others. Veril and Auria continued to go out into the deeper water where the defenders still fought, to help the wounded to safety, until at last Auria took a Zarnith arrow in her shoulder, and Veril used the last of her strength dragging her back into the house.

Outside the Zarnith still fought through the punishing hail, still climbed the cliffs and shot down at the floundering defenders. The smoke from the barricade lessened as the rising flood put out the lowest parts of the fire. Yet no more Zarnith swimmers came. The current underneath the barricade had grown too much for them, and the utmost of their strength and ingenuity was no longer enough to get them through. The upper part of the barricade still blazed furiously above the flood, fanned by the mighty wind and unabated by the rain and hail. It seemed to Brogal like the gate of Hell: blazing fire and black smoke beneath a stormy sky, luridly reflected in water thick with swirling corpses.

"Brogal," said Mudien in a calm and urgent voice. "Go up on the roof and bring down all the rope you can find. Tie from the pillars of the house to the trees across the stream, as strongly as you can so that the men may hold on to it in the flood."

Brogal did not understand what his father was preparing for, but he did as he was told with speed and skill.

He returned to his place to continue the hopeless fight. "It is terrible that it goes on," he thought, "but its end will be more terrible yet. I cannot laugh. It is dark; it is the end, and I can save no one."

The water was up to Brogal's chest. The flood was fast making archery impossible for the defenders. The Zarnith on the cliff edges continued to shoot downward into the teeth of the hail.

A loud crack sounded through the air, and a column of sparks went up from the barricade. Loud came Mudien's clear command, warm and strong above the storm, "Defenders, lay down your bows! Cling to the rope."

Brogal met his father's eyes. "Give up the fight?" he asked incredulously.

"Yes," said Mudien. "It is for God alone to fight for us now."

Brogal obeyed his father, for he was certain that he should. Yet it was the hardest thing he had ever done to let go his bow, and it seemed to him utter, hopeless folly. The bow drifted down on the dark water, and Brogal laughed bitterly at the thought that his bow would go down through the barricade for the Zarnith to use.

For a moment the Zarnith arrows kept slashing down among them. The wind roared, and the rain and hail fell, and all was as it had been before: hopeless. Then lightning struck the barricade. To the defenders down in the water it seemed to tear the earth and sky in two: a blinding column of blue-white light accompanied by a deafening crack of thunder, simultaneous, staggering, terribly and overwhelmingly beautiful. The barricade exploded into an enormous column of blazing coals and a vast cloud of deadly smoke. Flaming pieces of wood showered the defenders. They stood awestruck, their eyes dazzled, their ears ringing, while the burning fragments fell around them and the wild storm seemed a blank silence after that crash of thunder. The cliffs and the whole Gate of Hope were hidden in the spark-filled smoke. But the defenders did not stand and watch for long.

While fragments of the barricade were still falling, Brogal felt the first pull of the current. Instinctively he tightened his grip on the rope. An instant later he was swept off his feet, and his head went under. It took all his strength to cling to the rope against a force of water unlike any he had ever felt before. The barricade had been a dam, and now the dam was broken.

The cold, cold water rushed swiftly over him; he was held under by its force, and could not get to the surface though it was only an arm's stretch away. Strangely he felt no fear. Instead he gloried in the great power of the current and of the thunderbolt that had shattered the barricade. Above the blurring water the whole sky seemed to light up with flash on flash of lightning, and endless thunder came deafening even to his submerged ears.

* * *

Imranie sat near Eleanor, still near the window. She held wounded Auria in her arms, lamenting in her own heart the fact that she, mother of Ceramir, could do nothing more for her daughter now than this: nothing more than hold her in her pain, and speak useless words of comfort. Children crowded around Imranie and Eleanor, clinging to their skirts. The sound of crash upon crash of thunder burst painfully on cringing ears. The eerie lightning flashes stabbed their light through the cracks around the shutters, reflecting off the floodwater in the room and off wet clothes and frightened eyes.

The current was a new terror. For some it was the last straw, so that they broke down and screamed, or wept. It rose from nothing to its full power in a few heartbeats. First it was only a new sound in the storm, gathering force. Then they felt it in the room, and mothers grasped their children, trying to hold them from being swept away. Then they staggered themselves to stand against its force, while the whole stone house shook before its power. They wondered if it the strong old building would collapse, leaving only a ruin full of bodies when the victorious Zarnith swept in.

"Trust... Hope..." whispered Imranie to Auria, holding her hand, desperately wishing to bear her pain.

"Trust, and hope," said Eleanor, swiftly, urgently, to all in the room. "I do not know; I do not know, but hope, children of God. We are his..." her voice trembled, but then steadied swiftly, "we are his, and he has not abandoned us. I do not know what comes, but oh my sisters, my children, my mother, trust in God still, and hope."

* * *

Barnabas could not command; could not order his men to seek safety in cracks and behind large boulders as he himself was doing – the wind swept his words uselessly away. It was a wind such as he had never seen, even in this terrific storm. It screamed and roared; it blew boulders as large as sheep off the ridge and down upon the Zarnith. It had risen in a moment; his last arrow had missed because it was caught by the wind's rising. A heartbeat later he had been clinging with all his strength to a crack in the rock, while the wind tore his cloak off him and blew it away. He had struggled then to where he was now: a sheltered niche a man's height deep in the rock, a little away from the cliff edge. He lay there shivering while the wind screamed above him, its eddies carrying stinging rain and hail into his shelter. He knew that no more Zarnith would reach the cliff edge while that wind continued. Staggering lightning and thunder tore through the sky, much more than at any other time in the storm – so much that the lighting seemed to form a flashing wall around the Cloth of Joy.

A small, stunted tree that grew between the cliff edge and his shelter was struck by lightning. He looked around with ears ringing from the thunder-crash, and not a scrap of the tree remained, not even a stump. A moment later the crack in the stone where its roots had found their scarce purchase widened swiftly, and a boulder as wide and high as a standing horse leaned out and fell: greased with rain, loosened by lightning, blown out at last by the mighty wind. Barnabas heard it crash far below, and thought he heard the screams of Zarnith warriors there.

Barnabas huddled in his crack amid the staggering storm, expecting soon to die, either by lightning bolt, by mere exposure in the mighty wind, or by the spears of the victorious Zarnith. He thought of Hannah, perhaps far away upon the Luciyr road, or else mourning Naomi at Petrag. Barnabas prayed for her, thinking it might be the last thing he would ever do. He prayed with lips too cold to form clear words, and hands too numb to fold, in a place too small to kneel. He prayed that God would save her from evil men, and give her life and safety. He prayed that somewhere, somehow, she would find a measure of happiness, and live out her life in some good service despite the ruin of her world.

The wind stopped. The air seemed warm to Barnabas in the sudden stillness. The rain and hail fell straight down, but even they were swiftly decreasing. Barnabas stood and climbed clumsily with his numbed hands out of the notch of broken rock that had protected him. He went to the edge of the cliff and looked down. The rain cast only a light veil now, and despite the deep gray twilight of the storm he could see all the way to the foot of the cliff. The Zarnith were no longer attacking. He looked for a long time, not now feeling cold, unable to believe his eyes. They were retreating. He could see the dark lines of them, score on score, thousand on thousand, nearly undiminished despite their fearful losses. They were retreating. They were going away from the mighty cliff, eastward and southward out into the desert, leaving only their dead behind.

Hope leaped up in his heart – but then flickered and died. Despite the appearance, the Zarnith could not truly be giving up their assault. "The Gate of Hope or the western ridge is breached," he thought, "Ceramir has fallen. They are merely going to enter by the way that has been opened and take part in its destruction. Soon they will come up from the valley and kill us." He went to the other side of the ridge and looked down into the Cloth of Joy.

With the great decrease in the rain he could see clearly all the way to the western ridge, where Rangol had fought. There were no Zarnith there, though he saw no defenders either. He looked left then, toward the Gate of Hope, and he could not clearly see it. It was hidden in the trees, but a red glow seemed to rise from there, illuminating smoke and haze. "That is where the defense has been breached," he thought. "I will go down."

He hardly knew why he preferred to die alone on the valley floor, rather than fighting a last futile defense on the ridge with his men – if any still lived. As he climbed down the narrow path into Ceramir, he felt dazed by all that had happened – by the sudden silence, perhaps, most of all. He remembered that when he had climbed up this same way in the morning, he had not expected to go down alive. Now he was going down. It was something: a miracle of some sort, but it was not the miracle he had hoped for. Perhaps it was only a bitter coincidence in the confusion of war. He wondered as he went down what the

Zarnith did to their captives; whether they killed them swiftly or tortured them. They would kill him swiftly, at least, he thought: he would die with a sword in his hand, and fight them as long as he had breath or thought… As Jonathan had done, no doubt… Jonathan… the miracle that he had hoped for…

He was on the valley floor now, crossing, though he did not know it, the grassy clearing where Rennel had fallen sick so long before. The crack of a branch made him look up suddenly. A man was racing toward him, with dripping clothes that showed here and there the pink of blood mixed with water. He drew his sword in a swift motion, but then saw that the runner was Brogal. "Are you pursued?" he cried.

Brogal came to a swift stop, and leaned over with his hands on his knees, gasping for breath. "No," he panted. "Do we hold the eastern ridge?"

"Yes. The Zarnith retreated; I do not know why. But the Gate of Hope is breached?"

"No! But have you any news of the west? Could you see it?"

"The Zarnith have not won the west ridge," said Barnabas, "or at least they had not a moment ago when I was last high enough to see it. I saw no sign of fighting, nor of warriors on either side."

Brogal sat down cross-legged on the sodden grass, put his head in his hands, and laughed and wept and panted for breath all at the same time. "We have won," he gasped, "we have won."

Barnabas sat down on a log, unable to believe what he had heard. "We have won?" he repeated.

Brogal raised his head. His face was wet with rain and tears together. Laughter and joy danced in his shining eyes. "We have won," he said again, "or perhaps it is better to say we were on the winning side."

Barnabas still could not take it in. "They had so many," he said. "Why would they retreat?"

"Perhaps they knew what we have been most dreadfully slow to believe," said Brogal.

"What is that?" asked Barnabas.

"The ancient legends say," said Brogal, "that the honor of the Zarnith absolutely forbids them to fly from men. Once they begin a battle, they fight until they have either triumphed, or died to the last man. 'No man can conquer stone,' wrote Dradrag on the Cliffs of Doom – that all might know forever that he surrendered to the mountains, not to men."

Barnabas stood and looked up at the gray sky that had been filled with such overwhelming wind and lightning. "They do not fly from men," he said. "They have not flown from men today."

"No," said Brogal. For a long time there was silence between them. Light rain still fell softly, dripping off buds and branches.

"But where were you running so swiftly, when first I saw you?" asked Barnabas.

"To see if the Zarnith had overwhelmed your army or Rangol's," said Brogal, standing suddenly. "And now, indeed, I must find if my brother Rangol is still living. This business of war is bitter even for the victors."

"Yes," said Barnabas, standing also. "It is bitter even for victors – or those who fought on the winning side." He was silent for a moment, trying to sort through his thoughts and understand what he must do. He had, he supposed, abandoned the men up on the ridge, but surely they would not need his aid to see that the battle was over and that they should come down. There was only one thing he wanted to do. Brogal was still standing in front of him, not yet making for the western ridge.

"I need a horse," said Barnabas. "I need a horse to ride to the desert gap."

He met Brogal's eyes, and for a moment they held each other's gaze. "I understand," said Brogal. "It is bitterer for you than for us. And if I were Jonathan, I would want my father to do just as you are doing. There are horses in the barns against the northwest cliff. The black stallion Narlas is the swiftest. Watch lest some Zarnith still remain in the outlands, for the retreat of such a host cannot be swift. We would not want them falsely to conclude they have been fighting men after all." Then he was off again, running as fast as before, as though he could not tire.

Barnabas ran himself, stiffly but swiftly, across the rain-soaked fields of northern Ceramir to the barns. Soon he was galloping back across those fields, with Narlas' flying hooves striking up great splashes of mud. The dark shade of the great trees flashed by him swiftly, then the lake and the stone house. There were living men and women there, some working and some standing still in awe, but all alike seemed phantoms to Barnabas. Only Jonathan was real; only Jonathan and his desperate prayers.

He reined in at the Gate of Hope, awed by what he saw. The rocks were broken and the path was washed away. Large boulders that had not been there before littered the stream. Huge, black swaths of soot like the opening petals of some enormous dark flower stained the rock on either side of the gate. Barnabas urged Narlas cautiously forward through the rock-filled shallows.

What lay beyond the Gate of Hope brought him to a halt again. Several great trees were burning like enormous torches there, and the heat seemed to beat in his face with physical force. He looked at them in awe, wondering if the smaller fire at the barricade could possibly have set them alight. A large branch tore off one of the trees and fell in blazing ruin far down into the stream. Barnabas saw his danger but ignored it, and spurred Narlas on to ride through the trees. The brave and steady horse heeded its rider's will, and though the heat singed Narlas' mane, and Barnabas' hair and clothes steamed, they passed through unharmed and galloped on down the path beside the stream.

The trees flashed by again until he neared the village of Harevan – when cries and the low rumble of many horses came to him from ahead. He rode very slowly up a wooded hill that seemed to give some hope of seeing the Zarnith without being seen by them. Through a veil of gray vines, he caught a glimpse of the last thousands of their great host moving through the village without stopping to pillage or to burn, riding swiftly out toward whatever comfort the desert could offer its defeated sons. Barnabas slipped westward out of the forest, and rode at a thunderous gallop for the battlefield of the desert gap.

Meanwhile the Zarnith host assembled on the desert. They were not permitted to ride further until all stood in ordered ranks. Then, at a single shout, they swept eastward at a great gallop. Vadshron was a prudent commander. Having seen his warriors shockingly defeated, he was now reminding them who they were: the Zarnith, the Sons of the Desert, the horsemen of the unbreakable charge. Yet even in this not all went as the warlord intended, for the earth was wet with rain. The famous banner of dust, immemorial sign of doom for the foes of the Zarnith host, stubbornly refused to rise from their flying hooves.

Some of the men looked back uneasily, and saw that though dark clouds still filled the sky, though rain still softly fell and lightning flashed here and there in the clouds, a single shaft of sunlight cut through the rain and fell full and strong upon the entrance to the valley. They turned back to the desert, and spurred their horses on to faster speed. The shadow of their defeat lay heavy on them – and the terror of Nagryn gonk Wyrkriy, or whatever other immortal being had wielded the staggering force that drove them back.

* * *

Mudien had confirmed that all three Zarnith armies were retreating. He had sent men to bring in the wounded from the mountain walls. He had found that the great stone house was undamaged by the flood – though everything was wet except some medicines and other supplies that had been stored in closets on the roof. He had overseen the vital task of relighting the fires in the stone house, so that the wounded men who lay shivering in sodden beds might not die of cold. With all this accomplished, it was at last time to begin the main task: saving all who could be saved among the wounded.

He limped across the main room of the stone house, his own clothes sodden, his own hand and arm bleeding from the old wounds. He sat down heavily beside Auria's soaked bed, and looked across it into Imranie's face. Everything was wet, and he felt desperately weary. Yet for his daughter's healing, at least, he could gather sufficient strength.

"My wound is not mortal," she said in a voice that he knew was controlled against her pain. "There are others who need your help more: go to them; I can bear this longer. Ah! I confess: I am afraid of what you must do, and would have you help others first."

Mudien took her right hand. "You will live, daughter," he said. "Your brothers and sisters live, and victory is ours. Yet your wound is more serious than you know. Your courage is very, very great. Spring comes, and now we will live to see its coming. There are men in this room, dear Auria, who but for your courage would not have seen it." He leaned over her and took the arrow gently in his hands.

She forced a smile. "The roses..." she said. "Eleanor's roses will – Ah! – come back from the... the roots, even if – even if her house is burnt."

Then Mudien showed her the two pieces of the bloody arrow that he had removed while she spoke. The pain of it had shaken her whole being, and she spoke again, weakly. "I thank you, Father. Lady Eleanor lives... I wonder what has happened to the little girl, the one we called little fern. A strange name; she named herself when Ella asked her what thing she wanted to be like. A fern... is sheltered and made beautifully and intricately. Only those who care for what is small can have the joy of its beauty. Are you finished, Father?"

He had been bandaging her shoulder as she spoke. "Yes, dear Auria," he said, in a voice nearly as pain-wearied as hers, and choked with tears as hers was not, "yes, I am finished. There will be no need for me to hurt you more. You should drink this now." She drank the cup he gave her, a healing draught from a closet above the flood. A few moments later she was asleep.

Imranie gently let go her left hand, which she had held until then. She stood, and helped Mudien to rise as well. "Come with me out into the light, Beloved," she said.

"I cannot go," he said. "We are needed by scores of desperately wounded men."

"You are at the edge of your own strength, dear Mudien," she said. "Rest with me a moment, leaving the wounded in Eleanor's care, and Karlak's. Your strength must not fail, and it is good that you should breathe freely for a little now."

He yielded to her. They walked to the edge of the lake, and stood hand in hand looking out through the Gate of Hope. Dark clouds covered the sky in all directions, and rain fell soft and chill, but a broad shaft of sunshine rested on the entrance to the valley. The fires in the outlands were dying, without the wind to fan them. No Zarnith corpses remained in the Cloth of Joy, for although many had died there, the flood had washed their bodies down the river. The Gate of Hope was greatly changed. The path, along with soil, boulders, trees, and bushes, had been utterly swept away. The stream now ran broad and shallow, filling the whole width of the gate from one cliff to the other. A new stone path would have to be laid before it was as welcoming as before. Yet though the fierce power of the current had changed a dear, familiar shape, the gate's new form was as lovely as before, sculpted by the clean, strong force of water. And Ceramir was safe.

They walked forward and stood hand in hand at the Gate of Hope. The sunshine's warmth caressed them while the rain fell gently still. Despite their weariness, peace washed over them like the sunshine. They marveled in silence at the rescue of the valley they loved.

"I did not believe," said Imranie at last. "I knew our Lord would save us, but I did not believe he would defend us."

For a long time Mudien said nothing. He only held her hand, and looked at the sunshine, and the stream of Ceramir running out of the warm lake, sparkling and shimmering.

Finally he said, "The Zarnith, too, believed it at last. They fly before no man, and yet they have fled. They realized, then, that they were fighting more than men. Words I spoke when I warned them of the wrath of God, which at the time seemed over-bold to me, appear in fact to have been a prophecy. They did not heed it, to their loss, but maybe now some of them will remember."

"I do not want to think of their deaths," said Imranie. "I am glad I am not God, who had to choose whether he would slay them or let them slay us. Let us instead think of what God has saved. He has saved the Cloth of Joy and most of its people. Our lives will now be bound more closely to him than ever, because of what he has done for us. Greatly has he loved us. Forever we are his."

"It is true," said Mudien. He knelt on the mud and lifted up his hands in the sunlight that was still streaming down. "We praise you, oh God, for your mercy," he said. "We do not know why you should choose to save us, and we pray that you may yet save some among the Zarnith, but we praise you with all our hearts for what you have done for us. You have heard our prayers and done more than we asked. With awesome power you have defended us and spared us from destruction. Help us now to serve you forever, even more than before."

Imranie knelt beside him, and they stayed there still and quiet for a long moment. Weariness clothed them like their sodden garments, but peace was in their hearts. The ground of the home they loved was beneath their knees, while the soft rain, the warm sun, and the smell of spring were all around them. In the depths of their souls was a faith stronger than stone, from which flowed joy, like a spring from deep rock, fresh and clean. They knew the power and the love of God; knew it beyond a shadow of doubt. They had trusted him utterly, and had been willing to follow him faithfully to death. And they had seen beyond their hope, beyond their dreams, the power of his rescue and his love. They were still weary, as they stood slowly together to go back into the house. But the joy of Heaven was singing in their hearts.

As they entered they met Brogal and Rangol, coming from the western ridge carrying a wounded man between them. Rangol spoke swiftly to his father, and his words with their trust and honor seemed to Mudien to give him new strength. "I and more of my company than could be hoped are unwounded. Perhaps four score are dead, mostly Karolans, and as many wounded. The rest are coming here, carrying the wounded. Father, I would help you in any way I can, though I know my skill is nothing compared to yours. I have proved less brave and less strong than I had thought, but it is nothing: God has saved us. Tell me how I may serve you, Father, for your task and that of the other healers is long, and I have strength to aid you."

"My dear son," said Mudien, "I thank God that you still live. As for your offer of service, I must accept it, though I know you are weary. Through our diligent labor now, more may be spared to greet the spring with joy."

Chapter 25

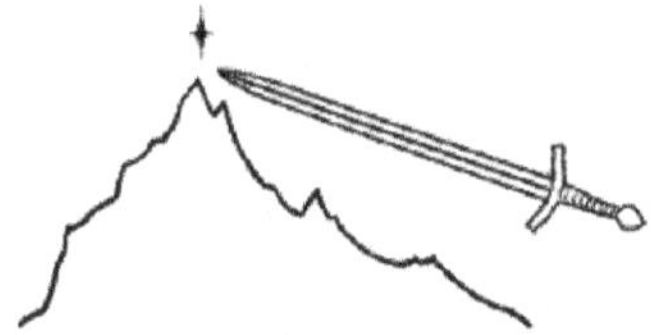

The River and the Quiet Voice

BARNABAS SEARCHED LONG AT THE SHATTERED barricade of the desert gap. The sun sank low, and on the west horizon a long band of clear sky opened up, glowing pale gold beneath the darkness of the clouds. It bathed the barricade in a strange yellow light – a light that was beautiful in itself, and yet seemed to make the brutal battlefield more hideous with its soft glow. It should have shone on harvest fields; soft new grass growing in the spring; great and lovely oaks in their shapely strength; or weary horses led home after a hard day's work. It was horrible that instead it should eerily illuminate this scene of death and chaos.

Barnabas was weary, shaken, full of grief. He had turned over scores of broken bodies of men who had marched over the mountains with him, whose courage he had seen, whose characters he had begun to learn. A few were alive, but he had no bandages or water or anything of use in tending them. Sometimes he tried to stop their bleeding, but besides that he could only hope that further help would soon arrive from Ceramir.

When he had searched the whole of the barricade, checking every body, and had not found Jonathan, he sat down on a splintered log and bowed his head. Vivid memories passed through his mind. He saw Jonathan as a small child, struggling to lift heavy hammers and half-made swords, yet laughing when he failed. He felt Jonathan's restless weight grow calm and still upon his lap while they listened to a wandering servant of God from one of the churches as he told stories from the Books of the Travelers. The child Jonathan had listened raptly then, Barnabas remembered, and he, looking down at his son, had never doubted that he would pass on his faith. Those stories... Joseph, betrayed by men, blessed by God, faithful, forgiving... Eleazar, who defied an army alone by God's power, and fought until his hands froze to his sword... the breathtaking story of Christ himself: authority in his voice, healing in his hands, love strong enough to break the curse of the world in his heart... Christ himself, the Prince, the Redeemer, the Hero who had dared a thing so terrible that it seemed to break the foundation of the world... immortal God come down, pure and holy, to die for mortal men who were twisted and broken beyond any healing save his death alone.

"Lord Christ," said Barnabas. "I praise you with all my heart for my life and for Hannah's and Naomi's – for our redemption. And if Jonathan is dead, I know that it was he who chose to fly from your love and escape your mercy. But Lord, the love in my heart for him is the purest echo I know of your love for me – an echo of the Father's love for all straying sons. I beg you for his life. I cry out with all my heart, asking you to claim him and redeem him. I dare even now to beg you for his mortal life – but most of all I ask that somehow you have made him yours. Lord Christ, holy Father... I beg you... I beg you... Alas... I trust you."

Barnabas felt a hand on his shoulder, and looked up slowly. Brogal stood beside him. "Is Jonathan dead?" asked Brogal.

"I do not know," said Barnabas. "I have searched the barricade for him again and again. I have found no sign of him, alive or dead. I do not know."

"I have come for the wounded," said Brogal. "Others are with me, to take them to Ceramir."

"Were you not wounded yourself?" asked Barnabas. "There was blood on your clothes when I saw you running up from the Gate of Hope."

"It was not my own," said Brogal. "I have escaped unwounded, as ever before, though better men than I lie dead."

"No man ought to rate his own worth thus," said Barnabas wearily.

Brogal smiled. "You quote back to me words I have said to others more than once before," he said. "We have seen God go to war for those he loves, today. The truth shines clear that it is his love for us alone, no courage or holiness of ours, that gives us life and worth. But as for Jonathan, the body of a man does not disappear…" he paused, and a shadow passed across his face, "…though perhaps a woman's did once: the direst failure of my life. Jonathan is not on the barricade. Would you find him before it, or behind it? Would he fly, or would he charge, when his shield was shattered in the hopeless fight?"

Barnabas stood, and looked into the west, where the band of yellow sky was still bright. "Those questions are easily answered," he said quietly.

"You will find him," said Brogal. "I go now to help the other wounded."

Barnabas stepped across the barricade, and the wet gravel of the desert crunched beneath his feet. Far ahead he could see the huge hulk of some upturned wagon or engine of war: a shapeless wreck, black against the golden light.

* * *

Jonathan drifted like a windblown feather, blind and confused, through strange dreams of aching pain. At last, like a feather coming to rest, he found that he lay on black mud, beside a dark stream, in a world of ashes and twilight. His senses and his thought were too dulled to feel very much, but with all that remained of them, with all of his faltering being, he was afraid.

The cold mud held him fast, and he could not move. The dark water was sinister. In this dreary world he could scarcely even remember beauty: all color, form, strength, joy, and light were lost to him. He could not even call their images into his mind, and all that remained to him was the fear of their eternal loss.

He was afraid. Time had slowed to a miserable crawl, and yet it was still moving inexorably on toward a moment when he would be annihilated. He felt that even when he dissolved into nothingness he still would not escape this torture of fear. He reached for anger and shame, always the companions of fear in his memory, but he was too weak to grasp them. He was left with nothing but fear: raw, dull, aching, inescapable, unalloyed fear.

Jonathan groped vaguely back toward memories of his faith, and, without fully grasping them, he was aware that he had always expected this in the end. "I will watch with a noble sorrow as everything I loved is lost to me, and at last I lose even myself." His mind was too weary to frame the words, but he could hold the thought, his own old thought, stated sometimes, shaken at others, but always affirmed in the end. That was what he had believed, and this was the end he had expected. The only thing to do was grieve for the inevitable ruin of all beauty, and for the fast-approaching end of his own bitter life. But it was not grief that ruled over the shattered remnants of his heart now. It was fear.

He looked into the dark river, flowing on with an oily sound, devoid of beauty. Its sullen waters reflected little even of the ashen twilight. It was a dead stream, a dead land, a dead sky, and he himself was either dead, or so close to death that it made no difference. He could not move or think. He was desperately afraid, though he knew nothing to fear.

He looked into the dark river. Vague thoughts took form in his dulled mind. The river seemed to him the proper end of the life he had expected. It seemed to offer him escape from fear. He could use his once-strong will one last time to roll over on the clinging mud. He would slip slowly and irresistibly into the river, grieving as his useless hands slid out behind him, brushing the mud with fingers that would never grip again. He must let go of fear, grasp at grief and despair, and go into the river. He must do this last act of courage: he must slip off the edge of death, and die. This, then, was what the cold, dark, unchanging world awaited. The path of courage and honor was still before him: not to lie unmoving and useless while one action was still possible. Not to turn back at the end through meaningless fear.

But he was desperately afraid – and cold. His loathing of the stream intensified. Facing it would be greater pain even than waiting here, tortured by fear. Yet there was nothing to fear: why should he be thus tortured? He did not know; he could not understand. He thought vaguely that the void, nothingness itself, was torturing him – and this idea deepened his fear, until he felt his very self was dissolving into it. There is no escape if nothing is the enemy.

Still he did not push himself off into the stream, because he was afraid. A thought came to him – vague and horrible as all his thoughts now were – that the stream had no bottom, and that in this world he could not drown. He thought of deep, unnatural depths of oily black water, filled with shapes of nameless, hopeless horror. He seemed to see them before his eyes as he lay in the black mud, monsters whose shapes cannot be named, whose terror cannot be comprehended. And yet that stream was the end of his road, and honor called him there. He must not turn back, or he was a weakling and a coward. He had accepted the joy in which he had believed, while the world still held joy. Now he must accept the grief and agony in which he had believed, which he had always known awaited him in the end. He seemed to hear those he had loved – he could not remember their names – crying out to him that he must not go into the stream. Yet he knew he must, or betray himself. He must hold the course he had set to its bitter end. If he had saved her – Naomi's name was not present in his mind, but the thought of her was there – he might have had another way to choose. But he had abandoned her, he had fixed his course for death, and he must follow it or betray his honor and his will. He must slip into the stream, or Jonathan would have utterly failed: Jonathan, whose will was all that now remained of what had once been a strong and joyful man. He must slip into that stream, or the foundation of his life, the end of the course he had set himself, was betrayed.

Fear tortured him. Fear threatened to dissolve him, and then still torture him. The stream was there. He had not rolled into it.

Then there were footsteps behind him, and a hand upon his shoulder. He could not move to see who had come, but he was more afraid even than before, and in a different way. His fear focused onto the unseen stranger who had touched him. He might now be in another's hands in this terrible place. His will, the last fragment of his being, might be broken before the will of another. He was terrified of losing the last choice, the last freedom that remained to him: the choice to slip into the dark river if he would.

"I have found you," said the voice behind him, a quiet voice laden with love and sorrow. "I have come to rescue you, for I love you."

"I am afraid of you," said Jonathan.

"Trust yourself to me, and let me bring you back to joy."

"I must not," said Jonathan. "I must go down into the stream."

"Why?"

"Because it is what I have chosen."

"Life and death are before you: I am life, the river is death. Both are before you. Therefore, choose life."

"Long ago I turned away from you," said Jonathan. "Long ago I chose a path that must end in death. I will not turn back now."

"Turn back now. You were wrong. Come with me, and I will give you joy."

"I do not turn back when I have set my course," said Jonathan. "I do not reverse my choices. I choose the river."

"Then the river lies before you."

There was a long silence, and Jonathan did not move. "I am afraid," he said at last in a low whisper.

"Do you know from whence your fear of that river comes?"

"From you?" asked Jonathan, barely breathing the words.

"Yes. From me."

"It is very wrong of you," said Jonathan. "To make people fear a thing they must do, so that they do what you want instead. It is very wrong. I wish that I could kill you. I wish that I could escape you."

"If you go down into that river you will escape me."

"I will," said Jonathan.

There was a long silence. Neither moved or spoke. The sky seemed to shake, and Jonathan felt that many things were happening above him, things of great consequence that he did not understand – while the river flowed sullenly the same, an arm's reach from where he lay.

"You have not slipped into the river."

"I am afraid," said Jonathan.

"You are mine."

His fear intensified, far worse than before – no longer dull now but keen and sharp as the Zarnith dagger that had pierced him. He felt the stranger's arms slide into the mud beneath him, and lift him up. Pain burst through him like a raging fire, until he sank into a darkness that was not loathsome, and that held no dreams.

* * *

Barnabas lifted Jonathan in his arms, and stood amid the wreckage of the wagon, which he had cut away with his sword to reach his son. He had no knowledge of Jonathan's dark dreams, and only the first words Jonathan had heard in them were his. He knew that Jonathan was alive, for the moment, but his wounds certainly appeared mortal. He fixed his mind on the problem of getting him to Ceramir as quickly as he could. He strode out from the wreckage of the wagon, carrying his son, and made for the barricade where he had tied Narlas.

His great strength was taxed, for he was weary and Jonathan was a heavy weight. Nevertheless he reached Narlas without faltering. He turned and paused a moment, breathing hard, before he lifted Jonathan onto the horse's back.

He heard hoof steps behind him, the steps of a weary horse coming from the east in the falling dusk. They ceased very near him just as he was about to mount his horse, and he stopped still at the sound of a woman's voice, very tired but steady.

"If you are my friend, I ask your help and mercy," she said. "If you are my enemy, kill me as you would any weak thing whose life was troublesome to you, for I will die soon whatever you do if I do not find the Cloth of Joy."

He knew her voice, and he could not believe his ears. He mounted his horse and rode up beside her. His voice was trembling when he spoke. "Hannah," he said. "Hannah, take my hand, and I will lead you into Ceramir."

She reached out her hand to him, hesitantly, as if he might be a vision that would disappear at her touch. He took her hand. Each felt the other's touch, as they had so many times before, as though they might be standing at the doorway of their cottage, long ago and far away, gazing up together at the beauty of Glen Carrah, or at Jonathan and Naomi running there to meet one another.

"I love you, Barnabas," said Hannah, bursting into tears. "I thought you were dead, and you live. But your hands are covered with blood, and there is Jonathan… at least I have come in time to see him buried. Naomi is also near death, I think, though she has survived the journey. She has not spoken… not spoken to me in long days."

"But God saved Ceramir, beyond our hope, dear Hannah!" he said. "There may be healing for her there – and Jonathan yet lives also, though his wounds are grave. Come, Beloved, let us hasten to Ceramir together. Come with me. Oh Hannah, thank God, we need not now be parted!"

"Joy and sorrow overwhelm me, and I… I can say no more," said Hannah, weeping. Naomi was before her in the saddle, alive but unconscious, gaunt with her long sickness. Hannah's tears fell down into her hair.

"Come, Beloved," said Barnabas. "Ride with me to Ceramir – ride like the wind!"

They pushed their horses on as fast as they could. Hannah was almost too tired to stay in the saddle, but with Barnabas beside her, and Jonathan and Naomi's lives perhaps depending on their speed, she was stronger than her strength. She held Naomi and herself on the horse, and urged it forward to keep pace with Barnabas as he thundered beside her.

All was strange to Hannah: the sudden appearing of great trees in the dusk; the kindly mist that blew off the warm river – and finally the great notch in dark cliffs ahead, through which warm lights were showing. Barnabas led her forward into the shallow river, and they paused there a moment with the warm waters swirling about their weary horses' hooves. All seemed still and peaceful in the dusk over the warm river.

"I do not know how any of this has happened," said Barnabas in a quiet voice. "It is as though God had plucked you up from beyond the mountains and carried you here. I know that in truth you have had an anxious and weary journey, but it seems a miracle nonetheless."

"And Ceramir was to be destroyed and you dead," she said softly. "And though our children may be at death's door, surely, after all God has done for us, we should have hope."

"You are standing at the Gate of Hope, dear Hannah," said Barnabas. "Come with me now into the Cloth of Joy." In the stillness of that night they went forward, each with a dying child, yet each with some small measure of hope – they went forward through the gate that had that very day been defended with the fury of rain, wind, and fire.

Here ends the third book.

IF YOU ENJOYED THIS BOOK...

-Tell your friends! This is a self-published book without the advertising budget of a big corporation behind it. If you think it's a good read, spread the word!

-Buy Book 4, <u>Darkness Gathers Round</u> – the triumphant conclusion of *The Epic of Karolan*! It's available from http://www.hopewriter.com, or from Amazon.com.

-You can order Karolan books for a friend or family member from either of the websites above. To contact the author directly, email ariheinze@hotmail.com, or call (832) 622-1114.

-Check the website, http://www.hopewriter.com, for interesting background about Karolan. News about Ari Heinze's next writing project may eventually appear there as well.